'Everything you need in a romance[...] hilariously witty banter, and that [...]
Colleen Oakley, *USA Tod[...]*

'I was hooked on the very first page of *How to En[...] Story*, the absurdly delicious debut from Yulin Kuang. The chemistry between Helen and Grant is pure magic, as is Yulin's gorgeous writing'
Carley Fortune, #1 *New York Times* Bestselling Author

'Impossibly tender, funny, sexy, and heart-wrenching, *How to End a Love Story* is a gorgeously original romance – and so much more – that will leave you laughing, sobbing, and desperately wishing that it would never end. This is the kind of glorious gut-punch of a book that you'll want to share with all your friends, and reread over and over'
Lana Harper, *New York Times* Bestselling Author

'A smart, sexy, and powerful page-turner. The insider's look at Hollywood is just as fascinating as the complicated characters who work in the writers room. I couldn't put this book down'
Jill Santopolo

'Two complicated people in an impossibly complicated situation, drawn to each other in spite of a deeply complicated past: *How to End a Love Story* is moving, compelling, and heart-flutteringly sexy'
Kate Clayborn

'Yulin Kuang has a wonderful voice, poignant and funny, she grabbed me from the first paragraph'
Jill Shalvis

Yulin Kuang is a screenwriter and director. She was once fired from a Hallmark movie for being 'too hip for Hallmark' and is the adapting screenwriter of Emily Henry's *People We Meet On Vacation*, as well as the writer/director of the forthcoming *Beach Read* feature film for 20th Century Studios. She lives and writes in Pasadena, California.

HOW TO END A LOVE STORY

YULIN KUANG

HODDER &
STOUGHTON

First published in Great Britain in 2024 by Hodder & Stoughton
An Hachette UK company

This paperback edition published in 2024

1

A CIP catalogue record for this title is available from the British Library

Paperback ISBN 978 1 399 71659 8
ebook ISBN 978 1 399 71658 1

Typeset in Janson Text LT Std by Diahann Sturge

Printed and bound in Great Britain by Clays Ltd, Elcograf S.p.A.

Hodder & Stoughton policy is to use papers that are natural, renewable
and recyclable products and made from wood grown in sustainable forests.
The logging and manufacturing processes are expected to conform to the
environmental regulations of the country of origin.

Hodder & Stoughton Ltd
Carmelite House
50 Victoria Embankment
London EC4Y 0DZ

www.hodder.co.uk

*For Zack,
this is a love letter.*

*And for eldest daughters of immigrant parents,
this is a love letter for you too.*

Author's Note

This story contains on-the-page discussions of complicated grief, suicide loss, and the death of a sibling.

One

All things considered, her little sister's funeral is a pretty boring affair.

Helen Zhang (the good one, the smart one, the *boring one*, according to Michelle, may she rest in peace) sits in the front row between her grieving parents. If Michelle were here, she would be snickering at something inappropriate, like the accidentally phallic floral arrangement draped over her closed casket. If Michelle were here, she'd be restlessly tapping her foot, anxious to sneak a cigarette in the bathroom, already plotting her escape to an afterparty. If Michelle were here—*it wouldn't be so fucking quiet.*

Helen's mother shakes with silent, rolling sobs and grips her surviving daughter's right hand so hard, Helen lost feeling in it during the pastor's welcome remarks. Her father stares at the wooden easel holding Michelle's sophomore-year photo. His gaze drifts first to the bland church window blinds (not for the first time, Helen wishes they were Catholic, for the vibes), then to the shoes of the pastor. Dad looks everywhere there isn't someone with a face to look back at him.

Helen used up all her own tears in the first forty-eight hours, shaking and crying alone in her room like some dumb wounded animal until her eyes were puffy slits, pondering existential questions too big to be captured in pathetic words. The well has dried up, and all that's left is a growing pit of resentment that threatens to swallow her whole. She hates the pastor's trite remarks trying to imbue Michelle's short life with *meaning*, hates Mom's tears, hates Dad's lack of them, maybe she even hates *herself*, but *why*? Really, if there's anyone she *should* be mad at, it's *Michelle*—

A door in the back of the church creaks open—a late mourner—and a sudden prickling at the back of Helen's neck says: it's *him*.

Hushed whispers dash up the aisle, and even though Helen tells herself not to turn her head, not to look—Mom isn't so lost in her grief as to miss the sudden shift of attention in the room. She turns and lets out a dramatic *wail* that Helen can't help feeling embarrassed by.

Helen turns around and her eyes confirm, it's *Grant Shepard, Grant Fucking Shepard. Class president, homecoming king, lover of parties and friends and teachers and football. And killer of my sister.*

That last part seems unlikely to hold up in a court of law—there were enough eyewitnesses to suggest sixteen-year-old Michelle Zhang darted in front of eighteen-year-old Grant Shepard's SUV shortly after two a.m. last Friday (and caused a grim traffic jam on Route 22) on purpose. There were enough "key search terms" in Michelle's internet history to confirm it. And the most humiliating blow for their parents: there was enough in the toxicology report to warrant the phrase *troubled youth* in the local news coverage.

About Michelle, not Grant.

Everyone felt bad for Grant: how sad, how tragic, how *selfish* that this girl—practically a stranger, some sophomore with a suicidal itch—would do something like this, forcing a bright young man like him to have to live with accidentally killing someone for the rest of his bright, promising life.

"*You*," Mom says, standing in the middle of the aisle, her mouth gasping for air like they're in a Greek tragedy.

Grant Shepard stands still, as if he exists just to be gasped at by grieving mothers and gawked at by middle-aged Chinese aunties and uncles.

He looks exactly the way Helen thinks of him—wearing a dark navy sweater over a crisp white button-down, as if he's on his way to a student council meeting after this to discuss grad night themes. His tie is perfectly knotted and his dark brown hair is neatly brushed and he looks too good—too young and handsome and *alive*—to be allowed in this room.

Grant's soft brown eyes dart around the church. He knows he's made a mistake coming here, she can tell. He probably thought it'd be okay, that they would understand why he'd want to pay his respects, maybe—maybe he even thought they'd forgive him.

What a supreme amount of ego it must have taken, to imagine his presence would be wanted here.

"*No*," Helen's mom is saying, her lips white but forceful.

Grant's hands come up, almost placating. "I didn't mean to—"

"She wants you to leave," Helen finally says, her voice firm. "Now."

Grant's eyes land on Helen. He ducks his head in understanding. As he turns to leave, he adds a mumbling sort of "Sorry."

It's all so dramatic, Helen feels an itch to shout at his retreating back, *And don't you ever show your stupid face in here again!*

Like they're in a movie, instead of a Presbyterian church they haven't attended in over seven years.

But it doesn't seem worth it, when the Grant Shepards of the world are so unlikely to cross paths with the grieving Zhang families of the world—gasping mothers, avoiding fathers, gossiping aunties and uncles, and all—ever again.

Instead, Helen leads her mother back to the pew. As she walks down the aisle, she makes eye contact with Michelle's smiling portrait.

I bet you liked that, Helen thinks, daring her sister to respond. *I bet that was your favorite part of your whole funeral.*

Two

When the phone rings on Tuesday morning, Helen already knows it's going to be good news. Her literary agent Chelsea Pierce sends bad news in sympathetic couplets over email—*they didn't go for it; fuck 'em*—but she picks up the phone for good news.

"I hope you hate your apartment because you're going to Hollywood!"

Helen laughs and immediately feels a rush of cautious energy flood her. *Don't get too excited, the paperwork isn't signed, everything could still fall apart.*

She's grown superstitious. When she published the first book in what would become the Ivy Papers series, she told herself, *Don't get ahead of yourself, people might hate it, or worse, maybe no one will even read it.* When it became a bestseller and the *New York Times* put her on a list of voices to watch in the young adult space, she admonished herself, *It doesn't really matter, the work is still the same as it was before it made the list, and what if they don't like the second book?*

Her entire career so far could be linked from cautious mental disclaimer to disclaimer, right up to the announcement that some fancy Hollywood people are turning her books about moody prep-school teens keeping dark, academic secrets into a soapier, sexier TV show.

"What do you do about imposter syndrome?" she once asked a much more successful, senior author over a celebratory brunch.

"Well, at a certain point, it becomes unseemly," he told her.

Six weeks later, as she opens the door to her new waterfront condo (all living expenses during prep and production paid for by the studio, plus per diem) across from the Santa Monica Pier—Helen thinks, perhaps, she's reached *a certain point*.

The place comes furnished in expensive beiges and smells like a trendy hotel. Late-September sunshine filters through the floor-to-ceiling windows that open onto her private balcony, and it makes Helen wonder if she could become a totally different person here, the kind with morning routines and inner peace. There's a shared common area on the top floor she can reserve for parties (Helen doesn't know enough people in this city to throw a party, but she nods politely at the building manager anyway) and her kitchen window looks out onto the patio of her temporary neighbor, Academy Award–winner Frances McDormand.

"How very *LA*," her East Coast friends say when she tells them.

"Who?" says her mom during their first bicoastal FaceTime.

"Frances McDormand, Mom," Helen sighs as she unpacks the groceries. "She's, like, an actress, you would know her. She's in . . ."

Helen pauses, as her mind suddenly erases the entirety of Frances McDormand's illustrious, award-winning career from existence. She was in *Miss Pettigrew Lives for a Day*, but Mom hasn't seen that.

"I think she played the Queen in something. Oh, and she's the mom in *Moonrise Kingdom*!"

"I don't know her," Mom says. "Never mind. What are you making for dinner?"

Helen dutifully recites her dinner menu—*just something easy, I still have to get more pots and pans, yes I'll add something green, thanks, Mom*—and is treated to another forty minutes of hand-wringing over the history of earthquakes in LA County.

"If the ground opens up, I'll jump right in so it'll be quick and painless," Helen says as she finishes off her tomato and egg rice bowl. "Don't worry so much. Love you, bye!"

She searches "moving into a new apartment in LA" on Spotify and puts on someone else's well-curated playlist over the state-of-the-art Bluetooth speaker system.

Helen has never been cool enough to be "a music person." She prefers leaving that up to strangers on the internet who've experienced the same specific soundtrack-worthy moments in life—"cozy October morning in the kitchen" or "driving toward my uncertain future"—and hoping they'll tell her exactly what songs would bring those feelings out best, like a purple scarf for green eyes.

As Stevie Nicks croons about time making her bolder and children getting older, Helen hangs her clothes up in ascending length in the walk-in closet and thinks about the times when life files itself neatly into chapters.

Travel is a way of turning the page, Helen reminds herself, reciting her therapist's counsel. *Maybe you'll finally be able to write something new.*

Helen mentally strikes out that *maybe* with savage determination.

She hopes this chapter is a short, productive one.

When the phone rings on Wednesday, Grant already knows it's going to be a shit conversation.

"Just take the meeting," his TV agent Fern wheedles. "What's the harm in taking a meeting?"

"I didn't like the book," he says, not untruthfully.

Prep-school teens and their sex lives aren't exactly his *area*, and Grant was hoping to break this unemployment streak with something more exciting, like a feature (which he's going to finish as soon as he has the time) or at least a development deal somewhere (it's not his fault he missed pilot season because his mom hired some shady contractors who did such a bad job he had to spend the entire summer back in New Jersey undoing and redoing her floors).

"So you didn't respond to the material—that's nothing we haven't gotten over before," Fern says. "If anything, it means you're a better candidate than some loser who's obsessed with the books. You can see its flaws, you know how to fix it, blah, blah—"

"I went to high school with the author," he says finally.

"That's perfect—"

"No," Grant says grimly. "It's not. She didn't like me."

"Well, that's ridiculous, everyone likes you," Fern says, sounding a little maternally offended on his behalf. "Besides, she's not going to be in the meeting; it's just the showrunner and executive producers."

"I . . ." He takes a steadying breath—*exhale longer than you inhale*—and shakes his head. "I don't want to talk about this right now. There has to be something else. What about Jason's spin-off show? That was a good meeting, wasn't it?"

"They don't have the budget for a writer at your level," Fern says evenly. "And you're not taking a pay cut back down to co-producer when we've finally clawed our way up to co-EP."

Grant's IMDb profile succinctly condenses each rung of his career so far into a one-line credit—*staff writer, story editor, executive story editor, co-producer, producer, co–executive producer.* Other writers he came up with never managed to make it past that first credit, and there really aren't many lines separating *him* from *them.* Grant knows he doesn't deserve the success he's had and it's always felt that much more precarious for it.

Grant downs an Advil and massages his temples. "What about features?"

"As soon as you've got a draft of that spec for me, I'm happy to read it. In the meantime, you're a TV writer. You make money for us both as a TV writer. And this is a straight-to-series, prestige"—he scoffs here, but Fern overrules him—"very *buzzy* TV show. The studio execs all loved your materials, the show-runner's already read your sample. Are you really going to make me tell them they wasted their time?"

Grant sighs. He knows, somehow, this is a mistake, even as he says, "Fine, I'll take the meeting."

That night he spends some time googling *Helen Zhang, YA author.* Her author photo comes up first and she looks more or less the way he remembers her, except older and more expensive. Her eyes are intelligent and assessing, her posture as straight as it was that day in the church at her sister's funeral. She's not smiling—Helen has never smiled in his memory, so that makes sense—and he can still see the stiff, serious editor-in-chief of the school paper in her, after all this time.

Their paths rarely crossed before the night that changed his life forever—Helen hung out with the nerdy, Ivy League–obsessed crowd and was not-so-secretly judgy about him and his friends on the football team and cheer squad, rolling her eyes at pep rallies and homecoming and everything that had given his life meaning when he was seventeen years old.

And afterward . . . afterward, Helen hadn't looked at him at all. She looked through him whenever they were in the same room.

Grant considers what Fern would say if he told her he couldn't take this job for "mental health reasons." He laughs to himself—Fern would probably remind him of his mortgage (he shouldn't have bought the bungalow in Silver Lake, but he'd thought *The Guys* would have at least one more season before its untimely cancellation) and dangle attractive numbers in front of him (*minus ten percent*) and tell him therapy costs money.

When he gets the call a few days later that they want to offer him the job, he's past the point of putting up a fight. Therapy *does* cost money, and if Helen Zhang has a problem with him being on the writing staff of her TV show, well.

She can take that up with his entertainment lawyer.

Three

Helen stretches in the parking lot at the foot of Fryman Canyon, the early-morning chill still hanging over all the cars like a shadowy blanket.

"I'm stupidly overbooked on meetings, but I'd love for you to join me on my daily morning hike," the email from Suraya, the showrunner, reads. "Fryman's a pretty one if you've never done it, and it's right up the street from my house."

Helen looks up Suraya's Studio City address on Zillow (purchased for a modest $1.3 million nine years ago) and clicks through all the photos of the interior with nosey curiosity. Further research reveals Suraya's partner is a "mixed media artist" and they have two darling elementary-school-aged children.

She thinks of texting these findings to her two closest author friends, Pallavi and Elyse. There was a time when she would have tossed that Zillow link into their group chat without a second thought, and they would have descended upon this new information like ants invited to a picnic.

Pallavi, Elyse, and Helen met when they were all young aspirings almost a decade ago, at an overcrowded bookstore event where it was impossible to hear the celebrated author's answers from the back. Pallavi had a meager YouTube following of twenty thousand subscribers at the time and Elyse had already published a collection of short stories. Helen had been an assistant at a publishing house that specialized in academic anthologies, fantasizing about the day when her bosses realized they had a literary genius crafting scheduling emails.

They weren't the type of friends who met up every weekend for brunch. Elyse thought Pallavi was kind of desperate. Pallavi thought Elyse was too judgmental. Helen was sure they both found her too serious to be any fun. But they all got their first book deals within months of each other—a coincidence that felt like fate in their early twenties, and theirs became a strategic sisterhood. They met up several times a month for "scheming sessions," where they swapped information on the details of their budding careers and answered each other's questions (*which author photo makes me look the most intriguing, would you actually pick up my book if it had this godawful cover*) with the honesty of young strivers who respected each other's grand ambitions.

These sessions grew fewer and further between over the last few years, but they still celebrated each other's book launches in person and on social media, they shared laughing texts over *this ridiculous thing* some mutual acquaintance said in an interview, they debated screenshots of emails (*am I crazy or does my new editor hate me*), and they found time at least once per tax quarter to get together for drinks.

"That's the mark of friendship in adulthood," Pallavi said at their last meetup in April. "Do I make time to see you at least twice a year in person? We're close friends. More than twice? We're basically family." They all laughed, and Helen had felt some relief—*this is just what adulthood feels like*.

But she's been less certain since the book-to-screen news came out. She texted them both in July when the deal first closed and received a short *Congrats! That's amazing!* from Pallavi and a confetti emoji from Elyse. She watched them get drinks without her on Instagram several times after that and wondered if she'd missed something obvious and if she could ask for an explanation without seeming pathetically needy (*no*, she concluded). She proposed getting drinks as a trio, but schedules never managed to align in the months preceding her departure for LA.

Helen has the sinking feeling that if she stopped texting Pallavi and Elyse, she'd never hear from them again.

She thinks this is the kind of thing she'd talk to a sister about—*a real one*, not the forced found-family type. The type of sister who grows up alongside you and understands without explanations *why* your faulty brain can't seem to process the subtly shifting dynamics of a social circle without a dramatic sense of tragic despair. But then, Helen suspects she wouldn't feel the loss of these friends as acutely if she *did* still have a sister to talk to, and she forces her thoughts in another direction before she can follow them down a dangerous old corridor.

New chapter, new problems.

When Helen sees Suraya the showrunner approaching across the lot ("Finally! Zooms really don't capture a person's *essence*, do they?"), it's hard not to feel starstruck and flattered that this busy and important woman wants to be in charge of her show. Suraya's shorter in person, which makes it all the more impressive how difficult it is to keep pace with her.

"You're the genius creative, obviously—forty weeks on the bestseller list speaks for itself," Suraya says as they pass a well-outfitted gaggle of young influencers on the trail path. "And we're so lucky to have you in the writers room."

Helen had requested a place in the writers room during her initial producer meetings, thinking the answer would be *no*—her agent told horror stories of authors getting into screaming matches with their adapting screenwriters, of projects falling apart because an author hadn't *stayed in their lane* and let the experts handle things. "We can ask, but I wouldn't press," Chelsea advised delicately. "It can be rough to watch a room full of screenwriters rewrite you."

Helen had been surprised when Suraya immediately said yes, they would love to have her in the room.

"I've been reading all the screenwriting books you recommended," Helen says now, eager to show she's done her homework. "And I know things are going to change from the books. I won't be super precious or annoying about it, I swear."

Suraya waves a hand. "Be precious and annoying if it's important to you, that's your role in the room. Protect the book when we've gone too far off the rails. It's no good to us if we put in all this work and your readers hate everything we've done."

Helen nods. "Of course. They won't, though. I trust you."

Suraya laughs as she looks sideways at Helen. "That's such a nice thing to say," she says. "I wouldn't go throwing that around casually in this town if I were you, though."

"Is LA so bad?" Helen knows she's coming across as a guileless bumpkin. But people will assume that of her anyway, so she might as well use it.

"It's an industry town, which if you're as obsessed with work as I am, that's a good thing," Suraya explains. "It's just that people have a way of being very friendly from the jump, and sometimes you forget your interests aren't necessarily perfectly aligned, and then all of a sudden you're in *Deadline*—it's an industry trade, if you don't read it, you should—because your project's fallen apart over 'creative differences.'"

"Oh," Helen says, unsure what to add.

Suraya looks at her shrewdly. "We both want this show to be good. Remember that, when the things we're saying in the room make you feel crazy."

"I will. But that won't happen. I feel lucky just to be here," Helen insists, and finds she means it.

"Aww, it will, though," Suraya laughs as they reach a peak in the hike. "I'm a very annoying person when you spend too many hours with me, which you will. And that's just me. We have six other writers in the room, and that's too many people *not* to have some interpersonal flare-ups in the next twenty weeks."

"I look forward to meeting them all," Helen says.

"They're great." Suraya waves a hand. "My assistant's setting up a dinner and drinks before the room starts so you're not going in cold. Are you excited? Are you nervous?"

Helen nods. "All the feelings. Like the first day of school."

She's pretty sure this is an honest response, though she isn't sure *feelings* is the best categorization for the tangled threads of thoughts in her head. She *needs* this to go well. She *needs* to prove this was a good decision, abandoning her life in New York for a Hollywood sabbatical. She *needs* to fix this uninvited mental block that has her starting and scrapping book proposals for new high-concept YA series with a frequency so alarming, she brought it up to her therapist. *What if I don't* have *any other stories?* she had asked, all the while wondering (stupidly, embarrassingly), *Who am I, if not a successful writer?*

Suraya smiles. "My youngest just started kindergarten last year. She was so excited, and then she spent the entire first day crying for us to pick her up because she didn't like the other kids."

"That won't happen to me," Helen promises.

"Of course it won't. That wasn't a metaphor; we're just talking about my kids now," Suraya laughs.

"Oh." Helen is slightly embarrassed.

"Occupational hazard," Suraya says. "We overshare and

mine our personal lives for work, and inevitably some useless information ends up on the table and you'll walk around LA for the next decade knowing some random detail about someone else's kids."

"Haha," Helen says, like an idiot.

"You'll get used to it." Suraya lightly taps Helen's shoulder. "Oh, if you look up there, it's George Clooney's house."

GRANT CHANGES HIS shirt three times before the dinner and feels stupid every time he does it.

He finally lands on a plain black T-shirt under a varsity crew jacket he bought at the Melrose flea market a few years ago with an ex-girlfriend. He never rowed crew in high school or college, but Karina had assured him that didn't actually matter. *"It'll look cool when you wear it on set."* And it did. She never steered him wrong in wardrobe, at least.

He's spent the last week and a half debating if he should reach out to Helen before the writers room starts, then puts it off until it's too late and he's in an Uber en route to a seafood restaurant on the west side wondering if the varsity jacket was a mistake.

Maybe this whole thing was a mistake, but it's too late to back down now.

When he gets to the reserved table and Helen isn't there, he feels a gnawing sense of dread instead of relief. *Something's* going to happen—he can feel the cosmic scales tipping against him—and he'd rather get it over with.

"Good, you're finally here," Suraya says, a mini–crab cake in hand. "Everyone, this is Grant, my number two."

It's a roll call of the usual suspects, Soapy Teen Drama Writers Room™ edition—the husband-and-wife writing team, the smart-funny-mean twentysomethings, and the mini-Suraya (her name is Saskia) who clearly reminds the showrunner of herself twenty years ago.

Suraya glances up and beams. "And here's our guest of honor, Helen Zhang."

The table cheers rowdily and Grant looks up.

It's her.

Helen Zhang, in the present tense. She looks—good. Her hair is swept back in a messy knot, the dark blue knit dress she's wearing flashes a hint of light blue pleating with every step that brings her closer. She looks intimidating, put-together, and *grown up* and he suddenly feels inadequately prepared in every way for this moment.

Helen smiles tentatively as she looks around the table and her eyes drift past him conveniently—he can't tell if this is on purpose or if she simply hasn't registered him.

"Helen, we've got Tom, Eve, Owen, Saskia, Nicole, and Grant."

Helen's gaze snaps to Grant immediately and he feels like an insect pinned to paper.

"We've met," she says neatly. There's a sharpness to her voice that suddenly calls to mind an image of dispassionate scissors, cleanly snipping away any thread of destiny that has the gall to show up right now. "Grant and I went to high school together."

SHE HAD NOTICED him immediately, standing next to Suraya like a cosmic joke. He still towers over everyone else in the room, though Grant Shepard's build has leaned out since his high school football days. *Is he wearing a letterman jacket?* For a wild moment, Helen wonders if this is some kind of messed-up prank.

The showrunner's brows lift and she throws Grant (*Grant!*) a bemused look. "You never mentioned that in your interview."

Grant shucks the jacket off and sips his water in an obvious bid for time. He watches her over the rim of his glass. She's perversely fascinated by what he could possibly say next and stares at the muscles of his throat (when's the last time she thought about *Grant Shepard's* throat?) working in anticipation. Finally, he swallows and sets the glass down lightly.

"Didn't feel like a fair thing to do. The school in the books is nothing like the school we went to," Grant says casually, his gaze flitting away from hers like it was never anything important. "Besides, I wanted to get the job because of how much you believed in me as a writer, Suraya."

"Kiss-ass." Suraya rolls her eyes. "He's the number two," she adds to Helen. "If I'm not in the room, Grant's in charge of running things in the writers room."

"Ah," says Helen.

Her mouth is dry and her pulse pounds violently in her head from the effort of *act normal, whatever that means here.* Grant looks up at her then.

Come on, his expression seems to suggest, *this doesn't have to be weird if we don't let it.*

It's as though he's using the kind of psychic connection that's only created by thirteen years of trying to forget the same thing, and she thinks she might be sick.

"You'll have to tell us embarrassing stories about Grant later," Suraya smiles.

"What are we eating?" Helen says instead.

And even as she feels with every fiber of her being that this is wrong, *that this can't possibly be happening*, that maybe there should even be *laws* to prevent this from ever happening again—she finds herself sharing endless appetizers and politely laughing at everyone's icebreaker jokes with *Grant Shepard* from opposite ends of the same table.

It becomes a silent game, who can seem more *normal* about this—maybe they'll even make it the full twenty weeks exchanging only polite, respectful glances across a table and no one will ever bring up Helen's dead sister or how she died.

Sometimes I wish you weren't my sister.

When Suraya suggests they relocate to the rooftop for after-dinner drinks, Helen goes up first to claim a spot while everyone else freshens up and makes phone calls to friends and babysitters. Grant reappears first, two drinks in hand— margaritas, which feel inappropriately festive. There's an air of slight hesitation in his stance that she finds to be *unlike him* and is suddenly infuriated by the thought.

"Is one of those for me?" she asks.

"If you want it to be." He sets it down.

Their natural lives should have taken them far, far away from each other, never to meet or think about each other again after graduation. Helen takes the drink and knows she's going to lose whatever game they're playing first.

"I think you should quit," she says abruptly.

Grant lifts his brows, then sips his drink coolly.

"Do you," he says, sounding bored.

She immediately hates how he does that, the way nothing she says or does seems to faze him, when she feels nothing but *affected*. She's vibrating from a sensation both familiar and strange—being in unexpectedly close proximity to *him*. Her heart slams against her chest in an impressive effort to meet the wooden deck floor, or perhaps to tackle her sister's mur- derer. *Not legally true*, she reminds herself. *It wasn't his fault.* Her wounded heart still tries to punch him through her chest.

"Yes. It's wildly inappropriate, not to mention *cruel*, for you to be here right now."

Helen is aware that she's doing that thing where she sounds

weirdly formal, like she was raised by Victorian ghosts or something, and immediately regrets saying anything at all.

"That's taking it a bit far, isn't it?" he says, like a jerk.

"No, it's not. How—how did this even happen?"

"They sent me your book, I took a meeting, Suraya's great, she thinks I'm great, here we are."

"You never should have taken the meeting," Helen says. She can feel her cheeks flushing from a heady mix of alcohol and anger. "You should have said no. Found something else. Anything else."

"Yeah," he laughs. "Well."

"Don't you feel like, like a terrible person taking this job?" she asks.

"No, actually, I don't," he says, knocking back the rest of his drink. "I have a mortgage and bills to pay and contrary to what someone who lucked into a cushy screenwriting job *two seconds* after landing in LA might think, jobs don't just fall out of the sky for the rest of us."

How dare you! the Victorian ghosts in her mind decry.

"I didn't *luck* into this job—this is *my* book," she says acidly. "And if you're having a hard time, that's too bad, but it's not really my problem, is it?"

Grant exhales and shuts his eyes tightly, pushing a finger against his temple. He looks like he's in pain, and she thinks, *Good.* When he finally speaks, his voice is controlled and quiet, and his eyes are on her.

"Helen, I didn't want to kill your sister and I've had to live with that every day since, and I'm not asking you to forgive me but you know just as well as I do, it could have been anyone's car she jumped in front of; it just happened to be *mine*."

Helen can't quite believe she's heard him right. She thinks she glimpses something desperate in his eyes, and bizarrely finds herself wondering what's happened in Grant Shepard's life since she last saw him.

"I don't *care*," she hisses. "It was *your* car. It was *you* driving."

Grant flinches and she feels a bloodthirsty kind of satisfaction. This night was supposed to be the start of a new chapter, a career highlight. The fact that she's thinking about *Grant Fucking Shepard* tonight seems like a cruel prank of the universe—that even from beyond the grave, little sisters have a talent for inserting themselves into places where *they weren't invited*.

"I don't want *you* on this show," Helen finishes.

She feels an itch to punctuate her words with a jab at his chest, but she thinks touching Grant Shepard might be the most inappropriate thing conceivable right now.

"Well, I'm not quitting," Grant says, his eyes full of cold, hard *nothing*. "So if you want to get rid of me, take it up with Suraya."

The sound of a small herd of TV writers clambering up the deck pulls them both out of the conversation. Grant slips on a mask of polite indifference as they approach. *What a monster*, Helen thinks automatically.

"I'm heading out early," he says to Tom, the husband in the married-couple writing team. "Great seeing you guys again. Everyone else, looking forward to working with you all."

He salutes Helen with a bitter twist of a smile and a glass of water, then heads downstairs.

The small Asian writer who looks like she's just out of school—Saskia—takes the spot Grant vacated and smiles at Helen in a hesitant, hopeful kind of way.

"It's so great to meet you," she says in a rush of energy, the most she's spoken all night. "I hope you don't mind me saying, I'm such a big fan. It's my first staffing job. I couldn't believe how lucky I was to even get an interview."

New scene. Helen clicks over to a fresh mental page and forces a smile back at Saskia. "It's my first TV job too," she admits. "I feel like I got thrown in the deep end."

"We can look out for each other, then," Saskia says eagerly. "I can't believe how young you are, to have accomplished so much."

Helen finds something familiar in this sentence. In the last few years, she's grown used to being approached by other young, female, Asian writers—at events, in her DMs, in her email inbox occasionally, when the intrepid ones manage to find a cracked door. They look up to her, they tell her. They want to know how she did it, they're proud of her, and maybe they're a little bit envious too. She used to respond to every request for advice—she was flattered, she was eager to help, and maybe it was a safe passage to channel some neglected guilt too. *I'm a good role model,* she told herself with every carefully crafted response. *I'm a good citizen in my community. I leave roadmaps and signposts for the ones coming after me.* But eventually it became too much—more success yielded a deluge—and she felt more guilt to push aside with every unanswered message.

She looks at Saskia now and tries to see something like a little sister.

Michelle would have hated you. The vicious thought comes unbidden. *Too desperate.*

Across the deck, Suraya gives Helen a *you good?* kind of look. Helen swallows. *I am not good.*

The thought pings through her heart and her mind and then her *entire body* insistently, and she imagines saying it out loud. She imagines how Suraya would look at her if Helen started tearing up her carefully selected, apparently beloved writing staff before they even started day one in the writers room. She imagines quitting and going back to Manhattan, tail between her legs—*turns out if you make it here, you can't actually make it "anywhere."*

She straightens her shoulders. She can handle this.

She's not going to give *Grant Shepard* the satisfaction.

Helen nods at Suraya and smiles. She's *great*.

GRANT MANAGES TO stave off the panic attack the entire forty-five-minute Uber ride back from the west side to Silver Lake. As soon as his home security system *beeps*, it all falls apart.

His vision is spotty and there's a faint ringing in his ears and there's not enough *air* in the room as he stumbles into the kitchen. He pulls out his cell phone with shaking hands and thumbs through his contacts list clumsily—he could call his therapist, but it's late and she has kids. Fern, his agent, is dismissed immediately. She's allergic to feelings.

He scrolls past more contacts—other TV writers, people he's poured his heart out to in closed, professional settings when they were all on the clock and opening personal veins while panning for story gold. None of them are personally invested enough to talk Grant through a panic attack at almost eleven o'clock on a Friday night.

Finally, his thumb swipes past the wet drops—*fuck, he's crying*—and lands on "Karina, wardrobe."

She picks up on the third ring.

"I have five minutes, then I have to go back to set. What's up?" she asks.

"I, uh, I'm . . . I'm having a panic attack," Grant says through the phone.

"Shit," she says. "Is there anyone with you?"

"No," he says, and feels like a loser.

"Breathe," she instructs him. "Longer exhales than inhales. One . . . two . . . three . . ."

She keeps counting on the phone with him till ten and his breathing is regular again.

"Thanks," he says. "Sorry to bother you at work. It's just . . . I have no one else to call."

"Do you want to tell me what happened?" she asks.

"Um." He thinks about how unfair this is to her, how they broke up five months ago, how he still has to return some of her vinyl records. "No. It's not important. You should get back to set."

There's a pause on the other side of the line.

Then she sighs. "You should find someone you can talk to, Grant. Not me, obviously, but . . . someone."

"Yeah. Thanks."

"Have a good night," she says, and hangs up.

Grant knows he could probably find *someone to talk to* easily enough. There's his therapist, for a start, and he's probably due for a session. But there was also a time when he might have thought eleven o'clock wasn't so late and he could have found himself at a bar, beside a pretty face with a sympathetic ear, before midnight. *Everyone likes you*, his agent had said and it's true, for the most part. He's easy to look at and just sad enough to be interesting.

The problem for Grant has never been beginnings. It's that none of his relationships ever seem to survive a second act. Dating him, living with him, loving him becomes *too sad*, he needs you *too much*, and he always seems to be attracted to beautiful, complicated women who are smart enough to eventually recognize *it's not their responsibility to fix him, though they truly hope he heals someday.*

As he brushes the taste of the failed evening out of his teeth, Grant wonders if Helen's told Suraya yet. He wonders how that conversation would go.

Do you know you've employed a murderer?

Suraya would gasp, she'd assure Helen she had no idea, she'd call Grant's agency and salt the earth with them for putting her in such a terrible position without disclosing it. He'd be dropped and unemployed not just on this show but for good, and everyone he's ever worked with would whisper, *We knew it, we knew there was something wrong with him, we all sensed it.*

He knows he's catastrophizing, that it's technically unhealthy, but somehow it makes him feel better. Imagining his past finally catching up to him, the day he's been dreading for so long finally here at last. He cycles through all possible worst-case scenarios until he reaches the oldest of his most suppressed thoughts, buried deep under years of therapy and friends' reassurances he doesn't believe nearly as much as the truth—*he could have stopped it from happening, if he'd only hit the brakes faster, if he'd been paying more attention.*

Grant knows he's right to feel guilty, that he should probably feel a little guilty forever—and it's not such a terrible price to pay, in the relative balance of things.

He should have apologized to Helen when he had the chance. He would have if he'd been in his right mind. He thinks maybe if he apologizes to her, he can salvage this. He decides he'll email her tomorrow.

This calms him enough to fall asleep, his last thought a hazy memory of Helen Zhang staring at him with coolly demanding eyes, first as a teenager, then as an adult, telling him firmly each time what he's always secretly known—that his presence isn't wanted, that he should leave before he offends everyone even more.

I know, he tells Helen in his dream-memory. *When will you stop reminding me?*

HELEN CAN'T SLEEP, so she gets out of bed and does what she always does when she can't sleep and doesn't love herself enough to stop. She retrieves her suitcase from under the bed, unzips an inner compartment, and pulls out an old (*haunted*, her teenage self always adds) hard drive. She plugs the haunted hard drive into her laptop and starts picking at an old emotional scab that never quite scarred over.

> Files ❯ 🗁 Michelle is Working
> > ❯ 🗀 AP Bio
> > ❯ 🗀 AP English
> > ❯ 🗀 Latin 2
> > ❯ 🗀 Pre-Calculus
> > ❯ 🗀 Phys. Ed.
> > ❯ 🗀 Photography
> > ❯ 🗀 World Cultures

Helen studies the files, the digital summation of her little sister's final semester of life. She clicks through the familiar folders. Michelle kept a diary for only a few days into seventh grade before Helen had admonished her, "Why on *earth* would you leave a written record of evidence for Mom and Dad to find?"

Helen will never forgive her fourteen-year-old self for that.

Instead of a diary, she's been left with a hard drive full of old essays and math assignments. Helen once had the romantic notion that it might be possible to understand her little sister better in death, that she would learn something new from the margins of Michelle's essay fragments on Dust Bowl–era photography and the lives of the Brontë sisters.

They hadn't been close enough to confide in each other after middle school—Helen had found her younger sister's existence slightly embarrassing to her new friends at her new high school, and Michelle, it seemed, had decided the feeling was entirely mutual by eighth grade.

In Helen's memory, Michelle is perpetually a surly teenage girl slipping behind the door of her cave-like bedroom, which always smelled vaguely of overripe fruit, in a towering mood across the hall over some perceived injustice enacted by her family, her teachers, or the world.

Secretly, Helen always hoped she'd eventually make the discovery of a lifetime in her archeological tours of her sister's old hard drive—something that would unlock the mystery of Michelle's last few years, in Michelle's own words: an early outline of a novel perhaps, or sketches of original poems, *or even a half-finished draft of a suicide letter*.

But nothing ever materialized and Helen abandoned the effort as a profoundly *stupid* version of self-harm that she was too smart to engage with. So smart, in fact, she wrote this search for lost letters into her own books—her books about brilliant, academic teens on the quest for long-lost academic secrets, in the wake of a tragic car accident that took the life of the protagonist's little sister. *And those books are getting turned into a TV show*, Helen reminds herself. She has spun this particular personal wound into gold many times over and it's time to let it go, its purpose as grist for the creative mill long since fulfilled.

Find a new emotional scab to pick—this is boring, Helen admonishes herself. *Tell a new story.*

But still, she sits in front of her laptop, and she clicks.

Maybe there'll be something she missed in the next folder.

Four

I like your name," the hostess says as she flashes Grant Shepard a smile across the check-in stand.

Helen thinks she might have to turn around and get back in her car immediately. She's standing on the sidewalk outside the alfresco restaurant in Mid-City where they agreed to meet and Grant is flirting with the hostess.

"I can't take credit for it," he says with an easy grin. "But thanks. I like yours too."

"We need another menu," Helen says irritably.

Grant and the hostess-with-the-name-he-likes (*Rose*, her name tag reads) both glance in Helen's direction, as if they've just remembered her.

"Of course," Rose the hostess says, shooting Grant a sympathetic look as she grabs another menu. "Right this way."

They're seated at a patio table that overlooks the street, under the shade of a vining bougainvillea. Helen is suddenly aware of how visible they are and regrets agreeing to this meeting. His (no subject) email had been short and unexpected—*Would like to connect before the room starts, if you're open. Lunch?*

She had forwarded the email to her agent's assistant, who understood the tacit assignment and coordinated a time and place without fuss or direct contact between them.

"So," she says, after the waiter has offered them both still and sparkling water, read off the day's specials (*beef tagliata, Italian wedding soup*), taken their lunch orders, and left.

Finally.

"So," Grant agrees, with a hesitant kind of smile. She imagines this must be his best weapon in any argument.

"What did you want to talk about?" Helen asks.

Grant pauses, as if considering his options.

"I didn't hear from Suraya after the welcome drinks night," he says, tapping his sunglasses on the table. "Just her assistant confirming my drive-on access details for Monday."

Helen looks out toward the street. She hopes he doesn't think she's forgiven him.

"If you don't have the decency to quit, that's on your conscience," she says. "I'm not going to sabotage the room with last-minute problems, even if I should have known about them sooner."

She sends him a look of pointed disgust. Grant's mouth twitches, like he finds this funny somehow. She hates that she always feels ridiculous trying to wear her own anger—like it's the wrong size after too many winters spent at the back of her closet.

"That's the thing about Hollywood," he says, pouring them both a refill of water. "Very few truly decent people left in our industry."

She gets the impression that he's laughing internally at her— poor Helen and her silly *morals*—and finds herself craving that feeling of bloodthirsty *victory* over him again.

"I bet you think you're decent," she says idly, as he lifts his glass for a drink. "*Sorry I killed your sister, let me buy you lunch.*"

Grant's glass freezes on its way to his mouth. He sets it down and she watches the veins on his neck work rather spectacularly.

"Helen," he says quietly. "I think we should set some ground rules."

"Ground rules," she repeats slowly. The shape of his words feel strange on her tongue.

"If we're both going to be in the room, it's in the best interests of the show for us to be . . . friendly," Grant says. "Writer to writer."

You're too good-looking to be a writer, Helen immediately wants to say out loud. *You didn't have an awkward teen phase that forced you to develop a rich interior life to compensate.*

His tousled dark brown hair looks almost chestnut in the sun and the dappled light casts just enough shadow to call attention to the sharp, attractive planes of his face. She thinks it's bitterly unfair that they share a profession, when he has that face. She remembers Grant Shepard the boy as handsome in a vaguely unattainable way.

Grant Shepard the man is painfully compelling.

"Friendly," Helen says. "Sure. Professionally, anyway."

If he notices the addendum, he doesn't seem to care much. He taps the linen tablecloth, thoughtful.

"We talk a lot about our personal lives in the room," Grant says. "Your books are set in high school—they'll probably ask about our shared experiences back then."

What shared experiences? They never spoke all that much before the accident and they certainly didn't speak afterward. She thinks that might have been by design, that their teachers and peers carefully steered them in opposite directions those last three weeks of school, as if afraid Helen would one day take out her carefully packaged grief and let it explode all over him inappropriately.

"It's supposed to be a safe space for discussion," he says, watching her carefully. "I want to know if there are any topics we're avoiding. For instance, I wondered how much from your own life you were pulling, with the sister—"

"Michelle is off-limits," Helen says abruptly. "I don't want to talk about her. Ever."

She swallows. She rarely says Michelle's name out loud these days.

He nods, curt—*understood*.

The familiar ghost of a thought drifts through her mind— *What was it like for you, afterward?* It's a thought she's always redirected herself from as quickly as possible—because the wondering would inevitably turn to imagining, and the imagining would turn to a moment of voluntary empathy, *it must have been fucking terrible for you*, and that empathy would mature into guilt—guilt that he even had to think about this thing that Helen herself absolutely refused to let determine more of her life than it already had. And then she would resent the guilt, because *she* wasn't the one responsible for him having that memory, and she'd find her way back to *anger* and the slammed door of her sister's suicide and *who are you really angry with?* and the unhealthy spiral would continue and continue until the past and the present blurred into the same reality, *reliving instead of reflecting*, as her therapist once called it. And so she always resurfaced back around to the general rule that it would be better not to wonder about Grant Shepard at all.

Grant Shepard in the present seems to be waiting for more and Helen tries to clear the haze of old ghosts long enough to find her place in the conversation again.

"Everything else . . . I guess . . . is fair game if it helps the show," she says.

Grant lifts a brow. "Everything?"

Helen shrugs. "Sure."

"Who'd you have a crush on in high school?" he asks, leaning back with a frown.

Helen shakes her head and laughs. "No one in your orbit."

"You'll have to do better than that, once we're in the room," he says, and she feels like she's just been judged in a competition she wasn't aware she'd entered. "Specifics are helpful."

"I know," she says, annoyed. "I *am* a writer."

The food arrives then (handmade pasta for him, a self-conscious salad for her), and she feels him watching her as the waiter sets down a fresh bread basket on the linen tablecloth between them.

"You don't think we need a safe word for when we're talking about high school stuff?" he asks, and she isn't tricked by his easy tone at all—there's a tense thread of something *careful* in his entire posture. "What if my feelings get hurt?"

It's not his own feelings he's worried about, she thinks, and stabs a crouton.

"I bet you're tougher than you think," she says. "Otherwise you wouldn't have gotten the job."

He barks out a laugh and picks up his fork.

"You know, I am *good* at my job," he says, taking a bite of pasta. "Some might argue you're getting me for below market price, at great value."

"If it were up to me, I wouldn't have you at all," Helen reminds him, and wonders how much longer they both have to endure sitting here before they can call the waiter for the check.

IF IT WERE up to me, I wouldn't have you at all.

Grant resists the urge to drag his hand across his face in case it catches and pulls off his mask of pleasant, barely restrained *politeness* to reveal how he really feels—like a hideous monster, whose own therapist felt the need to remind him, "There are things we *can* do, but it's good to ask ourselves if we *should* do them."

He knows he *should* quit. Helen had demanded it so regally of him that first night, he'd briefly imagined himself going down on one knee to kiss the ring and beg forgiveness.

But he's also pretty sure he *can* do a good job—a great job, even—and he muses philosophically that while he *should* have done a lot of things, he's here now, they're careening toward inevitability, and wouldn't it be more of a net positive for everyone involved if he started putting his energy into being *helpful*?

"Who's your favorite character?" Grant asks, hoping to put them back in safe territory.

Helen shrugs. "All of them," she says.

"I like to think I'm a Bellamy, with a Phoebe rising," Grant quips.

She frowns at him. "You're not," she says bluntly.

He's a little exasperated by this response. *We aren't talking about how you feel about me—we're talking about the art of adaptation!* he wants to say, like the pretentious artist he suspects he secretly is, under the Clark Kent disguise of this Hollywood hack. He has to find a piece of himself in someone else's work, that's the entire assignment. He's developed a talent for it— reading and quickly identifying *that part, that's the shard of glass reflecting back a piece of me.* The strangest thing about reading Helen's book was that he already knew what he was looking for, what he was hoping for, before he ever cracked the spine. *But she doesn't want to talk about that with him.*

"The word of god herself." Grant lifts his water glass, all deference. "Who do you think I am, then?"

"No one," Helen says, watching him with an unreadable expression. "You were never in the book."

"I guess I should be grateful for that," Grant says dryly.

Helen looks back out toward the street, silent.

It was in the early days—when he first started college— that Grant thought about Helen the most. It had been strange to know someone connected to the same tragedy as him was also going through the same off-to-college rituals as him—orientation week and moving into a new dorm and meeting her new roommate and learning her new city. He had wondered how all these experiences looked through her eyes, if she thought about that night as often as he did, or if she could suppress those memories better. Grant had no siblings of his own to fulfill the role of confidant. When he thought of who he'd want to confide in about the aftermath of that night, his thoughts always drifted strangely to Helen Zhang. He remembers one particularly stupid creative writing assignment, for which he had written out all the conversations he wanted to have with her as poems.

Somewhere on an old hard drive, he has shitty poetry about this woman.

Grant studies Helen from across the table now and thinks of how many more mirrored experiences they must have had in the last thirteen years, for them both to end up here. He has the impression that she holds all her real thoughts and feelings behind a shiny, impenetrable wall and it might take all the pickaxes in the world to chip a single hole.

He swings back a mental pickax and tries: "How do you feel about the first day of school on Monday?"

He thinks he catches a glimmer of humor behind her eyes.

"Fine," she says simply.

He wonders what it would take to make her laugh.

"I know you hate me," Grant says, stabbing more pasta on his plate. "But this could be fun, if we let it."

"Stop it," Helen snaps, and he looks up. She's angry and he's surprised by its vehemence as much as its sudden appearance. "I know what you're doing. You're being . . . charming, homecoming king, class president Grant Shepard, and I am the one person—*the one person*—that is not ever going to work on."

Are you sure about that? he wants to ask, just to get a rise out of her. *What if I try really hard this time?*

"Okay," he says instead. "No charm for Helen. Noted."

He sips his water and starts mentally counting down how many weeks they have left (*twenty, give or take a few holiday breaks*) until they can walk out of each other's lives again.

HELEN'S MOM CALLS as she drives her rental car back to the west side.

"Oh, you can hang up and call me back when you are not driving," Mom says, then proceeds to ask twenty "just before you go" questions about how it's going in LA, does she need one of Mom's friends in Yorba Linda to come check up on her, what grocery store is she buying her groceries from?

By the time Helen opens the door to her condo, she's giving a half-hearted account of her trip to 99 Ranch and listing Chinese vegetables while her mother grunts in approval or disapproval.

"You will need to make the water spinach soon," Mom says. "I will send you a recipe."

"Okay," Helen says. "Thanks. Is that everything?"

There's a pause on the other end of the line. Helen feels a touch of guilt, spooling from New Jersey to catch her all the way at the edge of the Pacific Ocean.

"Just call us back when you can. We know you are busy."

"Okay, I will," Helen promises.

She hangs up and rests her forehead against her cabinet doors. *She hasn't told her parents he's working on the show.*

She knows Mom and Dad have already experienced a few lifetimes' worth of undeserved pain. Sometimes it feels like she's spent her entire adult life carefully steering them away from sharp objects and despair.

Helen remembers the feeling of freedom when she finally left for college—she'd spent the summer ferrying food and water between her father, who watched Chinese soap operas nightly in the living room with dull, expressionless eyes, and her mother, who spent days at a time sobbing quietly in the master bedroom between her manic episodes of cleaning the house for the steady stream of visitors coming with food and condolences. Helen herself had stared at the closed door of Michelle's room every morning and every evening—willing it to open, for Michelle to reveal this had all been some sort of sick goodbye prank. *Come out, I dare you.*

College was Helen's first chance to write her own story from scratch. She had thrown herself into meeting new people, finding new routines, discovering new vices, and she had resolutely ignored the strange pang in her chest every weekend when her roommate would Skype with her brother.

She remembers with some embarrassment the first time she told a boy she loved him—they'd met the first night of orientation. They had been walking around campus in large packs, a bunch of teenagers trying on new adulthood for the first time. They heard the roar of a distant crowd and Helen had wondered aloud, "What's going on over there?" The boy next to her had said, "I dunno. Wanna find out?" and hoisted her above his shoulders, like something from a rom-com meet-cute.

That had been the start, when her weary heart had sputtered to life for the first time in what felt like forever.

She remembers being surprised by the intensity of their friendship, how they both insisted *it feels like time passes differently here than it did back home.* She learned more about him in a week than she felt like she knew about anyone from high school—his name was Ethan, he was from Pittsburgh, his parents were professors who never had time to teach their own son, he had a high school sweetheart going to school three hours away, *he was the best-looking boy who had ever smiled at her.*

"I love you," she had blurted out one night, just a week after they'd met. They had been sitting outside on the grass after exploring the campus after dark, as they had every night since the first night. She had told him about her parents, her sister, her pettiest thoughts and most shameful secrets, and he had listened and stroked her hair and held her hand, and she had thought, *I've never felt so understood before.*

"You *love* me?" he had chuckled, in a half-teasing, half-embarrassed way. "We've only known each other for a week."

That wasn't love, Helen admonishes herself even now. *You're not that stupid anymore. You don't fall for just anyone who smiles at you.*

She sometimes wonders if she's incapable of loving the way other people do, and if the ones closest to her can sense it.

When the TV deal was officially announced, Helen's agent took her out for a celebratory lunch. Chelsea had tittered gossipily when she saw Helen's ex from across the room—Oliver, a foreign affairs correspondent. They'd had a nice life together for two years—he had practically moved into Helen's place, the doorman knew him by name, and he knew all her favorite breakfast and dinner spots within a four-block radius. He told her he loved her just often enough to be reassuring instead of suffocating and he accepted that after two years, she still hadn't said it back to him. "Say it when you're sure," he always added.

But seven months ago on Valentine's Day, Helen had misinterpreted him reaching for his wallet for him reaching for a ring and blurted out, "I don't wanna get married." He'd blinked at her and slowly produced his credit card for the check and she had flushed almost as pink as the specialty prix fixe menus on the tables.

"Maybe we should take a break," Oliver said when they got

home, in a gentle voice. "Figure out if this is really something we both want."

She had nodded and hoped they could move past this, and a week later he had determined, "I deserve someone who can love me back. I just don't think you're capable of it."

"He must be regretting you right now," Chelsea had said, and ordered another round of drinks for the table. Helen found herself tearing up unexpectedly over her second martini.

"It's stupid," she said, and viciously swiped beneath her eyes while Chelsea graciously became fascinated with the tablecloth. "I'm just thinking about the life I almost had with him, and how it probably would have been nice if I'd just been able to say I loved him like a *normal fucking person*, but I'm being an idiot."

"You're not an idiot," Chelsea had said soothingly. "You're a number one *New York Times* bestselling author."

She hates how quickly that actually *did* make her feel better.

Helen takes special care to do her best by the few people she *does* love. She thinks ruefully of old friends who probably don't miss Helen's defective kind of love—*maybe throw in a sister too*—and she thinks of her parents, the ones who loved her first. She's never been able to completely erase the shadow of despair from her parents' eyes, but Helen has done the very best she possibly can.

This is not doing the best she possibly can.

She wonders if she can still call the whole thing off. She detected some familiar look of complicated *guilt* in Grant's eyes at lunch, and she thinks if she were to pick up the phone now, he'd answer. *I've changed my mind*, she'd tell him. *I need you off the show. Surely you owe me a favor or two.*

Then some contrary part of her decides, *no, it's too late now—he stays.*

Helen turns on the sink and washes last night's dishes as she determines, *it's not really about him at all*. It's about some private rebellion she finds herself relishing in the idea of keeping Grant on the writing staff, despite having spent their last two in-person interactions in open hostility.

What happens next? she keeps finding herself wondering in his company.

It's been a long time since she remembers feeling this interested in anything, even if it's an interest wrapped in some heady combination of *wrong* and *go away*.

It makes her feel like a different person—like she isn't a boring Goody Two-shoes who still writes young adult fiction mostly because she doesn't think her parents could handle reading "harder stuff," as her agent has called it. There's nothing in Helen's books that would suggest she's had sex or engaged in risky behaviors of any kind.

Her characters pine after each other with the tension of a nineteenth-century romance novel, while poring over long-forgotten eighteenth-century academic texts. The fictional dead sister died a saint, not a hint of heroin in her veins. "They could all probably use a good fuck and a few addictions," Suraya said in their first meeting, pitching her vision for the soapier series adaptation.

Maybe her parents will find out about Grant Shepard working on *The Ivy Papers* someday (*he could still set fire to himself professionally or die in a car accident, or his episode could get pulled by the network, for reasons beyond anyone's control*, she thinks optimistically), but someday won't be today, and she feels a new and thrilling kind of power in holding the reins on this piece of information.

She stares at her reflection in her glass cupboard and wonders what Monday—*the first day of school, he called it*—will bring.

Five

"Helen, would you like to say anything to start us off?"

She looks up, startled by the question from Suraya. *Was I supposed to have something prepared?* Helen has the sudden mental picture of herself giving a rousing inspirational speech to this room full of strangers (and Grant), and almost laughs. *Who do you think you are?*

"Um, no, I don't think so," she says out loud.

Suraya smiles at her in a *don't worry about it* way and turns to the room at large. "Well, you're all here for a reason, so don't be afraid to speak up loudly and often. We have some truly great source material to live up to"—here, she nods toward Helen—"and I'm excited we get to be the ones to introduce whole new audiences to these fantastic books. Let's do them, and the author, *who is watching us very closely*, proud."

That gets a few chuckles from the room and Helen hopes for the thousandth time that she isn't ridiculous for being here, that she shouldn't be somewhere in Midtown Manhattan with Pallavi and Elyse instead, sipping a martini and saying nonchalantly, *I think they're starting the writers room for my show today, isn't that cool?*

Then Suraya turns to her right and Helen feels a tingling sense of *things are about to get worse.*

"Grant, you want to add anything?"

Grant sits directly across from her, playing with a retractable pen in a way she finds vaguely familiar. They're separated by a long, oval table made from solid teak.

"Yeah." Grant clears his throat. "Be vulnerable. If I don't see each and every one of you cry before this room is over, you're fired."

That gets a laugh, which she finds surprising. Does he even have that kind of authority around here? He has the ear of the showrunner, which counts for something. But then, so does Helen.

She should have said something first, when she had the chance.

Grant glances at her for a fraction of a second and she feels a creeping warmth flushing up the side of her neck. It lasts even after he redirects his attention to the rest of the room.

"No, but honestly"—he grins in that friendly, *winning* way he has—"I feel lucky to be making art with all of you. Which sounds lofty, but that's what we're doing here, so I'll tell you my darkest secret."

Helen's throat seems to constrict as she stares at the side of his head.

"Which is that when I was nineteen, I had a sex dream about my mother, and my therapist told me that's very *normal*."

Helen blinks. *What?*

Nicole cackles, Saskia bursts into embarrassed laughter, and Helen clocks Suraya giving Grant a subtle, smiling nod of approval.

"Well, that makes me feel better about myself," the youngest male writer—*Owen*—drawls. "Is it my turn? My darkest secret is . . . hm, how deep are we getting here? Like 'I hate my brother's wife' deep?"

Owen launches into a story about his older brother's wedding weekend and Helen starts mentally counting down how

many people have to go before they get to her. This spontane-
ous bonding exercise seems to be happening only at the whim
of Grant Shepard. Surely if it was actually necessary, Suraya
would have started it?

Helen isn't even sure what qualifies as a dark secret. She's
reminded of all the times she's been a silent participant in ex-
cruciating group conversations that never seem to go well for
her. She always ends up waiting too long for a natural point to
interject, and when she finally speaks, it's usually something she
can instantly tell was the wrong thing to say—she's overshared,
or undershared, or asked a follow-up question that's too prob-
ing when she only meant to be polite.

The married-couple writing team—Tom and Eve—jointly
tell a story about Tom having a one-night stand with a former
child actress who Eve had grown up obsessed with, and how
they ran into her while on their first date, years later.

Helen chances a look at Suraya. The showrunner is nodding
and laughing. Helen tries to school her features into a fun, *I'm
actively listening* expression.

"Can we address the fact that you definitely wanted to fuck
me more after you found out?" Tom asks with a raised brow.

"Sometimes I picture you guys together and it's hot to me,
I'm sorry," Eve says.

Suraya interjects with an anecdote next, because they've
reminded her about a time her partner once pissed her off so
much, she almost walked out on their then-three-year-old
daughter.

Helen feels a prickling sensation at the side of her face and
knows that Grant is watching her. She tries to affect a *this
doesn't bother me* posture, propping up her elbow, resting her
chin in her hand, and resolutely not looking at him. She thinks
she hears a short *ha* of air from his general direction.

By the time they get back around to Helen, the room seems to be buzzing with the energy of newly discovered inside jokes, and she tries not to feel like she's at a disadvantage, going last.

"I don't know if I have any dark secrets," Helen starts.

"That's okay, we've spent enough time procrastinating," Suraya says, and turns to the giant, six-foot-wide glass dry-erase board on the wall. "Let's talk about our show."

Helen instantly feels both relieved and slighted.

Suraya stands and scribbles *courtyard, unearthing secret box* at the top left corner of the dry-erase board, then adds *courtyard, burying secrets + a body* at the bottom right corner.

Then she turns to the room and says, "Well, what happens in the middle?"

And they start talking about *whose body* (in the books, it's a teacher) and *how did they die* and the young female writer with cool eyeliner—*Nicole*—raises her hand and tells a story about her least favorite grandmother's death and somehow they're back on the dark secrets train and Helen thinks longingly of the bar in Midtown where she could be sipping a martini instead.

GRANT REMINDS HIMSELF he *did* try to warn her, over their lunch and in his general address to the room—that polite, serious conversation had very little use in a writers room. He watches as Helen's face flushes with distinctly East Coast embarrassment at a story he's certain Nicole has told at least a dozen times to complete strangers before.

This is the biggest difference between his interactions in LA and his interactions with old friends in Dunollie, New Jersey. He's spent most of his adult life in a city where erring on the side of blistering vulnerability is professionally rewarded— every working screenwriter he knows has an arsenal of three or four stories that make them sound like *terrible people*, like they're confessing *dark secrets*, when really, they cost next to nothing to reveal.

Grant finds the moments he enjoys the most in a writers room often come after everyone has run through their personal arsenal of stories. It happens after a few days, sometimes a few weeks if the room skews older, and there's always a bubble of quiet after the laughter from the last well-exhausted story dies down.

Finally, the good part, he always finds himself thinking.

It's the moment when a room full of relative strangers becomes a room full of people who have speed-run through the motions of friendship—they know things about each other that their own partners and parents and friends *don't* know, or at least haven't heard told like this.

And they've tricked themselves into thinking it doesn't *really* matter, that these are just the stories they tell as writers, to get the job done—but they've finally run out of stories that don't matter, and suddenly they're sitting in a room full of people who know actually *quite a lot* about them.

That's when they'll usually turn collectively to face the whiteboard, where they're puzzling over some story detail that just isn't *working*, and someone will say something like, "I just don't think that's how a person would actually *behave*, in that situation."

And they'd open it up to discussion, and someone would call bullshit on someone else's answer—*we all know you fucking love this shit, Shepard*—and someone else would bring up something that happened *last night* at dinner, and they'd tell the story haltingly, without any jokes, frowning as they examined their feelings in every beat of the interaction, while everyone else listening would try to figure out, *What would I have done, how would I have felt, in that situation?*

It's not true friendship—he knows he isn't *friends* with everyone he's ever worked with—but he likes *knowing things* about them. It makes him feel better, hearing the stories that stick in other people's brains, the interactions that keep them up at night, the things they obsess over and care about against their will. The things that make them feel vulnerable and human too.

He chances another look at Helen from across the table—she's smiling nervously in a way that doesn't reach her eyes as she listens to Nicole explain some detail about her dead grandmother's coroner.

Grant wonders sharply what it would be like to *know something* about Helen Zhang.

HELEN THINKS SHE might be allergic to this room.

By noon her skin is crawling from hours of listening, listening, listening. She thinks with a degree of nostalgic pining for her first job out of college, interning at a small publishing house in the city. How she would leave the building every day to eat lunch in the park across the street—sometimes listening to music, sometimes listening to nothing at all—and always blissfully *alone*.

Here, the writers' assistant takes their lunch orders, and about forty minutes later they're all sitting around the table eating and people are *still talking*.

"I wanna fire our pool contractor," Eve says, as she tosses the dressing in her salad bowl lightly. "But it's Tom's mom's friend."

"That's the worst," Suraya agrees. "Have you considered divorce?"

"This conversation is making me feel poor," Owen says as an aside toward the other end of the table, and Saskia and Nicole laugh.

Helen isn't sure how they do this—how everyone always seems to know exactly what to say next, striking some perfect alchemy of bitchy and interesting. It's an exhausting, constant volley of conversation. And she's bad at it.

They're so nice and so patient and so deferential, whenever she raises her hand with a self-conscious "Um, can I just— there's a thing we were talking about, I know we moved on, but . . ."

She feels their eyes on her like floodlights, everyone waiting for her to say something brilliant or at least relevant, and the idea that she might say something obviously *stupid* to these very smart and much more *experienced* people becomes a premonition of mind-numbing clarity. Her thoughts stutter and trip over each other on their way from her brain to her mouth, and she's angry at her words for betraying her in this hour of need.

She feels a stab of weird humiliation at the thought that Grant is witnessing all of this from a front-row seat. He has always been so much *better* at this than her, convincing a room full of people that his ideas are the best way forward. In high school, they were never group project partners or anything that pitted their ideas in direct competition, nothing so big or dramatic.

Her memories of Grant Shepard in classroom contexts mostly feature her sitting at a cluster of tables with skeptical classmates, then hearing sharp peals of laughter and clapping from across the room, and looking up toward the source to find *him*, always at the center of it.

She has the fleeting, *stupid* thought that she would like to show him a screenshot of her bank account balance, like, *hey, people actually pay me a lot of money for my brain now!*

Near the end of lunch, she catches this brief and potentially *nothing* of an exchange:

Grant types something in his phone and looks up in Suraya's direction.

Suraya checks her phone, then gives him a curt nod.

What are they talking about in a private thread without her?

Is it about her?

Helen tries to remind herself that her *least favorite thing* about herself is how much she cares about what other people think. And that they probably aren't thinking about her anyway.

Helen tries to believe this, but some warped and stunted little monster of ego in her brain insists, *Yes, but you're actually very good at guessing what other people think of you. You're usually right, that's probably why you're a successful writer.*

The day finally comes to an end sometime around five p.m. She hears Eve murmur to Tom, "Nice to have a room with shorter hours for once," and Helen thinks *short!* as she packs up her own bag.

She lingers after everyone else has filtered out, and hovers awkwardly by the door as Suraya and the writers' assistant review their board notes.

"Is there anything else you need from me?" Helen asks, trying to sound casual about it.

Suraya smiles in a slightly indulgent way.

"How do you feel about everything?"

"Oh, um." Helen pauses, because she never knows what kind of answer people expect to that kind of question. "Fine. Good, I think. It was a good first day, right? You would know better than me."

Suraya nods and starts packing up as well.

"It gets easier," she says. "As you get to know the rhythms of the room."

"Right, that makes sense," Helen lies.

Suraya looks up and considers her for a moment.

"If you're anything like me—and I suspect you are," she says, with a wagging finger, "you've got enough instant replay tape going on in your brain right now to last through the weekend."

"Ha," Helen says weakly.

"Try not to spend too much time looking backward," Suraya advises. "I promise no one's thinking about anything you've said as much as they're thinking about themselves and how they'll impress everyone tomorrow."

"Right," Helen says.

Suraya hesitates for just a fraction of a second before she adds, "You did well today. See you tomorrow."

Helen tries very hard not to replay that fraction of a second of hesitation over and over on her ride down the elevator.

She exits the building and collides immediately and gracelessly into the back of Grant Shepard, who's standing near the door with his phone to his ear.

"—not the best use of my time," he finishes into the phone, before he turns and catches sight of her. "Let me call you back."

Helen squares her shoulders—*I don't care*—and moves past him.

"Hey," he says, and they're walking side by side in a few short paces. "Helen, wait up."

"I have a lot of work to do at home," she says.

"Me too," he says, and she thinks, *crap, should I actually have homework to do?* "I wasn't talking about the room, on that phone call. My agent's trying to get me to meet on this other show that's not even for sure happening yet, and—"

"You should take the meeting," Helen says, as if she knows anything about this industry. "You know I wouldn't miss you."

Grant falters a step, then he lets out a huff of air and redoubles his pace alongside her.

"Thanks for that," he says dryly, an underlying note of *fuck you too* in his tone.

She knows she's being an asshole, but some part of her feels grossly relieved to find she still has a voice that isn't a stuttering string of *nothings*.

"You know, if you gave me half a chance, I could *help* you," Grant says.

"I don't *need* your help," Helen snaps.

"Coulda fooled me," Grant says as they walk toward the parking lot.

"I was just—being observant today," Helen says. "I don't feel the need to establish dominance in every room I walk into—you know what, I don't need to explain myself to you. Fuck off."

"Fuck you too," he snaps, and she feels a thrill of vindication—*I knew you were thinking it.*

Grant freezes, as if just realizing what he's said out loud. "*Fuck*, I don't mean that—dammit, Helen, I hoped we could be friends."

Did he really? Helen doubts that.

"We are friendly," she says. "In the room. Don't talk to me outside of it and we can keep it that way."

"Helen," he starts, in a painfully *soft* voice.

"Please stop," she says in a gasping rush, and hopes her eyes aren't as shiny as they feel. "Stop—stop trying to be nice to me, stop trying to explain things to me, stop calling us friends, stop trying to *help*. I don't want your help, I've *never* wanted your help, and this would all go *so much better* if we could please . . . just have as little interaction as possible, outside the room."

She stares at him miserably. Some unreadable expression flickers behind his eyes.

Grant swallows, then shakes his head.

"See you tomorrow, then," he says in a low breath that sounds almost like a laugh, and walks off.

Helen watches him go and feels some frustrated mix of pride and misery and an overwhelming need to *fix this*. She thinks of her earlier discomfort in the room and tells herself all she has to do is *get over it*.

She remembers a dictionary of English aphorisms her parents kept in the house to learn the language of their American peers; her parents' favorite phrase in it was *mind over matter*. "Mind over matter," they recited to each other, the way Catholics recited the Lord's Prayer. "Mind over matter," when she was fighting back tears as Dad taped up her skinned seven-year-old knees. "Mind over matter," when they were in that first cramped apartment that didn't have any air-conditioning because they couldn't afford it back then. *Mind over matter*, the entire funeral, when she was surrounded by so much parental grief, she couldn't find any leftover place to put her own.

Mind over matter. She'll finish her stint in LA, gain some fabulously interesting new stories to tell at dinner parties, and then she will have *fixed the problem*. She will return to New York and write and write and write, and then sell what she's written and edit it and edit it and edit it until she publishes it, and she'll be back in the swing of things. Helen is *good at winning*, or at least seeming like she is.

All I have to do is get over this, she reminds herself, and knows she will.

ONE WEEK DOWN, *nineteen to go.*

Grant stares at the clock above the door, ticking down the seconds until Suraya finally lets them go for the weekend. He ignores the impulse to look about two degrees to the right and slightly down, where Helen is currently drumming her fingers against the table.

"I just kind of . . . fundamentally disagree with everything you're saying," she says. She's using that awful, *friendly* voice she has whenever she's talking to him without looking at him. "It's a slow-burn thing. We'd be giving it up too early, moving that piece up from the finale."

"I hear you," he says. "But then we still need an episode-out that tees up *something* with Celia and James, or we're just killing time till the last episode."

"I hate to play this card, but they're *my* characters," Helen says stubbornly. "This is a hill I'm willing to die on."

"You can't die on *every* hill," Grant mutters.

"Okay, I think we've done a lot of good work," Suraya murmurs, and shuts her laptop. "We'll pick this up on Monday. I agree with Helen, though: the slow burn of it all works because it's surprising."

"Then we need something else, literally anything else, that'll make us care about the middle four episodes," Grant insists.

"Grant," Suraya says, her brows slightly lifted. *"Have a good weekend."*

Grant nods tightly. That's embarrassing. He's usually better at reading the room. Helen shoots him a triumphant look before she sweeps out the door. *I don't want to fight with you*, he wants to shout at her retreating back. The rest of the room files out, and the dull ringing in his head clears just enough for him to feel something other than shitty about this.

"Can I say something, between us?" he says, as Suraya waits for her assistant to take photos of the ink-covered dry-erase board.

"Make it quick. I'm thinking about my dinner menu," she says.

"Helen has a problem with me," he says, his voice even, his tone measured.

Suraya shrugs. "It's natural for you two to clash. Her loyalty is to her books and her readers; yours is purely to the show and the room. That tension is what keeps us in the pocket of where we should be. You're both professionals—I'm not worried."

Grant exhales shortly. "Okay, take me out of the equation. She's still not gelling with the room, and it's more than just nerves. Day one was nerves, we both saw that, but she's had *no* problems speaking up since. And whenever she does, there's an eighty percent chance it's dragging the flow of the room to a grinding halt. It's not an issue yet, but I can just tell, if she keeps going down this road, fighting us on every point . . ."

He shakes his head. "You told me when we first met, happy writers write better shows. *I* am fucking miserable, and maybe that's on me, maybe that's me and my own baggage here, but I can tell you for a fact that I'm not the only one in need of a pretty drastic morale boost after just one week."

Suraya purses her lips. "What are you suggesting?"

"I—don't know," Grant sighs. "It's like she can't fathom the idea of fun being productive. She's just *like* this, she's always been like this, since we were in high school. Someone has to talk to her about it and it can't come from me."

"That *is* you and your own baggage," Suraya says, clipped. "I don't think it's as bad as you're making it out to be."

"I'm reading the future," Grant says flatly. He watches as Suraya takes an eraser to the board, wiping it clean. A lump forms in his throat, some hopeless feeling he can't name. "I shouldn't have brought it up. I don't know. I'm sorry."

Suraya shakes her head. "I'm glad you brought it up; it's good that you're paying attention to things. I will monitor the situation, Grant. If it becomes a bigger issue, I promise I will handle it. Now go home and *have a good weekend*."

The feeling of self-righteous indignation carries him to the parking lot.

Then the bubble bursts. *What am I doing here?*

Grant knows he could just do his job to the point of technically fulfilling his contract: show up on time, make pleasant conversation at lunch, throw out a few ideas when they come to him, and throw up his hands if they get shot down, because at the end of the day, this is just a *job*.

He could easy-mode his way through the next nineteen weeks, and it would probably be better for the dynamics of the room.

But it wouldn't be better for the show.

He closes his eyes, and the image of Helen Zhang's unsmiling face appears instantly, annoyingly. She's as cool and uncaring as always in his memory, and just a little bit *brittle*.

Grant exhales and opens his eyes. He feels slightly ridiculous. He's not going to tank his entire reputation and career over one job he didn't even want that much in the first place.

He resolves that starting Monday, he will course correct.

He will be pleasant.

He will be *perfect*.

Helen Zhang won't be able to say a goddamn thing about him.

Six

"Fuck me, I love a good sandwich," Grant says as he tears off greedy bites from the lunch the writers' PA delivered.

It's their third week in the writers room and it's his turn to pick their lunch spot today. Helen registers that his pick is a hit with everyone in the room.

How annoying.

"It's pornographic, the way you enjoy things," Suraya says with comic disgust as she throws a tin of mints at Grant.

"I think you're sexy too, Suraya," Grant says, deftly catching the tin and popping Altoids into his mouth with a wink.

Flirting with their gay, married boss is something of a favorite sport in this room, Helen has discovered. Suraya rewards it with laughs, and those laughs turn into joke pitches that end up on the ideas board. Unsurprisingly, Grant is the best at it.

He doesn't have the decency to quit there.

Grant asks after Tom and Eve's weekend trips he's seen on Instagram, he brings DVDs and books for Suraya's kids "for their pop culture education," he laughs over gossipy internet feuds with Owen and Nicole, and she's pretty sure Saskia has a crush on him (*traitor*) because the chatty girl turns beet red and shuts up the second he enters the room.

The only person he doesn't spend his efforts on is *her*. To her, he is perfectly, infallibly polite. Never interesting enough to be charming or aggravating or *anything*.

"That could be something," he says, whenever she pitches an idea, waiting for someone else to boost or kill it.

"I could see that," he says, when she expresses concern over a stupid subplot that's growing like a weed.

"I hear you," he says, when she gets frustrated at something. "But . . ."

But, but, but. He couches his slings and arrows in politeness, then shoots down all her ideas one after another. She has a doodle of his face with butts all around it that Saskia drew her after one particularly frustrating day.

She can't understand how this happened, how she went from being the celebrated author who *created the series this show is based on*—to being the least important voice in the room, all in a matter of weeks.

Is this because she didn't go to Owen's drunken bacchanal of a birthday/early Halloween party when she was invited?

Helen hadn't thought much of declining—she was old enough to know herself, to know she didn't *like* parties with strangers and anyway it'd be a better use of her time to seriously contemplate her next novel. (She ended up marathoning a reality show about luxury real estate agents in Hollywood and falling asleep on the couch.)

Still, she'd thought she had saved everyone from some unnecessary, obligation-motivated awkwardness. But listening to Owen and Nicole recount the messy party the following Monday (even married-with-kids Tom and Eve had made an appearance!), Helen can't help but feel she's fucked up somehow and trapped herself in an old holding pattern that she thought she'd shaken long, long ago.

She feels like her presence here isn't *necessary*. She can sense it in the way everyone avoids eye contact when she talks, the way Owen and Nicole look to Grant like, *Was she this annoying in high school too?*

She hates how she can feel herself becoming a needy teenager again, looking to Suraya for approval, huddling with Saskia after class and bonding over how *everyone else is probably in a group chat without us*. She wonders what Michelle would say, then clicks off the thought like a forgotten porch light.

"I get where you're coming from," Grant is hedging now, "but I think, in the context of our *show*, Saskia's right: this opens up more story area for us down the road."

Saskia flushes and looks at Helen apologetically.

"I think we've done enough work for today," Suraya says briskly. "Helen, can you stay and chat about some casting stuff?"

Helen nods as everyone files out.

"You have a problem with Grant," Suraya says, when they're alone.

"No. I mean, I don't hate him or anything." Helen is flustered. "It's just every time I open my mouth, every time, he's there to shoot down my ideas."

"Hm," Suraya says, frowning.

"Am I doing something wrong?" Helen asks. "Am I being annoying, or talking too much, or not talking enough, or . . ."

"No, you're just—nervous," Suraya says. "Everyone can sense it. Saskia's a nervous baby writer herself, and she can sense it. And you being nervous makes everyone else nervous. They're thinking, 'What if we're wrong? What if she's smarter than us, and we're fucking everything up? What if this show tanks and we all go down with the ship and we never work again?'"

"They're not thinking that," Helen says. "Are they?"

Suraya shrugs. "What can we do to make you less nervous?"

Helen thinks. *Nervous.* She sees her performance in the room over the last few weeks with sudden, embarrassing new clarity.

"Probably nothing," she says finally with a laugh. "It's my baby, and this is the biggest thing it's ever done. It's like I followed it to college when I should have let it grow up without me. Maybe you should just fire me."

"Not on the table." Suraya rolls her eyes. "We're not going to be a house divided this early in the game. The studio would lose all faith in us."

"I'm just not very good at being *cool*," Helen says. "I'm never going to be like Grant."

Suraya laughs. "I don't need you to be like Grant; I need you to be like *you*. This nervous, scared girl, this isn't you. This is just . . ." She snaps her fingers. "This is just because you don't trust us yet. That's on me."

"No, Suraya, you've been great—"

Suraya holds up a hand. "I'm the boss, I get to say whose fault this is, and it's always mine. I should have known it'd take more than dinner and drinks to win you over."

"I'm won over," Helen says quietly. "I told you, I trust you."

"Babe, you have to get better at detecting your own bullshit," Suraya laughs. "It's fine. We'll fix this. Go home."

The next morning, when Suraya informs them they're all going on a mandatory "writers room camp bonding retreat" the first weekend of November, Helen feels slightly shamed knowing it's her fault.

"Yay," Eve says, shooting Tom a subtle *shit, we need a babysitter* look.

"Camping, like, in the woods?" Owen says, instinctively

reaching for his cell phone as if it were an emotional support dog. "With bugs and bears and, like, leaves and shit?"

"Dibs on the top bunk," Grant says as he swivels in his chair.

Did he already know this was coming? Helen wonders. She feels the hot sting of failure as Grant shoots her a bland, friendly smile.

Seven

Helen opts to drive herself to the cabin—it turns out everyone else lives on the east side or in the Valley, and she doesn't feel like driving forty-five minutes across town for a stifling carpool. Besides, she likes driving alone. Listening to music without worrying about what other people think of her second-hand playlists, switching to podcasts when she gets bored of her own thoughts, she feels more like herself than she has the entire time she's been in LA. The two-hour drive from Santa Monica to Forest Falls goes fast, the San Bernardino Mountains in the distance growing larger and larger until they finally disappear because she's driving in them.

The first person she sees is Grant, sitting in a lawn chair on the wraparound deck of a large A-frame cabin. He stands as she parks.

"Hi," she says uncertainly. They haven't had any one-on-one interactions outside the writers room since that first week in the parking lot. *Have you ever willingly spoken to Grant Shepard outside of official classroom time? No, of course not, Your Honor.* "Who else is here?"

"Everyone else left fifteen minutes late and got stuck in traffic," Grant says.

She walks around to the trunk to grab her bag.

"I can get that—"

"No thanks," she says, hefting her weekender bag out.

"Don't be stupid," Grant says, and takes it anyway.

The inside of the cabin isn't what she expected—there's really only one room. It's an open floor plan with two large pullout couches downstairs and four bunk beds in the loft area upstairs. There's a large chandelier made of antlers that throws ghoulish shadows on the wooden walls, which are covered from inch to inch by framed landscape paintings.

Grant follows her in, her baggage in tow. "The downstairs bathroom is definitely haunted," he says. "By spiders. I'm in one of the bunk beds upstairs. Where do you want to sleep?"

"I'll take one of the pullout couches. I can share with Saskia," she says.

Grant tosses her bag down and they both realize at the same time that there's nothing to do now but wait for everyone else to arrive. It occurs to her that she might be overdressed for the setting, in a black turtleneck and leggings. He's wearing a faded gray sweatshirt and sweatpants and he looks like—*someone's boyfriend*. The thought comes unbidden, and she scrambles for an excuse to look anywhere else.

"Is there tea?" she asks, and moves to the kitchen without waiting for an answer.

She opens cabinet doors at random and finds mugs and tea but no kettle. She feels the sudden, solid warmth of his body behind her as he reaches above her to grab a tarnished silver kettle from the top shelf.

"Here," he says, holding it out to her.

She takes it and turns to the sink. She hesitates, then—"Do you want some?"

He looks up, surprised. "Sure."

She fills the kettle and sets it on the gas range and, after a few seconds of struggle, manages to get a fire going.

"Suraya thinks you don't trust us," Grant says.

Helen doesn't turn around. "So she did tell you that."

"Yeah," he says. "Do you want to talk about it?"

Helen exhales. "Not with you."

Grant shakes his head. "Why are you always like this?"

"You'll have to be more specific," she says.

"You make things harder for yourself. You're prickly and defensive when you don't have to be."

"What, should I try to be like you and campaign to be everyone's favorite person in the whole entire world *all the time* instead?" she asks dryly, as the kettle starts to whistle.

"Don't be a dick," he says, and the door opens.

It's Tom and Eve, looking travel-worn and smelling of In-N-Out burgers.

"Traffic was *insane*. I almost made us turn around and call in with food poisoning but it would have taken longer to get home," Eve says. "Oh, this place is weird."

"I feel like I'm at summer camp in the seventies and this is the sexy, haunted counselors' cabin," Tom says. He jogs up the stairs. "There's actual bunk beds up here!"

Eve rolls her eyes at Grant and Helen. "He's going to want to sleep in one."

"I'm totally sleeping in one!" Tom shouts from above them.

SURAYA ARRIVES JUST before sunset, equipped with apologies, tales of traffic nemeses, and booze. Grant is slightly resentful about their fearless leader arriving so late to her own mandatory trip; he's spent the better part of the day playing host against his will, as her second-in-command. Part of him suspects she did it on purpose. Suraya is the type who would—some Machiavellian calculation about people getting more socially acclimated without the boss around, and how many of them would arrive late due to traffic. He's helped Tom and Eve set up their side-by-side bunk beds ("We can role-play sexy camp counselors," Tom said suggestively, and Eve smacked him with her pillow), pushed the couches around upon request for Saskia and Nicole to compare their witchy arsenals of tarot cards and crystals and sage, and hunted down his iPhone charger for Owen, who forgot his own.

And there's Helen, who retreats further inside herself with every new arrival.

"Hot toddy," he says gruffly, handing her a new mug. "Suraya's special recipe."

She looks up at him from her spot bundled on the deck chair, the one he sat on for half an hour before anyone else arrived. "Thanks," she murmurs.

Everyone else is inside, enjoying the last of the homemade dessert Nicole brought. Helen had excused herself for some air, and he caught the disappointed look in Suraya's eyes before she nodded.

Grant wishes there was some way to break down Helen's defenses. If she were anyone else, he's pretty sure he could. He'd say something funny and a little stupid; he'd find a way to show that he was paying attention to the jokes she said in the room, always too quietly and self-consciously for anyone else to hear them.

She wraps a throw blanket around herself tightly, and he doesn't think he's ever seen someone so badly in need of a hug in his life.

"You hate this," he says finally.

"It's so much time being around people, *all the time*," she says. "I don't know how you can stand it."

"Easy, I like people," Grant says simply. "You don't."

Helen scowls.

"There's a reason some people become celebrated, *New York*

Times bestselling authors, and other people become screen-writers," he says. "You're a writer, you write for a living. I'm a Hollywood hack. I'm just good at talking in rooms."

Helen lets out a short, dismissive exhale.

"You are good at that," she says finally.

He sits down across from her. "I tried to write a novel once," he offers.

She doesn't respond.

"Aren't you going to ask me what it's about?"

She scoffs. "Everyone's tried writing a novel once—my dad's fishing buddy tried writing a novel once. Trust me, it's better if I don't know what it's about. If it's good, you'll be afraid I'll steal it. And if it's bad, I have no poker face."

"I know," Grant says. "I can tell by the way you glare at me over lunch every day."

"You're very annoying at lunch," she says, tetchy in a way he almost finds endearing in its familiarity. Almost. "It's the part of the day where you campaign your hardest to be everyone's favorite writer-man."

"Well, the election's coming up soon, so."

Helen gives a derisive snort-exhale that sounds not unlike a laugh.

"I never should have come here," she says finally. "I'm not built for this kind of—Hollywood thing."

"Sure you are," Grant says. "Everyone's jealous of everyone here. You thrive on thinking people hate you. I remember high school."

She meets his gaze evenly. "I remember high school too."

It makes Grant uncomfortable, how her stare seems to cut through all his layers of hard-won polish to the raw grit inside.

"I have context for you," he clarifies, trying to find his footing again. "That's what I meant."

"I wish you'd stop bringing it up. I don't like the context you have for me."

He exhales shortly. He doesn't like the context *she* has for *him* either, but it seems counterproductive to bring that up now.

"Fine," he says finally. Remembering why he came out here, he adds, "You have to make more of an effort with everyone else, though. For the sake of the room, or for your books, if you don't care about the rest of us."

He turns on his heel and leaves her alone to sulk.

OWEN BRINGS OUT a Ouija board after everyone's in their pajamas.

"Who wants to talk to some ghosts?" he asks. He's had a few hot toddies and an alcoholic hot chocolate too. They all have. "I got this in a discount bin after Halloween."

There was a period of time a few years after her sister's death when Helen was consumed with wondering whether it was possible to communicate with the dead. Her parents were scientists who held the scientific method more sacred than the smattering of Sunday school classes she and Michelle attended (for concerns of socialization and assimilation, rather than their immortal souls). So Helen wrote a college research paper on the subject to exorcise herself of the obsessive wondering, and she now recalls a paragraph on Ouija boards.

She'd found the concept of them silly, like a slow phone connection to the afterlife.

Make more of an effort.

"You know, Ouija boards were created as a Victorian parlor game so people could flirt," she says, tentative.

"Why would we know that," Nicole says.

Helen wants to shrink down until she disappears into the

cracks of the floorboards, but next to her, Tom says, "I knew that, because I'm not uncultured swine."

Nicole barks out a laugh. "Fine, then I want to flirt with a Victorian ghost."

Grant stokes the fire as the rest of them kneel around the floor, the Ouija board laid out in the middle of the coffee table.

"Grant, get over here, we're gonna booty-call a ghost for Nicole," Owen shouts.

Helen suddenly wonders if Grant Shepard believes in ghosts.

"You guys have fun with that," he says. "I'm gonna sit this one out."

He swings his long legs onto a love seat and pulls out his Kindle.

"Lame," Eve heckles him.

"Everyone, put a finger on the planchette," Owen says, reading the instructions. "Then we ask a simple question, like 'Are you friendly?' or 'How many spirits are with us tonight?'"

"Are you friendly?" Saskia asks the antler chandelier.

Helen glances in Grant's direction. He doesn't look back at her and she can't remember the last time their eyes met without some awful thing passing between them.

The planchette beneath their fingers moves slowly, slowly, to the *Yes* on the upper left corner.

"Oh, that's nice," Saskia says. "Hi, ghost . . . ghosts? How many are there?"

They look at each other as the planchette travels across the board.

"I'm not moving it," Tom says.

"It's a psychological thing," says Eve. "Everyone unconsciously moves it a little toward the answer they want."

"Stop being so logical," Suraya says. "Ghosts are talking."

The planchette lands between *2* and *3*.

"So there's . . . two and a half ghosts here? Or twenty-three?" Helen frowns.

"I like two and a half," Nicole says. "Which half? The bottom?"

The planchette stays still.

"I don't think the ghosts liked that question," Saskia says.

"Did you die here?" Tom asks.

The planchette moves to the *Yes*.

"Spooky," Owen says.

"Were you hot?" asks Nicole.

The planchette stays on the *Yes*.

"So we've got two and a half hot ghosts who all died here," Nicole says. "I feel like a ghost orgy is the way to go."

"We should ask them about dead people we actually know," Owen says.

Helen glances up at Grant. She could have sworn she felt the prickling heat of his gaze, but he's determinedly reading his Kindle.

"Do you know my grandma Ruth?" Nicole asks. "She died last year."

The planchette moves to the *No*.

"Well, that makes sense. There's probably a lot of ghosts in the spirit realm," Nicole adds. "Anyone else wanna try?"

"Helen, do you have any ghosts you want to talk to?" Suraya asks.

Helen swallows. She's reminded suddenly of those awful hours spent in the school counselor's office her last few weeks of senior year, when she'd heard whispers follow her every step—*can't believe she's even here, her little sister, I know I wouldn't be coming to school like normal if it was me*. She remembers the adults trying to help her, asking her so patiently, so condescendingly, "And what would you say if you could talk to your sister now?"

You have to make more of an effort, Helen thinks to herself miserably.

"I've got a ghost," Grant says abruptly. "Move over."

He squeezes between Suraya and Owen and puts his finger on the planchette. Helen looks up at him, which is a mistake because Grant's brown eyes are instantly on hers. She registers the stirring of some raw, terrible, *unspoken* thing clawing up inside him, before he snaps his gaze away. *Come back here*, she wants to say. *I want a better look at you.*

Grant clears his throat. "My uncle died last December. Fred Shepard. He's got a bunch of boxes in the basement we still have to go through, and I think we should just throw them out. That cool?"

The planchette moves to *G . . . E . . . T . . .*

Owen yanks his hand off. "Nope, nope, nope. This is getting too spooky for me."

"*Get* is too spooky for you?" Grant laughs.

"We don't need to know how that sentence finishes," Owen insists. "I'm done, I'm sleepy. Let's bless this mess and go to bed."

Saskia insists on burning some sage in the room before they clean off the board. Helen has the strange feeling that she should thank Grant for some reason, but he heads off to bed without a backward glance at her. So she stays to help clear the room of stray mugs and empty bottles of alcohol instead.

"We drank a lot more of this stuff than I thought," she says, a warm and spicy feeling in her belly as she examines an empty bottle of Southern Comfort.

"Suraya's special recipe," Saskia mumbles.

A *thunk* upstairs catches their attention. "Ow," Grant's familiar rumble sounds.

Saskia giggles. "He's too tall for the top bunk."

Grant appears before them a few moments later, bundled in

his comforter. "I'm sleeping out there," he grumbles, moving toward the door.

Helen blinks. "You can't sleep out there. There are—bears and shit," she says.

Grant looks sleepily amused. "Bears and shit," he murmurs.

Helen jerks her head toward the love seat between the two pullout couches. "Sleep there."

"And wake up a human accordion? No thanks," he says, and moves forward.

"We'll take the bunk beds, then," Saskia says. "You can have our pullout couch. Right?"

She nudges Helen.

"Right," Helen says.

Grant yawns. "I'm too tired for chivalry. There's two empty bunks up there," he says, and drops onto the nearest mattress.

Saskia and Helen head up the stairs. Only two top bunks are left, and Saskia takes the one closest to the bathroom. Helen turns off the light and clambers up her own, careful not to wake a gently snoring Owen on the bottom bunk. She realizes her mistake as soon as she gets there—it's Grant's, and he brought the comforter with him downstairs.

"Grant Fucking Shepard," she mutters to herself.

She climbs back down using her cell phone as a flashlight and tiptoes downstairs. She shuffles through the furniture in the darkness, until she finds the pullout couch. Grant's breathing is shallow; his eyes are closed and his features relaxed. He's already asleep.

Helen shines her flashlight nearby and finds spare sheets piled near the discarded couch cushions. She creeps past him to retrieve them, when strong fingers suddenly catch her wrist and pull her forward.

She throws up her free hand to stop her fall, it lands on bare skin, and her pulse stutters.

Grant sits up, radiating heat, very much awake.

"What are you doing?" he asks in a low rasp.

"The bedsheets," she manages. "You took the comforter with you."

She is painfully aware that her right hand is still pressed to his chest, and if anyone were to throw on the lights, they would look like a tawdry pantomime of a romance novel cover.

He looks down, as if just waking up to their surroundings. He laughs to himself. "Right. Sorry. Give me a second."

He releases her and she feels the cold air rushing back to her body in his absence.

"I can just take the sheets," she murmurs, moving for them.

"No, it's fine, just—take the comforter." He throws it at her. She catches it and drops the bedsheets onto his mattress.

She pauses at the foot of the bed. "Um, good night," she says.

Her eyes have adjusted to the darkness, and she can see his eyes glinting in the blue shadows.

"Night," he says back finally.

Helen turns and runs upstairs. She can't help but feel like she's fleeing the scene of a crime, which is ridiculous. She spreads her looted comforter onto the top bunk, crawls beneath it, and—

She's instantly wrapped in the scent of *Grant Fucking Shepard*.

Her breath catches—it feels too intimate to breathe in; she feels too exposed even in the dark. She pulls the duvet over her head, creating a full cocoon as her senses are flooded by *Grant*. She can smell the wood from the burning fire he stoked downstairs, the salt of his sweat mixed with his aftershave— something spicy and woodsy at the same time.

Her mind replays the millisecond of him asking, "What are you doing?" on an insistent loop, a mental record skip as her wrist feels the phantom sensation of his grip. In her mind's eye, he seems to pull her just a hair closer each time.

I'm a pervert, she thinks as she takes a final deep inhale of his comforter before pulling it down below her shoulders.

If she's careful, if she doesn't sink into her pillow too much, if she turns and keeps from burying her nose in the fabric surrounding her (*why* does every instinct in her body tell her to do it?), she can avoid *him*.

After a few slow breaths, she becomes either too sleepy or too used to it to notice the woodsy, intimate smell of Grant Shepard in her bed anymore and drifts out of consciousness.

She dreams of warmth and a solid chest and a strong body surrounding hers, overwhelming her senses.

"What are you doing?" she asks in her dream.

"What do you think?" he answers, as he moves against her, mouth covering flushed skin, every touch a fevered kind of promise.

She wakes up with a jolt, on the brink of an orgasm, and bites her lip to stop from weeping in frustration. It's early morning and she can hear creaking downstairs as people get dressed. She exhales shakily, inhales, and steadies her breathing before she sits up.

She comes downstairs and finds Grant sitting up sleepily on the pullout couch, his brown hair still tousled with sleep, as Tom and Eve bustle in the kitchen.

"Morning," she says, hoping her face isn't as red as it feels.

"Sleep well?" he asks casually.

"Mm," she says, as if any more syllables would betray her.

She glances at the bathroom door behind her. "Do you need . . ."

"You go first," he says, glancing down quickly. "I need a minute."

"Oh. Okay." She rushes into the bathroom as her brain flashes a neon sign advertising the sudden pressing knowledge: *Grant Shepard has an erection right now.*

Eight

It's a tricky scramble here," Suraya calls back to them.

They go on a hike after breakfast for their second day of the retreat and Helen has never been more certain she is not a fan of the great outdoors. She enjoys the occasional nature walk, but steep inclines and roads less traveled hold little practical romance for her.

"I'm with you, girl," Owen says, as she audibly whines at the sight of the scramble.

He's wearing a necklace beaded to read "Happy Camper," yet is decidedly anything but. He reaches into his pocket and pulls out a brightly colored bag of gummy candies.

"Edible? It'll kick in when we get back to the cabin so we can forget this godforsaken mess," he offers. "Plus I heard a rumor there's s'mores waiting for us back there."

"Ooh, are we sharing? I want one," Nicole says, and Owen passes her an innocuous-looking dark purple gummy.

"Um," Helen says.

Her one experience with cannabis was in college, when she unsuccessfully tried to smoke with her roommate and spent a full hour repeating, "I don't think it's working." She was labeled a buzzkill and never invited to participate again. She still associates marijuana with a slightly bohemian, laissez-faire, underground lifestyle that's cooler than she ever will be, though she knows it's been legalized in California for so long that driving past high-end cannabis dispensaries that could front as Apple Stores has become a normal part of her daily routine.

"I don't usually do edibles," she says, hoping she doesn't sound painfully uncool.

"God, I know, I just pass out and I'm completely useless after I take one," Eve says behind them. "On the bright side, that might get me out of the next corporate bonding exercise."

Owen offers Eve the bag of gummies. "They're ten milligrams each."

"Oof, I'm old, I'm gonna have to split it," Eve says. She takes a bite of half, then taps her husband on the shoulder. "Here," she says, and feeds the other half to him.

"Did you just drug me?" Tom asks.

"All the cool kids are doing it," Eve says, and jogs ahead, laughing.

"It's cute how they keep the spark alive in their marriage," Owen says, then shudders. "Couldn't be me. Helen?"

Helen blinks. *Don't be the buzzkill.*

"Well, if all the cool kids are doing it," she says, and gamely takes an edible.

The gummy tastes like a blackberry Sour Patch, with an unmistakable hint of *weed* in the aftertaste.

"How long do you think it'll take to kick in?" she asks.

"I dunno, maybe forty minutes, maybe two hours?" Owen shrugs.

Off Helen's expression, Owen laughs suddenly. "Oh, babe, tell me this isn't your first edible?"

"I'm from the East Coast," Helen answers.

Owen claps an arm around her. "This is gonna be fun," he promises.

Helen laughs, feeling strangely light—surely it's too early for the edible to be working already?

As Nicole and Owen help her up the scramble, she realizes—it's not the edible, it's the feeling of *acceptance*. It suddenly seems to mean a lot, that she was invited to participate.

She's never felt particularly secure in her friendships back in New York—Pallavi and Elyse had friends they seemed slightly closer to, outside of their trifecta. And there was always an air of competitive friendliness in Helen's wider YA author circles that often made her doubt if any of them actually *liked* each other, or if they were just performing for their readerships on Instagram. She could never quite shake the feeling that she wasn't a particularly vital member of any group—she wasn't the fun one, or the good-at-planning-things one, or the model-hot one.

So she threw herself into her work and presented her achievements like bargaining chips in her social circles—*See how useful I am as a friend? Don't I seem valuable as a long-term investment, even if I'm not that fun?* More than one person has introduced her as "Helen, my most *impressive* friend."

She hasn't been particularly impressive in this writers room, though.

Maybe being bad at things in front of other people is the secret glue of friendship.

The thought lights up like a Christmas tree in her stomach, and that's when she realizes the edible *has* kicked in.

Oh no, she thinks with a laugh, *I'm thirty-one and peer pressure still works on me.*

ABOUT AN HOUR into their hike, Grant is painfully aware that about half their party is high off their asses.

"Do you ever just think . . . *Trees!*" Eve says, making jazz hands as she looks up at the canopy of golden leaves above them.

Tom snorts. "You sound so dumb right now. *Trees!*"

"No, it's like, they're so big and so old and so *beautiful*, like, they're the same ones that have been standing since, like, the old times," Eve says. "It's like me and some Victorian lady both could have experienced these *same trees*."

"No, I know what you mean," Tom agrees. "We should do a rewrite on that western spec."

"*Yes*." Eve snaps her fingers.

"Keep up," Suraya says, moving briskly up ahead with Saskia at the front of the pack. "We're almost at the view, and then we can go home to s'mores."

A collective excited murmur sounds behind him at the word *s'mores*.

He's surprised to see Helen hanging with the stoned half of their group. She's laughing at a joke Nicole has just whispered in her ear and glances up at him before bursting into a fit of giggles. She looks happier than Grant's ever seen before.

He feels an involuntary tug at the corner of his mouth, and quickly forces it down into a neutral expression. He offers his hand to everyone passing by, helping them up the slight incline.

"Thanks, Dad," Nicole says, then she and Helen burst into another round of giggles.

"I can do it on my own," Helen says, waving him off.

"Of course you can," Grant says, eyeing her brand-new hiking boots that have zero traction on them.

He reaches to support her elbow, and she swings away from him. "I said I have it."

The force of her swing throws her off balance, and Grant lurches forward on instinct to catch her by the windmilling arms.

"Oh," she says, staring up at him. "I guess I didn't have it."

She laughs then, and the shock of it makes him lose his own footing, and suddenly they're *tumbling downhill*.

"Fuck," he groans, trying to take the brunt of the damage.

"Nonononono," Helen says, her breath coming out in short bursts on his neck.

They end their fall at the bottom of the leafy hill and look up to see six figures peering down at them.

"Shit," Helen says, springing up. "We're fine!" she calls up at them.

Grant pushes himself up and feels the stinging protest of his palms as he stands. He looks down to find them raw and pink.

"Oh, fuck," she says. "You're not fine."

"I'm fine," Grant waves her off.

"Grant's bleeding!" she shouts up at the others.

"I'm fine!" he shouts back.

"He's not fine, he needs—medical attention," Helen says, shouting half up to the others, half at him.

"She's being dramatic," he shouts up at them. "I just need to wash my hands."

"You wanna head back to the cabin first?" Suraya shouts down at him. "It's just a few more steps to the view anyway. I can lead the way."

"You shouldn't go back alone," Helen says heroically. "What if something happens?"

Grant lifts a brow sardonically. "Are you offering me your protection?"

"I'll walk with him," Helen shouts up. "I hate hiking anyway."

Grant can tell by the cheers uphill that she's not the only one that feels this way.

"Don't eat all the s'mores without us!" Owen shouts down at them. "Lucky bitch."

"Come on." She pats Grant on the chest. "Let's go."

Grant lets her lead the way a short distance before deciding it'd be safer if he was at her side.

"What?" she asks, when she senses his presence.

"You're high," he says finally, trying not to laugh. "I just . . . never thought I'd see the day."

"Someone brought gummies," she says with a frown. "I succumbed to peer pressure."

Grant *does* laugh at this. "Mrs. Granuzzo would be so disappointed right now," he says, thinking of their pinched-faced D.A.R.E. teacher. "Did you forget to 'just say no'?"

"I was trying to make more of an effort to be like everyone else," she says, surly. "Some people told me that was important."

"I didn't say be like everyone else; I said make an effort *with* everyone else."

"But not you, because that'd be a waste of time," she agrees.

"Right," he says.

"Aw," she says, looking sideways at him. "I hurt your feelings."

"Don't be ridiculous," he says.

"I'm so mean to you," Helen says suddenly. "And you're so— effing—nice. I'm awful."

"You're not awful."

"I am, I'm the worst," she says in a rush, sounding like she might cry. "I'm selfish and I'm obsessed with seeming like I'm winning to people from high school that I don't even *talk* to anymore and I'm *not*, I'm so far from winning it's laughable, like, why do I still *care* about high school and why are you always around when I feel like . . . like . . ."

"I'm always around when you feel like?" he prompts.

"Like I'm not super awesome and successful and winning," she finishes, pathetically. "Sometimes I do, you know."

"Some people just bring out the wrong colors in each other," he says.

Helen sighs and looks around.

"It *is* pretty," she says, talking sideways now. "I didn't think it was possible to see fall colors this close to LA."

He's game for the conversational U-turn from deeper emotional waters.

"There's a few places for that," he tells her. "There's a botanical garden called Descanso that's just twenty minutes away. I go there when I miss the East Coast."

"Are you going back for the holidays?"

"This year I am," he says. "Have to help my mom clear out my uncle's house."

"Oh, right," she says. "Sorry."

"He was kind of a dick," Grant says. "Not that anyone deserves a heart attack at sixty, but . . ."

"Hm, actually let's not talk about this. I'm thinking about my heart and my organs too much now," she says, rubbing a fist against her chest. "Thump, thump."

"What do you want to talk about instead?" he asks.

"Nothing," she says. "Let's just . . . enjoy the walk."

"Okay," he agrees, and they walk in silence the rest of the way. He glances over at her a few times and wonders if she's actually enjoying walking with him. His head feels a slight dizzying pressure from the wondering.

By the time they get back to the cabin, Helen seems to be vibrating with energy. She tilts her head back and forth like Meg Ryan in a rom-com but on a sped-up loop, and begins a familiar butterfly tapping motion, her arms crossing in the front as if giving herself a hug while she pats her own shoulders in an alternating pattern.

"My therapist has me do this sometimes," she says. "When I'm too aware of my organs."

"Have you been thinking about your organs this entire time?" he asks, incredulous.

Helen pauses, then shakes her head. "No, but now I am. You need to wash your hands," she reminds him.

He goes to the sink and hisses slightly as the water touches his raw palms.

"Ouch," she says, watching him.

"Can you get the first aid kit?" he asks.

She brings it to the couch, and after drying off with a towel, he follows. She's poured isopropyl alcohol onto a gauzy pad and holds out a hand expectantly.

"We need to disinfect it," she says.

"I can do it myself," he says, then yelps, "Ow!"

She grins at him—she's placed the gauze pad onto his palm, sandwiching his right hand between both of hers.

"Gotcha," she says, and his stomach does a funny sort of flip at this. He can't remember the last time someone else took care of his cuts and bruises like this, and makes a mental note not to catalogue the feeling of the pads of her fingertips skating across his hands too much.

"Gross," she says, when she removes the gauze to look at the raw skin. There's a yellow stain on the pad now.

He snorts. "Thanks."

He moves to take his hand away, but she holds on to it. "Neosporin," she says grimly.

"I can do it—"

"—yourself, yes, I know," she says, rolling her eyes as she squeezes the gel onto his cuts. "Would you just let me feel helpful for once? It's my fault you're hurt."

"I'm not hurt," he says as she circles an index finger to spread the gel. "And if it's anyone's fault, it's whoever gave you that edible. It was Owen, wasn't it?"

"Not telling," she says, and blows gently on his palm.

"He should have known better than to do it while we were on a hike," Grant says, annoyed. "Asshole."

"Hold still," she says. She retrieves a Band-Aid from the kit.

"You're lucky you didn't get seriously hurt," he says. "You shouldn't take drugs for the first time out in the fucking woods where anything could happen and no one's paying attention to you."

"You were paying attention," she says, smoothing the Band-Aid over his palm. "Give me the other one."

He offers up his left hand, which isn't nearly as cut up as the right hand, but she seems determined to subject it to the same treatment anyway and who is he to stop her.

She touches the pink skin softly and stares at it for a long beat. His throat feels suddenly tight and scratchy, and he's aware of the weight of his hand resting heavily in hers.

She draws a finger soothingly across his stinging palm, then leans forward and presses a light kiss to it. The sensation shoots through him and goes straight to his dick, which wakes up with an awareness that's almost comical. *What's happening?* it seems to demand. *Is this real?*

Helen looks up at him, her gaze hazy and soft for a moment, before comprehension seems to dawn and she looks horrified.

"I—I didn't mean to do that," she says. "I was just—high."

She scrambles away, tossing his hand back at him as if it's scalded her. He laughs.

"It's fine," he assures her. "It's—it's a nice gesture. I can't remember the last time someone tried to kiss and make it better."

Helen draws a throw blanket over her head dramatically.

"Helen," he says gently.

The Helen-shaped figure under the blanket shakes her head. "Don't look at me. I'm gonna die."

"I'm gonna make s'mores," he says, standing up and readjusting himself. "I'll make one for you in case you survive."

He pats the outside of her thigh lightly—*friendly*—and gets off the couch.

THE HOT TEA spreads warmly in Helen's stomach and the fire pit on the deck blazes cheerfully. She feels enveloped in warmth in a way she's never experienced before, as if she's aware of each molecule in her body heating up, one at a time.

"Sorry," Owen says next to her, looking contrite. "I should have given you a half dose for your first time."

Helen waves a hand, her entire body feeling warm and liquid and comfortable. "You didn't know," she says. "And I'm having fun."

She leans back and rests her head on Owen's shoulder.

"See, she's having fun," he says, looking up at Grant, who passes around s'mores.

Grant doesn't acknowledge this and coolly admonishes, "Careful, they're hot."

As he moves off, Owen snickers. "I think he's still mad."

"Does Suraya know?" Helen asks.

"Do I know you're all high as balls?" Suraya says loudly, across from her.

"I'm not high," Saskia says, looking alarmed. "Who said we're all high?"

"Just don't tell the studio," Suraya says. "Liability waivers and all that."

"We should tell scary stories," Nicole suggests, stretching her hands over the fire.

"Boo," says Helen. "I don't wanna be scared."

"You know the rules," Suraya says. "Don't break an idea without fixing it."

She's referring to the golden rule of the writers room, and Helen feels proud of herself for remembering that at a time like this.

"Um," she says. "First kiss stories?"

"What, first kisses ever, or with each other?" Tom asks, as Eve gently snores into his shoulder.

"Obviously the first—the rest of us haven't kissed each other," Nicole says, then winks at Saskia. "Yet."

Helen glances at Grant, who she's surprised to find is already looking at her. He frowns and she looks down quickly.

"My first kiss was when I was seventeen," she says.

"Late bloomer," Owen says.

"His name was Ian Rhymer," she says, and Grant lifts his brows.

"Really," he says.

"Really," she answers. "It was in the travel section of the library where I worked. He ran cross-country, and he'd cut through the library sometimes to see me during practice."

"God, that's some wholesome shit," Nicole says. "Mine was in the parking lot of a Starbucks with a guy whose name I don't even remember anymore. I do remember hooking up with his best friend Derek a week later—he was my dealer."

"My first *technical* kiss was my best friend Bethany in kindergarten," Owen says. "We both wanted to see what it was like. My first *real* kiss was when I was sixteen, with this guy from math camp."

"Mine was Brittany Clark, seventh grade," Grant says. "At a spin-the-bottle party."

The others catcall and whistle at this.

"Didn't you date her best friend in high school?" Helen frowns.

Grant shrugs. "Yeah, in junior year—it was a lifetime later."

"What was Helen like in high school?" Saskia asks.

"Yeah, did you guys ever . . ." Nicole nudges Helen. At Helen's scandalized expression, Nicole scoffs, "What, like we weren't all wondering?"

Helen balks at this. "Who's been wondering??"

Owen raises his hand, and so does Tom, who also raises snoozing Eve's hand.

Saskia raises her hand with an apologetic shrug. "I mean . . . not like in a serious way. Just in like a 'ooh, is there any gossip there?' way."

"There was no gossip there," Helen says. "We barely talked in high school. I was—"

"Mean," Grant says. "And super judgy about popular kids."

"I wasn't mean," Helen says. "I was . . . shy."

Grant shakes his head. "You told Mindy Fielding she wasn't trying hard enough as the features editor and maybe if she spent less time partying and more time working on her articles, the paper would have a chance at the regional student paper awards."

"Nerd!" Owen coughs.

"Yeah, well, we placed fourth in Central Jersey the first issue after she quit the *Ampersand*," Helen grumbles.

"See? Mean." Grant grins.

"You were the literal homecoming king," Helen says. "No one needs to feel sorry for you."

"Homecoming kings have hearts too, Helen," Grant says, feigning an arrow to the chest.

"Stop flirting. It's too wholesome," Nicole says.

Helen flushes. "We aren't," she says. She addresses Grant, more directly. "We *weren't*."

The laughter in his eyes fades, and he ducks his head to stoke the fire. "Don't take things so seriously. I flirt with everyone."

Helen isn't sure, but she feels like she's just undone something that was on the brink of mending.

"It's her sister, isn't it?" Tom asks him as they clean up after dinner.

"Hm?" Grant asks. He's washing the dishes. It's his favorite chore—mindless, repetitive cleaning.

"That story you told, when we were in the *Edendale* room a few years ago. About that accident that happened when you were in high school," Tom says. "The girl who died. She was Helen's sister, wasn't she?"

Grant stops scrubbing, his ears ringing. "How did you know?"

"I googled Helen," Tom says. "She's mentioned her sister in a few old interviews."

Grant starts scrubbing at a stubborn, congealed bit of ketchup on the plate. They should have soaked it sooner.

"Pretty fucking wild situation, huh?" Tom adds, when Grant doesn't say anything.

"Yep," Grant says.

"Are you . . . okay?" Tom asks. "I can't imagine . . . I mean, if you ever need to talk to someone . . ."

"Thanks, man," Grant says, trying to keep his tone friendly and *normal*.

"Yeah, of course." Tom glances around the kitchen. It's damn near pristine. "Look at us, a pair of domestics."

Grant wipes his hands. It's late for how early he wants to get on the road tomorrow—almost midnight.

"Night, then," Tom says. "Night, Helen."

Grant turns and sees Helen standing under the kitchen light in flannel pajamas.

"I came to get some water," she says as Tom heads off.

Grant nods. He grabs the Brita filter from the fridge, half expecting her ever-present refrain of "I can do it myself." But she just waits for him to pour it into an empty mason jar and takes it from him with downcast eyes.

"Night," he says, and moves to go past her.

"Hey," she says, and he stops. "I'm sorry about . . . about earlier."

"There's nothing to apologize for," he says brusquely.

"I don't want things to be awful between us all the time," she says suddenly.

He stops, surprised.

"It's not . . . it's not fair. To you, to the show, to . . . anyone. I'm just . . . I'm just *so* tired," she says, sounding small. "I wish I knew how to make things easier."

"Tom knows about our history," Grant says. It suddenly feels important that she knows this, that he's not keeping it from her. "Years ago, I . . . I talked about stuff, in my past, when we were working in another room together. And he googled you."

Helen laughs shortly. "Right. So that means Eve knows. Which means between the four of us, half the room knows."

He can't tell if this is a good thing or a bad thing.

"I'm sorry it's been hard for you," he says. "A lot of that's probably my fault."

"Don't give yourself so much credit. I'm in a new city, on a new coast, in a new job. Which I only took because . . . because I can't seem to do my actual job anymore," she says in a rush. "I've been working on the Ivy Papers for seven years, and I want to do something new, but every time I sit down, nothing real comes out, and I never wanted to be one of those authors who doesn't know how to let go and *move on* from their first series, but I can feel it happening—the only ideas I have are set in the same world, but they're *worse* ideas, they're smaller and lazier and—and I just thought . . . maybe, if I work on this as a TV show, I'll finally be able to . . . close the chapter."

She shakes her head and drinks her water.

"For what it's worth," he says slowly, waiting for her to look at him because he wants her to know he means it. "This job, it's not *easy*. You're handling the stress better than I ever did in my first writers room. And even if you never write another word and this show falls apart and never makes it to air . . . you'll still be the most impressive person I know."

"Thanks," she says, looking at the floor.

"I mean it. Not just because of everything you've accomplished so far, though that's impressive too. But because I have a fraction of an idea of how shit your senior year of high school was. And to go through all that and be as . . . tenacious as you are, as strong as you are—that's fucking big impressive, Helen. I know I'm the wrong person to say all this, and mine is the last opinion you care about, but I think you should know, I . . . I admire the shit out of you. As a person."

Helen wipes her cheeks. "I never know what to do when people comfort me," she says softly. "I think I must be broken because it always makes me want to . . . to . . ."

She takes a short gasp and he realizes she's crying.

"Fuck," he says, and reaches out before he knows what he's

doing. He presses her into his chest, tucks her under his chin, and rubs her back slowly. "Sorry."

He feels her wet tears at the neck of his T-shirt. She doesn't take to hugging naturally—she's angular and stiff, resisting where others would soften. After a moment, she seems to give way—he feels her forehead collapse against his neck, registers the slow inhale and exhale of her breaths as she seems to melt into his body. He isn't sure how long they stand this way, pressed together like pages in a book. Then suddenly, her fingers, smashed into his chest, harden and push him off. She breathes in and out slowly, then looks up at him through red-rimmed eyes.

You idiot, he thinks to himself. *She just said she doesn't like when people comfort her.*

"I, um," she wipes her nose. "I should get to bed."

They both look toward the stairs behind her, which seem far away in this moment. She turns to go, then pauses.

"Thanks for the water."

She takes a steadying breath and walks away from him. He ignores the tug in his stomach that seems to follow her.

Nine

I still think we should move the piece with Bellamy and Phoebe sooner," Eve says. "We already have the angsty slow-burn pining with Celia and James; we need another flavor."

Helen studies the enormous glass dry-erase board, covered in blue and red and purple writing.

"Hm." Suraya leans back in her chair, considering. "Where, though? If we move it any earlier, they still hate each other."

"I mean, that could be hot, right?" Nicole says. "I vote episode three. Who hasn't wanted to have hate-sex with their nemesis?"

"Do they even know each other well enough to be nemeses at that point?" Owen counters. "Phoebe only hates Bellamy because of what he did to her ex–best friend. That's not personal enough for it to be full-blown hate-sex."

"I was trying to tell a story about forgiveness with them," Helen says. "Whereas with Celia and James, it was more . . . horny."

"I mean, it's horny in the books," Eve agrees. "But if we boil it down to what they actually do, they're just . . . *staring* at each other. Which is hot, but not necessarily horny in an 'I can't watch this with my parents in the same room' way."

"Could it still be a forgiveness story if they have sex earlier?" Nicole asks. "Like, I've totally hooked up with people and kept doing it because it made me feel like shit and that's what I felt like I deserved at the time."

"Aw, babe," Owen says, squeezing her shoulder.

"Fuck off, I'm in therapy," Nicole rolls her eyes.

"I'm with Nicole on this," Grant says. He grabs a blue marker and writes *Bellamy/Phoebe hate-sex??* at the end of a taped-off cell on the dry-erase board. "If we make it our end-of-episode-three cliffhanger, that gives us a bigger secret to drive a wedge between Phoebe and Iris, and it changes the dynamics of the Fall Ball too."

"So instead of getting closer before they hook up, they're doing it in reverse." Suraya scans the board. "I like it. Helen?"

Helen feels the sudden burn of all eyes on her. She's noticed that Suraya has taken to checking in when they pitch bigger differences from the book—never more than once, and always with a short "Helen?"

"Yeah, I think it'd be fun to watch," she says. "I guess I'm just trying to work out what that looks like. Who initiates it, who wants it more, who makes it happen a second time."

"You and your obsession with second kisses," Eve laughs. She's referencing a conversation they had a few days ago, when Helen had insisted *the first kiss is just an icebreaker.*

"They're a bigger deal than first kisses!" Helen says. "They turn something that could be a one-off into something that could be significant."

"Okay, but they're not just gonna kiss," Owen says. "All that tension built up."

"I think she initiates it," Grant says, staring at the board. "She's feeling low, she's looking for a way to get back at her best friend, she turns a corner, and boom, he's there right when she needs an excuse."

"I don't know," Helen muses. "I think it's hotter if he makes the first move. It's more . . . villainous."

Grant lifts a brow. "And that's hotter?"

Helen flushes. "Yes."

"I'm with Helen," Saskia says. "You kind of want it to feel like he's doing it to piss her off."

"And then she surprises them both because she's into it," Eve adds.

Tom holds up a hand. "Hold up—is this not gonna land us in a minefield of consent issues?"

"No, okay, I have it, I have it," Nicole says. "He follows her into the bathroom after the drama in the library. She's like, 'blah blah, I hate you, fuck off, whatever.' Then he's like . . . looming over her, being intimidating on purpose, and it's like a game of chicken; neither of them wants to back off."

"Yes, yes, yes," Suraya nods. "He kisses her first. . . ."

"Thinking she's gonna hate it and he'll just leave," Saskia adds.

"But then she pulls him back in and it's *on*," Helen says.

"Hot, clothes-on, self-loathing bathroom sex," Eve nods.

"I should call my ex," Nicole says.

"Is this hot to women?" Tom asks.

"Yes!" Helen, Nicole, Eve, and Saskia shout at him.

"In fiction, babe," Eve says, patting his arm. "In real life, I much prefer a nice boy who can cook a mean lasagna."

"Be . . . meaner . . . to . . . women. . . ." Grant says, and feigns typing into his notes app.

"Like he needs the help," Owen says, and snickers.

"I haven't gone on a second date since Labor Day," Grant objects. "And Helen would agree: it's the second one that makes it significant."

"Only if you're looking for something deep," Helen says.

"I always go deep," Grant winks at her.

"Oh my god, unless you're gonna fuck one of us on this table while the rest of us get to watch, please shut up," Nicole says.

Helen laughs. She realizes she must be acclimating to the rhythms of the room, because she would have been shocked into silence by Nicole's outburst a month ago.

Instead, she says, "Nicole volunteers as tribute."

"Please, he's too wholesome for me," Nicole says. "Besides, we all know Helen has a homecoming king kink."

Grant lifts his brows, then turns over his shoulder and bites the marker "sexily." "What do you say, Helen, do I have your vote?"

Helen snorts and dissolves into laughter with the rest of the room.

TOM AND EVE invite everyone to their annual Christmas potluck right before the room shuts down for the holiday season. Helen makes sure to attend, after a somewhat sad Thanksgiving spent marathoning *Gilmore Girls* and watching everyone else go to their individual Friendsgivings on Instagram. She had thought maybe someone would invite her along, but no one in her cell phone contacts seemed to be hosting a dinner of their own. Suraya went out of town to her in-laws' home ("pray for me, I've been assigned green beans") and Grant had been in Vegas with his visiting father (not that she'd been expecting any kind of invitation from him). She'd ended up FaceTiming her parents and telling them she was going to meet up with some friends later, and then hung up to watch Lorelai and Rory roadtrip to Harvard.

Helen drives along the Silver Lake Reservoir now, looking for parking. She loves driving, but she hates parking. Her first week with the rental car, she tried to parallel park on Ocean Avenue and ended up scraping the entire right side of her vehicle in the process. She left a hasty note on the windshield of the other car and drove home directly, then ghosted the guy from Hinge she had been supposed to meet.

She's made only the barest of attempts at dating in LA—frankly she finds the game of swiping and messaging and flirting to be somehow both tedious and embarrassing. There shouldn't be a written record of her rough-draft attempts at dating.

She finally finds a single spot that she's pretty sure she'll fit her hatchback Prius into and pulls up alongside the front car. As soon as she reverses, she realizes she's misjudged—there's no way the front of her car will make it. She tries to pull out, but it's already too late—she's somehow trapped herself.

She whines and allows herself a moment of self-pity before she opens the door and walks to the front to inspect the damage. There's at least an inch of space there. Maybe she can maneuver her way out, centimeter by centimeter?

"Need some help?"

Helen looks up to see Grant standing across the street, on the sidewalk. He's holding something wrapped in tinfoil (crap, she forgot the cookies she bought) and wearing a dark coat that looks like it'd be more at home on the East Coast.

"I can't get out," she says.

"You're leaving the party this early?"

"No, I mean, of this spot. I won't fit."

He tilts his head and inspects the space. "Sure you will."

She exhales shortly. Hangs her head. An admission—"I can't parallel park."

Grant lifts a brow. "Didn't you pass driver's ed with the rest of us?"

"Are you going to help me or just stand there and heckle?"

Grant grins as if that sounds like exactly what he wants to do. Instead, he jogs across the street and stops directly in front of her, a hand on the frame of her car. He peers behind her at the driver's seat. "Do you want me to do it for you, or do you want me to tell you what to do?"

He's suddenly very close for comfort—close enough for her to smell his aftershave (cedar + bourbon) and see the shadow of stubble on his jawline. *Do you want me to do it for you, or do you want me to tell you what to do?*

She swallows hard. "Um, you can do it."

She moves out of the way and he hops into the driver's seat. He adjusts the chair, checks the mirrors, and deliberately navigates her car into the parking space. He parks, exits, and drops the keys into her palm.

"Thanks," she says.

"I remember now," he says. "You failed the driver's ed test."

"I didn't fail, I just had to take it more than once. It wasn't a priority," she huffs. "I didn't have anywhere I needed to be."

Grant laughs. "How many times?"

Helen pauses. "Three."

Grant shakes his head as they walk up the steps. "*Helen.*"

"I was focused on my SATs!" Helen protests.

The door swings open.

"Oh look," Eve says, wearing a bright red knit dress and cherry earrings. "Grant and Helen are here. Tom! Grant and Helen are here together. And they brought—"

Grant holds up a sugar-crusted pie. "Blackberry pie."

Helen flushes. "I forgot to bring something."

"Oh, that's fine, we have way too much stuff anyway," Eve says as she pulls them into the house. She deposits the blackberry pie onto a table as Tom brings over two mugs. "They brought blackberry pie."

"Grant did. I'm just a terrible houseguest," Helen says.

"Yeah, jeez, Helen, stop trying to take credit for my pie," Grant says.

Tom hands them each a mug. "Mulled cider for you. It's barely alcoholic."

About an hour later, Helen is pleasantly warm from the cider and caught in a conversation with Nicole and her date, Ben ("this guy I'm dumping as soon as the weather gets warmer"). He's surprisingly *normal* for Nicole, and Helen can see in the way he looks at her that he's smitten and completely wrong for her.

"You guys went all the way to Forest Falls and didn't go to Big Bear?" he's saying. "Oh, we should do a trip together sometime. Maybe February."

"Can you get me another one of these?" Nicole presses an empty mulled cider cup into his hand and he dutifully walks off. She shakes her head at Helen. "We are *not* going to Big Bear with Ben."

She shudders.

Helen smiles. "He seems . . . fine."

"Yes, exactly," Nicole says. "He's someone my mom would love me to date. I swear he seemed more . . . tortured when we met. You can have him if you want."

Helen laughs. "I think I'm good."

"Did you bring anyone?" Nicole asks, casting an eye around.

"No," Helen says. "I'm taking a break from . . . meeting people."

"Good for you," Nicole says. "If you need recommendations for a good vibrator, I've got you."

"Thanks," Helen says, glancing around for Tom and Eve's kids.

"Do you think you'll stay in LA, after the room finishes?"

"Well, I'll be around for filming," she says. "And then . . . I don't know."

"Don't know what?" Grant says, approaching with a slice of

pie and two forks. Ben returns and hands Nicole another mug of cider.

"She's debating whether or not to flee back to the East Coast once the show wraps," Nicole says. "Because she hates LA and sunshine and everything us Hollywood elites stand for."

"I like LA," Helen says. "More than I thought I would, actually. It's just that I've always seen myself as an East Coast person. I grew up in New Jersey, I went to school in New Hampshire, I moved to New York as soon as I could. Ninety percent of my wardrobe only works ten percent of the year out here."

She takes a fork from Grant and takes a bite of blackberry pie.

"Buy new clothes," Grant says with a shrug.

"Plus I think I'd miss the weather."

"That is my great cross to bear," Nicole says. "I'm a winter person—I belong where it's winter. I swear, one of these days, I still might fuck off and move to Canada."

"You can drive to weather, though," Ben says. "And if you're from the East Coast, you can always go back."

"You're going back this year, right?" Grant says.

"Mm," Helen nods. "I wasn't going to because it's only been a couple months, but my mom called, and . . . the holidays are hard for my parents."

Grant's expression flickers and she resists a strange urge to reassure him of something.

He clears his throat. "Which airport are you flying out of?"

"LAX?"

"Rookie move," he says. "I always book out of Burbank if I can for domestic flights. Half the wait time—it's my favorite airport in the world."

Helen laughs.

He lifts a brow.

"It's just, in high school . . . I never thought I'd know Grant Shepard's favorite airport in the world."

"They went to high school together," Nicole jabs her mug in their direction as she explains to Ben. "Supposedly they never even fucked, though I still find that hard to believe."

Helen chokes on the blackberry pie. Grant slaps her back.

"Stop embarrassing her, Nicole," he says. "Or we'll never tell you about spring break sophomore year."

"Haha," Helen says weakly.

"Remember what I said about vibrators," Nicole says. "I've got recs for multiplayer games too."

Two hours later, Helen attempts to slip away without saying goodbye to anyone. Her flight's the day after tomorrow, and she still hasn't packed at all. As she heads down the hallway, the front door swings open—Grant appears, with a bag of ice.

"They were out, so I made a run," he explains. His eyes flit over her, taking in her coat and purse. "You heading out?"

Helen nods. He hesitates in the doorway, as if debating whether to say something. Instead, he says, "Night, then."

As she walks out the door, she hears people cheering his name behind her and it's a reminder that no matter how far they leave the past in the rearview mirror, some things really never seem to change.

GRANT SHOWS UP at Terminal 7 of LAX with his one carry-on bag and a grim determination to get on a flight out of this god-forsaken city, one way or another, before midnight. After missing his first flight from Burbank because his elderly neighbor needed help retrieving her escaped cat from under the porch and then having his second flight canceled due to thunderstorms in Texas, he books a direct flight from LAX to Newark and vows never to fly the week of Christmas again.

It's just after four p.m. when he tips his cabdriver and heads for the security checkpoint, only to find that the line to go through airport security wraps clear into a second building. *Of course.*

It's past six by the time he finally gets through security and heads for his gate. His stomach grumbles that it's time to eat, but he'll be damned if he misses a third flight today.

As he stalks with purpose toward Gate 27B, he hears, "Grant? Grant Shepard!"

He turns to see—*Helen*. She's sitting at the terminal's wine bar, wearing a soft, gray, loungey travel outfit. Her cheeks are slightly flushed from calling out his name, and he feels a lick of surprised pleasure that it's *her*. He frowns then—his flight plans can still get fucked.

"I missed my flight," he says, checking his watch. "Then it got canceled. So now I'm here. I have to get to 27B. It's boarding in—"

"Two hours," she says. "It got delayed."

His face must be one of utter devastation, because she pats the seat next to hers and orders another round.

"I hate flying out of LAX," he mutters as he finishes off the wine she's slid his way.

"It's not so bad," she says, looking around. "There's good Wi-Fi and plenty of outlets."

"And overpriced food, and miles of walking to get from one checkpoint to another, and a million shops that exist just to take your money while you're trapped here," he grumbles.

"You don't travel well, do you?"

"I try to avoid it when I can."

"When's the last time you went home?"

"Home is LA," he says, inspecting the menu and frowning at a thirty-two-dollar pizza. "But I get back every other year, usually."

He orders a burger and checks his phone. Nothing new besides three texts from the airline.

"Are you looking forward to seeing everyone?"

Grant shrugs. "Not really."

"That's surprising," Helen says, tucking into an overpriced crème brûlée. "I'd have thought—"

"What, that I love reliving my glory days in a basement with all my old football pals?" Grant raises a brow. "Give me some credit, Helen."

She dabs at her mouth with a napkin. "I always got the impression you guys all stayed friends," she says. "From Facebook and whatever. Like I always saw a post every year of you hanging out with that old crowd."

Grant gives her a wry smile. "Been keeping tabs on me?"

Helen scoffs. "I just mean when *I* go home, it's . . . it's not like that."

Grant frowns. He doesn't like to think of her lonely in their small town.

"I did keep in touch with the old crowd," he says. "Kevin Palermo throws a New Year's party that I usually end up at when I'm in town. And I see a few of the others around then too. But the last few years, it's like . . . our lives have been moving in different directions. They're all getting married, having kids, buying houses."

"You have a house," she says.

Grant laughs. "Yeah, a two-bedroom bungalow in Silver Lake. Not a four-bedroom colonial with a two-acre backyard and room to grow with the family."

"Do you ever wish you had what they have?"

Grant considers the question. "I'd like to be married someday. Have a family. But not right now."

"Too busy sowing wild oats," she says sagely, sipping another glass of wine.

"You leave my oats out of this," he says, and she laughs. "No, I just . . . I have some work to do on myself. I don't think it'd be very fair for someone to be saddled with all of this in a permanent way until I've figured some shit out."

He feels Helen's assessing eyes sweep over him warmly.

"Saddled with all of that, right," she murmurs with pursed lips. He lifts a brow and she says dryly to her wineglass, "I bet the women of LA don't mind so much."

He chuckles and the corner of her mouth twitches up, and he wonders if that means what he thinks it does.

"I get it, though," she says into her chardonnay. "My mom's been sending me photos of all her friends' kids' weddings every chance she gets. Not so subtly hinting about grandchildren while she's still here to hold them."

"You want kids?"

"I've been thinking about it a lot. Most of my writer friends are either married with kids or freezing their eggs. I used to assume motherhood would be a given, but as I think about it more, I don't know." She tilts her head. "I guess I'm afraid of being responsible for someone who never asked for me. And I don't want to do it alone."

She looks down then, and it occurs to Grant that he doesn't know much about Helen's personal life. He's never heard her mention anyone waiting for her back home.

"No current prospects?"

"No," she says, and he can't tell if she feels any type of way about that.

"What about Ian Rhymer?" he asks. "I hear he's still kicking around Dunollie."

Helen laughs. "I know, I usually stop by his pizzeria when I'm in town. But he got a Mohawk in senior year and I never really got over that."

"So shallow," Grant grins.

"What about you?" she eyes him as he finishes off his burger. "Do you ever hit up any of your old flames when you're back home?"

He looks away, and she hits his arm with delighted shock. "You do! You have a hometown sex friend!"

"Let's talk about something else," he says. "What are you doing for Christmas?"

Helen snickers. "I bet I can guess who it is. Brittany Clark. No, wait, Desiree Evans."

"Desiree got married last year," he says evenly. "I sent her a nice card and money for her honeymoon fund."

"Who was that other girl, the one you were with senior year for a hot second, the one with the bangs—"

"Lauren," he says quietly. "Lauren DiSantos."

"Right, her," Helen says. "I always forget about her because she wasn't a cheerleader. It's her, isn't it?"

It feels weird to talk about Lauren and Dunollie, New Jersey, when he's still on California soil. He feels slightly itchy thinking about it, like he's a bad person and he's not sure who he's disappointing here. Lauren, maybe, though he doesn't think she'd mind being discussed outside of New Jersey. Maybe he's just disappointing himself.

"I haven't seen her in a while," he says truthfully.

"But you'll see her this trip?"

He shrugs a shoulder noncommittally.

"How did it start?" Helen asks.

"I don't know. I was home for winter break in college and she didn't mind the company," he says. "Why are you so curious?"

"It's kind of romantic, in a fucked-up way," Helen says. "You're the hometown boy who made it big, she's your high school sweetheart who waits for you to come home every Christmas, hoping you'll stay for good this time."

"Stop projecting," he says, feeling a twinge of annoyance. Lauren isn't waiting and hoping for him; they both know what it is.

"She doesn't ask too many questions and you like that, but that's just because she googles you the rest of the year."

"Stop," he says. "Lauren's a real person, not one of your characters we're gonna punch up."

Helen looks stricken, and he wants to kick himself for causing that wounded look in her eyes.

"Sorry," she says. "You're right, it's none of my business."

"It's fine," he says, and looks away.

"I have a hard time with people from high school," she says finally.

"I know," he says, and when he glances back at her, she's looking at him too.

"I didn't like myself very much back then," she says. "And I worry, when I see people who knew me then, that they still see me the same way. So I make up mean stories about them in my head and they become less important, and it doesn't matter because I'll never see them again."

The corner of his mouth lifts at this.

"You didn't have to make up mean stories about me, though, did you?"

She's saved from having to answer, as an announcement tells them their delayed flight is now boarding.

ON THE PLANE, Grant convinces the older woman next to him to swap seats with Helen.

"It's my friend's first time flying, and she gets nervous," he says.

The woman agrees happily, saying something about *adorable*, and Helen rolls her eyes as she takes the seat beside him. "Your ego couldn't take being the one who gets nervous flying, huh?"

Grant shrugs. "Window or aisle?"

Helen prefers the window. She likes looking out over the wing to see the moment they leave the ground.

"Works for me. I hate moving over people to go to the bathroom," Grant says.

They share snacks that Helen bought back at the terminal, and after trading barbs about each other's initial media choices on the flight—*Die Hard* for him ("so obvious") and *The Great British Bake Off* for her ("what's the point if you can't taste the food?")—they agree to watch the same thing.

"I love this movie," she says, placing one earbud in her left ear as he takes the other and places it in his right.

"It's a classic," he agrees. "And a Christmas movie, though no one ever seems to count it as one."

As three small mice appear on the screen to narrate the first chapter of *Babe*, Helen sinks farther under the thin, airline-supplied blanket and lets herself feel *cozy*. She glances up at Grant, who looks rapt by the adventures of an animatronic pig, enough that she can study him without feeling too easily caught.

He looks younger from this angle, she can see the teenager

in him still like this. The Grant Shepard she's spent the last ten weeks with is sharp and funny and wears his charisma like armor. This Grant sitting next to her now seems less guarded— tired, a little travel-worn, and somehow less self-conscious and more easily delighted.

Don't be ridiculous, she admonishes herself. *It's the same Grant, there's only the one.*

"I actually love the evil cat most of all," he says. "Where's her movie?"

Helen laughs and redirects her attention to the screen. The warmth of his right arm presses comfortingly into her left shoulder, and when her stomach does a funny flip, she blames the turbulence.

SOMEWHERE OVER CHICAGO and a half-hearted twenty minutes into *Babe: Pig in the City*, Helen drifts off to sleep. Grant supposes this isn't the first time he's been in close proximity with a sleeping Helen, but it's the first time he's been close enough to register the way she falls asleep with a slightly furrowed brow. As if even in her dreams, she finds something to disapprove of, something that could be nudged to become slightly *better*. So very like Helen.

"Drink?" The flight attendant pushes her noisy cart beside their aisle, and he waves her off quietly.

Helen frowns as she turns her head into her headrest, making a soft, whimpering *"Hmmph"* that crawls into the cracks of his chest and fills him with a strange and unfamiliar yearning.

So he quietly unplugs the earbuds they're sharing from the middle armrest. When her head lolls to the side, he shifts his arm over slightly and she falls onto his shoulder. She turns her cheek then and faintly burrows into him. He resists an urge to drop his nose into her hair—*don't be a fucking creep, Shepard*—and instead pulls out his Kindle from the seat back in front of him.

He's pretty sure he's read the same paragraph twenty times when the pilot announces over the intercom that they're preparing for descent into Newark.

"Hm," she says into his neck.

"We're landing," he answers, nodding slightly in her direction.

He can almost feel the second she comes back to full consciousness—when the warm, soft sleep in her body leaves and is replaced by a certain sharp stillness he associates with Helen Zhang.

The lights in the cabin come on and she abruptly lifts her head. She glances at his shoulder. He holds his breath.

"You're a shit pillow, Shep," she says finally, yawning as she adjusts a crick in her neck.

He laughs. "You're a drooler," he returns. "I'm sending you my dry cleaning bill."

THEY DISEMBARK AND Grant watches her bags while she stops in the restroom to brush her teeth.

Helen stares at her reflection in the mirror and wonders if there's something about being in New Jersey that makes her hair look duller, her face more tired and drawn. She runs her fingers through her hair and flips the part in one direction, then the other, in a vain attempt at creating some volume.

Forget it, she admonishes herself. *No one that matters is going to see you like this.*

She feels a hot flush of embarrassment creep up her neck as she thinks about how Grant saw her on the plane—the evidence of that needy, drooling puddle on his shoulder. She wishes she could forget the first sensation of familiar warmth and cedar-scented aftershave that flooded her senses when her conscious brain started to come back online, the way her synapses fired energetic reminders: *This isn't the first time you've slept cocooned in the scent of Grant Shepard!*

"Do you need to stop?" she asks, when she finds him waiting for her beside the water fountain.

He shakes his head, and they walk together down the long hall to the baggage claim.

"You have checked bags?"

"Just one," she says, and he nods.

He waits with her as she scans the baggage claim. They pass the woman who traded seats with them—*adorable*—and see her reunited with her husband and son.

"It's that one," she says, indicating a large mint-green suitcase that matches her carry-on.

Grant leans forward and pulls it off in a swift, decisive motion for her.

"Thanks," she says.

He glances at the signs for the taxi stands.

"How are you getting home?" he asks.

"Cab," she says. "My parents are probably sleeping by now, and I have a key. You?"

"Same," he says.

Neither of them moves. It occurs to her that with every step, they seem to be moving further and further into the past. Further away from the easy banter they've developed over the past few weeks, and back to a world where the Grant Shepards and Helen Zhangs of the world have no reason to exchange passing glances, let alone share earbuds and armrests.

The thought makes her unbearably sad for some reason.

"We should get going," he says, and they walk to the cab line.

They wait in silence—he checks his phone, and she checks hers. She can't help wondering if they're both doing it on purpose—in case anyone sees, in case it's important that no one who drives past notices anything interesting about these two near strangers on the curb.

She reaches the front of the cab line first and the driver moves her luggage into the trunk. Helen turns to find Grant watching her with a slight frown.

"Well," she says finally. "Have a good break."

He nods. "You too." He hesitates, then adds, "Call if you get bored."

"Ha," she says. "Okay."

She gets in the cab then and it drives off, taking her farther and farther away from Grant Shepard and his strong, warm shoulders.

Ten

The truth is, Helen hates coming home for the holidays.

She feels a lot of guilt about it, and that doesn't help. There's a memorial for Michelle set up in her former bedroom turned study, and it's always Helen's first stop during a visit home. She has no idea when in that first year her parents decided to change Michelle's bedroom, and Helen still remembers the whiplash of coming home for summer break and seeing that long-shut door suddenly opened to a room she had never seen before.

Why didn't they ask before changing it? She'd been pissed on Michelle's behalf. *I should have protected you from that.*

The walls are lined with clean white IKEA bookshelves: The first shelf to the left is full of textbooks on organic chemistry and Chinese test-prep books from the eighties—relics of her parents' graduate studies. A large section—two bookshelves' full—is devoted to Helen's own novels, each row boasting at least a dozen copies of each book in the Ivy Papers series, along with various translations and special book-club editions. Below the one window in the room, a shorter shelf holds the small collection of books Helen and Michelle shared between them—a combination of science-fiction classics that Dad would read to them as children and their own carefully considered Scholastic Book Fair purchases—and on top of that short shelf rests a neat row of silver-framed photos: deceased grandparents, and Michelle.

Helen lights two sticks of incense and bows, then she places the slow-burning incense in the waiting pot next to Michelle's portrait. The heady scent always paints a memory in the smoke of the first time she did this ritual—with Michelle, when they were visiting China at ages twelve and ten. They were in the countryside with distant relatives and paying their respects to long-dead people they'd never met, at a fireplace memorial in an otherwise bustling kitchen. Helen recalls affecting a serious expression and acting as if she knew what she was doing, and Michelle carefully copying her movements as their elderly relatives clucked approvingly in the background.

If you were here, we'd be at a bar catching up.

The thing Helen struggles to imagine most is her sister today, if things had been normal. It's as though her brain stumbles, suddenly flummoxed every time: *This is the end, you are leaving the city limits of imaginable things.*

Michelle would have been anticipating turning thirty next year, but what would that have looked like? Would she be single or possibly married? Would she have a pet? What city would she live in? What would her apartment look like? Helen can't picture any of it—every conjecture feels half-hearted and paper-thin, less real than all the fictional characters she's created.

The real Michelle didn't want to be here.

Helen sits in an armchair by the window and picks out a book—*The Tenant of Wildfell Hall*. She keeps reading from where she left off, her last trip home. Sometimes she'll find a dog-eared page or an underlined passage telling her where Michelle once left off too. Helen has read through their entire shared collection twice (just in case she missed something).

The other homecoming routines will be mundane from

here. Mom always scrubs the floors down to their varnish in anticipation of a visit and has a meal of all of Helen's favorite home-cooked dishes ready to greet her, no matter what time she arrives. Dad is more gruff—they usually run out of conversation by her second day home ("How's work?" "I saw this article about another Chinese author . . .")—but grunts approvingly whenever Helen updates them about life and work.

She shares only the good things—a book announcement, a positive review, news about the show's development, a writing retreat with friends. She hates the look of *worry* in their eyes; it reminds her too much of a childhood stifled by parental concern and gives her a wooly, claustrophobic feeling that makes her want to run and run and run until the pavement turns into the California beach beneath her feet.

Helen has never introduced them to any of the men she's dated over the years. The thought of having to tell them about a breakup is so impossible a concept, it's laughable.

The white friends in her author groups would balk at this, while her Asian friends would often nod and commiserate.

"But—*never*? Like not even one?" Elyse had exclaimed with wide eyes.

"They can meet when there's a ring on her finger," Pallavi had said, waving it off. "Otherwise, what's the point?"

Elyse would say *the point* is so that your parents know what's going on in your life. But Helen has created a very special window into her life that's just for her parents. *Don't look there, the view's not as good*, she would say, pulling the drapes over a messy fourth date, a failed situationship, a bad breakup, and a drunken night out. She stores up bad news like acorns in the winter and metes them out in small doses, when she finally has good news to soften the blow. "The revision's been tough, but I finally turned it in and my editor loved it!" "I hadn't heard from Elyse in a while and thought she was mad at me, but it turns out she's expecting her first child and she wanted to surprise everyone!"

"You feel a lot of responsibility for other people's feelings," her therapist once told her, as she described the careful little ways she frames her life for her parents.

She supposes that's true. Her mother's knuckles still turn white from gripping the steering wheel whenever they drive down that one stretch of Route 22 on the way to the mall. Helen once boldly asked why they didn't just move somewhere else, somewhere they weren't as burdened by the knowledge that there should be two Zhang sisters moving through the world.

"What's the point?" Mom had said. "We know this place and we're too old to start new somewhere else and have to learn everything again. Besides, your sister is here."

Helen knows she doesn't mean Michelle's ghost. Her mother is unfailingly turned off by any kind of superstition. She means Michelle's body is here, in a cemetery over the hill on the other side of the mountain that carves out the boundary of Dunollie, New Jersey, from its neighboring townships.

Helen looks around the study, trying to feel Michelle's ghost here.

Nothing.

ON HER THIRD day home, the day before Christmas Eve, Helen tells Mom to take the night off from cooking. She drives to Rhymer's Pizzeria and orders two large pepperoni pizzas and a bundle of garlic knots from the pimply-faced teenager behind the counter. A few moments later, her first kiss, Ian Rhymer, appears from the kitchen, his eyes crinkled in their perpetual smile, his arms stretched out for a hug that she submits to happily.

"It's my famous author friend," Ian says. "I heard you moved to LA and you're a Hollywood big shot now."

Helen snorts. "You sound like a cartoon right now," she says. "Hollywood big shot, fuck off."

Ian grins and pulls out a chair to sit down with her. "I feel like it's been ages. What's going on in your life?"

"My life is the same as always," she says. "Writing, hating my writing, revising, convincing myself I'm a genius, then doing it all over again. Tell me about your life."

Ian shakes his head. "Nuh-uh, you don't get off that easy. You moved across the country, where they don't even have good pizza. How are you doing?"

"Honestly? The farther away I am from my parents, the happier I am."

She says this glibly, the kind of joking thing they would have said to each other as teenagers. But does she actually mean it?

"So you like it out there."

Helen thinks of her condo in Santa Monica, of the podcasts she listens to on her long commutes in the morning, of the bright blue sky and the palm trees and the sound of trucks unloading on the studio lot as she walks to the writers room.

"I do," she says.

"That's great, Helen," Ian says. "It's nice to see you happy."

Helen smiles, then nudges him. "What about you? You're a *family man* now."

He grins and whips out his phone to show her pictures. "Deanna's hoping to go for a second kid next year," he says. "But look at this little fluff ball. He had so much hair when he was born, Dee almost cried laughing."

As Helen carries the pizzas and garlic knots to her car, she thinks about how much fatherhood makes sense on Ian Rhymer.

He's not the skinny kid cutting track practice to kiss her in the library anymore; he looks more solid and dependable now.

Like he's grown up, she thinks, and feels the ache of something bittersweet stretch up.

"Hey," a familiar voice calls out when she reaches the parking lot.

She turns to see Grant standing across the lot, next to an unfamiliar gray CRV. He clicks the keys to lock the doors with a chirp.

"Hi," she says, placing the pizzas on the hood of her car. "Fancy seeing you here."

He looks a little amused at her old-fashioned turn of phrase, and she kind of wants to disappear into the woods.

"What'd you get?"

"Pepperoni. And garlic knots," she says.

"I never got the garlic knots here before," he says.

"You should try them."

Grant looks up at the sky. It's a thick kind of light gray. "Think it's gonna snow later," he says.

She cranes her neck and looks up too. "I think it's already snowing on the other side of the mountain."

"Better get my pizza order in soon then," he says.

"I better get home before they get cold," she says.

He nods and heads toward the pizzeria. He pauses at the sidewalk outside and turns to wave at her. "It's good to see you," he says.

"You too," she says, and gets into her car.

WOULD HAVE BEEN nice to find out you were in town sooner.

Grant stares at the text from Lauren on his phone, the one he hasn't responded to yet.

He's been busy and he knows she would understand if he told her. He's been shuttling his mother from their home to his uncle's house in the next township every day, spending hours at a time in Fred Shepard's basement sorting boxes of old family photos, saved receipts, and letters—a lifetime of paper.

It's emotional work for his mom and Grant wishes sometimes they could dump all the boxes in the street with the rest of the trash after Christmas and be done with it. Instead, Lisa Shepard insists on seeing each picture, clucking and cooing over it, explaining to him who each acquaintance featured in the background *might* be, *she thinks*, and sighing.

"It's just such an awful reminder that this is where it all ends up," she says, looking around the damp basement. "Where we all end up. And then your family ends up going through your boxes, deciding what to keep and what to throw away."

It's not even his mom's brother. Fred was Grant's dad's brother—but Lisa grew up next door to both of them, and as Fred never married, they folded him into their family as a bonus member on family vacations, birthdays, and celebrations. "*He needs to socialize more*," Grant always heard his parents whispering to each other.

Grant is pretty sure Uncle Fred had resented their concern and he's wondered more than once if there were an alternate universe where Lisa had married Fred instead of his brother. If it would have worked out better that way for everyone involved, instead of in a marriage that fell apart (or maybe just stopped keeping up appearances) as soon as Grant went off to college.

Would have been nice to find out you were in town sooner.

The truth is, Grant hasn't wanted to see Lauren during this trip home. It's been over a year since he last saw her (she was on vacation in Aruba when he was here in the summer), and part of him thinks—*aren't we getting too old for this?*

He never intended for this to keep going for as long as it did. It started as a way to pass the hours back home when he was in college, and somehow, over a decade later, it occurs to Grant that this might qualify as his longest relationship.

He always assumed one of them would find a reason to break it off—he'd start dating someone seriously or she would get engaged and he'd see it on Facebook. Instead, she's become as familiar a landmark in Dunollie to him as Washington Rock, the viewpoint at the top of the mountain where George Washington supposedly observed the British troops once. Possibly.

His sense of decency won't let the text—slightly accusatory in tone—go unanswered, and a few hours later, he's leaving the house to meet Lauren at the one bar in Dunollie that's open after ten p.m.

"You look different," she says, her eyes raking from his hair to his chest, as they sit across from each other in a booth.

She looks the same, her dark hair pulled back in a clean ponytail. She's wearing leggings and a warm, oversized sweater.

"You look good," he says, searching for something to say. "I saw you ran a marathon in April."

She smiles. "All the girls in the office signed up," she says. She works in a dentist's office in the nicer part of Dunollie and she's been there since graduation, he's pretty sure. "I got the best time, though."

He nods and a waiter comes by for their drink orders.

Hers is the same as always—an amaretto sour with two cherries, something so sweet and sugary the taste would linger when he kissed her. He doesn't really want to drink now—he thinks about ordering a beer so she doesn't feel self-conscious about her own drink, but finally orders a decaf coffee instead.

Lauren raises a brow. "You're not drinking?"

"I have to get up early tomorrow," he says. "There's guys from the storage facility coming for Uncle Fred's stuff."

Lauren nods. She tilts her head as she looks at him. "Are you seeing anyone these days?"

Grant shakes his head and makes a small sound of dissent. "You?"

Lauren shrugs. "No one permanent," she says.

He's comfortable around Lauren, he realizes. His body is re-laxed in a way it hasn't been in weeks. He wonders if this feeling is love, then randomly thinks of the way Ian Rhymer had shown him pictures of his family when he stopped by the pizzeria ear-lier this afternoon.

He gets an itchy feeling as he remembers seeing Helen in the parking lot, and their conversation about Lauren at the wine bar in LAX.

"Do you ever wish . . ." he starts, then thinks better of it, then decides to ask anyway. "Do you ever wish you could find someone more permanent?"

Lauren laughs. "Why, are you trying to set me up?"

Grant shrugs. "What are you looking for? Maybe I know someone."

She quirks a knowing brow at him, and it would be easy—so easy—to take this conversation down a familiar, flirtatious path.

"My mom's selling her house," he says instead, changing the subject. "It goes on the market in January."

"I'm not in a position to buy," Lauren says, frowning.

"Yeah, no, I was just . . . sharing," he says. "She wants to move to Ireland once it's done."

"Ireland," Lauren says, brows lifting.

"Apparently she always wanted to live there at some point in her life, but it was never the right time."

"Oh." Lauren studies him for a moment. Then, "Why do you think we never fell in love?"

Grant finds he isn't surprised by the question. "I don't know," he says. "I don't . . . I don't want you to think I don't care about you. I do."

She smiles at him a little sadly.

"I know you do," she says. "I don't mean with each other. We were never meant to last past high school. I mean, why do you think we never fell in love with other people?"

Grant wants to conduct a thorough investigation of this question—he wants to tape it off and walk its perimeter while he examines it from every angle. But he knows, before he can even untangle the thought, *there's probably something wrong with me.*

"I don't know," he says finally. "Maybe it's just not in the cards for us."

"I'd like it to be," she says. "It seems like it'd be nice."

He remembers suddenly the first blush of their own romance—that weekend in a rented beach house after prom. He had broken up with his girlfriend Desiree because he knew he was going to college far away and he didn't want to draw it out, but he'd taken her to prom first because he felt like he owed it to her.

"You're such an idiot," she had said, after he'd tried to gently end things in the car on the way to Seaside Heights. She'd made him pull over at a rest stop so one of her friends could pick her up and drive her to the same beach house instead.

Lauren had been someone else's date that weekend—he doesn't even remember whose. She wasn't part of their usual crew. She ran more with the stoners and future art majors. But as the end of high school drew nearer, those clearly defined lines separating their friend groups seemed to blur and he remembers drinks in a hot tub, a game of truth or dare, and a first kiss with damp, clinging hair and searching mouths.

She was the first person he'd called after the accident a week later; she stroked his hair while he cried in her lap. He'd been embarrassed to ask so much of someone he barely knew, but Lauren hadn't seemed to mind. It had connected them, in a strange way.

"Do you want to get married?" she asks. Then adds, "I'm not proposing. Just wondering, generally."

Grant laughs and thinks of what he told Helen back at the airport. *I'd like to be married someday.* He meant it and he thinks maybe that's why he's telling Lauren about his mom selling the house. Lauren is a dangling thread that keeps him tied to this place and it doesn't seem very fair to any of them.

"I do," he says out loud. "Someday. I should probably do something about that."

Lauren smiles as she tilts her head. The action is so familiar, his heart kind of aches for it.

"I hope you do," she says.

When they walk out of the bar, Lauren lingers as she searches for her keys.

"Are you good to drive?" Grant asks.

"I'll be fine," she says. "The drinks get weaker here every year."

She considers him. "Are you heading home?"

There's an invitation in that question, somewhere. *One last time, maybe?*

"I am," he says. "Get home safe."

"You too," she says.

She reaches out and touches his cheek softly, brushing a thumb against his stubble.

He catches her hand suddenly and presses a kiss to the back of it. She laughs, surprised.

"Well, that's the most romantic thing you've ever done," Lauren says. "Merry Christmas, Grant."

It starts snowing as she says it, and he feels like they're living out the end of someone else's rom-com. Maybe every movie ending has extras in the background just trudging through toward the rest of their lives.

"Merry Christmas," he says back to her.

She opens her car door, then pauses. "You deserve to be happy. I hope you know that."

Lauren smiles and Grant feels a complicated knot in his stomach tug as he tries to return it. After she gets in her car and drives off, he stays standing there, fat snowflakes floating down from the sky and dusting his hair, his shoulders, and the ground beneath his feet.

He pulls out his phone and numbly swipes until he finds the name he's looking for. He presses dial before he can talk himself out of it, and he realizes he's holding his breath, because it releases as soon as he hears the voice on the other end.

"Hello?" Helen says, her voice low and quiet.

"Do you want to get lunch tomorrow?" he asks, as if this is normal for them, as if he calls all the time. "I have to finish clearing out my uncle's house in the morning, but I'm free afterward and I think I might lose my mind if I spend another day at home alone."

There's a pause, then the *click* of a door shutting in the background. Helen sounds closer to the phone when she speaks again.

"Send me the address," she says.

Eleven

She tells her parents she's going to meet up with a friend and drives to a bagel place in the next township over. Helen makes a mental note to bring back a half dozen bagels and prepares a story of breakfast sandwiches shared with an old friend from the *Ampersand* who's unexpectedly in town. It feels almost like espionage, if the stakes were toasted cinnamon-raisin bagels. She feels a fluttery kind of nervousness when she walks through the door and sees him standing in line—their rendezvous point.

"I haven't been here in forever," she says, trying not to sound like she's read too many spy novels. "We used to get giant bags of bagels here to sell at our morning fundraisers for the school newspaper."

"I remember," he says.

They order breakfast sandwiches to go and drive to Washington Rock to eat them. There's a short, pitiful excuse for a nature-walk trail by the far end of the parking lot, and he suggests they take it. It's a gray, gloomy Christmas Eve, and it seems unlikely they'll see anyone else there. There are patches of snow on the ground from last night, though not enough to hide the muddy, leaf-covered path.

"My mom's selling her house," he says. "I met her real estate agent this morning."

"Oh," says Helen. "You guys have been in that house a long time."

She remembers passing Grant's house on their daily school-bus route, back before any of them had cars. It was a beautiful Victorian near the top of the mountain with perfectly lined-up windows that captured spectacular light at sunrise and sunset, and she used to look forward to the part of the morning when she would see it approaching on the horizon.

"I'm surprised she stayed as long as she did," he says. "She's talking about moving to Ireland and working on a sheep farm. I think she might actually do it."

Helen tries to remember Mrs. Shepard, who she met only a handful of times at parent-teacher fundraising events. She remembers a tiny blond woman in a pink cardigan with gold jewelry.

"Your dad lives in Boston now?" she asks.

"For the last twelve years," he says. "Pretty much since they separated."

"Do you ever visit him?"

Grant shrugs. "He prefers to come visit me. He likes the sunshine and the beaches."

Helen nods.

"What about your parents? How are they?"

She kicks a pebble in the path. "They're good. Dad's taken up golfing and Mom's waging a war with some squirrels in her garden. I don't think they'll ever move."

Grant nods and tosses the wrappings of his bagel into a nearby trash can. They've already reached the end of the trail.

"Short walk," he says, looking around.

"I don't think I've ever gone on it," Helen says.

"Me either. What do you usually do when you're in town?"

"Pretty much nothing," Helen laughs. "Sulk in my bedroom

and regress into my teenage self, mostly. It's like time doesn't pass in our house."

They turn and walk back toward the parking lot. Helen can't help but feel like this has been a dud of a meetup, and wouldn't blame him if they parted ways and didn't speak again until they're safely back in LA.

When they reach their cars, Grant turns to her and asks, "Do you wanna go see the high school?"

"Sure," Helen says. "You drive."

HE DIDN'T REALLY expect her to say yes when he asked, let alone volunteer to carpool with him.

She hops in the passenger seat, and the sound of 106.7 Lite FM's Christmas classics comes on the radio. She smiles at that.

"My parents always have that station on in their car too," she says.

He drives them down the back of the mountain, past the houses that used to be as familiar to him as the faces of his friends and teachers. Some of them have changed in the years since he left—a fresh coat of paint here, a new addition to the wraparound porch there—and he always experiences a slight shock of unwanted surprise, to discover his old small town keeps changing and moving on without him too.

He parks them in the upper parking lot behind the north side of the campus. It's where he used to park every day on his way to morning football practice.

"Wow," she says. "I haven't seen it in so long."

"They added another wing," he says. He hasn't turned the keys out of the ignition yet; he's reluctant to burst their bubble of warmth in the car.

"Do you think we can get inside?" she asks.

Grant pops open the door. "Let's find out," he says.

The first door they try is locked and so is the second. He's about to suggest they just walk around the open track, when he remembers the side door by the teachers' lounge hallway, where his friends used to sneak back in after cutting class.

"The lock's broken on that one. All it needs is one good— *yank*."

The door gives way, and with one metallic *clank*, they're staring into the empty hallways of their old high school.

"It's so . . ." Helen says, as she steps inside. He follows her and shuts the door behind them. "Empty."

"Where do you wanna go?" he asks, tucking his hands in his pockets. He feels nervous suddenly, like they might get in trouble, like she might think this is just as lame as the nature walk at Washington Rock. Like she might think he's a loser for even suggesting this.

"I wonder if the cafeteria's changed," she says, and leads the way down the hall.

They find the old cafeteria quickly. The floors look like they've gotten an update, but everything else—the tables and chairs, the walls, the windows, the inexplicable scent of *graham cracker* that permeates the air no matter how many greasy pizzas were eaten here—is all the same.

"They took out the vending machines," Helen says, as they wander inside. "We used to have a coffee cart over there."

"I don't think they're allowed to serve coffee to minors anymore," Grant muses.

"I used to put three packets of sugar in my iced coffee," Helen says, looking around with slight amazement.

They keep walking the perimeter, until Helen stops at a table near the window. "I used to sit here at lunch. Do you remember where you used to sit?"

Grant turns and points at the opposite corner. "Over there."

Helen nods, staring at his old table as if she can see their past lunching selves. He sits down on "her" table, his legs swinging off the edge. "Nice view from this table."

"I liked having a window so close," she says.

"Colder in the winter, though," he notes.

She shrugs. "I usually wasn't here this late in December. Where do you wanna see next?"

He votes for their junior-year English classroom, but the door is locked and they can only peer through the window in the door.

"I don't recognize any of these teachers' names," Helen says as they walk down the English wing. "I guess all of our teachers retired."

"Did you keep in touch with any of them?"

"No. I should have," she says. "I heard my favorite teacher, Mr. Choi, the faculty rep for the *Ampersand*, he died a few years back. Right before I published my first book."

"I'm sorry," he says, and means it.

She tries a door at random and it opens—it's a closet-room full of old, dusty books. School-edition hardcovers of classics like *Great Expectations* and *Shakespeare's Tragedies* and Norton's Anthology compendiums of the American literary canon—there are piles of books so high, they tower over Helen.

"Jackpot," she whispers, and walks in. She opens one book and laughs, then tosses it at him. "First page."

He opens it and sees the register of the names of students who once held this particular copy of *A Portrait of the Artist as a Young Man*. Sandwiched between students from the classes of '07 and '09 is *Lauren DiSantos* in a cramped cursive scrawl.

He laughs and thinks about taking a picture to send to Lauren. But would that be weird?

"I don't even remember which ones we read which year," he says instead, setting the book down.

"We did Shakespeare senior year," she says, picking through the books. "Austen and Brontë sophomore year. And I don't remember the rest. I wanna see if I can find my *Wuthering Heights*. If I do, I'm taking it."

He opens a copy of *Wuthering Heights*, scanning for familiar names. A few names tickle the back of his memory, but nothing solid. He opens another, and a name stares back at him in bold Sharpie.

"Here," he says thickly, tapping it.

"You found it?"

She moves over, then stops when she sees the name he's pointing at. *Michelle Zhang, '10.*

"Oh."

"You want it?" he asks, trying to keep his voice low and neutral.

Helen touches her sister's name.

"No," she says finally. "It's better off here, living its life, educating high school students." She laughs ruefully. "That probably sounds insane."

"No," he says. "That makes perfect sense."

She smiles at him in gratitude, and he swallows hard. "What now?"

"Where did you spend the most time when we were here?" she asks.

He thinks, then jerks his head outside. "Football practice.

But it's pretty cold. I guess when it was winter, we'd do some drills in the north gym."

"Okay," she says, and he leads the way.

WALKING THROUGH THE empty halls of their old public high school feels like walking into a memory. She trails her fingertips along the solid walls to reassure herself they're real. There's a strange, dreamlike quality to the day, and if she could, she'd reach out her fingers and touch Grant to check if he was real too.

"That was my favorite mirror," she says, pointing at a mirror on one of the hallway intersections on their way to the gym. "I always checked my hair and clothes in it on the way to class."

The first door to the gym is locked too, but as Grant tries the other door, Helen spots something that makes her shout in delight.

"Look at you!" she exclaims, and points up at a dusty, framed photo on the wall by the trophy case. *Dunollie Warriors Varsity Football Team, 2007–2008 Season.*

Grant walks up and he's beside her before she realizes it.

"Huh," he says, staring up at the team photo.

Helen turns to watch Grant studying the photo. "It must be weird to see yourself become a part of the background scenery here," she says. "I remember walking past these photos all the time and not really seeing them. And here you are."

"Weird," he echoes.

Helen takes out her phone and snaps a photo of the framed picture.

"I'm sending this to the room," she says. "Merry Christmas, one and all."

"Wait, no, that's not fair," Grant says, and grabs for her

phone. "Not unless there's one of you and the newspaper club dorks around here somewhere."

Helen acts on instinct and hides the phone under her sweater, out of reach. "They didn't appreciate our accomplishments as much as yours. You're lucky to be immortalized on the walls of our school!"

Grant laughs and seizes her by the shoulders from behind.

"Give it to me," he says, his voice a low growl in her ear.

He has one arm looped across her chest, trapping her against his body. A strange thrill shoots up her back, and she feels him swallow hard.

"*Oy!*"

Grant releases her and she drops the phone with a clatter.

A middle-aged man strides toward them from the far end of the hallway. His walkie-talkie beeps from his belt and he points an accusing finger at them.

"How did you get in? I'm talking to you!"

Helen glances at Grant.

"Run," he says, and grabs her hand, before sprinting for the closest door.

As it turns out, running wasn't the smartest idea.

"You tripped a silent alarm," Vice Principal Peters tells them in the parking lot, where he's waiting with two security guards. "What were you doing in there?"

Grant watches Helen transform into a helpless female before his eyes.

"Oh my gosh, this is so embarrassing," she says. "We graduated from here years ago, and we just wanted to come see the school."

"By breaking and entering?"

"We didn't break anything," Helen says, and looks at Grant with wide, innocent eyes. "Did we? The side door was unlocked."

"Yeah, I remember we used to sneak in through that door when I was a senior," Grant says, pointing at the offending door. "The locks were broken even back then. You guys should probably get that fixed."

"We're not gonna get in trouble, are we?" Helen turns back to the vice principal anxiously. She looks at him as if he has their fate in his hands, which Grant thinks is laying it on a little thick. "I swear, we didn't take anything. We just wanted to see where . . . where we first fell in love. Right, babe?"

She smacks Grant on the arm.

He clears his throat. "Yeah. Such a romantic, this one. I told her we'd get in trouble, but . . . you're married, you get it."

Grant nods at the ring on the vice principal's left hand.

"Are you two married?" he asks, warming to them.

Helen looks to Grant wildly. "No. I don't have a ring."

Grant pulls her to his side. "Not yet, anyway. We keep arguing about how she wants me to propose. I'm still pitching football field at homecoming."

Vice Principal Peters beams. "Well, that'd be a hell of a story, two Dunollie alums getting engaged at homecoming. I bet you'd even make the front page of the *Ampersand*."

Helen huffs and Grant grins at her. "You hear that? We'd make the *Ampersand* front page."

After exchanging email addresses with the vice principal ("in case you *do* decide to do something at homecoming") and some thorough apologies for disturbing the peace on Christmas Eve, Grant and Helen walk silently back to the car in the north parking lot.

"Don't laugh," she says. "He's still watching."

"What do you think the headline of our engagement story would be in the *Ampersand*?" he asks as they approach the car.

Helen rolls her eyes. "I'd never have let a story like that on the front page. Maybe a blurb on the sports page."

"'Ex–Homecoming King Finally Finds His Queen,'" Grant pitches, hopping into the driver's seat.

"'*Ampersand* Standards Plummeting; A Former Editor-in-Chief Reports,'" Helen responds.

"'Town Daughter to Wed Her Sister's Slaughterer,'" Grant says.

A stunned silence follows this as Helen turns to look at him.

Grant freezes. "Sorry," he says immediately. "Sorry—"

Then she bursts into laughter.

"Oh my god," she says, wiping tears from her eyes. "You're going to *hell*."

"And you're riding shotgun with me," Grant says as he throws the car in reverse.

THE SUN IS setting by the time he drives her back to her car at the top of Washington Rock.

"That was fun," she says. It feels like giving something up when she says it—some part of her flutters anxiously, as if to say, *What if he doesn't agree?*

"Yeah," he says, smiling at her in a way that does funny things to her stomach. "What are you doing tomorrow?"

"Christmas? Helping my mom clean the house, then cooking for all the Chinese aunties and uncles coming over for dinner."

"Sounds like a good Christmas," he says.

If he were anyone else, she'd invite him over.

"You wanna do something the day after?" she asks instead.

He nods. "Sure. You pick the time and place."

He's leaning against the car door, his arms folded across his chest as he watches her face. It occurs to her that there's something incredibly *dear* about him standing like this, and she's aware of a sudden gladness that he's here with her.

A thought bubbles into her mind, and it grows insistent.

"Would you . . . would you come with me to see my sister?"

He stills and she thinks maybe she's made a mistake reading him. It's too big an ask for so new and fragile a . . . *friendship*? What are they to each other?

He clears his throat, then nods.

"Sure," he says finally. "If you want me there."

She thinks about the day of Michelle's funeral, of him showing up in a sweater and tie to the one room where his presence wasn't just unwanted, it was firmly rejected. She wonders if he's thinking about it now too, as his brown eyes seek out hers.

"I do," she says.

"Okay," he says softly. "I'll be there."

Twelve

Christmas in their mostly agnostic Chinese household has become a familiar mishmash of traditions. Every year, Helen wakes up at eight a.m. with the sun, to the sound of porcelain plates and bowls moving downstairs. As she brushes her teeth and washes her face, the smell of this morning's *tang* floats upstairs—some warming blend of bone broth, jujubes, and ginger.

By the time she comes downstairs, her mother has set aside a quick breakfast for them to eat whenever they wake up. This year, it's steamed and salted taro root, already peeled and waiting in a thin plastic wrapper. Helen has never actually woken up early enough to see Mom eat on Christmas morning—she's already mopping the floors.

Helen helps tidy up the living room and dusts the framed photos above the fireplace. Something always twists in her stomach when she reaches the single framed photo of her with Michelle. They're in middle school, at the peak of both their awkward phases, and wearing bright neon snowsuits for a random ski trip they took with Mom and Dad's work friends. They look happy and nothing like themselves—Helen doesn't think they ever went skiing again and those work friends eventually faded from their lives like so much background noise.

They don't have stockings or wreaths or any decorations

like that—she remembers going to another friend's house in December and being awed at the feeling of stepping into a Hallmark Christmas card. At their own house, Christmas is confined to a single room by the front door—they put up a fake tree they bought at Target twenty years ago and decorate with the same plastic ornaments every season.

Still, there's a festive feeling in the air when she gets the red tablecloth out from the basement and helps Mom expand their dining room table to accommodate more guests.

Her own contribution comes in the form of a mulled cider this year, which she brews in a Crock-Pot according to the recipe that Tom from the writers room emailed her. She puts on the "Yule Log" broadcast and listens to Christmas music over the new speaker system her parents bought last Black Friday. Dad vacuums all the carpets while Mom puts a roast duck in the oven. When Helen opens the fridge, it's full of frozen tiramisu from their nearby Costco.

Sometime around three p.m., the first of her parents' friends arrive, holding dishes whose names Helen has never learned but that have become familiar enough that she's made up her own for them—*that black-ear mushroom dish everyone likes, the flowery greens with the good dark sauce, the thin clear spaghetti with the stripey green vegetables and minced pork.*

Everyone greets her and gives her a *hongbao*—a red envelope stuffed with crisp new bills—at the door and Mom nudges her to remind Helen to say thank you, as if she's still twelve years old. It occurs to Helen that she's getting to an age where it's maybe embarrassing to still be accepting these cash envelopes—surely her parents were in their early thirties when they started distributing them to their own friends' kids.

Sometimes the other parents will bring their kids with

them—kids who are, at this point, full-grown adults like Helen. This year it's Theo Jiao, in his third year of a post-residency fellowship at—*some teaching hospital*; Helen tuned out when everyone started saying "med school" more than once in the conversation. Inevitably, there's the moment when the dinner conversation turns into a humble-bragging competition between parents—"Helen is so busy all the time with her TV show, she never calls anymore." "Theo isn't sleeping enough, he's overworked at his cardiology fellowship"—and then the not-so-subtle joking-haha-not-really part of the evening when they wonder why Helen and Theo don't just date each other and get married and have babies already.

After dinner Dad turns on the TV and the grown-ups (Helen still thinks of them as grown-ups) all chatter idly while she and Theo watch *Titanic*.

"That's cool they're making a TV show out of your books," Theo says. "I remember you were always reading at these things when we were kids. My mom donated your books to our local library."

Helen feels bad now for not paying more attention to Theo's residency talk.

"That's really nice of her," she says. "My parents are proud of you too. They sent me photos when you graduated med school."

Helen wonders if Theo is actually single or if he's got a girlfriend waiting for him to call after this is all over. Theirs was always a friendship of convenience—someone to talk to during these endless Chinese family gatherings, someone who understood this world without needing explanations. It probably *would* be easier if they would just fall in love, and Helen remembers vaguely a period when they were teenagers, when she thought she might have a crush on him and practiced her flirting with him. It never came to anything, though—maybe knowing their parents wanted it so badly sapped it of any real potential.

Theo checks his phone and Helen takes that as a sign that it wouldn't be rude to check hers as well. There's a string of *Merry Christmas* texts, from her YA author group chat and from the *Ivy Papers* writers room, which is currently litigating an ugly-sweater-off happening at Owen's family Christmas. She sends a festive emoji to the group chat and votes for Owen's uncle. Her phone dings, and it's a text from Grant, to her individually—

On for tomorrow?

Merry Christmas, btw.

GRANT REMEMBERS WHEN Christmas at their house was a not-to-be-missed event of the season. His mom would deck the halls and hire landscapers to string up a spectacular lighting display that made him proud to claim the house at the top of the hill as his home. She'd make him put on a suit for Christmas Day church services and then they'd host all the extended family for a catered Christmas dinner.

They kept it up for the first year he was back from college, but by the second year, his parents were separated and his mom said it was too much bother to manage on her own. Instead, they went to one of her book club friends' Christmas parties. In the last few years, she hasn't wanted to venture out ("the roads are icy, and it's so much work for a boring party"). Grant still spends Christmas dinner at home, but it's a simple meal for two now.

This year, though, his mom seems more in the holiday spirit.

She hums as she prepares the Christmas roast and offers him wine.

"It's our last Christmas in this house," she says cheerfully. "Falalalala!"

It occurs to Grant that this may also be one of his last trips to Dunollie, if the house sells as quickly as the agent promises it will.

"Mark anything you don't want tossed," his mom had told him when he first arrived. "And I'll ship it to you when the time comes."

Grant doesn't have room for all the souvenirs of his childhood in his house, nor does he particularly want them.

But he caught his mom crying over one of his Pop Warner football trophies the other day ("We were *so proud* of you . . .") and he knows she'd balk at the thought of throwing everything out to the curb with this year's Christmas tree. She'd probably hang on to all of it in a storage facility somewhere, spending unnecessary money preserving insignificant memories.

So he puts Post-its on things at random—his old yearbooks, a few books, a random football. It'll be easier to throw them out once he has full ownership over them.

His phone dings with a message and he violates the old rule of no cell phones at the dinner table because Lisa Shepard is currently dancing in the kitchen to Bobby Vinton.

It's from Helen.

> Is 4 p.m. too late? Have to help clean up in the morning.

He gives the message a thumbs-up, and her next message is a dropped pin for Somerset Grove Cemetery, followed by:

Meet you in the parking lot at
the bottom of the hill.

A thumbs-up feels almost too whimsical for the conversation
now and he thinks for a moment on an appropriate response
before he types back:

Thanks for inviting me.

Thirteen

Grant buys flowers from the supermarket at the last minute, because he isn't sure what the right thing to do is but he'd rather err on the side of bringing something. The checkout lady smiles indulgently at him when he places the flowers on the conveyer and he feels uncomfortable at the thought that she's misinterpreting the gesture.

He pulls past the wrought iron gates of the cemetery and sees the parking lot is pretty full. It makes sense, he supposes, that a lot of people would want to visit their loved ones during the holidays.

Helen waits outside her car in a woolen winter coat, and he feels bad that she's been standing in the cold waiting for him.

"Sorry," he says, and holds up the flowers. "I wasn't sure whether I should bring something."

"No, that's . . . really nice," Helen says. "It's up this way."

She leads them up the gravel path, past the oldest headstones covered in lichen and the craggy trees that must create a more picturesque scene in the spring and summer, but currently give the place a haunted winter feeling. The snow from a few days ago has melted by now, and the dirt beneath their feet is still wet and dark with moisture.

Helen wears heeled boots and he catches a glimpse of dark sheer tights under the swishing skirt of her long camel coat.

They reach the top of the hill and Helen slows her pace so

they're walking side by side, their elbows occasionally brushing as they navigate the bumpy path.

"How was your Christmas?" she asks.

"Good," he says, then thinks about it, really. "Fine. Underwhelming. Just dinner at home. But I didn't mind. I always get my fill of Christmas spirit in LA before flying back."

She nods. "Christmas in LA seems like it'd be so different," she says. "No snow."

"There's no snow here this year either."

"Yeah, but there's a chance of it and that makes a difference, I think."

"There's fake snow at the Grove," he says, referencing an upscale outdoor mall in Mid-City. "They run it every hour or so, with soapsuds."

"That's not the same, though."

"No, but it's fun anyway."

Helen smiles, then slows her walk. She points directly below them, at the nearest row of headstones. "She's over here."

Grant's heart beats a little faster and his body tenses. Helen looks up at him with eyes that always seem to see too much.

"Come on," she says softly, and slips her hand in his as she leads the way forward.

They stop in front of a dark marble headstone.

MICHELLE ZHANG
May 24, 1992–June 7, 2008
Beloved daughter, sister, friend.

HELEN WATCHES AS Grant crouches down and places the supermarket flowers across the bottom of the headstone. The flowers are wrapped in festive cellophane and it feels almost as if he's saying *Merry Xmas, Merry Xmas, Merry Xmas* to her dead sister. She sits down on the grass in front of the headstone, and he sits beside her.

"Why did you come to the church that day?" she asks.

He hesitates and she becomes aware that they're holding hands still. He studies their gloved hands as he contemplates an answer.

"I felt like I should," he says. "I didn't really want to. I just felt like . . . I owed it to her, or something. It was stupid, in retrospect. I was thinking about me and not how it'd make your family feel. My dad tried to talk me out of it, to be fair."

"It must have been hard for you," she says. He laughs mirthlessly.

"Hard for me," he murmurs. "You lost your sister."

Helen turns back to look at the headstone as he gives her hand a slight squeeze.

"My parents asked for my input on the inscription. I gave them the blandest, most generic one on purpose." She studies the headstone for what feels like a long time before she looks at him. "You know if someone in your family dies by suicide, your chances of being suicidal increase?"

Grant turns to look at her sharply. Helen exhales.

"One of the school counselors told me that. I spent the rest of that summer paranoid every time I picked up a knife or scissors. Which was stupid, honestly. Because after all this time . . . I still don't understand how she could do it."

They stare out at the same view, as if an answer might materialize before them.

"After she died, I became so, *so* angry at suicide prevention organizations. I know that sounds strange," Helen says. "Everywhere I looked, it seemed like there were messages to reach out if you were worried about someone, to tell them you loved them, to tell them they weren't a burden, to help them find help. It infuriated me. The idea that they all seemed to believe there was something *I* could have done to keep Michelle from killing herself."

Helen picks at the grass with her free hand, then presses her palm into the dirt.

"It's the life-and-death stakes. Everyone wants to believe they could save someone else's life, if they saw the right signs, had the right tools. Like maybe, if I say the right words, in the right combination this time, she'll *choose life*. But that's not how it happens." She laughs, a short brittle one. "What happens is your sister withdraws and becomes distant, but not all the time, and you think, *she's just being a teenager*, and then you find out she's doing things you'd never *dream* of doing—she had a boy-friend and a drug dealer before I even had my first kiss—but you want to be *cool about it*, you don't want to seem like you're overreacting, and you don't want to get her into trouble, and she's a fucking *asshole* to you back, and you start checking in and checking in and she pushes you away and pushes you away and finally you're like, *Fine! And fuck you too!* And then suddenly she's dead."

The letters on the headstone are still sharp and easy to read, and Helen has to look away.

"I refused to feel guilty, after she died," she says to the ground. "And no one knew how to talk to me. Everyone knows how to say, 'It wasn't your fault.' But if you say, 'I know it wasn't my fault, it was *hers*,' people get uncomfortable. And maybe they're right. Maybe—maybe it wasn't Michelle at the steering wheel of her own body, that night. She died without ever having gone to a therapist, so I have no idea what disorders might have been driving her. She was probably an addict—she didn't look like one, like how I pictured addicts before: desperate, homeless strangers on the street. She lived in our house. She was smart, and she had people who loved her, and it *still* wasn't enough . . ."

Helen swipes away a frustrated tear. "I called a suicide hotline, the Monday after she died. I didn't want to kill myself," she says. "I just wanted to talk to someone who was used to talking to people who did. I remember asking him—'Do you think if everyone on earth went through the training you did, learned how to talk about suicide without all the—the *stigma* and the self-consciousness, do you think then we'd live in a world where no one would ever kill themselves again?' I wanted to see if there was a way to cure it, like cancer. And I'll never forget—the man on the other end of the line said, 'No. I can almost guarantee you, some of them still would.' And I hung up after that."

Helen draws a shaky breath.

"I took her suicide really personally," she laughs, and it comes out a stifled, wet sound. "It felt like she took all the love I had to give and said, *no, it's not good enough*. Which is probably not the healthiest way of looking at it. But—I am so sick of always being the healthy one."

Her breath comes out in shaky spurts now, and Helen becomes aware of the warmth of Grant's body, his left side pressing against her right as she commands herself *do not cry*. Grant shifts his arm slightly—not enough that it's wrapped around her, but enough that she feels the support of it against her back.

"Did you know her at all?" she asks thickly.

"No," Grant says, his voice hoarse. It feels like a long time since she last heard it. "She might've been friendly with some people I knew, but I didn't really pay close attention to things like that, back then."

"She was—loud and bright and unpredictable," Helen says, thinking of squawking arguments in long car rides and sudden unexpected displays of sisterly affection. "It was like Michelle felt all her emotions, good and bad, at a higher saturation than anyone else in our family. She could be really funny too. We'd get into fights—*you borrowed my sweater, you were a bitch about something when I was really upset*, sister shit—and she'd come up with these incredible, really *mean* one-liners, just in the moment, that were so funny I'd have a hard time staying angry because I wanted to laugh so hard. She probably could have become a comedian, if she'd wanted. But I have no idea what . . . what she actually would have wanted."

"Was there a note?" Grant asks, his voice quiet.

"Not a physical one," Helen says, and feels strangely grateful for the chance to tell him. "But I always thought if she'd tried to write one, she would have done it on her laptop—she was so obsessed with that thing when she got it. I have her hard drive all backed up, and I've looked and I've looked but I've never found anything."

"I'm sorry," Grant murmurs, and she wonders what he's apologizing for.

"We buried her in the Chinese community section of the cemetery. So she's spending eternity with all the old grandmas and grandpas and Saturday-morning Chinese school principals who never approved of her. If ghosts exist, she's probably giving them hell."

"Do you think you'll be buried here?" he asks.

It's a blunt, existential question. One she's thought of before.

"No," she says. "I always liked the idea of having my ashes scattered in some significant place. The problem is I've never really felt that strongly about anywhere. I like a lot of places, but enough for eternity? Then again, it probably wouldn't matter. I'm overthinking it, I know."

"I read somewhere that you can get your remains turned into organic mush and they'll plant a tree over your body," Grant says.

It feels macabre to be talking about bodies turning into mush when he feels so warm and solid and *alive* against her. She drops her head against his waiting shoulder.

"What kind of tree would you be?" Helen asks.

"I don't know," he says, and she feels the deep rumble of his voice against her body. "I guess I feel the way you feel about places, with trees."

Helen lifts her head slightly and studies Grant Shepard from closer up than she ever has before. "I feel like you'd be an oak tree. It's like the golden retriever of trees."

Grant laughs, a genuine laugh this time—the sound is jarring in the cemetery. Helen looks out at the view and tries to see a peaceful park instead of a final resting place.

"I haven't been back here without my parents since the week we buried her," she says. "I was really mad at her, for a long time. And it's kind of depressing here."

"Thanks for bringing me," he says, and smoothly presses a kiss against the side of her brow.

They're both quiet then, and for a moment she listens to their synchronized breaths, inhaling and exhaling with the wind.

"It's not a big deal," she says finally, and looks away. "We should get going, though, before it gets dark."

He offers her a hand up and she takes it.

"Are you hungry?" he asks.

"A little," she says, even though she isn't.

The path is rocky and he touches her elbow lightly as she climbs back up the hill.

"You should come over for dinner," he says. "There's always too much food anyway."

"Would that be okay?" She lifts her brows.

"Yeah," he says. "Come over."

Fourteen

Helen types Grant's address into her car GPS, even though she knows she could get there by memory from years of school-bus routes still mapped in her brain. Eastbound on Route 22, then up the mountain, past Washington Rock, past the cul-de-sac of newly developed (now not-so-new) homes, just after the stop sign on the right.

She rings the doorbell and she can tell by the bright way that Mrs. Shepard greets her, Grant has already told her who to expect.

"It's so good to have you here," Lisa (*she insists!*) says. "Grant's just washing upstairs. Can I take your coat?"

Helen tries not to gawk at the interior of this old Victorian. It looks vaguely familiar for a place she's never been—she remembers seeing the lush peacock wallpaper in the drawing room ("aren't we fancy!") in the background of photos of parties she never went to, on Facebook. There's an antique umbrella stand near the front and a cheerful little plaque that reads, "God bless this home with love and happiness." *This is where Grant Shepard comes from.*

She washes her hands in the downstairs bathroom and studies herself in the mirror. She's thankful that she woke up in a mood to accessorize—the black sweater dress is on the casual side, but the gold necklace and earrings save it from being too much of a lazy funeral vibe. She pulls her long hair back into a ponytail with a scrunchie after some debate. Then she texts her parents—

At dinner with friends, don't wait up.

Grant is helping set the table when she walks in. He's wearing an old Dunollie Warriors crew-neck sweatshirt that she has too, buried somewhere in the back of her closet.

"Can I help?" she asks, gripping a chair for something to do with her hands.

"No, no," Lisa says, bringing over a steaming platter of green beans. "You're our guest. Oh! Wine. We need a good wine."

Lisa disappears into the kitchen and Grant grins at Helen lazily.

"She's going to bring back the good stuff she's been saving," he says.

"Oh no, tell her not to—"

"We have to get rid of it before she moves anyway," he says. "And she doesn't like drinking alone."

"Here we are," she says, and returns with two bottles. "A nice red, but also, I found this lovely white while I was rummaging around and I thought, *why not.*"

Grant rolls his eyes. "Helen will think we're trying to get her drunk, Mom."

"Well, if she does get drunk, she can take a nice nap on the couch," Lisa says, with a roguish wink. "That's what I do when I've overindulged."

Over the course of roast potatoes, green beans, leftover pot roast, and a surprise bottle of port that comes out before dessert, Helen learns more about Lisa Shepard than she's ever known about Grant himself. She tells them about the sheep farms in Ireland that she's been researching and how she's narrowed her choice down to two likely options. One that's a longer commitment and a bit farther from the parts of Ireland she's interested in; another that's a shorter commitment but maybe that's a blessing in disguise—"You never know what could be waiting for you at the end of an opportunity rainbow." Lisa tells Helen about her childhood in Bucks County, Pennsylvania, and growing up as the girl next door to the Shepard brothers. "Very handsome, *very* in demand." She reminisces about her wedding, and brightens when she remembers she found her old bridal portrait in the basement the other day.

"One second," she says, and dashes downstairs.

Helen glances at Grant and can't help laughing at his pained expression.

"Sorry," he says. "She doesn't get to talk to new people very often anymore."

"She's charming," Helen says. "I see how you learned to talk to people."

"I'm good at getting other people to talk," Grant says. "She's good at talking about herself. There's a difference."

Lisa reemerges with a framed photo of herself on her wedding day, in a Victorian-revival gown with puffed sleeves and a lace collar. "That was the style back then," she says. "I remember feeling like the prettiest girl in Bucks County that morning."

"You were a beautiful bride," Helen says honestly.

"Mm." Lisa nods, staring fondly at the photo. "I was a picture. Which ended up in the basement! Ha! That's where these things end up sometimes."

Grant sighs audibly and Lisa laughs at him.

"He's embarrassed," she says. "It's so nice to be able to embarrass him. It's been ages since he brought any of his friends over."

"Mom, can we wrap up the show-and-tell before midnight?"

Lisa looks at the old clock in the corner and claps her hands. "Oh my god, it's after nine! Well, time flies when you have good company."

"And three bottles of wine," Grant mutters under his breath, and Helen laughs.

"Helen, do you want some decaf before you get on the road?"

Helen presses her hand to her cheeks, feeling a flush of warmth from the wine. "That would be great, Mrs. Shepard."

Grant glances at her warily when Lisa leaves the room.

"You shouldn't drive. My mom practically poured a gallon of alcohol down your throat."

Helen lays her head down on her linen placemat, feeling a warm kind of sleepy.

"Yeah, why'd you let her do that?" she yawns, and her eyes drift shut of their own volition.

Grant laughs—it's a familiar rumble now.

"I'll give you a ride once you're more sober. You can get your car in the morning."

Helen opens one eye and squints at him. "Such a sturdy oak."

"Mom, bring the coffee upstairs," he shouts into the kitchen, then leans over to rap the table in front of her. "Come on, if you fall asleep, I can't give you the grand tour."

THEY WALK UP the stairs slowly, ostensibly to look at the old family photos and framed childhood paintings on the wall, but also because Grant wants to be sure she doesn't tumble over the railing, forcing him to explain the unexpected death of a second Zhang sister on his watch.

"You grew up in my childhood dream," Helen murmurs as

he leads her past the lounge area on the second floor. "I begged and begged my parents for an old house like this."

"It's not as romantic as you think it is," Grant says. "None of the doors fit their frames, the heating system sounds like four ghosts ate a cat, and it's colder than a witch's titty in the mornings this time of year."

Helen cackles, then pushes past him into the next room.

"This is your room," she says with slight amazement. She looks around with such naked enthusiasm, he feels an urge to take a picture of her—unvarnished Helen. "You have a whole couch in it."

"Yep," he says, leaning against the doorway as she inspects his bookcase.

"A lot of sci-fi," she says, scanning his paperback collection.

"Hard fantasy," he corrects reflexively.

She laughs, then glances up at him with a suggestive smile. "Dirty."

He feels something twist in his stomach and turns instead to a box by the bed.

"This might be interesting to you." He pulls out a thick, leather-bound yearbook. "I think there's even an issue of the *Ampersand* in there."

"You're kidding," Helen says, and hurries over.

"Knock knock," his mom says, and they both look over at the door. Lisa holds a silver platter with a pot of coffee and cups. "Oh, you found your old yearbook—how fun!"

"Mom," he says.

"I'll leave this right here," she says, and sets it down beside the couch. "Have a good night."

She pulls the door half shut behind her. Grant shuts it affirmatively. He tries to ignore the mounting headache that's been building since dinner, watching his mother reveal layer after layer of their home life to Helen. *What did you expect when you invited her? Why would you bring her here?* Grant ignores that too, as Helen flounces onto the couch with the yearbook.

"I don't even know where mine is," she says, tossing her legs across the couch cushions casually.

His fingers itch with a strange need to squeeze her stockinged calf. He nudges her over and sits on the opposite end of the couch instead, so her head is next to his thigh. She seems to interpret this as a transitional position and shifts back again until her head rests in his lap.

Well, fuck. His hands hover awkwardly for a moment as she adjusts her grip on the yearbook so they can both see it. Finally, his left hand settles in her hair, while his right hand steadies the yearbook.

"Oof, we really over-tweezed our eyebrows back then," she murmurs, flipping through pages of senior portraits.

His thumb sweeps along her temple, barely grazing her eyebrow.

"Looks like yours grew back all right," he says, and he feels the rumble of her laughter.

"There you are," she says, flicking his senior portrait.

"Hm," he says, and watches his fingertips slowly scrape through her hair. She closes her eyes and exhales with a contented little "*hmmph*" and he forces his fingers to stop before he does something stupid.

"Flip to the extracurriculars section. My arms are tired," she says, nodding at the yearbook.

He takes the yearbook and dutifully flips the pages for her. She uses her freed hands to release her hair from its velvet scrunchie, then leans back into his lap and takes the book from him.

His left hand resettles of its own volition in her hair. This time his fingertips comb through and massage her scalp.

"I hated my outfit in this picture," she says, studying a group photo of the school newspaper club. "My sister borrowed the shirt I was going to wear."

"You looked cute anyway," he says, his voice sounding gravelly.

Helen laughs and looks up at him. "That would have made my year, if you'd said that to me back then."

Grant smiles and tips her chin back down to the yearbook. His right hand lingers there, then settles and brushes the knuckle of his index finger back and forth along her jawline. It might be his imagination, but he thinks she leans into his touch like a cat starved for affection.

She flips the pages until she finds the student council photos.

"There you are again," she murmurs.

"Here I am," he agrees, and his knuckles brush past her jawline to skate down her neck, lingering at her fluttering pulse point. He doesn't imagine it this time—she leans in and rubs her cheek against the inside of his wrist.

"Do you remember what you ran your campaign on?"

"No," he says, his breath caught as he drags the backs of his fingers along her face, sweeping light contact against her skin and lifting just before her lips.

"I do," she murmurs, and the movement brings her full bottom lip in contact with the edge of his thumb.

He swallows, his thumb lingering just between her top and bottom lip.

"What?" he asks, unsure what they're talking about.

She drags her lower lip along the side of his thumb and suddenly he's never been so hard in his life. It'd be embarrassing if he wasn't so turned on. She turns her face slightly and presses a slow, warm kiss over the top of his thumb. *What the fuck.*

"You said you'd reform the parking space lottery, and raise funds for new Astroturf on the football field."

She looks up at him and he swallows hard.

"Oh," he says.

He drags his thumb down past her lips and settles it at her collarbone instead, trying to cool the mounting hot tension in his gut.

"I interviewed your campaign manager for the paper," Helen is saying, and he can barely make sense of the words. She taps at a girl in the group photo. "I think she had a thing for you."

His hand expands and contracts at the base of her collarbone, flirting with the inch of skin just below the neck of her sweater dress.

"You could have interviewed me," he says, his voice rough.

She shakes her head slowly and he thinks it would take a miracle for her not to feel his pressing erection through the denim.

"You didn't get back to me in time," she sighs. "I was on a deadline."

"Poor Helen," he says, and his right hand has entirely given up the pretense of respectability and is now slowly running a rogue finger under her left bra strap. He stays on the path of the elastic, as if this proves something. "Always on a deadline."

"Grant," she says, with a whiny rasp to her voice that he suddenly discovers is the sexiest noise in the entire goddamn world.

"Hm?" He draws slow circles along the outside of her shoulder. *Circle, circle, dot, dot.*

She laughs. "Do the hair thing again," she murmurs.

He slowly removes his right hand from the fabric of her sweater and pulls both of his hands through her scalp.

"That feels so good," she whispers.

He doesn't trust himself to respond and focuses instead on adding pressure as he runs his fingertips along her scalp again.

She drops the heavy yearbook on her chest, and one of her hands reaches up, her fingertips seeking out the side of his face.

He tilts his head and tries not to audibly groan at the feeling of her warm palm against his stubble. Her fingers drift innocently toward his lips, and he can't help expelling a short, low laugh. He brushes a quick kiss against her index finger, then she drags the rest along his mouth *just so*, lingering long enough for him to kiss the tip of each finger.

He can't resist pulling her pinkie into his mouth and running his tongue along its underside.

She taps an admonishing finger against his lips as soon as he releases it, as if he's broken some unspoken rule.

He laughs and mutters, "Sorry."

He takes the opportunity to kiss the inside of her palm, and she pulls her hand away. She grabs his own hands instead, and uses them to pull him down *just enough* so he's hovering over her. Her eyes are closed, but he's pretty sure by the rapid tattoo of her pulse that she's just as awake as he is.

She takes a few slow, staggering inhales and exhales. The furious beat of blood in his veins slows down just enough to register her quiet sigh.

"Can I sleep here?" she asks, as his thumbs keep brushing against her skin. *Back and forth, back and forth.*

"If you want to," he says, his voice a low gravel. He waits for a response, but none arrives. He feels her pulse again—it's slow and steady; she might already be asleep. "I'll get you a blanket."

He tilts his head back against the wall for a second. *Get a grip, Shepard.* Then he slides her gently off his lap and stands. *Down, boy.* He downs a cup of cold decaf coffee, then walks down the hall to the upstairs bathroom. He finds a blanket in the closet and walks back to his room.

He frowns, confused, at the Helen-shaped indent on the couch. A *thud* downstairs brings his attention to the window, and his eyes adjust to the dark just in time to see her car pulling out of his driveway.

Well, fuck.

Grant shuts the door and drops the blankets on the couch. He notices a soft scrap of black velvet on the cushion—her scrunchie.

He leans over the couch and fumbles with his zipper until he releases himself. He shuts his eyes and strokes as he thinks of silky hair, *Grant, do the hair thing again, that feels so good*, soft trailing fingers, *sorry*, full lips and the barest hint of a tongue dragging against his thumb, *that feels so good*—

He comes with a quick, shuddering gasp, panting over the couch as his orgasm rocks through him.

. . . Fuck.

Fifteen

Helen drives home and concentrates doubly on the road instead of the insistent *thump thump thump* of her heart. The numbers on the clock tell her it's just after one a.m.—she's spent almost nine full hours in Grant Shepard's company today, yet somehow it feels like everything has happened in the span of minutes, then heart-racing seconds.

She isn't sure when their idle conversation about a yearbook turned into something more, something flirting dangerously close with seduction. She laughs as she stops at a red light. *If that was flirting with seduction, I'm screwed.*

Her cheeks flush with heat as she remembers the sensation of Grant's fingers skating across her skin—slowly, innocently, just staying on this side of plausible deniability until . . . *until you basically fellated his thumb.*

If anyone escalated things, it was her and her brazen mouth. *Not fair*, she protests to herself. *He wanted it too.*

She remembers the insistent press of his erection against the denim of his jeans, and tries to ignore the embarrassing answering dampness in her previously respectable cotton briefs.

Technically—*technically!*—nothing has happened that they can't explain away.

She laughs at this train of thought. *Remember when we held hands at the cemetery? This was just like that, but . . . more.* He'd kissed her forehead then too. *Kissing fingers and kissing foreheads is basically the same thing. Chaste gestures between friends.*

She combs a hand through her hair, hoping it isn't too much of an incriminating mess.

Can I sleep here?

The words had slipped out innocently enough, but she may as well have just said, *Please will you fuck me so hard we both forget our names?*

She embarrassed herself with how easily, how quickly and certainly, she would have thrown herself at him if he'd leaned down just a fraction of an inch closer. *And then what?*

Helen shakes her head as she pulls into the driveway of her parents' house. There is no *and then what* with Grant Shepard. There's no world in which a night of temporary, sanity-obliterating horniness ends in anything but regret and awkwardness and avoidance and . . . *and what if it's too late and this ruins everything once we get back to LA?*

She sits in the car, tapping her finger against the steering wheel. She thinks about those first uncomfortable weeks in the writers room, when they barely ever looked at each other—as if it was the last month of their senior year all over again.

No.

It's not too late. It's fine. Technically, nothing happened. We didn't cross any lines that can't be uncrossed. In a few months, Grant will forget this next-to-nothing even happened.

Helen nods to herself, takes a steadying breath, and heads into the house.

She's avoiding him.

Grant glowers at the call log on his phone. He hadn't called on the morning of the twenty-seventh. He had needed time to think and, if he was honest, replay the events of the previous night a few more times until it was permanently tattooed in his memory.

He *did* call on the twenty-eighth, but she didn't pick up and he thought he'd give her a full twenty-four hours to call him back. Twenty-four turned into thirty-six. He knows she's still in town—he saw an Instagram story she posted getting bagels. He tried texting her—a carefully considered *what are your new year's plans?*

It's around nine a.m. on the thirtieth now and she still hasn't responded.

He thinks about driving down to her house and banging on the door like a caveman until she answers. *And then what?*

And then he'd drag her back to his cave and finish what they started.

He laughs at this surprisingly primitive thought. But he doesn't know where she lives—somewhere at the base of the mountain, across the highway. And what if someone else answered the door? What then?

He pushes away the *what then*. *What then* doesn't matter if she won't even fucking talk to him. Does she expect to be able to avoid him until they're back in LA? *What then?* Are they supposed to sit in a room and pitch storylines and jokes and pretend he didn't jack off three times this weekend to the thought of other things he could have done to her warm, willing body while she was still beneath him?

His phone dings and it's embarrassing how quickly he grabs it, only to relax when he sees the name—*Kevin Palermo.*

Heard you're in town! NYE party at my spot, come thru.

It's followed by a second ding—a cheesy graphic inviting him to Kevin's Rockin' New Year's Eve Party, along with address details.

Grant exhales. He doesn't want to go to Kevin Palermo's Rockin' New Year's Eve Party—it gets sadder every year as more and more of their old friends have kids and babysitters to get home to. He can think of a hundred things he'd rather do than sit in Kevin's parents' basement listening to a Spotify playlist of pop hits from the early 2000s. At least ninety of those things involve Helen Zhang and her interesting mouth. Screw it, all one hundred of those things.

On the other hand.

He tries to think past the angry haze of lust. Maybe a passive, neutral approach would be best.

Grant thinks of the way she tapped her finger—so prim and admonishing—against his lips when he violated whatever insane rules she had privately determined for this game of "who can make the other person hornier without technically running any bases."

> I'll be at Kevin Palermo's new years party tomorrow.

> Come if you're around?

He forwards the graphic invitation along and ignores the feeling in his gut that says *she might not come, she might be done with you already.*

HELEN CALLS HERSELF a fool at least twenty times in the Uber to Kevin Palermo's house. Does Kevin even know she's coming? Does he remember who she is? Would it be worse if he did?

She fidgets and pulls the skirt of her dress down slightly. She only packed so many clothes for this trip, and none of them particularly appropriate for a New Year's Eve party. After debating a last-minute trip to the mall and nixing it for being too pathetic to entertain, she decided on a black silk slip dress she packed as a nightgown. It's honestly too cold for a slip dress, but it clings to her ass in a flattering way and her pride won't let her show up in a shapeless sack of a sweater dress, as she did the last time she saw Grant. She added a leather jacket and a spritz of perfume, laughing at herself the whole time. *What for?* She told her parents she was going to an old friend's house, and they didn't mind because they had plans of their own with Theo's parents in Edison.

Helen rings the doorbell and a pretty brunette in a clingy silver turtleneck dress answers the door. She tilts her head, studying Helen, then her pouty lips break into a smile.

"It's you," she says.

Helen runs the smiling brunette against a mental Rolodex of possibilities and arrives at—

"Hi, Lauren."

Lauren DiSantos looks Helen up and down.

"Long time no see," she says.

Grant Shepard's hometown sex friend is gatekeeping me from this party. Helen wonders if it'd be more mortifying to turn and run back into the Uber and tell the driver to take her home. Or to Siberia. Maybe the North Pole.

Except if she did, Grant would definitely find out. And that would be worse.

"It's really cold out here," Helen says.

"Well, let's get you a drink," Lauren says, yielding and opening the door.

Helen follows Lauren into the kitchen, trying not to crane her neck a full 180 degrees searching for Grant in every room of this mid-century house that looks like it was last decorated by someone's grandmother. They pass clusters of adult strangers with vaguely familiar faces and Helen feels like a sophomore playing dress-up at a party full of cool seniors.

"There's cheap champagne or boxed wine on the menu," Lauren says.

"I'm fine with either," Helen says.

Lauren smirks.

"Or . . ." She stoops and pulls out a bottle of sixteen-year-old Lagavulin from beneath the sink. "There's the good scotch Kevin hides and forgets about every year. You'll get warmer faster."

"That'd be great," Helen says.

Lauren pours them both glasses of scotch, neat.

"Cheers," she says, and clinks their glasses.

Helen isn't a scotch drinker but she thinks she might become one after this, as the smoky taste of aged whisky melts down her throat and travels straight into her belly.

"So," Lauren says. "What's new?"

"Um," Helen says, taking another sip of scotch. "Not much."

Lauren laughs. "Babe, we haven't seen each other in fourteen years. Not much?"

"Maybe too much, then," Helen says. "I wouldn't know where to start."

She's anxious and jittery. Suddenly she's reminded of how much she hates parties and staying out late with people she doesn't know that well and *why the fuck did she come here.*

"I heard you're working on a TV show," Lauren says. "That's pretty big."

"Yeah," Helen says into her drink. "It's exciting."

"Is anyone famous gonna be in it?"

"Um, I don't know," Helen says. "I think they're still figuring out . . . contracts, and stuff."

Lauren studies her and takes a sip of her scotch. "Grant's working on that show, right?"

"He is," Helen says, and looks down.

"Must be weird for you, given everything. How is he to work with?" Lauren asks.

"He's . . . fine," Helen says. "High school was a long time ago."

Lauren studies her curiously. Helen hopes she won't press on the subject.

"It was," Lauren finally agrees. "You know Grant's here, somewhere."

"Yeah, I know," Helen says. "He told me about the party."

He told me about you, she thinks, and wonders if there's something he didn't tell her. Maybe she's been overthinking things. Maybe he's already forgotten about what happened the day after Christmas. Maybe he took her lack of response to his calls and texts at face value and just threw out the invite to be friendly.

Maybe he's already planning on going home with Lauren.

"I wondered. We've never seen you around here before," Lauren says. "So you guys are friends?"

"Something like that," Helen agrees.

"Grant and I were 'something like that' once too," Lauren says casually. "Not so much now, though. I think he's changed, since I knew him."

"That makes sense," Helen says, not entirely sure it does.

"You're different too, than how I remember you."

Helen feels uncomfortably warm under Lauren's direct gaze.

"I hope so," she says, telling herself to grow a spine. "I have tried."

Lauren smiles.

"I get it," she says finally. "I'm trying to change too. Old habits, though, you know."

Is Grant an old habit?

"I think he's downstairs," Lauren says. When Helen blinks, Lauren nods toward the carpeted stairs to the basement. "Grant. If you want to say hi."

"Oh," Helen says, and her pulse quickens. "Thanks. I will."

"Hang on," Lauren says. She sets down her drink and holds Helen's chin in place with one hand, then dabs at her lips with a napkin with the other. "Your lipstick's smudged. Wouldn't want that, would we?"

Helen waits for Lauren to finish, then pulls back.

"Thanks," she says uncertainly.

"No problem," Lauren says. "Girls gotta look out for girls. Good luck."

She raises her glass in a slightly sardonic toast.

GRANT DOESN'T LOOK up when Kevin leaps off the couch and yells, "Bruh!" for the fourteenth time tonight. Another long-lost face from his past, probably.

"I haven't seen you in fucking forever, man," Kevin says.

"Yeah, well," a crisp female voice answers. Grant whips his head so fast, he's surprised he doesn't break his neck. It's *her*. "I don't usually have a lot of free time when I'm back home."

"You look *great*," Kevin says, in the understatement of the century.

She's wearing a silky black dress that looks like it's a few molecules thick, which is ridiculous in this weather and also *fucking hot*. Her long hair is brushed and curled and his hand itches with a desire to wrap those curls around his knuckles. *And then what?*

Helen flushes at Kevin's pathetic compliment in a way that makes Grant want to knock his old friend out cold.

"Thanks," she says. "I tried. You look great too."

Her eyes flit to Grant and suddenly the air seems to have left the room.

"Hi," she says to him.

"Hi," he answers, trying to keep his voice even.

"So what's new, man?" Kevin says, fucking oblivious. "Can I get you a drink?"

"I, um, had one," she says. "Lauren, upstairs, gave me some of your scotch. I hope that's okay."

She mumbles that to the ground and Grant frowns. He thinks she must be uncomfortable here, with so many people she doesn't know. He hates Kevin suddenly, and Lauren, and everyone in this building that's keeping him from having a straightforward conversation with her.

"Yeah, yeah," Kevin assures her. "Lauren's an old friend. She knows where we hide the good stuff. And now you do too! Funny how people become old friends, isn't it?"

"Yeah," Helen says, looking over at Grant.

"So how *are* you?" Kevin asks again.

Grant stands and walks over to them, because he can take only so much before he does something drastic.

"I'm good," Helen says. "I've been busy with . . . writing stuff. How have you been?"

"Same old, same old," Kevin says. "Had a job, lost my job, got a new one, didn't work out, but that's cool because I'm gonna take some time off to go hang with my cousin in Lake Michigan in January anyway."

"I hear it's beautiful there," Helen says.

"Yeah, we're gonna work on his boat," Kevin says. "I've never worked on a boat before, but, you know, sounds like a good time. Maybe it'll be my calling."

"I think the ball's gonna drop soon," Grant says. "You should probably . . ."

"Oh shit, yeah," Kevin says, and claps his hands on his head. "We have this big projector outside so we can do sparklers and shit, but it's been glitchy as fuck this year. I mean, we can watch in the living room upstairs, but no sparklers, no fun, you know what I mean?"

"Yeah," Helen says.

"Catch you guys later," Kevin says, and heads upstairs, leaving them alone.

Finally.

"So," Grant says. "You came."

Helen nods. She seems far away, and he has the somewhat whimsical impression of a stray cat contemplating crossing the street. *I'll come to you, if it's easier.*

"I wanted to see . . . what it'd be like," she says, as he advances slowly on her.

"And?" he asks, as her pulse flutters rapidly at her neck. He stops in front of her, close enough to touch. "How are you finding it?"

She looks around at everywhere but him.

"I remembered I hate parties," she says.

"And people, and talking to them—and me," he says, his voice low. He places a hand on the wood-paneled wall behind her, mentally commanding her to tilt her chin up to look at him. "Right?"

"I don't . . ." She starts, then stutters as he finally, *finally*, reaches out to stroke the skin on her shoulder. There are goose bumps on her arm—because it's cold, and her dress is flimsy. "I don't hate people," she says softly.

He huffs slightly and the hair in front of her face moves from his breath. His hand at her shoulder drifts down until he's just lightly holding on to her elbow with his thumb and forefinger.

"People," he repeats. "Okay."

"I don't know what this is," she says, looking up at him.

"What do you want it to be?" he asks, and tugs her closer, closer, until she's practically arching into his leaning body.

"Nothing. I mean—I don't know," she says.

He laughs and drops his head to her shoulder. Her hand floats up and tangles in his hair, scratching slowly. *Good boy.*

"Help me out," he says against her skin. "I don't know the rules."

"The rules?" Her voice is small, and he skims his lips across her shoulder. Not enough pressure to be called a kiss. But—*something.*

"Of this game we're playing," he says. His fingers dig into the cool satin of her dress, and he can feel the heat rolling in waves off of her. "What do I get if I win?"

"There's no winning," she says.

He lifts his head, then flicks the thin strap of her dress off her shoulder. "No?"

"It's not . . . possible," she says, breathing heavily as he lowers his head to the newly exposed millimeter of shoulder. He presses his nose to her skin and brushes it back and forth.

"I'm enjoying it all the same," he whispers, his lips brushing her collarbone.

"What else are you enjoying?" Helen asks, her voice tiny.

His fingers flex against her hip and she gasps.

"I'm enjoying this dress," he says. "If you can fucking call it that."

She presses forward against him and feels a gratifying answering hardness below the belt.

"I meant," she gasps, as he presses his knee between her legs and pulls her down, whispering silk across the hard denim. "Are you enjoying . . . anyone else?"

Abruptly he leaves her and she finds herself shivering in the relative cold of the basement without Grant Shepard's body heat.

"What do you mean," he says, staring at her, "by 'anyone else'?"

"I saw Lauren upstairs," she mutters, and looks away. "And I wondered, if maybe you guys were . . ."

He lets out a soft *ha* of air.

"Not during this trip," he says. "Not in a while, honestly."

"Oh," she says, and colors. "Okay."

He tilts his head, then grins. "You're cute when you're jealous."

She scoffs and looks away, but doesn't deny it. Not when she can still feel the hum of satisfaction in her body processing the apparently very important information that (1) he thinks she's cute, and (2) he's not going home with Lauren.

"So that's a rule, then?" he asks, studying her. "No enjoying anyone else?"

She thinks she must look ridiculous right now, her hair mussed, her skin flushed, her dress wrinkled. *Fuck this.*

She's too smart for this.

She comes off the wall and reaches out to press a hand against his chest, taking back some control. He doesn't put up a fight, and within a few steps, he lands against the back of the couch he had been sitting on when she came downstairs.

"It would be easier," she says softly, "if we could say nothing's happened."

"Nothing *has* happened," he says quietly.

Her palm slides down from his chest and stops at his belt.

She pauses, then slowly brushes the back of her hand against the front of his jeans. He exhales sharply.

"I want—"

"I don't want to know what you want," she says, and slides her hand off.

"Okay," he says, his breath ragged.

She feels powerful then, like he might do anything she asks, just now. Her fingertips skim his outer thigh, then she dips a hand under his belt, into his jeans.

"*Fuck*," he exhales.

She leans forward, her breath a warm suggestion in his ear as she strokes him through the soft fabric of his boxer briefs. She can feel a damp spot, and heat. His throat muscles seem to go taut.

"There's no way to win with us," she says, stroking, squeezing, pulling. "There's just . . . this."

His breathing comes out in short, ragged bursts. He's close, she thinks—it would be so easy to reach out and taste him. *He probably tastes like something she can't afford.* Grant cups the back of her head and brings her close enough to rest his forehead against hers.

"Look at me," he says, straining. "You want this?"

She watches him through glazed eyes, and the tip of her tongue comes out to wet her lips, which suddenly feel dry. A muscle ticks in his jaw and his eyes flicker, but he keeps watching her with a strained kind of intensity, until she gives a fraction of a nod. He isn't going to last much longer.

"I want this," she whispers.

"You can have it, then," he gasps. "I have to come."

"Come for me, then," she murmurs, and he does, dropping his head to her shoulder and stifling a groan as his shaft jerks against the fabric into her hand. He drags his mouth—*lips, teeth, stubble*—against her skin so hard as he climaxes, she thinks it might leave a mark. "That's what I wanted."

IT WOULD BE easier if we could say nothing's happened.

Grant cleans himself up in the bathroom to the best of his ability. So far, he could say Helen Zhang is responsible for two of the quickest, hottest orgasms of his life. But she's careful with him, the way that she's careful with everything. Her hands never strayed to the skin, no matter how determinedly his dick pressed against the placket of his boxer briefs. When he finished, she let him linger against her for a few harsh, precious heartbeats before slowly extracting her wandering hands from him and murmuring, "There's a bathroom over there, I think."

She never kissed him either, at least not on the mouth.

Well, he thinks grimly, he never kissed *her* either.

She's two up on him, though, and *that* bothers him.

Come for me, then. That's what I wanted.

What about what he wants? He wants to bury his face between her legs and find out if she comes undone loudly without inhibition or with quiet shaking sobs. He wants to fuck her against a wall, then again in his bed, and maybe in a car afterward too.

I don't want to know what you want.

Grant remembers the fire in her eyes when he asked her if *she* wanted this. If she wanted him.

I want this.

A feeling of hot, masculine pride surges in his chest at the thought that this woman—this prickly, particular woman, wants him. Or some parts of him, anyway. He isn't sure how much she's willing to give, but he suddenly finds he's willing to take whatever he can get, for as long as it lasts.

There's no winning.

Bullshit. He wipes his hands and stares at himself in the mirror. He looks like he just ran a marathon. He feels like a horny teenager, and like he could build a house with his bare hands. He's Grant Fucking Shepard. And before Helen Zhang came into his life, he was always good at winning.

So that's what he'll do. He exits the bathroom to find the basement empty. He goes upstairs and is completely unsurprised to find out she left already. He locates his coat and quietly slips out as well. He doesn't need to stay for the ball drop. He needs to make a plan.

Sixteen

"Helen has a daaaaaaate," Owen announces triumphantly as he sits down.

"Let's not do this," Helen says, settling into her chair and getting out her laptop.

"But it's such good *gossip*," Owen says.

It's really not but Owen likes to overstate things.

They've been back in the writers room for three, going on four days now and there's still an uncomfortable churning sensation in her stomach every time she accidentally meets Grant's eyes from across the table.

She flew back on January 1 and soon learned (from a close reading of the comments on Grant's last Instagram post) he was staying in Dunollie for another week to help clear out his mom's house. He didn't call her, text her, or respond in any direct way to her messages in the writers room group chat wishing everyone a happy New Year. After a minor sulk and soak in her bathtub about it, she concluded he was leaving the ball in her court.

And she would let it bounce there until leaves collected and rains came and everyone abandoned the game. There are nine weeks until the close of the writers room—surely that's enough time for things to get back to normal between them, and just short enough that she can endure it.

Because the truth is, she knows it would be a mistake to take this—*thing*—between them any further. She's never been very good at casual hookups and she suspects she already likes him too much to throw up the barriers completely against any traitorously soft, warm feelings that threaten to come up every time they're in close proximity.

Like a useless sixth sense, she always knows immediately when he's in the room. The air feels different and her eyes seek out the safe areas to look (anywhere he isn't) like a reverse heat map. She also knows when he's staring at her, though she can count on one hand all the times she's looked at him directly this week.

Right now, for instance, she knows he's playing with a rubber band ball and watching her intently.

"What's the gossip?" Eve asks.

The gossip is that Greg, their casting director, has apparently been carrying the slightest torch—matchstick, really—for Helen over the past few weeks and very chivalrously waited until principal casting on the show was completed to shoot her a very sweet email with a link to a Google Forms survey asking her out on a date, along with multiple-choice options of the possible dates they could go on.

"Well, *obviously* we have to help you fill out the survey," Suraya says.

Helen reluctantly texts the link to the writers room group chat.

"Be still my heart, modern romance isn't dead." Eve grins as she scrolls through the Google Forms survey.

"'Level of Fancy: athleisure, casual, business attire, semi-formal, full tux/ball gown,'" reads Nicole. "I vote you say 'full tux' and show up in athleisure. Or vote 'casual' and show up in a ball gown."

"I like that he has venue options but also leaves a space for suggestions of your own," Saskia says. "I don't know about

'Malibu beach date,' though. That's kind of an all-day affair—
it's a lot for a first date."

"I'm putting all my chips on bowling," Tom says. "If he's
good, then you know he wants to show off and that his most
impressive skill is bowling, and if he's bad, you see how he reacts
to stressful situations."

"Interesting thought," Eve says. "I would have voted for the
home-cooked meal for similar reasons."

"Yeah, but what if he makes the wrong choice of menu and
that ruins an otherwise potential-filled date?" Owen says.
"Controversial opinion: eating is too personal a thing to do on
a first date. Like, gross, I'm gonna show you how I sustain and
nourish my body?"

"I think the important thing here is what will make Helen
feel like she's in her comfort zone," Suraya says. "Then she can
assess accordingly if Greg's being additive or not to her general
mental and emotional state."

"My comfort zone is at home with my laptop, at a seat with a
nearby outlet and no windows or doors behind me," Helen says.

Grant makes a noise that sounds suspiciously like *of course*.
She looks up at him then, but he's scrolling on his phone with a
slightly bored expression.

"Grant, would you like to share with the class?" Suraya asks
patiently.

He lets out a quiet "*huh*" that she's pretty sure no one else
hears, and his eyes flicker up to her face before he returns his
attention to his phone screen.

"My vote goes to full tux/ball gown, so you can find out if
he owns a tux, bowling because Tom's right, and tacos because
you can leave early if it's a bad date or prolong the night if it's a
good one."

He sets down his phone and smiles placidly at Helen. She

senses that he's issued her a challenge of some sort, and feels a sudden itch to rise to the occasion.

"By George, I think he's got it," Owen says. "That's perfect, no notes."

THEY FINISH BREAKING the story for the second episode of the season that afternoon and Suraya sends Grant off to outline and script. Helen doesn't think much of this, until he doesn't show up in the room the next morning.

"Where's Grant?" she asks, trying to sound casual.

"Writing," Suraya says. "We send writers out of the room when they're on script."

"Oh," Helen says, feeling silly. Of course. Why had she imagined they'd all sit and type scripts shoulder to shoulder, in the same room till the bitter end, like they were studying for finals?

She finds herself walking by his office on her way out that day before she can stop herself. The writers' individual offices are a line of glorified walk-in closets along the back wall of the bullpen. She's never seen Grant in his room before and she's surprised to catch sight of him through the open door. He's frowning at his laptop, leaning back in an ergonomic swivel chair.

"Knock knock," she says, and is immediately embarrassed.

His eyes flit over to her, then return to his laptop screen.

"I just wanted to check in and see how it's going."

He looks up and she feels the full intensity of his stare for the first time today. She thinks suddenly of a time when she was young and running inside from the winter weather: a rush of warmth, followed immediately by the unpleasant jolt of falling against a cold, hard floor.

"Not great. I've been distracted."

"Oh," Helen says.

She lingers in the doorway, uncertain. The corner of Grant's mouth kicks up as he watches her.

"Shut the door," he says.

Helen hesitates, then pulls the door shut behind her. Grant taps a pen idly on his desk, still watching her silently. She leans back, holding on to the handle of the doorknob a little anxiously.

It occurs to her then that he might have meant for her to shut the door on her way out. Shit.

"I, um, I should let you—"

"Come here."

Her legs obey the command before her brain has time to argue, and suddenly she's standing in front of him, her knees a few centimeters away from his, the fabric of her wrap dress flirting with the denim of his jeans.

Grant looks up at her, a lazy tension in the way he leans back into his chair.

"When's your date?" he asks.

"Six thirty."

He glances at a clock on the wall, where it reads a quarter past five p.m.

"So I have a little time," he murmurs, and stands as he pulls her into him.

Helen suddenly finds herself pressed against his chest, which rises and falls as he buries his face in her hair and inhales deeply. His fingers spread into her back; they rub up and down in a soothing, stroking motion that pulls her steadily closer, *closer* into the frame of his body, as if the goal is to eliminate all space between them. It's so *much* and not at all enough. Her body faintly hums at the contact—*we missed this*, her limbs seem to be singing, and her skin prickles with awareness.

"I'm sorry," she says, though she's not sure what she's apologizing for.

He laughs into her hair and she feels him press a kiss to her temple.

It's soft, a peck. She could still extract herself from his arms now and leave, she thinks, and that would be that. They could move forward without too much awkwardness, a hug and a kiss on the forehead saying what words can't seem to.

Start walking, she tells her limbs, but they don't seem to want to listen.

"Poor Helen," Grant murmurs, and presses another kiss, this time to her brow, then another over the corner of her left eye. "So conflicted."

His thumb draws slow circles against her arm, and he brushes his lips to her cheek.

"I don't know why . . ."—she trails off as he moves to kiss her other cheek—"I keep ending up here."

Grant drags a knuckle slowly across her lips, staring at her mouth with naked want in his eyes. He swallows, hard. Then he bends his head and kisses her on the jawline instead, moving up toward her ear.

"Maybe you missed me," he says, and she exhales sharply as he catches one of her earlobes between his lips.

She shakes her head slightly—or maybe she's just shaking, full stop. "I've seen you every day this week," she says.

"Hm." His fingers run up her arms, leaving pale marks against her flushed skin. "I remember it differently."

He presses a soft, lingering kiss to her pulse point and her hand flies up involuntarily to bury in his hair.

"I've seen *you*," he says into her neck. "I can't seem to stop, in fact."

He pulls away from her abruptly and she wants to cry from

the loss of contact. Her hands lean back and grip the edge of his desk, so they don't reach out for him.

He drops down into his chair then, and she thinks maybe she's about to be dismissed. Instead, he studies a bit of yellow floral fabric in his hand and she realizes he's holding on to the edge of the tie string to her wrap dress. Suddenly there doesn't seem to be enough air in the room.

"How much am I allowed to see, Helen?" he asks softly.

Slowly, so *slowly*, she lifts a palm off the desk and pulls at the other dangling piece of the wrap dress tie front. It loosens the bow and she feels the dress slacken against her body, held loosely in place by gravity and a sorry excuse for a knot.

Grant's eyes seem to flare with something hot and cold and dangerous and he tugs at the fabric in his hand until the loose knot disintegrates. He releases it and she whispers a silent thanks to the gods of wardrobe that she put on matching underwear today as her dress falls open and exposes a straight column of skin and black lace to him.

He swallows hard.

"You're my favorite thing to look at in that room," he says suddenly, and drops to his knees in front of her.

He presses a trail of kisses from her stomach to the elastic lace band of her underwear.

"And no matter how hard I try"—he presses more kisses against the lace triangle front now, insistent, hot, *seeking*, and she gasps—"you never look back at me."

"That's not true," she mumbles, her fingers tangling in his hair as he licks her boldly through the fabric. "I—I look at you."

He lets out a short, hot breath that seems to go straight to her clit. *Fuck.*

"Are you looking at me now?" he murmurs, and she bites her lip to stop from groaning at the delicious friction of his tongue and lace.

Grant looks up at her as he builds a steady rhythm that has her panting. There's a blaze of heat in his eyes and the lightest sheen of sweat on his forehead. She feels worshipped.

She's so wet, she's certain she's soaked through the fabric, and he practically *growls* into her.

"You taste so fucking good," he says, and the wet heat of his mouth sucks against her. "I could dine on this pussy every night and come back for dessert."

A strangled whimper comes out of her, and she thinks that if anyone were to walk in, she'd be completely incapable of doing anything but pressing his glorious mouth closer.

"Grant," she whispers.

"I'm right here, sweetheart."

"I want . . ." She bites her lip as the thin ridge of his tongue presses against her clit through the fabric. "I want to come on your tongue. Please."

In a fluid motion, he pushes the lace of her underwear aside and presses his tongue against the folds of her tortured skin. Her hand reaches out blindly and lands on his jawline, feeling his stubble and the tension of his jaw as he works his mouth against her.

She lets out a shuddering gasp and feels a wave of oblivion rock through her, as all the world disappears beyond a single spot on Grant Shepard's miraculous tongue. *Yes, yes, yes, yes.*

She comes back into her body gradually, and when she looks down at him, he's watching her with hungry eyes as he brushes the back of his hand against his mouth.

He drops a swift kiss to the inside of her thigh and she shivers.

He stands then and she feels herself arching under his leaning body as he reaches past her. She can't help but notice a dark
spot of pre-come on his jeans and the muscles working on his
neck, begging to be kissed. He grabs a thin blue dry-erase
marker from a cup of pens and uncaps it.

"What are you doing?" she murmurs, as he drops back into
his swivel chair lazily.

He presses the felt tip of the marker to her inner right thigh
and starts writing.

"Giving you my address," he says. "In case Santa Monica is
too far to drive after your date."

He looks up at her then and she catches a glint of humor in
his eyes as his hand lightly squeezes her thigh.

"It's washable marker," he says, and her heart does a funny
kind of flip. "If you're worried about it."

She *is* worried about it, though not about the washable blue
ink. She's worried that even after she washes it off, her skin will
refuse to forget the feel of him. She's worried they're careening
toward something inevitable.

GREG THE CASTING director meets her at a bowling alley in Burbank, near the studio lot.

"There's an ice-skating rink and an equestrian center nearby,
if we need ideas for a second date," he says.

Helen smiles, and picks out a marbled purple bowling ball
that suddenly reminds her of the bath bomb she used to sulk
over Grant's radio silence last week. She forcefully redirects her
thoughts to the charming, perfectly fine man in front of her.

"Do you bowl often?" she asks.

"No," Greg says, and rolls an impressive spare anyway.
"Damn, that was just dumb luck."

"So what was the thought process behind the survey form options?" she asks. "I'd love to know."

"Well, the thing about dating is that it should be fun," he says. "I came up with the form a while back as a way to make it fun for myself. I tried to come up with options of things my friends and I are always saying we've been meaning to do, but never get around to."

"It's novel," she says, and rolls a gutter ball.

"There's an optional exit survey," Greg says. "I have the email on auto-send so I don't chicken out."

"Sounds like you're collecting a lot of data," Helen says.

"Not as much as you're thinking," Greg laughs. "I'm not that kind of fella, Helen."

She laughs and thinks to herself that Greg would probably make someone a good boyfriend. He's funny and easy to talk to, always ready to fill a pause in the conversation with an anecdote from work or a thoughtful question. She learns that he has two older brothers, one who also works in the industry and another who works in information systems in Vegas. She tells him about how she's been thinking of other possible book series ideas to pitch to her agent.

"Maybe something with a league of teen bowlers," she says, and manages to knock a paltry few pins down.

"Do you want some pointers?" he asks, because he really is better than her.

"Sure," she says, and suddenly he's next to her, adjusting her stance and touching her arm. She tries not to think about the blue ink that seems to be burning an address-shaped hole into her inner right thigh.

"Just pull your hand back and . . . release," he says, stepping back an appropriate distance to watch her go. He's so *appropriate*, Helen thinks.

They watch her ball roll into the gutter, and they both laugh.

"I told you I didn't actually know what I was doing," Greg says.

1847 ROTARY DRIVE.

It's dark by the time Helen drives past the Silver Lake Reservoir and turns onto one of the winding streets nearby. The streets are cramped, and she tells herself that if she can't find parking, she'll make a U-turn at the top of the hill and drive straight home and never mention this part of the night to anyone.

But there's a spot right out front next to the driveway, and she pulls into it easily, her heart pounding.

1847 Rotary Drive is a light yellow, Spanish-style bungalow covered with bougainvillea, and a warmly colored porch light is on when she walks up and rings the doorbell.

Seventeen

Grant opens the door to find Helen standing on his porch, holding a brown takeaway bag.

He crosses his arms and leans against the door frame, inspecting the details of her. She's smiling, a little nervously, but smiling nonetheless. She's thrown on a winter coat over the familiar yellow dress underneath, maybe because January desert temperatures quickly run from hot to freezing after the sun sets. She looks buttoned-up and proper. *She came on his tongue a few hours ago.*

"How was your date?" he asks.

"Fine," she says. "Good."

His jaw tenses and he tries not to think too much about what *good* means.

"Think you'll see him again?"

Helen tilts her head, considering the question. He wonders what calculations are happening in her sharp, beautiful brain right now.

"I don't think so," she says softly. "No."

"Hm."

She smiles slightly and his chest feels tight. He wants to touch her again. But she already knows that.

"I brought dessert," she says, holding up the bag. Then, a little more uncertainly—"Can I come in?"

He stares at the woman on his porch, whose hidden layers

he's just starting to unravel, and he gets a sharp, strange sensation in the back of his lizard brain that he might be in some danger here, which is ridiculous. After briefly considering sending her home—*ha*—he nods gruffly and leans back to let her pass.

She looks around his living room with naked curiosity as he takes her coat from her.

Seeing her existing in the familiar space transforms it—he's grateful he listened to the real estate agent who suggested custom wood blinds instead of cheap ones from Target, and whether or not his couch is worth keeping suddenly seems to hinge a lot on the next few hours. He thinks he might be losing his mind.

He doesn't have enough hangers in the nearest closet, so he throws her coat on top of one of his.

"Do you want anything?" he asks as he moves into the kitchen.

"Tea, if you have it," she murmurs.

She's running her hands across his wood dining table now, and an image of her palms pressed into the wood while he presses into *her* flashes across his brain.

Tea.

She's flipping through his mail when he returns with a mug of chamomile.

"You get a lot of mail," she says.

"Most of it's junk."

"A lot of DVDs." She holds up a few screeners for some Oscar hopefuls of last year.

"You're welcome to any of those," he says, ignoring the bubbling thought that she's welcome to anything in his house that she wants. He flips the floor lamp on and retreats to the kitchen to get plates.

"I'm impressed you have so much framed art on the walls," she says, her voice carrying from the dining room to the kitchen. "I still have things I need to hang back in New York."

She's studying his gallery wall of framed paraphernalia—a cast-signed copy of his first produced episodic script, a screenshot of his first on-screen writing credit, behind-the-scenes photos, posters for old movies.

"I can make you a frame if you need one," he says. "I made probably half of those."

"That's so impressive," she says, and he's slightly embarrassed by how much he likes hearing her say *impressive*.

"I started watching woodworking tutorials to fall asleep a few years ago. Frames are easy; it's the glass that's tricky."

She's silent for a while and he turns his attention to the dessert she brought—cinnamon-dusted dough balls. He tries not to think about whether Greg the casting director is at home with his own portion of the same dessert and warms them up before setting them out next to a dipping bowl of sauce. He sits at the head of the table, and after a quick scan of the seats, she takes the chair nearest to him.

"I stopped at a beignet food truck on the way here," she says. "Didn't want to show up empty-handed. But I wasn't sure what you like."

He swallows at this.

He'd happily spend hours telling her his likes and dislikes and cataloguing hers in return, but he has the distinct impression that isn't what she wants from him.

"I like everything," he says instead, and picks up a beignet. She plucks up another one and clinks it against his in a whimsical move.

"Cheers," she says, then pops it in her mouth and moans slightly. "Fuck, that's good."

He catalogues this moan as a new one, and picks out another beignet.

"What'd you talk about on your date?" he asks casually.

Helen looks up as she licks cinnamon-sugar from her fingers. She stretches out a smooth bare leg until it lands on his lap. His left hand slips down to squeeze her shin.

"The usual stuff," she says. "Where are you from, what do you do for fun, where do you see yourself in the future."

"Hm," Grant says, massaging her calf. "Did you kiss him?"

"I don't usually kiss on a first date," she says, leaning back and dropping a second leg in his lap. She closes her eyes as she murmurs, "That feels good."

Grant swallows. He pushes her legs off of him and stands. Helen opens her eyes and blinks up at him, looking like a cat who just got shoved to the floor from a perfectly acceptable lap.

"What?" she asks.

He frowns. "Nothing."

She tilts her head. "You're annoyed with me."

"You kept me waiting," he mutters, glancing at a clock. "Maybe I want to go to sleep."

"Do you want me to leave?" she asks.

He lets out a short, dismissive breath. He grips the back of the chair, because his hands can't be trusted around her. He has the terrible feeling that he's played almost every card he has, and she's barely even started.

"Why did you come?" he asks finally.

"I wanted to see where you lived," Helen says. "I wasn't sure when I'd get another invitation."

HELEN HOLDS HER breath, waiting for him to kick her out. She wouldn't blame him—it's late, and she's committed the terrible sin of showing up to a meeting without first knowing what she wants from it. Suraya had warned her early on to always have an agenda in mind ("otherwise, it's a waste of everyone's time, and yes, they'll remember").

Why did you come? She hadn't expected him to ask her so directly, not when she hadn't even asked herself the question yet. Honesty seemed like the best move, but as she watches a muscle tick in his jaw, she thinks maybe it's time to excuse herself and flee before the humiliation of him sending her away becomes inevitable.

Instead, he says, "Let's play a game."

This is how she finds herself sitting on an ottoman across from Grant on the couch, playing Connect 4 on his coffee table.

"I used to play this game in the basement of a church in Westfield," she says as they build the frame of the grid, slotting polished wooden parts against each other because it's a nice, adult version of Connect 4, just like everything else in his house feels like a quietly decadent combination of *nice* and *adult*. "My parents were always the last ones to pick me up from summer camp, and the nuns who ran the aftercare program only had three games—chess, checkers, and Connect 4."

"I never got to go to a real summer camp," he says, sorting the red and black chips out. "I was always in some kind of forced football training regime."

"It wasn't what I hoped it'd be, if that helps," she says. "I always imagined camp being cabins in the woods, canoes, and crushes. This was more like school if the classes were all electives. I took pottery and band and a poetry workshop."

Grant lifts a brow. "So there are poems, is what I'm hearing."

"Pretty sure I burned them all," Helen answers, then grabs her portion of red chips and drops one into the left side of the grid. "Your turn."

Grant frowns at the game. "I wrote some poetry once. It was about you."

She looks up at him, and he studiously drops a black chip on the opposite side.

"Liar," she says, and drops a red chip.

"I'm serious," he says, and she catches the ghost of a smile at the corners of his mouth as he drops a black chip. "'All the Conversations I Want to Have with You.' That was the title. It was a creative writing assignment, my freshman year of college. We were supposed to write poems addressed to someone we wanted to talk to, but couldn't."

"I don't believe you," she says, and drops another chip. "Can I read them?"

"No," he says. "They're on an old hard drive my laptop isn't compatible with anymore."

"I bet we could salvage them—the technology exists," Helen muses.

"I'd rather just talk to you now," Grant says, and her stomach does a funny flip when he looks up at her. He taps the frame. "I got this game as a wrap gift. They had a whole thing with Connect 4 on this show I worked on and they gave all the writers customized Connect 4 sets after production."

Helen picks up one of her red chips and inspects it.

"*The Guys*," she reads, and drops her chip to block his.

"It was my first big show as the number two," he says, and drops another black chip nearby.

"Like you are on our show."

"Kind of," he says. He blocks a run of three of her red chips with a decisive drop, and she doesn't think she's ever been so attracted to someone while playing Connect 4. "It's different on every show. That one was created by these two brothers, Dan and Chris. Good guys, good writers too. But I don't think they were very good at handling the politics behind the scenes, and we got canceled pretty quick. Paid for the down payment on this house, though."

"Would you ever want to do your own show?"

Grant laughs. "Sure, that's the dream, isn't it?"

"Why don't you?" Helen drops her chip near the middle.

"It's not that easy convincing people with power and too much to lose to trust you with millions of dollars and years of their lives," he says, and drops his chip to the right of hers. Then, with a flash of humor in his eyes, he adds, "Congrats on getting them to do it on your first try, by the way."

She tries not to preen at the compliment and studies the board.

Grant shuffles his remaining chips. "Anyway, I don't mind helping other people realize their visions. Maybe I'm better at it than coming up with my own."

Helen drops a chip to the right, and he immediately counters it.

"I think you'd be good at the top job," Helen says. "When you run the room for Suraya, we get more done."

She drops a chip, and he drops his own immediately on top of hers. He reaches out and taps a diagonal pattern of black chips with his index finger—*one, two, three, four.*

"Ah," Helen says. "I guess that means I lose."

Grant lifts a brow. "What do I win?"

There's a bitter twist to his smile, and she wonders what he thinks she's trying to do here. She has the distinct impression that he believes she's in control of this—whatever it is that's come up between them. And she feels more like a pilot realizing miles after takeoff that the navigation system is on the fritz and they're flying into a storm.

Helen suddenly wants nothing more than to wipe that too-knowing, slightly *sad* smirk from his face.

She stands and walks around the coffee table. He watches as she places one knee on the couch cushion next to him, testing her weight, before she straddles him and settles into his lap. His hands rest at his sides, deceptively still while his heart beats rapidly against her palms on his chest.

She leans in to press a slow kiss to his earlobe—fair play, he did the same in his office.

She feels him inhale sharply at the contact.

Helen turns her head to brush her nose against his. His lips barely brush by and she imagines she can feel the shifting of the molecules in the air between them. She lingers there, daring herself, daring him. He makes a strained sound at the back of his throat.

"Don't . . . tease me," he says.

"I thought you liked when I tease you," she says.

He laughs shortly and his eyes flit to her lips.

"I can only take so much, Helen," he murmurs. "I'm just a man."

The gravelly need in his voice does something to her insides and she leans forward, giving him a quick, impulsive kiss on the lips. His lips are soft and warm and *gone*—she pulls back before he almost catches hers again. He exhales slowly and looks up into her eyes. She wonders if he sees what she's seeing in his— darkness so inviting, she wants to dive in.

Then in a swift motion, he captures her by the wrist and pulls her down for a second kiss—her eyelids flutter shut and she falls into the sensation of being thoroughly, deeply *kissed*. She feels like she's sinking and evaporating at the same time. It's slow and drugging and when she starts to retreat, Grant makes an insistent noise as he chases her lips. *You don't get to run this time.*

His tongue pushes into her mouth and she whimpers as she remembers what that tongue did in his office. She answers his implied challenge and shifts in his lap, and his bottom lip falls away in a gasp. She nips lightly at his lower lip and he laughs, then he cups her face with his hands and kisses her slowly, persuasively, as if they have all the time in the world—before he slows down the kiss that she's already starting to call *the best damn kiss of her entire life* and it retreats from present tense into memory.

Her breaths are coming out in short puffs as he pulls back, his face flushed with exertion, a familiar hardness pressing into her from below.

"You're killing me," he says finally, and his hands run down her shoulders to her hips to her shins, roaming, kneading, squeezing along their path.

"Maybe that's the end game," she says.

Grant lets out a short *"ha"* of air, then looks up at her.

He brushes a stray piece of hair from her face and tucks it behind her ear, and she remembers the heat of the scotch she drank that night in Kevin Palermo's kitchen, the way it traveled a warming path from her mouth to her insides. Grant pulls her back to the present with a slow, insistent *back* and *forth* brush of his thumb on her Achilles.

"Serious question," he says. "Is there an end game?"

Helen huffs and bends to kiss him. *The end game is to kiss him as many times as possible.* He submits to one, two, three—*ha, almost four*—kisses, then pulls back. "Helen?"

She suddenly feels very exposed. She swallows, studying the micro-movements of his face. Her hands itch to unfurrow his brow and smooth out the tension around his grim mouth. But she keeps them fisted at the neck of his T-shirt, as if they'll help her hold on to him better this way.

"I don't know," she says. "Does there have to be?"

He draws slow circles on the backs of her thighs, and she feels like she's sleepwalking off a cliff.

"I don't like surprises," he says. "If you have a destination or an expiration date in mind, I'd rather know now."

Expiration date. Like they're bread, or the watery Greek yogurt she has in the back of her fridge. Helen taps an index finger against his lips, shushing the thought.

He presses a slow kiss to her finger, and there's something warm in his gaze she can't quite bear.

"I can't think when you're touching me like this," she murmurs, her eyes closing.

"Hm," he says. "I know what you mean."

She leans down and kisses him again, this time with an urgency that he matches, his grip going from featherlight to viselike in an instant. It's a searching chase of a kiss, it's a kiss that knows they *don't* have world enough, or time, for all the ways they want to lay claim to each other, at least not tonight. Somewhere, in the darkened corridors of her mind, she thinks it might be fun to play this kissing game with Grant forever, changing tempos and rules until they've circled back to that first, perfect kiss. When he pulls away, she's the one who falls forward slightly, and she's annoyed by how quickly she's learned to chase after the feeling of his lips on hers. He laughs gently.

"Let me know if you figure it out," he exhales. "I'd like a fighting chance of survival."

HELEN IS STARING at a spot in the hollow of his clavicle, stroking the inch of skin there with a single-minded frown of concentration on her face. He swallows, and her eyes flicker at the movement it causes.

"Helen," Grant says, trying to get her attention again.

"Hm," she answers, her hand coming up to examine his stubble.

"Why did you leave, after you asked to sleep over that night in New Jersey?"

She stops stroking his skin and her frown is now directed at *him*. Well, he's used to that. He feels a sincere need to reach up to smooth out the crease of her brow.

"I thought if I stayed, I'd do something very . . . foolish."

He laughs at that. *Foolish*. She's so proper, even at a time like this. He tightens his grip on her waist, and in one smooth motion, he flips them over horizontally onto the couch. She's flush under him now, and her mouth is a perfect, surprised *O*. Some primal part of him is briefly satisfied. *So this is what it's like to have her body under him.*

"Helen . . ." he says, pressing his unmistakable erection against her thigh. "We aren't going to have sex tonight. I'm not in the mood."

She laughs as he drops his face to her neck, so she doesn't see just how badly he wants to fuck her into the next weekend.

"Can you sleep over now?" he asks her neck.

"Hm," she says. Half an eternity seems to pass before she says, "I have nothing to wear, though."

He lifts his head. "You're a fucking evil woman, you know that?"

She cackles, and he rolls off the couch before he does something . . . *foolish*.

"I'll give you a shirt," he manages as he walks off into his bedroom.

HE GIVES HER a soft, heather-gray T-shirt that she's pretty sure she's seen him wear before while sitting across the table from her, and a pair of boxer shorts she's grateful for because her lace panties have been soaked through to an embarrassing extent.

He leaves her the privacy of his bedroom to change, which she thinks is a polite and wise gesture until she realizes she's been left alone *in his bedroom.*

His bedroom that he sleeps in. Probably has had sex in. Probably, if she's honest, will have sex with *her* in, because they've driven so far past the city limits of *a matter of time* that it's laughable. Somewhere in the back of her mind, she reminds herself that this morning, she was determined to let that ball in her court bounce until it was lost and forgotten. *And then* . . .

He knocks on the door before he enters and she feels like a mirrored reflection of their past selves in his office. His eyes sweep over her, from the loose fit of his shirt on her to the barest sliver of his boxers peeking out beneath the gray fabric. He swallows hard, and she realizes her nipples have turned to pinpricks under his shirt.

"Grant?"

"Hm?"

"You knocked."

"Jesus Christ," he says, and laughs at himself. "Yeah. I have a spare toothbrush for you. If you want it."

There's a strange sort of intimacy she feels brushing her teeth side by side with Grant, though he's still fully clothed and she's wearing his clothes. It feels like they're laughing at some private joke as they stare at each other in the bathroom mirror and brush.

"What?" she asks, when her mouth is clear.

"Nothing," he says. "You look good in my clothes."

She goes back to the bedroom first, tucking her knees up as she waits for him. When he returns, he has a spare pillow and throw blanket under his arm.

"You'll be fine on the couch, right? There's only one bed and it *is* mine, so . . ."

She chucks a pillow at his head.

He ducks it and laughs. "Sorry. Couldn't resist," he says.

The laughter in his eyes diminishes with each step he takes toward the bed, and by the time he reaches the edge of the bed, she's kneeling up and waiting for him to get close enough to drop her arms around his neck.

"You're staying here, then," he says, when they finally reach each other, and it feels like a question.

She pulls at his shirt in response, and he lifts his arms so she can pull it off him.

Ah. Grant Shepard's solid chest, in the flesh. Her hands return lightly to his shoulders and one adventurous finger drifts slowly down to explore the ridges of what looks like must have been *hard work*. She's never been much fascinated by men's built, naked torsos—she's always preferred a certain bundled-up cozy sweater vibe that makes her feel like she's living inside a men's J.Crew catalogue. But as she feels every hard muscle of Grant Shepard's perfect chest expand and contract to her touch, she thinks maybe that's just because she never thought she'd encounter a body like his in the flesh, when she had permission to touch and explore and, as his labored breathing suggests, *titillate*.

She thinks vaguely she must have seen him shirtless before, running and passing her in gym class, maybe, and wants to shout back at herself, across the void, *"Run faster!"*

"How does something like this even *happen*?" she asks, as her hand runs down his abdomen, and he laughs.

"Working out clears my head," he says. "Sometimes I think too much."

She wants to lick every inch of him until he doesn't have a thought left in his brain.

He must see some trace of it on her expression, because he

swallows hard, then watches her face for a reaction as he lowers his hands to unbutton his jeans. Helen inhales, then turns around sharply. She hears his chuckle and the soft *thwump* of fabric hitting the floor.

"I'm trying to be polite," she says. "Stop laughing at me."

She hears drawers opening and shutting, then feels the mattress dip below her and the warm weight of his knee on the bed. She turns around and he's wearing sweatpants. He settles so that they're sitting up facing each other and hooks one leg behind her, pushing her closer into the frame of his body.

Suddenly the cold January air vanishes into radiating heat and she feels like a dumb bunny caught in a trap.

He brings up a hand to her hair, and his thumb brushes her temple.

"Sometimes," he says softly, "I think you're afraid of me. But you always have the upper hand."

She doesn't feel like that's true at all. In the entire history of their knowing each other, he's been the one everyone listens to, the one who seems to be comfortable everywhere she feels out of place. The one who can see right through her, all these years later.

If she had the upper hand, she'd have answers for his too-honest questions that continue pinging back and forth through her bones. *Why did you come?* She still isn't sure, but she's starting to forget it was ever an option not to.

"I'm not . . . I'm not trying to date anyone for real right now," she says, in a rush. "Not when I'm going back to New York in a couple months."

Grant makes a slight "*hm*" sound as he tucks her hair behind her ear. "So Greg the casting director wasn't real, then."

She feels certain he can see the rapid tattoo of her pulse trying to fly through her skin.

"Just a way to pass the time," she agrees. "I thought I could use a distraction."

"I could distract you," Grant murmurs, as his knuckles run down her arms. "What do you need a distraction from?"

"I, um," Helen exhales. "I can't remember."

"See," he teases, and his words bring him tantalizingly closer, but *not close enough*. "It's already working."

She's about to close the gap between them but Grant looks down instead and lets out an amused "*huh*" when he sees his address scrawled on her inner thigh.

"Sorry about that," he says, his thumb brushing her flesh. "Went a little caveman there."

"I didn't mind it so much," she murmurs, and the corner of his mouth kicks up.

"So." His eyes flit to her lips and she licks them in anticipation. He swallows. "Wanna watch this forty-five-minute cabinet-building tutorial with me?"

As it turns out, woodworking tutorials on YouTube are a very cozy way to spend a Friday night. She sits beside him, not quite touching, as he explains the inside jokes being dropped by the dry-humored, grandfatherly woodworker on the screen.

"Ha," she laughs, feeling sleep tugging at her senses as she sinks down into the pillow. "Never show me these videos again, please."

Grant chuckles. "Okay," he says, and captures her chin to brush a quick kiss to her mouth. "I'll put in headphones."

Some warm, unfamiliar feeling floods her chest, and she pushes it down as she nudges her way onto his shoulder, his right arm curving around her as his left reaches for the headphones on his nightstand.

She watches him watch the video for a while, one earbud trailing onto his chest, and she thinks of their time together on the plane, when he looked younger and less invincible, watching *Babe*. She thinks perhaps this is the only angle from which to catch a glimpse of this version of Grant, slightly off to the side and looking up toward him. *It might be her favorite view of him.*

"It's a pretty good view for me too," he says, and slowly she realizes she must have said it out loud before drifting off to sleep.

Eighteen

When Helen wakes up, the sun is streaming in through the windows and Grant's arm is slung heavily across her, trapping her body against his. It's a warm, welcome weight and she feels a kind of delirious relief that it's still *there*, that she didn't fever dream the last twenty-four hours. She stares at his far bedroom wall, registering the way it looks different in the daylight—less cozy and safe and more like a normal, everyday wall. She swallows and wonders what they could possibly say to each other this morning, after last night. Gradually, she senses his breathing go from slow and deep to shallower, and something hard nudges against her backside.

"Hm," he rumbles sleepily, and his hand drags down her stomach over his borrowed T-shirt, then slips below the fabric.

"I think I've had this dream before," she murmurs, and feels his answering chuckle against her ear as his thumb brushes the few inches of skin above her belly button. "When we were at the cabin."

"What happened in the dream?" His hand flexes, and it causes his thumb to scrape just below the swell of her breast. She exhales shakily; so does he.

"It was your comforter," she says, pressing back into him, and hears a gratifying "*hm*." "It smelled like you, and I think I was incepted somehow to crave this."

He pushes up against her again, and the fabric of her boxer

shorts shifts so she can feel the ridge of his erection against her bare ass cheek. His hand slides out from under her shirt and lands on the curve of her hip, his fingers seeking purchase.

"What else are you craving?"

She squeezes her thighs together for the friction, and he groans into her neck as he pulls her back by the hips. She rubs herself slowly up against him, and he exhales.

His hand slips over her hip and slides down to press against the damp, hot heat of her through his borrowed boxers.

"Fuck," he says. "You're wet."

"Mm," she answers, biting her lip and pushing up against him.

"Could you come like this, sweetheart?" He growls the question into her ear, as his hand presses insistently against her.

"I," she gasps, as he pushes up against her clit through the fabric, then eases off.

"You," he prompts, repeating the motion.

"I want your fingers," she says.

"Thought you'd never ask," he answers, and slips his middle finger between her slick folds.

"*Oh*," she groans, as she adjusts to the feeling of him *inside* her.

"*Fuck*," he says, and resumes the slow, upward pressing movement of his fingers.

"Grant," she exhales, drawing herself against him in tight circles of pressure.

"You gonna ride my finger like a good girl?" He kisses her neck.

"Yes," she gasps, as she squeezes him back with her inner muscles.

"How about a second?" he murmurs.

"Yes," she says again, as if there are no other words. She lets out an involuntary moan when he pushes another finger into her.

"How did your dream end, Helen?"

"I wanted to come," she whispers. "But I couldn't, because you were downstairs."

"That's right, I was," he rasps. "If I'd known this was waiting for me . . ."

Helen lets out a soft, keening "*hmm*," and he crooks his fingers inside her, beckoning.

"Please, Grant," she gasps.

"I like the way you say that," he growls.

"Please, Grant," she echoes needily, and he rewards it by repeating that quick, beckoning motion deep within the slick heat of her—again, again, *again* until she's thrumming from *want.* "Can I come now?"

"You can come when I say so," he says, his voice low. "In five . . ."

She exhales slowly.

"Four . . ."

He presses against her again.

"Three . . ."

His fingers press to the hilt.

"Two . . ."

The heel of his palm pushes against her, and she whimpers.

"One."

He crooks his fingers and hits *that spot* and her world explodes behind her closed eyes, and she's faintly aware that the desperate sobbing sound is *her. Ah, ah, ah.* She clutches at Grant's wrist, pressing it against the front of her. *Please, Grant.* Behind her, she feels his breath coming out in short gasps into her hair and knows he's climaxing with her.

Afterward, when they both come back to earth, she shuts her eyes tightly and pretends to snore. Grant laughs behind her, his breath still expelling as a shallow, labored pant.

She turns around, and he's watching her closely.

"That's one way to avoid morning breath," she murmurs, and he pushes a hand into his eyes sleepily as he laughs.

"You're funnier than I thought you'd be," he says. "Before I knew you."

Something twinges in Helen's heart at *before I knew you*, and she wonders what he means by that. How far back does his memory go? Before their trip home for Christmas? Or earlier? Before she moved to LA? Before that one night that linked his name forever to her family history?

She wonders how often he thought of her back then, *before he knew her*—if he thought about her at all. She knows she had a reputation for being a humorless bore in high school, but it still hurts to think he probably thought so too.

The laughter fades from his eyes as he watches her.

"I'm sorry," he murmurs. "I was an idiot for thinking that."

She smiles faintly and shrugs. "I didn't give you or anyone else any reason to think otherwise."

He reaches out and brushes the hair from her face, and she thinks suddenly of how improbable it is that they're both *here*, in his bed, after all this time. She thinks they must have both taken a few accidental wrong turns somewhere and feels a pressing, surprised kind of panic as she realizes how close they must have come to never having this happen at all. She feels like this bed and this morning and this *something* between them exist only in a precarious bubble, and it might burst into nothing as soon as she leaves.

"There you go again," he murmurs, tracing her cheek with his knuckle. "Thousand-yard stare while I'm right in front of you."

"It's just . . ." She pauses, and leans into his touch. He's *so good* at touching her, she thinks she might miss this forever. "Brain goes vroom vroom. But I'm still here."

The corner of his mouth turns up at this. "I know. That brain of yours never stops, does it?"

"I think maybe it did for a second there, just now."

He laughs (she likes being responsible for it), then studies her. "What are you doing today?"

She shrugs.

"I need to get a coatrack," he says out of nowhere. "Come with me."

Nineteen

The place he wants to buy a coatrack from, as it turns out, is an antiques market that runs every weekend out of a retired airport hangar in Santa Monica (about twenty minutes from her condo). It gives her an excuse to leave as he heads into the shower, so she can go home to her own shower and bath products and makeup and oh god, her hair probably looks like a rat's nest.

She texts him her address before she has time to overthink it and gets on the road.

She passes at least two other flea markets during her long drive back home and wonders why he suddenly wants a coatrack.

When Helen opens the door to her apartment, she's slightly surprised to find everything exactly as she left it yesterday morning. The same marble countertops, the same beige furniture, the same generic art on her walls. She thinks of how worried her mother was about earthquakes in this city and wonders if emotional earthquakes have the same kind of internal fallout—rattled bones, shaken foundations, everything hanging on the walls slightly askew. She wonders if *he* feels like this too, and what he's thinking about right now.

Helen steps into the shower and hugs herself slowly under the hot water. The hazy steam from the humidity drifts up, fogging the glass, as she submits to the quiet, cleansing meditation of water falling down her body.

She allows herself a moment to look back and properly *ruminate* on the events of the past twenty-four hours.

She's kissed Grant Shepard.

She's slept in his bed, in his arms.

They've traded orgasms at least three times since that New Year's Eve party in the basement, though she's not so sure of the score anymore.

This won't end well, a small voice in the back of her head reminds her. *It can't.*

She isn't kidding herself. She knows she's lucked into something she could never possibly keep—*Grant Shepard's undivided attention.* Keeping Grant in her life in any *real* way would be tantamount to setting fire to a tapestry she's spent the better part of the last thirteen years carefully weaving. Her parents would never be able to understand or accept it, and every time they saw him, they'd be reliving the same old hurts she has worked *extremely hard* to help them heal and move on from.

So no, this battle of her base wants and old needs can't end well.

But also, also, she's just as sure it can't end *yet.*

Not yet, she protests. *Shouldn't we get to enjoy this before we have to give it up?*

She's already enjoying it too much, perhaps.

HELEN CHANGES INTO jeans and a white button-up and she has just enough time to blow-dry her hair when her phone vibrates with a text—it's ridiculous, the buzzing thrill that shoots through her when she sees his name on the screen.

I'm here.

When she opens the door, she sees him before he notices her—he's leaning against a parking sign, wearing sunglasses and a navy hoodie she remembers seeing hanging in his closet. He scrolls through his phone, and she's tempted to snap a photo of him like this—some evidence of him waiting for her, something she can look back on as proof it all happened when she's old and gray.

He looks up just then, and it's like the sun comes out only to highlight Grant Shepard's smile. He looks like he belongs in a movie and she self-consciously plays with the strap of her purse as she approaches. He stands up a little straighter as she gets closer and puts his phone away.

He reaches out a hand and pulls her in for a kiss—slow, determined, *sure*. She exhales slightly when he releases her, resting his forehead against hers as her pulse hums in a contented buzz.

"Just checking," he says.

She feels a clinching sensation around her heart, as if someone's just squeezed it.

"Are you driving?" she asks.

He nods and heads for the driver's side of his gray convertible. She slips into the passenger seat and realizes it's the first time she's been inside his car in LA. She doesn't know anything about cars, but she's seen enough movies to know that girls like her—*nice girls, girls who listen to their parents*—don't ride around town in convertibles like this.

"So," he says, as they pull into traffic. "What do you like to do for fun?"

"I, um," she starts, and realizes she's nervous for some reason. "I go on long walks and listen to podcasts hosted by stand-up comedians."

Grant chuckles softly as he makes a left turn. "Why stand-up comedians?"

"They're good at talking to people, and I'm not," she says. "So I like listening to them having conversations with other people. I usually listen to a podcast before my meetings, as a warm-up reminder on how to talk to people."

"You're not as awkward as you think you are."

"It's working, then," she murmurs, and he laughs.

"What about you?" she asks, as he shifts gears on the car. She glances down at his hand and wonders what he'd do if she reached out to touch it.

"I play hockey sometimes," he says. "A couple of the guys in a room I did a few years back started a league. They needed more people so I joined to have something to do."

"Did you skate in high school?" She frowns, trying to remember.

"No," he says. "I took classes as an adult. I was on the ice with all these little kids, like a giraffe in hockey skates."

She tries not to think too much about Grant Shepard on the ice surrounded by children—her ovaries can't take it.

"You're such a team player," she says. "Football, hockey, writing TV. What do you do when you're alone?"

Grant glances at her and his hand catches hers idly by the wrist. His fingers slip up to entwine in hers.

"Hm," he says. "Woodworking, if a friend has a project for me. Go to the gym. Read things my agent sends me. I don't know. I guess I'm pretty boring on my own."

He brings her hand up to press a quick kiss to the back of it as they stop at a traffic light. She holds her breath—he slowly brushes her thumb with his.

"I don't think you're boring," she murmurs, and her heart pounds wildly in agreement.

"That's a good sign," he says.

THE SANTA MONICA antiques market is a relatively small flea market. Still, Grant knows it's a good place for people watching and talking while zigzagging up and down the stalls, each one boasting something slightly different and interesting to anyone with a romantic fascination with the past.

Helen stops at a used-books and rare art-prints stall, and spends a good deal of time talking to the older man who runs it—Yanis, a former computer programmer who quit his job in the nineties to pursue his true passion, art dealership. She walks away with a few rare bookplates and an 1800s edition of *The Vicar of Wakefield*, and he can tell she's in a good mood by the way she touches his shoulder sometimes to point out some new interesting thing every few steps.

They find a few coatrack options and he soon learns that Helen haggles like it's an Olympic sport.

"How much?" she asks. "Hm. There's a little damage there, but it's beautiful otherwise. Maybe we'll come back."

They settle on a vintage coatrack from a seller with much bigger furniture pieces to worry about. Helen talks the price down to $60, then whispers to him it would probably go for upward of $125 online. The seller winds the coatrack in shrink wrap and hands him a ticket to pick it up later. Grant leads the way back through the market to the parking lot.

"Why do you know so much about vintage furniture pricing?"

She shrugs.

"One of my author friends back home—Elyse—she furnished her entire town house going to random flea markets and estate sales," she says. "And I became a little obsessed. We never had anything old in our house growing up; my parents always said flea markets sounded dirty."

"Hm," he says. "You think the East Coast will always be home?"

Helen pauses. "I've never really thought about living any-where else," she says. "Not seriously."

"Could you see yourself staying in LA, for any reason?" he asks.

"For the show," she says. "If it does well, maybe. I like the weather. I like being on a different coast from my parents, as terrible as that sounds. They worry about me and I don't . . . feel it, as much, from here."

"Did they visit you a lot, in New York?"

Helen shakes her head.

"They just kind of expected me to come home a lot, and I was close enough that it felt like they were right and I should." She shrugs. "Anyway, the studio's paid for my condo through the end of production in April, so I have some time to make decisions."

He wonders if he'll factor at all into those decisions.

"Hm," he says out loud.

They reach the car and he brings it around to the items pickup area.

"How are you going to transport it?" Helen asks.

"Carefully," he answers.

They hand his ticket to someone in an orange vest and wait by the entrance, resting against a parking lot barrier near the gate. He looks askance at her—her cheeks are flushed and her hair has acquired a windswept quality from walking outside for the last two hours. His heart squeezes slightly with a sudden desire to pull her closer—she's so damn *pretty*—but she's kept a respectable distance since they stepped out of the car.

He looks down to study their hands—his rests next to hers on the granite parking barrier. He nudges her pinkie slightly with his and she answers by lifting her pinkie to cover his own. Not quite holding hands in public, but—*something*.

"Grant Fucking Shepard! Oy!"

He turns toward the entrance and feels Helen snatch her hand away, and then the heat of her presence leaves his right side.

It's a trio of familiar faces—Andy, a camera operator from the last show he worked on; his boyfriend Reese; and . . . *Karina, wardrobe.* Karina smiles at him, her eyes flitting briefly to his side.

"Hey," he says.

"What, we don't hug anymore?" Karina asks as she leads their crew over, and he gives her a one-armed hug, as well as Andy and Reese.

Grant turns and finds Helen hanging back at a polite distance. "This is Helen. Helen—Andy, Reese, Karina. Andy and Karina worked on *The Guys* with me; they're camera and wardrobe department. And Reese is—"

"Newly engaged," Reese says, flashing his ring finger. "As of last week."

"Holy shit." Grant grins. "Congrats, you two."

"Well, it felt like time," Andy says.

"What a romantic." Reese rolls his eyes.

"What do you do, Helen?" Karina asks.

"I, um, I'm a writer," she says. "Grant and I work together."

"That makes sense," Karina says with a slow smile as she tilts her head. "It's nice to meet you, Helen."

Grant suddenly regrets everything he's ever told Karina and the existence of ex-girlfriends, as a concept.

"We should get going, before all the good stuff gets got," Andy says. "It's good to see you, man."

"You too," he nods and waves them off.

It occurs to Grant that he doesn't really have *friends*, for all his agent claims that everyone likes him. He had thought of Andy as a friend, but he's realizing theirs was the kind of casual friendship of convenience that came from working together for months on end, twelve plus hours a day. They're friendly now, but they're not friends—not in the sense of keeping up with each other's lives or going out of their way to see each other outside of work.

They had all hung out as a unit back then, Andy and Reese, Grant and Karina. But once the show ended, so did most of the things they had in common, including his relationship. He thinks this might be a character flaw of his, this ability to fall into friendships and relationships so easily, when they never seem to last once the initial trappings of what makes him temporarily relevant in people's lives passes. He isn't sure how to fix it.

"Did you . . ." Helen starts, looking back at them. "Never mind."

She's frowning and he thinks of how she looked asking about Lauren DiSantos in that basement on New Year's Eve—like she'd been annoyed she was even bringing it up. He wants to reassure her suddenly, though *of what*, he's not even sure.

"Karina and I used to date," he says. "It wasn't very serious."

Helen nods. "Right."

Someone brings over his coatrack and they manage to maneuver it into the convertible with the top down. It creates a perfect barrier between him and Helen on the drive back.

THEY STOP FOR lunch at a drive-through In-N-Out and sit in the parking lot with their burgers and fries under a line of palm trees.

"I don't get the secret menu thing," she says as she polishes off the last of her animal-style fries. "Why make everything harder?"

"It makes people feel cooler," he says. "Knowing things not everyone knows."

Her phone rings then, and she freezes slightly.

"It's my mom," she says. "I should . . ."

She picks up and he suddenly finds himself holding his breath.

"Mom? Hi," she says, and turns slightly away from him. "No, I'm just out to lunch with a—friend . . . yeah."

A friend. Grant wonders what he would call Helen if his mom asked. She had lifted cool brows when he'd told her who was coming for dinner the day after Christmas, then she'd calmly asked if Helen had any dietary restrictions. The day before he flew back, she'd asked him if he would see Helen again soon. "We do work together, Mom," he'd said. She'd given him a funny look and said, "I hope you know what you're doing."

Helen is speaking in a jumbled mix of English and Mandarin now—he can pick out occasional American phrases like *the show* and *production office* and *the Sheraton in Santa Monica*—and he wonders what he *is* doing.

He had left New Jersey with a single-minded determination that they weren't done with each other yet, and he spent the days after New Year's Eve weighing his options in case Helen might not agree. He opted for a slow and subtle approach—if he'd done anything else, it would have been too easy for her to take any scrap of evidence of disconnect (*you don't use punctuation in your texts, this is doomed*) and build it into an insurmountable wall between them.

She's sitting in his car now and there isn't a wall between them. But there is a coatrack. And he can't help but feel the stupid thing is a spindly little metaphor for *something*.

"Okay. Yes. I will. Bye." Helen hangs up and looks over at him.

"Good phone call?" he asks.

"My parents are coming to town in a few weeks, for the start of filming," she says. "They wanted to see the set and take pictures and brag about me to their friends."

"Seems pretty worth bragging about to me," Grant says.

She looks up at him, worry clouding her eyes.

"I haven't told them you're working on the show," she says, a dent of concern forming between her brows that he wants to smooth and kiss away.

"No, I figured as much," Grant says.

"I kind of thought I could tell them later, after everything was over, once the episode was definitely going to air." She laughs at herself. "I know that sounds stupid. But it's kind of how I handle everything . . . tricky with them. Wait till the last possible minute to make sure the conversation is absolutely necessary, and then rip off the Band-Aid and move on when it's too late for them to do anything about it."

He brushes a stray piece of hair behind her ear patiently.

"It doesn't sound stupid," he says. "It sounds like you found a way to make your relationship with your parents work."

"Yeah," she says, and looks off, before glancing at him again. "Even if you're not on set, you're going to be on the call sheets as a co-EP. Maybe I can make sure they don't see one. Everyone on set technically works for me, right?"

Grant laughs out loud. "Yeah, let's just kick that can farther down the road."

He ignores a twinge of *this might hurt more later*, somewhere under his ribs.

Helen groans. "This one time I had to pick them up from the airport to take them directly to my apartment in college, then I remembered my parents are my parents and I had to frantically text my neighbor to break into my room and clean it out of anything incriminating."

"What was so incriminating?"

"Oh, just . . . the usual stuff. My diary. Lingerie. Sex toys."

Grant lifts a brow and she gives an embarrassed shrug.

"Well, the difference is you're an adult now," Grant says, trying not to think about Helen's lingerie and sex toy collection. "With your own apartment and your own disposable income, and your own TV show."

"Yeah," Helen says, nodding. She's quiet for a moment, then looks up at him with wide-open vulnerability. "I still don't want to hurt them, though."

Grant feels strangely like he's just lost something. His jaw tenses, and he nods.

"I do love my parents," Helen says, a little haltingly. "Sometimes I think it sounds like I don't. To people who come from other types of families. Families that know how to love each other out loud. Mine never did. None of us ever told Michelle we loved her, that's for sure."

Grant watches her. "Did anyone ever tell you?"

Helen looks down and lifts a shoulder. "I started saying 'I love you' to my parents whenever I hung up the phone in college. It always feels kind of forced and they only say it back like fifty percent of the time, but . . ."

She smiles and waves a dismissive hand, like, *What can you do?*

Grant waits for her to continue.

"It wasn't like I ever missed it or anything. I used to cringe whenever people said *love* in books and movies," she says. "*I love you, making love,* anything with *love* . . . it always seemed so unimaginable to me, that someone could actually say that out loud without, like, immediately dying of embarrassment."

"What did you say instead?"

Helen shrugs. "Let's have sex," she says.

The stutter in Grant's brain must be visible, and Helen stifles a laugh. "I meant that's what I said instead."

"Right," he says. "Of course."

"Anyway, I didn't want you to think I . . . I don't love my

parents, or something," she says quietly. "I know how to love people. *I love, Helen loves, she-slash-it loves*. That's, um, a joke I had, with my best friends in New York. I was a robot, Helen-the-Machine, and she-slash-it was sometimes trying to become sentient between all her dumb achievements. It was stupid."

Grant frowns. "Who are your best friends?"

Helen rubs her temples and shakes her head. "We don't have to talk about them right now. They don't really talk to me anymore, anyway. I think they'd be surprised to hear I even called them that."

Grant studies her carefully as she looks out the window. She looks fine, like she doesn't need whatever reassurance he suddenly feels compelled to give her. He decides to say it anyway.

"I know you're human, Helen," he says. "And I'm sure you know how to love people, even if you don't say it out loud all the time."

He's surprised by a sudden warm grip on his right hand—she's snuck her own hand under the coatrack to squeeze his. He looks over at her and she's watching him with soft eyes.

"Thanks," she says quietly.

He exhales and starts the car.

"Let's get you home."

IT TAKES ABOUT forty-five minutes to drive from Helen's condo in Santa Monica back home to his own house in Silver Lake, and Grant spends most of it running mental laps around the same track of problems.

"Do you wanna come up?" she asked him when he'd pulled up to the loading zone outside of her building. "There's guest parking in the garage."

She'd looked so hopeful, inviting him. He'd looked up at the building and thought about the hours he could spend there, seeing where Helen ate and slept and dreamed.

"I should get this home," he had said instead, patting the coatrack.

It had been an act of self-preservation.

The first problem, he determines, is that he *likes* her. She's smart and she's funny and she's sexy as hell when she wants to be. When she's paying attention to him. When she's not. She makes him feel like he has to be smarter and funnier and *better*, so she'll let him stick around.

And that's the second problem. He is quite, quite certain that she *won't*, not in the long run. There are a million Grant Shepards in this city alone and it's a matter of time before she meets one she likes just as much, who doesn't come with his particular brand of personal baggage.

He isn't sure how long he has, or how easily she'll cut him out of her life when the time comes. Grant feels a pressure building in his chest at the thought.

As he gets the coatrack into his house, he hears a faint ringing in his ears and his vision grows spotty. He knows he's on the verge of having a panic attack.

You should find someone you can talk to.

He thinks about what Karina told him on the phone a couple months ago. He had assumed she meant a therapist (and he does have one; he had one even back then), but maybe she meant someone more like a friend. Does Helen count as a friend? The word seems pathetically incomplete, applied to her.

He hasn't told his therapist about Helen yet. Or rather, Helen post-Christmas. It had felt too new, too complicated, to get into during their monthly check-in.

He walks on unsteady legs to the couch and grips the back of it. He shuts his eyes and exhales. He remembers sitting on this couch last night—waiting, watching, *wanting*—trying not to move a muscle as Helen came toward him. Willing her closer— close enough for him to make a compelling argument for her to stay. *And she did.*

The ringing in his ears subsides slowly and he stands, frowning against the afternoon light.

What was he doing?

Oh right, the coatrack.

He frowns at the thing, not entirely sure why he bought it. He walks over to the closet and opens it, and he remembers. There were no hangers available last night, when Helen came over. He woke up this morning feeling like he should make some space in his life for people with long winter coats.

He frowns, staring at all the jackets and old hoodies hanging in the dim light.

Maybe, he thinks, *I should just get rid of things I don't need anymore.*

Twenty

Helen hosts a single-girls-only sleepover at her condo the following Friday.

"I was gonna make fun of you for moving to the west side like every other East Coast transplant, but this . . ." Nicole throws open the windows to gaze adoringly at the perfectly framed Santa Monica Pier, lit up like a carnival at night in the distance. "This is worth it."

"Where's your wine opener?" Saskia asks, opening and closing drawers in the kitchen.

Helen isn't enough of a wine drinker to own one in a temporary apartment, and they have to watch a YouTube tutorial on how to uncork a bottle using car keys and a pen.

They put on *Cruel Intentions* because Saskia's never seen it, and halfway through explaining just how truly iconic the cast is, including platinum-blond Joshua Jackson ("You mean Jodie Turner-Smith's husband?"), Nicole pauses the movie.

"Okay, we aren't watching another second of this movie until Helen agrees to tell us about her date."

Monday had been an embarrassment of attention from everyone in the room. They were all too invested in her survey-form date. Grant had been there when it came up—he'd popped in to join them for lunch, taking his usual seat across from Helen, and he'd loudly pulled the tab of a Coke Zero as Nicole demanded date details.

"It was fun," Helen told them. "We bowled."

Owen called her a story tease and Saskia wanted to know if he gave her butterflies and Grant asked her to pass him a mint.

Ultimately, Helen told them she wasn't going to see Greg the casting director again, to the great disappointment of Eve and Saskia.

"But why?" Nicole had demanded.

Then Suraya had started looking at the glass dry-erase board in the way Suraya did when she felt like lunchtime conversations were going on too long, and Helen cut off the chatter with a promise to tell them later. Grant left for his office and she had slipped out to use the restroom before they started their afternoon session of breaking episode four.

She made it two steps before Grant's hand reached out, and suddenly she found herself pinned against the wall behind the writers room and thoroughly, *extremely* kissed.

"Come over tonight," he'd said, his voice low and vibrating in a way that made her want to press against him harder and again and *more*.

"No," she'd told him. "I don't have clothes."

"I'll buy you new clothes," he'd said, nipping at her lower lip.

"Go write a good script," she'd answered, "and maybe then I'll come over."

She slipped away from him then, willing herself not to turn around when she heard his low chuckle behind her.

She's proud of herself for sticking to it—for the most part, a few daily detours to his office purely to check in on the status of his writing notwithstanding.

On Thursday afternoon, her inbox chimed with an email from Grant.

(No subject)

Come over.

Attachment: *The Ivy Papers*—Episode 102—Grant
Shepard—Draft 1.pdf

She had flushed so noticeably, Nicole asked her what was
happening on her phone. She had been too flustered to think of
a better lie and said, "I think I have a date this weekend."

They had been treated to a heavy *this doesn't sound relevant
to breaking the story* sigh from Suraya, and Nicole had extracted
a promise from Helen to make good on her earlier promise to
share all date-related gossip. They settled on a Friday-night
sleepover, which Helen figured would buy her some time to figure out what, exactly, *coming over* would entail.

"Helen," Saskia whines now, wineglass in hand. "I thought
we were friends. Why are you being so cagey about this?"

Helen ducks her head and tries to grab the remote from
Nicole.

"Because she's relishing in the fact that she has gossip," Nicole answers, shoving the remote under her shirt. "Stop being
a cunt and tell us what the deal is with your date. Is it with
Greg?"

"No, I told you I wasn't seeing him again," Helen says.
"It's . . . I don't know. A weird new thing."

Nicole eyes her shrewdly.

"Why is it weird?" Saskia asks.

"Um," Helen says.

"Is it someone we know?" Nicole asks, her eyes narrowing.

"I—"

"Holy shit, you're fucking Grant," Nicole says.

Helen turns beet red, which doesn't help her case as she denies, "No, no, no. I'm not. We're *not* fucking."

"But you want to!" Nicole says, and smacks Helen with a throw pillow. "Bitch, I fucking knew it!"

Saskia looks between them, her mouth agape. "No . . . no, really?"

Helen drops her head into the throw pillow in Nicole's lap and lets out a muffled groan. "It's . . . complicated."

"Yeah, I bet," Nicole says, patting her hair. "When you bang, is he the one in charge, because he's Suraya's number two? Or are you, because it's your books and therefore your show?"

Helen snorts at this.

"How did it start?" Saskia asks, sounding a little awed.

"I don't know," Helen says. "We went home for winter break and it was . . . different."

"Hot," Nicole offers supportively.

"But now we're back here, and it's . . . I don't know." She flips up and stares at the ceiling, as if she's lying on her therapist's couch. "It's like the whole time we were in New Jersey, we were in this twilight zone of not the past and not the present. Nothing felt real—maybe that's why it was even . . . possible. Ever since we've come back to LA, it's felt like . . . like there could be real consequences."

"Consequences like what?" Saskia prompts.

Helen considers. Probably something like—liking him too much to walk away at a sensible time and getting stupidly attached and forcing herself into an entirely avoidable, impossible situation.

"I don't know, I'm just talking absolute shit," Helen mutters. "It might not even be a date. His email just said, 'Come over.'"

Nicole snorts. "Yeah, he means on his dick."

"I would like to do that," Helen says with an air of tragic

resignation, and Nicole and Saskia burst into laughter. She feels a giddy, unexpected sensation of relief then—as if sharing this secret has somehow made it easier to bear, though she knows none of the vital facts have changed.

"What you need is a good, old-fashioned terms-of-services agreement," Nicole says at last. "That way, everything stays aboveboard and everyone's on the same page. Extremely vital in any situationship. The earlier you talk it out, the better."

It makes enough sense that Helen texts him shortly before midnight—

> If I come over tomorrow, can we talk terms of service first?

The response is almost immediate—

> What services are you interested in?

She flushes, thinking of him awake in his bed, waiting for a response from her. She debates the pros and cons of a teasing versus a serious answer, but a second message comes from him first—

> See you in the a.m.

GRANT OPENS THE door before she has a chance to knock.

It's Saturday morning and he's still wearing sweatpants, an old T-shirt, and a sleepy kind of expression as he combs a hand through the tousled mess of his hair. He leans against the doorway idly, and suddenly she wants to plant herself face-first into his chest, so she can hear the rumble of his laugh as she rises and falls with his breathing.

But that would be an insane thing to do, so instead she nudges his slippered foot with her sneaker.

"Fuck, you look good in yoga pants," he says finally, and pulls her inside the door as she laughs.

"I haven't read the script," she murmurs, between kisses that taste like peppermint toothpaste.

"Who cares," he says, burying his face in her neck.

"Grant." She tries to bring his head back up but succeeds only in tangling her fingers in his hair instead.

"Who decided on a five-day workweek?" he says, kissing his way down to her collarbone. "Let me go back in time and murder them."

"I missed you too," she exhales, and after a brief pause, he rewards her with a bruising, hard kiss on her mouth as he pulls her into his body.

Her hands slip under his T-shirt to rake nails down his chest, and she feels the vibration of his growl of approval.

"We should talk about—this," she murmurs against his mouth.

"Stop kissing me, then," he answers, impossibly.

She slides a hand from the back of his neck to smooth down the front of his T-shirt, finally separating them. From the lips, anyway—he drops his forehead to hers and fiddles with the bottom of her cropped sweatshirt.

"I'm worried," she starts, then stops as she feels his other thumb brush across the pulse point at her neck. "I'm worried we might be starting something that could end . . . badly."

"Hm," he says, and brushes his thumb slowly back and forth on that one spot. "Go on."

"I think maybe we should talk about some . . . ground rules."

"Ground rules." He nods against her forehead.

"I don't want it to affect our work. Maybe it is already."

"But how would you know if you didn't read my script?" he teases her, and his lips seem to bait her closer.

"I was going to," she murmurs, and it feels like her pulse is beating faster just to chase the feel of his skin. "But I don't have a printer."

"Hm." He smooths his thumb over that one spot, then presses a quick kiss to the corner of her mouth. "Fine. Let's go."

She frowns as the warm heat of his hands and body retreat from her. "What?"

He walks away from her down the hallway, into his bedroom.

"Let's go to the office," he says from the other room. "We can talk about how this will or won't affect our work there. I just have to put on some clothes."

"But . . ." She walks a few steps and stops outside his bedroom door. He's in his boxer briefs, and he lifts a brow at her appearance.

"Helen," he says firmly. "If you come in here, I'm gonna fuck you on my bed until you forget your name, my name, and whatever very smart and important questions you have brewing in that beautiful head of yours because you can't think straight from how many times I've made you come. So if you *don't* want that, you should stay . . . put."

"Oh," she says softly, and falls back against the wall. "Okay."

He laughs, and shuts the door in her face.

THEY DON'T TALK much in the car as Grant drives them to the studio lot. She's entirely too *aware* of him, and though he isn't touching her, she feels her cheeks flush every time he glances in her direction. The weekend security guard waves them by after they flash their drive-on badges, and she isn't sure what to do with her hands. Grant shoots her a crooked, reassuring smile that seems to wedge right into a wobbling corner of her heart. *Almost there*, it seems to say.

They walk past the usually bustling soundstages and rows of empty white trailers. It's a sunny January day in Burbank and Helen is grateful for the excuse to wear sunglasses beside him.

"Have you ever been here on the weekends?"

"No," she says.

"There's usually some people working in the offices in the building," he says as he holds the door open for her. "Not a lot, but . . . showrunners are a type A lot."

"Oh," she says.

"Suraya has a decent work-life balance," Grant says as they walk into the elevator. "Thank god. The last showrunners I worked for would never break the room before eight p.m. I think they must have hated their families."

The ride is a short, tense one and when the elevator doors *ding* open, they observe the ghost town of the bullpen outside their writers room.

"Come on," he says, and leads the way through the familiar office space. He unlocks the door to the writers room, then shuts it behind them with a soft click, and Helen shivers.

They sit down across from each other, in their usual seats.

"So," he says. "You're worried it's going to affect our work."

"How could it not?" She crosses her arms. "I have to sit here and look at you every day for the next seven weeks."

"Four weeks," he counters. "After that, you'll be on script, writing your episode, and when you get back, we'll be at the point in the season where everyone's 'in the room' but basically working remotely on their scripts all the time. Then production will start, and you and Suraya will always be wanted on set for something or other, and then after *that*, the room will be officially over and you'll just be on set all the time."

"And you won't be there?" She frowns.

"Not unless Suraya needs me, but she's more the on-set type," he says. "My reps are already sending me materials for next shows to consider."

"Oh," she says.

"You said you had ground rules," he says, tapping his fingers together in a way she's seen him do in exactly this manner, when they're working on a story beat just before he's about to pitch something that throws the entire thing into the trash.

"Yes," she says. "First of all—we both know this can't . . . go anywhere."

Grant nods slowly, tense. "Fair enough."

"Either of us can end this, at any time," she says.

He snorts at that. "So like any relationship, then."

"This isn't a relationship."

Grant lifts a brow. "We're negotiating the terms of how and when I get to fuck you," he says. "I would say there's some kind of relationship here."

Helen swallows. He's right, she knows.

"Not a real one," she says. "Not a public one. Nothing on social media."

"Fine," he says.

She pauses. "Nicole and Saskia know we're . . . something. I think maybe they suspected before I said anything," she says.

He lifts a shoulder. "Considering I've been staring at you like a teenager with a crush for weeks, that's not surprising."

She flushes then, the word *crush* lighting up in her brain like a Broadway marquee sign, and she clears her throat.

"We set an end date after the writers room wraps in March," she says. "A week afterward, maybe."

"With an option to renew if both parties consent?" Grant counters. "That's pretty standard language in most of the contracts I've had my lawyer write up."

Helen taps her fingers on the desk nervously. "Option to mutually renew on a week-to-week basis."

Grant lets out a short exhale that sounds like a laugh. "Fine."

"But there's a hard cutoff on contact once production ends and I'm back in New York," she feels the need to add. "The goal is that when this is over, no one can say they were surprised by anything and it's quick and . . . and painless as possible."

SOMEHOW, GRANT DOESN'T think *painless* is going to happen, but he doesn't say it.

"So once you leave town, we both move on and pretend this never happened?" he clarifies. "No tortured three a.m. drunk voicemails, no texts when one of us is in the other's city, no . . . anything."

"Correct," she says.

"Hm," he says. "When would we start?"

Helen swallows. "Now, if you want."

He taps a pen on the desk, watching her intently. "I want."

She tilts her head, as if considering her next move. He thinks suddenly of playing Connect 4 with her, the lazy concentration on her face as she'd studied him and the grid. He'd won that game, but maybe she'd been playing something else entirely in her mind. Then she reaches for the bottom of her cropped sweatshirt and he stops thinking at all. She slowly removes the sweatshirt, revealing a thin sports bra underneath. He can just make out the shadow of her hardened nipples as she walks around the table toward him. He swallows as she stops a few inches from him.

"I have some addendums," he murmurs, staring up at her.

She kicks off her shoes.

"No more casting directors," he says. "Or actors, or camera operators, or other writers. Or anyone. If we're doing this, it's just me and you."

She nods as she hooks a finger into the elastic of her yoga pants and peels them down, before stepping out of them. She's wearing plain black cotton underwear, the same material as her thin sports bra, and he's never been so turned on in his life.

"If I do something you like, you have to tell me," he says, as his hand reaches out and traces the side of her thigh.

Her eyes drift closed and she bites her lip, then nods.

"And if I don't, you tell me that too," he says, lifting her hand and pressing a kiss into her palm.

Helen hums her consent.

"And finally—while we're together," he murmurs, his lips skimming her stomach, "I don't want to talk about how it's going to end. I'd rather not waste the time I have."

HELEN NODS, HER hands gently falling to his shoulders.

In a fluid motion, he lifts her up and places her on the table in front of him. He looks up at her like she's a feast and he's deciding where to start. Her legs dangle off the edge and he massages her calf, then bends his head and kisses the inside of her knee.

She exhales at the unexpected pressure and he stands, his hands running up her thighs and brushing past cotton and along her sides. His thumbs catch at the bottom of her bra and she shudders at the feeling of his fingers teasing under the elastic band.

He watches her intently, his thumbs sweeping the swelling sides of her breasts.

She inhales sharply as she meets his gaze—some molten-hot feeling floods her insides.

"More," she tells him, and his thumbs brush her nipples beneath the fabric.

She used to be self-conscious about her small breasts and remembers worrying in high school about the moment she'd have to be naked in front of someone else for the first time, revealing a disappointing lack of soft curves. The men she's been with in the years since have never said anything, often skimming past them after an initial curiosity-satisfying exploration and dwelling instead on her other, more welcoming parts.

Still, there's a moment of hesitation every first time, as she braces herself for inspection.

Grant pauses, in the middle of pressing a kiss to the side of her face.

"What is it?" he asks.

"Nothing," she says. "It's stupid. I just . . . don't like thinking about how my boobs measure up to other boobs."

Heat flames her face as he pulls away to look at her. She's painfully aware it sounds like she's fishing for a compliment and decides the best way through this is to reassure him quickly, "Forget I said that. I love my body. You're very lucky to be here. Come back."

Grant listens. She submits to another long, drugging kiss, and his fingers come up to sweep her jawline and skate down her neck and shoulders.

His lips follow his fingers, and he kisses down to the scoop neck of her sports bra. She feels the warm, soft lick of his tongue against the fabric, scraping onto skin. She inhales sharply, and she's certain he can hear the insistent tattoo of her heart against her chest.

His other hand brushes down her stomach, down past her

underwear, and onto the tops of her thighs, finally drawing slow circles on the inside of her knees. She becomes aware of a keening sound that's coming from the back of her own throat.

Grant lets out a low, answering growl as he runs his hand down to grip her ankle, and brushes his thumb over her Achilles, then her ankle bone.

"Why does that feel so good," she breathes.

He follows the path of his hands again, dropping a kiss to her stomach, then the inside of her thigh—*where he once wrote his address*, she remembers suddenly—then her inner knee. Finally he kisses the inside of her ankle, resettling back into the chair, his gaze hot on her even as he maintains contact only around her ankle.

GRANT LEANS BACK, his jaw tensing, his breath coming out in sharp, ragged pants.

Helen is most sensitive on the soft spots of her inner thighs, knees, and ankles, and he relishes in the knowledge of the discovery. He keeps drawing a slow circle around her ankle bone, unwilling to break contact completely—he feels like he's just started a new favorite book and he can't put it down or he'll lose his place.

"I don't think you realize," he says slowly, "how often I've imagined this."

His eyes rake slowly down her body; he can see the rise and fall of her rib cage.

"How often I've come into my own hand at the thought of you on this table," he murmurs, and watches her eyes flare with heat.

Grant pulls his shirt off then and it drops in a heap on the ground.

"Do you ever touch yourself, Helen?"

She watches his hands moving toward his belt with such intense concentration, he can almost feel the heat of her gaze on his knuckles. She nods slowly.

In a few short movements, he unbuckles his belt and shoves his free hand—the hand that isn't still drawing slow circles on her inner ankle—down his pants. He squeezes himself and lets out a shaky breath. His cock surges against his own hand, as if to remind him there's a warmer, sweeter place for it right in front of him.

"Take off your bra," he says, "and cup your breasts for me."

She watches him as she takes the bra off, finally, *finally* revealing pebbling brown nipples and peaked globes that make his mouth suddenly water like a man starved. Her hands move up to cup them obediently, her eyes flitting from his eyes to his hand working slowly, rhythmically below his belt.

"Pinch your nipples," he says, and is gratified to hear her gasp as she complies. She closes her eyes to the sensation as her head falls back, but he squeezes her ankle. "No, don't close your eyes. I want you here with me."

Helen opens her eyes then, her lips falling open in a pornographic pout.

"They're so pretty, I want to lick them while you come," he says, giving himself a harder tug.

She lets out the softest whimper, and he has to force himself to stay in his seat and ignore the all-consuming desire to dive forward.

"Do you ever think about me when you touch yourself?" he asks.

Helen exhales and nods.

"Show me," he demands.

One hand drifts down her body, and she slides a flat palm

against the front of that maddeningly enticing triangle of black fabric. She hooks a thumb against the elastic, while her other hand continues to work her breasts.

"I thought about you like this," she says. "Sitting in your chair. Watching me."

She squirms against her own hand, her mouth forming a perfect *O* at the sensation, and he can tell she's close from the glaze of her eyes, the unselfconscious way she rocks against the table.

He drops a quick kiss to the inside of her knee, his hands flexing around her ankle and his cock at the same time. He has to slow down, he knows, but he can't resist a final tug before he stands up between her legs. His pants fall to his ankles, and he thinks it must be very undignified but can't be fucked to care when he can feel the heat radiating from her perfect pussy through the fabric.

"Helen, I think you're going to make yourself come for me now," he whispers into her ear, his fingers gripping the sides of her thighs. "And I'm gonna lick your nipples till you beg for me."

She whimpers then, as he presses the hot flat of his tongue against one peaked brown nipple. He licks her like ice cream—slow, dragging, savoring the taste of her.

"I . . ." she pants, still writhing against her own hand, and it's the hottest thing he's ever witnessed. She lets out a tortured sob. "Please, Grant."

"Please, Grant what," he murmurs against her breast.

"The other one now," she breathes, and he complies.

"I'll give you anything you want, sweetheart," he murmurs. "You just have to ask."

She whimpers again, and he suckles her areola into his mouth, scraping his teeth gently against the nipple. She gasps then, and he feels her grind against her own hand once, twice, and her other hand flies up blindly to grip his hair as she comes apart on the table. He feels her shuddering against his tongue, under the iron grip of his hands at her thighs, and she lets out a single tortured groan before her breaths turn to shallow pants.

Her hands pull at his hair and urge him up until she's kissing him desperately, as desperately as he feels like he's drowning in her.

"I love your body," he says, between bruising kisses. "I'm so fucking lucky to be here."

She reaches down between them, slipping into his boxer briefs and *holy fuck her hand is on his cock*.

"I want to feel you," she murmurs into his mouth. "Please."

A strangled groan escapes his throat as she runs a thumb across his weeping head and squeezes his shaft.

"I have to—" He pulls away from her, thinking of the condom in his wallet, somewhere on the ground.

"I have an IUD," she says suddenly. "I . . . please, Grant, I need to feel you."

He gasps as she tugs him free of his boxer briefs, and tries to clear the pounding in his brain long enough to think. *I have an IUD. I need to feel you.*

"I had a physical at the end of last year," he pants. "I haven't been with anyone since—since—"

He can't seem to finish the thought, because her nails are raking softly against his balls as she pulls gently against them.

"*Fuck*," he says instead.

"Yes," she says, and lifts off the table slightly to slide off her underwear. He looks down, slightly stunned, and watches as she guides the head of his cock against her folds. "Just—slow."

He grits his teeth at the feeling of her taking him in, the tight heat enveloping him in slow, sliding millimeters. *I'm fucked*, he thinks, as he looks up to see her gasping at the sensation of him pushing into her. *I'm going to need this forever.*

HELEN STARES AT Grant's face, thinking through the fog, *so this is what you look like when you do this.*

His jaw is tense from concentration, and impossibly, he's still sliding into her, the slickness of her heat making him surge forward faster now.

"Oh," she gasps, as she squeezes involuntarily around him. He groans, as if pained, then jerks and tilts his hips, and suddenly she's filled to the hilt by *Grant*. She gasps at the sensation of him inside of her, foreign yet growing more and more familiar—*unforgettable*—by the second.

His breath expels hotly by her temple, and his hands grip the sides of her hips as she rocks experimentally—*once, twice*—into him. He drops a restrained kiss on her lips and rests his forehead against hers, his eyes closed in concentration, and she thinks suddenly of how unfairly *beautiful* he is.

"Mm." He exhales, and she becomes aware of him slowly pressing her into him, then easing off, then repeating. They both look down at the point where their bodies are joining and rejoining—her breath catches at how primal it looks.

"I . . . I can't believe you're fucking me on this table," she says, and he lets out a short gust of laughter.

"I can," he says. "I've thought about it so many times, it feels like I was remembering this."

He runs a thumb down past her peaked nipple and slides himself out a little farther this time, before surging back into her.

"You feel so fucking good," he exhales into her ear. "How dare you."

She lets out a throaty laugh that turns into a gasp as he slams into her again.

"Grant," she pants needily into his ear. "I think I'm gonna come again."

His thumb slips between them, pinching her clit insistently, unrelenting even as she whimpers. She gasps, arching into him, and suddenly white-hot stars explode in her vision. He groans as she feels the pulsing wave of pleasure sweep over her body, rocking through her, and she's forgotten to be quiet as she releases her orgasm in racked sobs.

Dimly, she becomes aware of him lowering her back onto the table, and she watches him with lazy fascination as he runs a thumb from her lips down her sternum. She bites her lip as he pulls back, then slams into her, the cold table rocking beneath her, then he pulls back again.

She reaches a hand up, and he captures her hand and kisses the inside of her wrist—a surprisingly tender gesture that catches her by surprise. He slides into her once, twice—she stares with wonder at the sweat on his brow—then he jerks out of her with a groan and she feels a hot stream of his come land in spurts across her stomach.

He drops his head to her neck and exhales in slow, ragged breaths as he comes back into his body. He kisses her shoulder, and laughs in a low, raspy way that makes her belly feel tight with some kind of unfamiliar wanting.

"Let's do this every weekend," he says into her shoulder, and she laughs.

HE CLEANS HER stomach off using wipes for the dry-erase board, and she already knows she's going to blush anytime she looks at the prosaic plastic container (still bearing its $3.99 sticker from Staples) on Monday.

She puts her underwear and her clothes back on and remembers a vague conversation she had with Suraya in the early days of the writers room.

"Some writers are bad in the room, but great on the page," she had explained. "It's harder for them at the start, but when people discover them, they *work*."

Helen had wondered if Suraya had meant to imply that Helen herself was bad in the room, so she had better be great on the page.

"But the vast majority of TV writers are good in a room, and somewhere between decent and pretty good on the page," Suraya had gone on. "It's an easier path to what a lot of people want."

Helen had gone home that weekend trying to catalogue the writers in their room, rereading their spec samples that she had only skimmed when Suraya first forwarded them after the welcome drinks night.

Saskia was quiet in the room, but her sample had sparkled with heart. Nicole was consistently funny in the room, but had a tendency to run her mouth to the point of annoying Suraya—and Helen found her sample to have a similarly distinct voice. Owen, Tom, and Eve were *good* in the room—always funny and ready to build on the energy at the table, drawing connections from seemingly totally disparate conversational threads throughout the day. Their writing rose to the occasion too—more confident and capable than either Nicole's or Saskia's, but perhaps less *special*.

And Grant. She knew even then, he was *great* in a room. He always had been, and she had flipped through his sample expecting something hovering between adequate and good.

Then she read his sample pilot. She tore through his writing the fastest that night, drawn against her will into the tangled web of complicated relationships and secrets and lies binding his cast of characters together in a small seaside town of South Jersey. It wasn't even the kind of TV show she'd ever willingly watch, yet when she reached the last page, she felt a stupid compulsion to text him to ask what happened next. (She didn't, of course.) She'd been unpleasantly humbled by his work and the knowledge that no matter how *great* on the page she eventually was, he'd always be one up on her for being capable of both.

As Grant drops a collated printout of the first draft of his episode on the table in front of her, she feels a rush of nervousness. Not about his writing, but about *hers*. About the thought of him having spent a week intimately exploring the characters she had once dreamed up in the privacy of her own mind, in her first cramped studio apartment in New York, in coffee shops in Brooklyn, in public libraries around the city.

She worries that reading his script, she'll catch an honest glimpse of how he sees *her*, and she's afraid then it might ruin whatever burgeoning thing is happening between them. It feels more intimate than him being inside her body, somehow, and she catches a claustrophobic sensation building against her will.

"I'll read it later," she says finally. "Let's go back to your place."

He offers her a hand and she stands. He tilts up her chin to kiss her gently, and she feels a dizzy kind of warmth in his arms.

"Your heart's pounding," he murmurs. "Anything I did?"

She laughs.

"Pretty much always," she answers, and he lets out a satisfied "*hm*" that fills her with a nervous kind of yearning.

Twenty-One

"I don't know why you can't just be happy," Helen says to her mom over FaceTime. "It sounds like it was really nice."

Her mom is calling from the road after leaving the farewell brunch of Helen's cousin's wedding in Canada, to tell her that the wedding was beautiful but felt more like the wedding of a work friend's daughter than family.

"Not enough Chinese people," Mom says. "Everyone is French; everything is French. I think your cousin is embarrassed to be Chinese."

Helen rolls her eyes and pulls up her cousin Alice's tagged photos on Instagram.

"She put up a neon double-happiness sign and they had a lion dance, that's pretty Chinese, Mom."

"It is not the same. I know her mother is a little sad, even if she is happy. You would not understand." Helen thinks Mom's right about that, at least.

Back in college, when she had vague aspirations of being a great voice on the American literary-fiction scene, she wrote a lot of short stories about the quiet tragedies of immigrant-kid assimilation, of the sense of disconnect she felt every time they visited her parents' hometowns in China over the years, of the way she'd catch her grandparents tsking at her in their native Cantonese and not being able to understand them because of decisions her parents made before she was even born. She thinks sometimes if she ever wanted to pivot, she could still write an entire book of poems about all the ways she breaks her mother's heart in a day.

"When you get married, just make sure you invite more Chinese people," Mom is saying. "My sister is so sad. All she has is your uncle and me and Dad."

"Uh-huh," Helen says, "I will keep that in mind."

"You will keep that in mind, ha! You don't even bring anyone home for us to meet," Mom says. "At least Alice is married."

Helen nods at this entirely logical leap to being Team At-Least-She's-Married Alice.

"I bring friends home all the time," Helen says, and it's mostly true. Her friends in New York still rave about the soy sauce salmon Mom made for them three years ago.

"You know what I mean," Mom says. "A *special* friend."

"Oh, a *special* friend," Helen says, and thinks impossibly of Grant and the breakfast he made her this morning. She'd been impressed by his ability to poach an egg. "Mom, you spent two and a half decades telling me to focus on school and work and not to think about boys. Maybe the reason I'm not married is because I'm such a *guai nui*."

Such a *good girl*. It's one of the only Cantonese phrases she knows, the one her parents and her grandparents would say to her as a compliment—when they were in front of their friends, when she did something they approved of, when they were reassuring each other in hushed tones after the funeral that Helen would never do something like this.

Helen has always been a good girl. She remembers her frustration watching Michelle move through the world and finding ways to upset everyone, all the time. She had envied it a little bit too—the idea of just *not caring* seemed so foreign to her, she sometimes couldn't believe they had the same parents. She recognizes an uncharitable feeling of resentment rise against her little sister, even all these years later.

You had it so much easier than me, Helen thinks. *You had me. And you still couldn't stick it out?*

Helen's mom is in the middle of a monologue about the tragedy of having a daughter who claims to listen but doesn't, really.

"It's the natural order of life, Helen, your children are supposed to grow up and start a family and have children of their own," Mom says. "You need someone in your life too, to take care of you when Mom and Dad aren't here anymore."

"I can take care of myself—I *do* take care of myself," Helen reminds her. "I'm doing really well."

"I know, I know," Mom says. "Such a modern woman."

Helen sighs. "If I ever meet someone who's worth bringing home, I'll let you know," she says finally. "Just let me live my life in the meantime."

"Hmph," Mom says, as if that's up for negotiation too, and Helen closes her eyes against the impending headache and wishes things were just a little bit *easier*.

GRANT FIDDLES WITH his phone and tries not to interfere as Helen moves through her kitchen, looking slightly frazzled as she opens drawers looking for random tools.

It took them two weeks to get to the point of home-cooked meals, because they'd always become too preoccupied with other activities from the moment she stepped through his door and then it'd be too late and they'd be too exhausted to whip something up from scratch. *Stop trying to distract me*, he'd said this morning, heading straight for the kitchen. *I bought eggs just to make you breakfast.*

She insisted on returning the favor for dinner and he gets the distinct impression that she feels vaguely competitive about it.

"We're doing salmon and rice, and green beans with a black-bean garlic sauce," she announces. "I thought about doing this tomato-egg thing that's really good, but it doesn't work as a side dish for only two people. Maybe for breakfast, though."

He thinks about suggesting they invite more people over then, but abandons the idea when she hands him a glass of white wine and kisses him on the corner of the mouth in a casually possessive way that tugs at some secret spot hiding just under his ribs.

"I'm linking to your Bluetooth system," he says, and puts on a random playlist for cooking at home.

She looks up at him over her shoulder, with a sudden grin. "Is this the 'cooking with friends' playlist on Spotify?"

"Do you know it well?" he asks dryly, taking a sip of his wine and thinking she looks fucking adorable right now.

"I listen to it all the time when I'm cooking with friends," she confirms. "I like looking up really specific vibes and then putting on someone else's playlist for it. This is one of my favorites."

He feels himself mentally tuck this information away, information that will be useless to him in a few months' time but he's fairly certain will stay lodged in his brain for much longer.

"What are you most looking forward to this week?" he asks, as she manages a beeping oven. "And what are you most dreading?"

"Meeting the pilot director in person," she says. "Supposedly she's really cool and young and Suraya convinced the studio to take a big swing on her. And dreading . . . the notes call with the studio on Thursday. They hate me."

"They don't hate you."

"I'm like an extra limb they have to deal with—they never know what to say to me before Suraya gets on the call," Helen says, spooning steaming rice into bowls. "It makes me feel like two inches tall."

She drops a bowl of rice on the ground, then yelps.

"Hm," he says, getting up from his seat to help her in the kitchen. "I thought maybe you would say you were most looking forward to seeing me back in the writers room."

When he reaches the other side of the kitchen island, she grabs him by the collar to kiss him against the sink cabinets.

"You're so fucking corny," she murmurs against his lips, and he can feel her smile.

After dinner, they sit outside on the fake grass on the floor of her balcony. He leans against the wall and she drops between his long legs to lean back against his chest. His body seems to hum slightly with the contact and he bends to press his nose into her neck, a gesture he's identified as one of her favorites by the way she always lets out a breathy little sigh as she nudges back with her cheek like a needy cat.

"You'd make a good boyfriend," she says to the air.

He pulls back from her neck suddenly.

"Thanks," he says, unable to keep the sharpness from his voice.

"What are you doing on this balcony with me instead of being all boyfriended up with some nice, appropriate girl out there?" She gestures vaguely at the street and the Santa Monica Pier ahead of them. She turns her face to look up at him shrewdly. "What's your damage, Grant Shepard?"

He laughs shortly.

"Well, my therapist says I have anxiety," he says. "And a fear of being unworthy."

Her hand squeezes the heavy arm that's draped over her shoulder, and her thumb brushes his forearm in a quick, reassuring sweep.

"That's not so bad," she murmurs. "You could get over that, I bet."

He drops his head back into her neck and she releases another shaky little sigh.

"You think I should get a girlfriend?" he murmurs into her neck.

"Only one who deserves you," she says, her voice low and soft. "I could vet the candidates for you."

"What about you?" he asks, and his stomach gives a funny flip like he's on the ancient, rickety roller coaster ride on the pier.

She's silent for a moment, and her voice is quiet when she finally speaks.

"You mean, why am I entangled in this sexy situation with no real future instead of finding a nice young man to settle down with?"

That's not what he meant at all, but he waits for her to answer her own question.

"Guess I'm just not ready to be healthy yet," she says finally. "Someday, though."

Grant frowns at this puzzle of a sentence. He has a feeling if he were to examine it further, it'd fall to pieces, and maybe this fragile thing between them would too.

"Helen," he says finally, kissing her shoulder. "Stop talking absolute shit. It's too late and I'm too tired to keep up."

She laughs and tilts her head up so he can kiss her on the lips. It's a slow, lazy kiss, but somehow—and he isn't sure who starts it—it becomes hot and searching. It feels like they're arguing, and when she turns to cup his jaw in her hands, he stands and pulls her up with him, until she's trapped between his body and the wall.

She kisses his neck, then looks up at him with some soft *something* in her eyes, and it feels like shrapnel lodging in his gut. His hand lifts to brush her hair from her temple, then slides down to palm her left breast. She gasps, and he frowns, squeezing harder, pinching her nipple.

"Am I hurting you?" he asks, his voice low.

She shakes her head, and bites her lip.

"I like it when you hurt me a little," she whispers, and his lips come crashing down on hers, harsh, bruising, wanting. He thinks maybe if he kisses her long enough, he'll chase away the taste of bitterness and *hurt*, though where that's come from, he isn't sure.

"Helen," he murmurs against her mouth. "I don't want a girlfriend."

She nods, whimpering slightly as he nips at her lower lip.

"And I don't want to talk about this ever again," he says, his voice ragged. "Understand?"

She doesn't answer, chasing after his lips insistently, so he pulls away, resting his forehead against hers. "Did you hear me?" he says.

"Yes," she says. "I heard you."

She captures his lips again and he kisses her back this time, and for the rest of the night, the conversation consists only of soft gasps and each other's names.

Twenty-Two

O n Tuesday, Helen is surprised to be the first one in the office. It's the day after Valentine's Day (she spent last night getting dinner with Nicole and Saskia, then driving home alone on principle) and there's a seven-car pileup on the freeway, apparently, which traps everyone else in the traffic going north to Burbank. Suraya texts instructing them to start without her, whenever Grant arrives. About forty minutes later, she texts them again to say they're basically done breaking episode 109 anyway and she has too many preproduction meetings so she's going straight to the production office instead and they can all just work from home today.

Helen's about to turn and head home when the elevator doors open and Grant appears. He's wearing a hoodie and a baseball cap, and she can see his shoulders heaving up and down unnaturally as he walks out.

Something's wrong.

He sees her, but he's walking in brisk strides toward his office instead.

"Grant?"

"Water," he says croakily, and jams a mug under the office water cooler.

He presses the hot water accidentally first, and curses before he switches to the cold water. She reaches his side then, and up close she can see he's pale and sweating.

"What's wrong?" She touches his hand gently.

"Panic attack," he says grimly, closing his eyes as he leans back against the wall.

"Tell me what you need now," she says.

"I need to count," he says. "Letters on signs, or—or something . . ."

"Should I count with you?" she asks, and points at a poster on the wall. "That sign?"

He nods, and she holds his hand as they both count upward. "One . . . two . . . three . . ."

By the time they reach five, his breath is coming out in slow, racking sobs, and she slides her arm around his waist to wrap him in a hug. He drops his face into her hair, and she can feel the damp heat of his breath and tears as he inhales and exhales, accepting her comfort without hugging her back.

"What happened?" she asks, when his breathing slows and she feels him straighten.

She runs her palms up and down his upper arms, trying to warm him.

"It's stupid," he mutters, and she presses a kiss against his neck, willing him to go on. "Traffic on the five north, because of the pileup."

"The big car accident?"

"There was a second one, a few miles after the big pileup. Someone in a sheet on the ground," he says.

"Oh."

"I kept thinking about how they made it past all that traffic, just to die a few miles later," he mutters. "Or maybe it happened before and caused the other big pileup. I don't know."

"And you had a panic attack?" she asks, looking up at him.

He wipes his face with his hand, and she takes the hand from him to press a kiss into his palm.

"You've done that before," he says, and swallows.

"You were hurt then too," she murmurs, lacing her fingers through his hands.

He exhales shortly.

"Sometimes I get like this," he mutters. "I don't know why. The most random fucking triggers, it's embarrassing."

"Is it about . . ." Helen doesn't finish the question, but he hears it anyway.

"Probably," he says. "I mean, it definitely fucked me in the head, if that's what you're asking. It took so long for the paramedics to get there, I still remember the traffic."

"Come on," Helen says, and tugs his hand to lead them toward his office.

She shuts the door and sits on the couch against the wall. He removes his baseball cap and leans against the door. He's cold and pale, and she aches at how vulnerable he looks.

"Come here," she says, and when he moves to the couch, she urges him down until his head is in her lap. She brushes a hand through his hair, repeating the motion in soothing strokes.

"Do you think about that night a lot?" she asks.

"I try not to," he mutters. "I feel so fucking useless whenever I do."

"There was nothing you could have done," she murmurs.

"You don't know that," he says quietly.

"There was nothing you could have done," she repeats, shaking her head. "It wasn't your fault."

"I thought I was going to jail," he says, and laughs in a choked kind of way. "I was mostly worried about me."

"That makes sense," she says. "You were just a kid. You didn't know what could happen. It was scary."

Grant presses the heels of his hands into his eyes.

"You . . . of all people . . . should not be comforting me. My life has gone really well since then," he says. "It's so fucked-up."

She covers both his hands with hers, hoping the extra weight feels comforting even in the darkness of his vision, and after a moment, he silently laces their fingers together.

"You can tell me, you know," she says, so quietly she feels compelled to repeat it. "You can tell me about that night. If it helps to have someone to—to remember it with."

They're both still for a moment.

Grant takes a breath, and then he starts.

Twenty-Three

Whenever Grant remembers it now, it always feels like flash-backs, like—and it sounds so dumb to him, out loud—like his memory turned into a montage.

He remembers the party he was at, a last-minute decision to attend Brianna Peltzer's last-minute party, celebrating nothing but another Friday. He had vague plans to see Lauren DiSantos afterward—but the party wasn't Lauren's scene.

He remembers the bottle of Pabst Blue Ribbon someone handed him at the start of the night, the sweat on the glass, the way having a beer in his hand always made him feel older and more world-weary, like he was already at college. He remembers looking up and seeing his ex-girlfriend Desiree, and the forbidden attraction of *ex-girlfriend*, as a concept. She'd picked up his hand in a knowing sort of way and pulled him onto the dance floor. They danced. They kissed.

"Give me a ride home," she whispered against his ear.

He'd had only a sip of his beer, while everyone else at the party was still drinking.

It had seemed like the right thing to do.

They pulled up to Desiree's driveway shortly after midnight. There was the familiar oak tree out front where they'd taken prom photos a week ago. Grant and Desiree had been together since sophomore year. It suddenly seemed strange and sad that they weren't together anymore. Desiree looked over at him from the passenger seat, and he knew she was thinking the same thing.

"I'm scared of what happens next," Desiree said. "After high school."

"Me too," Grant said, even though he'd never thought so before. He'd gone through most of high school with the impression that he hadn't met the real version of himself yet; he was excited to start the next chapter. But seeing Desiree in his passenger seat, in her old familiar driveway, he suddenly knew he was telling the truth.

"Do you want to come in?" she asked.

Grant doesn't remember exactly what he said. Instead, he remembers the fullness of Desiree's lips and the way they curved up a little at his response. He remembers brushing back the hair on her shoulder, the soft light of the driveway breaking through the curtain of blond. He remembers laughing as they dodged the sprinklers on her parents' lawn, and the way her finger looked pressed against her lips as they tiptoed upstairs to her bedroom. He remembers feeling a stab of guilt as he thought of Lauren DiSantos—he'd said he would be at her house by midnight. He could be a little late.

He remembers the sex being good, and sad, and maybe good because it was a little sad.

"I can't do this again," he said, as he stood on the other side of Desiree's bedroom door for the last time. "I have to go."

"I wish you weren't so sure," she said. "That's the part that hurts the most."

Grant wishes now he'd been less sure.

GRANT DOESN'T REMEMBER the song on the radio, or the color of the car in front of him, or the flavor of soda he had in the cupholder of his mom's minivan.

He remembers the time—
2:03 a.m.
    and the weather—
cloudy, with a chance of showers
    and his destination—
Lauren DiSantos's house,
but maybe his own house,
he didn't have to decide until after the next stop on Route 22.

He remembers the speedometer—
60 MPH—
    and looking up to see—
A PERSON, SHIT—
65 MPH

Grant doesn't think he should tell you this part, but you want to hear it.

GRANT REMEMBERS OPENING the door to the smell of smoke in the air and the crunch of glass beneath his feet. He remembers the car not showing much damage—he thinks, *but that might not be true*, his parents got rid of the car the following week. There were other people—their faces and clothes and genders all blurred by memory now—silhouetted by blinking hazard lights formed in an arc around him.

"Did you see who the driver was?" he heard one person saying to another.

"Just some kid," they answered. "He looked terrified."

Grant wanted to ask, *Are you talking about me?*

But he had to check on the victim first.

He remembers his approach being stopped by the firm grip of a stranger, a man in his late forties who looked the way Grant imagined *fathers* were supposed to look. (This didn't make any sense because Grant *had* a father, one who looked nothing like this man, but that was neither here nor there.)

"Son," Grant's not-father said. "You don't want to go over there."

"I have to," Grant said. "I have to see if they're okay."

The man shook his head. "We all saw what happened. It wasn't your fault."

Grant remembers a sudden, swooping dread filling his stomach.

"Am I in trouble?" he asked.

"What's your name, son?" the man asked in response.

Grant remembers wondering for *one wild second* if he should lie.

"Grant," he answered, and it sounded like he'd run a long distance just to tell the truth. "Grant Shepard."

"How old are you, Grant?"

"Eighteen." He was crying by then, because behind the man he could see a limp figure in the dark being covered by some Good Samaritan's dark green coat. The coat had clear glass buttons, and he could see them catching the light, along with the glass on the ground.

"Look at me, Grant," his not-father said, and Grant wiped his tears and obeyed, focusing on the stranger in front of him instead of the dead girl—*he was pretty sure by then it was a girl, by the size of her*—a few feet away. "You been drinking?"

"No, sir," Grant said, and he remembers feeling like he was lying, though the Breathalyzer test he took later said he wasn't.

HELEN THINKS OF all her memories of that night as locked in a single, flooded room in the back of her mind. Before she opens the door, she always tries to remember the good things first.

How AS A toddler, Michelle had been a strangely sweet shadow following her everywhere, always willing to share her toys and candy. How she'd been obsessed with animals, and how they'd spearheaded a joint campaign to adopt a chocolate Labrador puppy, or an orange tabby kitten, or maybe just a pair of parakeets, *it doesn't matter what color, we swear* (all unsuccessful). How much Michelle loved the strawberries growing in the backyard of that first cramped duplex apartment in Union, New Jersey, where they'd shared a bedroom—and how she'd cried the entire car ride as they left the plants behind to move to Dunollie, with its better school district and much-needed space.

In the brief sixteen years of their sisterhood, Helen estimates they were too young to remember the first two years, close as adolescent sisters could be for ten years, and at near-constant odds for the last four years. In the balance of things, it seems like a ratio she should be able to wield in her favor, to ward off the memory of one tragic night.

But it never seems to work out that way.

Helen remembers being left behind while her parents went to the morgue.

She doesn't remember how she felt—*sad*, is what she told the school counselors who asked, a week later—she remembers only an overwhelming need to *clean Michelle's room now, now, NOW before Mom and Dad get back*. It was a mental directive so imperative she could feel it itching in every skin cell still touching her comforter as she lay in bed waiting for the sound of the garage door to shut behind her parents' car. A family friend was on their way to the house to watch over Helen; she didn't have much time.

She remembers racing into Michelle's room and feeling silly once she got inside. The room smelled like confirmation that Michelle was *still very much alive*, like she'd burst in at any moment pissed that Helen had gone through her things.

Helen knows the word *suicide* hadn't occurred to her yet—that would come later. Even as she fumbled with the empty battery compartment of Michelle's Hello Kitty clock to retrieve those little knotted plastic bags full of powder, Helen thought it was still possible everyone was wrong, that the body they'd found on Route 22 in that terrible accident *wasn't* Michelle's. If they'd *known*, why would her parents have to ID the body? Or maybe it *was* Michelle, but she wasn't *dead*-dead—didn't people come back to life in ambulances all the time, in TV shows?

Either way, Helen remembers feeling like *the world's best sister* as she combed through all of Michelle's favorite hiding spots and flushed all evidence of anything that might suggest *substance abuse problems* down the toilet.

That was when she remembered the last words they'd said to each other.

IT WAS AFTER dinner, less than six hours ago. Helen had been sitting up in bed, Facebook stalking her fellow classmates in the incoming Dartmouth Class of 2012, as if knowing enough about them would allow her to astral project herself three months into the future, when this suffocating house and everyone in it would be nothing but a distant memory. Michelle had come in to curl her hair, *because Helen's mirror was better than hers*. She had plans to sneak out to a party—Helen didn't approve, but *Helen never approved*. Michelle wanted to borrow a necklace, and Helen said no.

"But it's just for a few hours," Michelle said.

"Assuming you don't lose it, like you lose *everything*," Helen muttered, not looking up from her laptop. "The answer's no. Popo gave me that necklace. I'm bringing it to college."

"The only reason I don't have a necklace from her of my own is because she *died* before my sixteenth birthday," Michelle said.

"Bummer for you," Helen said. "Get out of my room."

"You're always so mean to me," Michelle complained. "And I do *nothing* to you."

"Well, I won't be living here soon, so you won't have to suffer much longer, will you?"

Michelle was silent for a beat. Then, cruelly: "Sometimes I wish you weren't my sister."

Helen looked up from her laptop at last.

Freeze it right here, Helen always wants to tell whoever's playing the film reel of her life. But the scene continues relentlessly:

"Well, I was here first and I never asked for a sister. If it were up to me, I wouldn't have one."

Michelle stared at her mutinously, jaw working on some response that never came. Helen remembers feeling a stab of regret, but—*hadn't Michelle started it?*

Then Michelle yanked the hot curling iron from the wall and hurled it across the room at Helen.

"What's *wrong* with you?!" Helen shouted, dodging the hot metal.

Michelle ran out and slammed the door shut behind her.

HELEN REMEMBERS OPENING Michelle's laptop and the screen being a little blurry—she must have been crying, though she doesn't remember crying—as she deleted a secret folder full of Michelle's favorite erotic Lord of the Rings fan fiction. Michelle didn't write any fan fiction, as far as Helen knew, but she liked annoying Helen by reading the saucy sections out loud whenever she wanted Helen to leave her alone. Michelle was annoying like that. *Michelle was too annoying to be dead.*

She opened Michelle's internet browser history, with the intention to clear it of any porn or incriminating drug-related searches. And she remembers what she found.

"WHAT IS THE likelihood of survival if hit by a car at 55 mph for a 95lb female" 1:38 a.m.

   "what happens when you die medically" 1:39 a.m.

   "10-Day Weather Forecast Dunollie NJ" 1:41 a.m.

IT FELT MORE like finding a noose than a note.

Helen remembers thinking viciously, *I'll never forgive you, if this is all you left behind.*

She didn't delete it just in case it was. She scanned the room for anything obviously intended to be read in this situation.

Nothing.

The silence in the room became eerie.

Helen remembers convincing herself then that searching for a physical note was silly. Of course Michelle wouldn't have done that, of course it would have been too old-fashioned for her, of *course* if she'd written any kind of suicide letter, she would have done so on her laptop and left it somewhere to be unearthed digitally—in her email drafts or in a password-protected file buried deep enough on the hard drive that only Helen would know how to access it.

Of course Michelle wouldn't have left this earth without getting the last word, even if it was just one final *fuck you* to the only sister she'd ever had.

Helen remembers being impressed by her own sense of regained calm as she copied the entirety of Michelle's digital legacy onto a hard drive to be searched thoroughly, exhaustively, at a later date.

Once she was sure Michelle was really dead.

GRANT WANTS YOU *to know what happened after he left the funeral.*

HE REMEMBERS STEPPING outside into the humid, gray summer afternoon, with Helen's voice still ringing in his ears. *She wants you to leave, now.* He remembers a choked, horrible lump in his throat, and a burning in his lungs, and thinking he *absolutely must not cry* while he was still visible to anyone inside the church. He didn't want to be seen lingering about the premises, as if he didn't understand perfectly what she'd been saying. *Leave. Now.*

So Grant left and drove to the old pizza shop up the mountain, because he didn't want to go home and tell Dad he'd been right about the funeral. He remembers wondering what became of the man (not Dad) who had stood with him reassuringly while the police questioned him at the scene. That man disappeared at some point, and Grant never saw him again.

He remembers the smell of warm olive oil and dough in the air as he ordered a slice of pepperoni pizza with a can of Coke. He remembers the pretty redhead behind the counter smiling at him, and then hearing his name—*"Grant?"*—and turning to see Kevin Palermo, sitting with other graduating seniors from the football team.

"Good to see you here, man," Kevin said. "It's been a minute."

Grant hadn't seen any of them since the party at Brianna Peltzer's house, the stupid party he shouldn't have gone to.

"I'm sorry," Grant said, and the lump in his throat seemed ready to choke him.

"Grab a slice with us while you wait for yours," Kevin said, and stood so the others could shuffle to make room behind him. Grant still isn't sure if Kevin was being nice or oblivious when he said it—*you've met him, he's always been like that.* "Hey, you hear they made frickin' Tommy Hariri team captain next year? Those poor freshmen."

"Tommy Hariri," Grant remembers saying, and sitting down as if Michelle Zhang, *beloved daughter, sister, friend*, wasn't being lowered into the ground a few short miles away. "No way."

"*Way*," Kevin said.

Grant remembers discovering he had a terrible new power that day in the pizza shop.

That he could get away with killing someone and everyone would still treat him the same as always, as if he hadn't done it at all.

Twenty-Four

I'm sorry," Grant gasps, and his breathing becomes erratic again. "I'm sorry, I'm sorry, I wish . . . I wish—"

He can't seem to finish his sentences and Helen thinks of all the times she wondered (all the while wishing she didn't), *what was it like for you, afterward,* all the times she briefly allowed the next thought, *it must have been terrible,* and the guilt, and the resentment, and the anger, and the present pain turning into the past hurt over and over again until her insistent heart beat out a never-ending rhythm of *hurtpainhurtpainhurtpain.* She's spent a good fraction of her good fortune on therapy, training that terrible recurring poem of her heart to dull its thud, enough so she can hear her own thoughts over it, enough so she can think about something other than her still-beating organs.

She suspects she always imagined some version of this for him too—an echo of her own emotional scars, whenever she imagined *what was it like for you.* But seeing it, *feeling it,* from his cold skin to her not-cold-enough heart, is so awfully different.

Helen slips out of her shoes. She stands and slowly resettles herself above him, one knee on the inside of the couch, the other dangling above the floor.

"Would you hold me?" she asks, and after a beat, he nods.

She drops down more fully, her legs stretching over his, her body covering his body like a weighted blanket as his arms come around her. She is suddenly, bizarrely grateful that she can give this to him, that maybe she's the only person in the world who *can*.

"I think I forgave you long before I ever forgave her," she murmurs finally. "I still haven't, really. I don't know if I ever will."

"You shouldn't forgive me," Grant says. "It's not . . . you shouldn't be mad at your sister forever. That's not how it should be."

"It's how we left it," Helen says. "We were supposed to grow up and get over ourselves and meet on the other side of the mountain as friends. Closer than friends—I see old classmates hanging out with siblings they grew up with and I wish I had thirteen more years of memories, I wish I'd said something else in that last moment, or *she'd* said something else, and I wish—I wish she'd wanted to live more than she wanted to die in that final instant. I wish I could tell her what a *dick move* the last thing she ever did was, and I wish she could respond. Anyway, it's not your fault. I don't blame you for any of it, Grant Shepard."

She listens to his heartbeat slow down as she draws slow circles on his chest. She thinks he might be drifting off to sleep, when he mumbles, "I'm sorry I need this so much. I wish I didn't."

Don't be sorry, she thinks, a little desperately. *I want you to need me*.

When she looks up, his eyes are closed. She isn't sure why her heart feels like it's breaking, when it hasn't been working properly in years anyway.

GRANT WAKES UP and it's afternoon, and he hears a reassuring, soft *click-clack* of Helen working on her laptop behind his desk.

"How long was I out?" he asks grimly.

"A few hours," she answers. "It's almost one thirty."

He sits up, rubbing the sleep from his eyes. Embarrassment too. If he looks up and she's looking back at him with pitying eyes, he'll get in his car and drive to Canada.

"I think you should buy us lunch," Helen says, still typing. "Or we could go somewhere."

"It's your turn to pick lunch," he says.

"Then I pick that sandwich place everyone likes," Helen says. "Let's go."

He drives and she sits in the passenger seat as she updates him on the work that the others have done since this morning— Owen's delivered his outline, Tom and Eve have delivered their first draft, Nicole's sending in her revision, and Suraya sent the first three episodes along to production.

Helen mentions she's getting nervous about them reaching her episode, the penultimate one of the season, and he covers her hand briefly with his while the car idles at a traffic light. She looks over at him, a fond smile in her eyes, and his heart squeezes in a way that's becoming altogether too familiar.

They order a variation of the same combo and sit outside in the sun as they wait for their orders. Helen sips from a glass bottle of sparkling water, and as she sets it down on the spindly round metal table on the sidewalk, he thinks sharply—*I could love you.*

She eyes him warily.

"You look like you're about to say something stupid," she says.

"You're a mind reader now?" He lifts a brow.

Helen shakes her head and the waiter brings them their sandwiches in red plastic baskets.

"I'm a Grant's face reader," she says, opening her bag of chips and dumping them into the tray. "You get this look in the room sometimes, right before you say something like, 'Wild pitch, what if we change everything and toss all the hard work we've been doing for the past six hours out the window.'"

Grant laughs. "I'll keep it to myself, then."

Helen sips her water, then sets it down again. "Why didn't you tell me your birthday is next week?"

Grant frowns and squeezes a packet of ketchup into a corner for his fries. She steals one of them deftly, popping it into her mouth.

"I saw it on the tax forms on your desk," she adds.

"Okay, creep."

"You shouldn't just leave those out," she answers. "What do you wanna do for your birthday?"

"Nothing," he says, biting into his sandwich. "You."

Helen rolls her eyes. "Do you have a favorite cake? Or a restaurant?"

He leans back in his seat, considering. "You'd go with me to a restaurant?"

"We're at a restaurant now."

"We're at a sandwich shop on a lunch break," he mutters. "I mean an actual restaurant, with snooty waiters and tiny plates and dressed-up people on dates."

"Sure." Helen pauses. "We could invite the whole room."

Grant chuckles lowly as he wipes his mouth. "Right, the whole room. And drive home in separate cars?"

Helen shrugs.

Grant studies her. He feels like maybe there's a way to solve this, but he hasn't hit upon it yet. Maybe he needs a room full of professional screenwriters to workshop it out. He laughs at the thought, then something occurs to him.

"I know what I want," he says slowly. "I want you to throw a birthday party—a dinner party—at my house. Invite everyone from the room. Come early to help set up. Stay late to break it down. And I get to touch you whenever I want, until you walk out the door."

Helen flushes. "What, like, in front of people?"

Grant lifts a shoulder. "You asked me what I want."

"THAT MAN IS in love with you," Nicole says, reading over a draft of Helen's email inviting everyone to Grant's birthday party. "What even is happening here?"

Helen flushes. "A birthday party invitation, that's all."

She would be lying if she didn't suspect *some* feelings—she's caught him looking at her with that warm, soft expression a few too many times, and there was that moment on her balcony last week, talking about hypothetical girlfriends he should be dating instead, when her heart had jammed into her throat—*What about you?*

"Which you're sending, because you're . . . such great pals that you're hosting it at his house?" Nicole sips her wine skeptically. Helen is starting to regret accepting the invitation to come over to her house for "wine and whining." "If I'm wrong, then he's a psycho for asking. Are *you* in love with him?"

"No," Helen says firmly. *No.* "We're having fun, it's easy and convenient for now, and then it'll be over. It's just . . . I think sometimes it gets confusing. Because we knew each other before, under kind of intense circumstances, and it's impossible not to see each other all the time when we work together."

Everyone in the room knows about Grant and Helen's tangled connection from the past by now. It seems silly to her in retrospect that she thought they could keep it a secret for so long when Google exists. Helen still remembers the day they realized everyone else knew—some stupid plot point about a deadly car accident had come up in the room. A thick silence had descended over the table. Owen shot Tom and Eve a meaningful look, Saskia coughed lightly, Nicole was being *suspiciously* silent, and Helen suddenly realized, *everyone is avoiding eye contact*. She remembers looking up to see Grant having the same realization and sharing a private, laughing look with him. Suraya had been the last one still obliviously staring at the dry-erase board, only to turn around and instantly snap, "*What the fuck did I miss?*"

Only Nicole knows the full picture of past and present, though. (Saskia probably suspects too, given their last conversation at the precipice of everything, but has been too polite to ask.)

"You trauma bonded your way into mutual attraction." Nicole nods. "Healthy."

Helen laughs, then groans. "I think . . ." She pauses, carefully considering her words. "I think *he* might think he's in love, or not even love, but catching inconvenient feelings. I think he's the 'falling in love, catching feelings' type. You've met him."

"Yes," Nicole says dryly. "I have. You know, I do *like* Grant, as a friend. Maybe I should ask you what *your* intentions are here. I'd hate to see him heartbroken and left in the dust at the end of all of this."

Helen shifts uncomfortably.

"Grant knows what's happening," she says. "This is just . . . it's like a game we play. I keep us on track and he's always trying to push and see what's the most he can get. It's like we're negotiating, all the time, and it's . . . fun, I guess, otherwise we wouldn't both keep coming back. It forces us to pace ourselves. But he knows the rules. He wouldn't . . . he wouldn't ask for something he knows is impossible."

"Hm," Nicole says, and sips her wine. "Not gonna lie, that sounds confusing and kind of hot, but maybe you should be a little careful here, Hel. You're smart, but you're not smarter than dumbass lizard-brain feelings. You can still get hurt with your eyes wide open."

"That's a good line," Helen says. "You should put that in something."

"I'm such a *writer*," Nicole says, and they laugh, and Grant and his unspoken, tricky, possibly-there feelings don't come up again.

IN THE ROOM the following Monday, Suraya declines the invitation ("You'll have more fun without the boss around") and has her assistant ask for Grant's home address so she can send a bottle of champagne. Everyone else accepts.

"Nice of you to put this together, Helen," Tom adds, and Eve jabs him in the ribs.

"I'm, um, trying to make up for being so mean in high school, apparently," Helen answers, as Grant watches her from across the table with *I fucked you against a wall this morning* eyes.

"Anyway, production starts next week, and then the room's going to end pretty soon after that," Grant says. "It'd be nice to see you all not in this room, for once."

They spend the night at her place on Friday, so she can pick from the full scope of her wardrobe for the party tomorrow. She wears a silk robe as she lifts options in the absurdly large dressing room adjoining her bedroom and auditions them against her body for him.

"I like it," he says, when she holds up a flirty black dress.

"I like that one too," he says, when she pulls a vintage green dress.

"My prom dress might be around here somewhere, think you'd like that one too?" Helen huffs, and he laughs. He stands from the dressing room bench and pulls her back against his body, kissing her neck. "You're absolutely no help."

"I like watching you get dressed up," he says. "But it's late, and there are other things we could be doing."

She shivers against him and turns, and her arms lazily clasp around his neck as they sway gently to music that isn't playing.

"What time is it?" she asks.

He glances at the clock on her bedside table. "A little after midnight."

"Happy birthday," she says, and rises on her tiptoes to kiss him. He lets out a satisfied little "*huh*" before he kisses her back. The sound washes over her, and the familiar yearning feeling in her stomach returns. When he pulls back, her breaths come out in shaky little spurts.

"Sometimes I feel like I miss you when you're right in front of me," she says as he nudges her cheek with his nose. "Isn't that weird?"

He laughs, and tilts her face up to kiss her again instead. His hands slide down her arms and soon she finds herself lifted up, her legs wrapped around his waist as he walks them back into the bedroom. She helps him pull off his shirt, and by the time they fall onto her bed, all that's separating them is a thin layer of his cotton boxer briefs and her silk robe.

He hums slightly with thoughtful *hm*s as he pulls the tie of her robe and the bow comes undone quickly. He brushes the robe off her skin easily, like wrapping paper, and follows the path of his hands with his mouth.

She's shivering, she realizes, even though it's warm and his lips are hot.

"Do you miss me right now?" he murmurs against her stomach, and kisses softly down past her belly button, drifting maddeningly toward the tops of her thighs.

Her fingers tangle in his hair and she nods without thinking as she redirects him to where she wants him.

"Yes," she gasps, as he laves attention to the soft, secret spots of her. "It's so good, it feels so good."

He builds a slow and steady rhythm, then suckles against the tiny, sensitive nub he's become so familiar with, and she's surprised by her own sudden orgasm.

"*Fuck*," she gasps. "I didn't know . . . I was so close."

She looks down and he's watching her with fevered eyes; he looks *hungry* and *satisfied* at the same time. She thinks maybe this is how she looks at him too.

He drops another kiss on her inner thigh, then moves up until he's above her. Her hands drift down and she can feel a wet, sticky trail of precome against her leg, and the dampness of her own orgasm. It's messy, the way they want each other, and she doesn't seem to care.

"I've never wanted anything as much as I want you," he gasps when she squeezes him, as if he can hear her thoughts.

He grips her by the hips then and rolls them over so that she's perched above him, her hands on his shoulders. She sinks slowly onto him as he guides her down, reveling in the way he exhales and scrapes her skin with the force of his grip as she takes him farther into her body. She moves her hands up her own body because she knows he likes to watch her touch herself, and his eyes gleam with wanting as she cups and squeezes her breasts.

He grabs her hands then, and lifts them above her head as he leans forward to kiss her. There's a strange kind of intimacy in being pressed against him like this, as her hips draw slow circles below them.

He gasps against her mouth. "I'm not gonna last much longer."

"Me too," she murmurs. "Can you wait for me?"

He makes a small, pained sound at the back of his throat, and nods. "What do you need?"

"Just this." She squeezes him with her inner muscles, and his breathing goes ragged. "This, and you, and this, and you. . . ."

"Helen," he rasps into her neck. "You have me."

She falls over the edge then and feels him climax too. He comes in shaking waves, and she's surprised to feel tremors still racking through him when she returns back to earth. She holds his face in her hands and kisses him then, loving the taste of salt and *her* on his tongue.

"You have me too," she murmurs against his mouth.

He doesn't say anything, but drops his head to press a reverent kiss to her shoulder, and she feels the strangest sweep of melancholy wash over her. He chuckles when he looks back up at her.

"Missing me?" he asks, tucking a piece of hair behind her ear. She nods.

"But you're right here, crackerjack," he says, squeezing her ankle. "Happy birthday to me."

She laughs then, and he scoops her up and carries her into the shower, and she doesn't think about it again for the rest of the night.

Twenty-Five

It's remarkably easy to imagine what it'd be like to love Grant Shepard.

Helen sets up the dinner table with placemats he has because his mom forced him to take them back to California after Helen made a passing comment about liking their place settings. They're made from a plain linen fabric and feature a scrolling embroidery border ("stitched in the 1920s by his great-grandmother Margaret!") and are unlike anything Helen ever had growing up.

Grant cooks his own birthday meal—he's using old family recipes from a box she found in his kitchen a while back, and she once took an edible and separated out each dish she wanted him to make for her. Folded in between instructions on hot cross buns and Christmas roast and steak Diane, there are newspaper clippings boasting of local events featuring Grandma Vicki's famous German-Irish apple cake and Grandpa Carl judging a "nicest ears" competition. There's even a photo of seven-year-old Grant and Grandma Vicki in the kitchen, covered in frosting and bad sweaters and perfectly joyful smiles.

"I wish I knew you then," she says, touching the smiling Grant in the photo.

She thinks of where she must have been at the time—*in that first cramped apartment in Union, New Jersey, sharing a bedroom and learning about mind over matter, probably*—and feels some familiar ache stretching up.

Present-day Grant brushes a kiss to the side of her head and gently nudges her away from the stove to stir some delicious molten thing.

"You gotta stop saying things like that out loud—everyone will know," he says, a teasing note in his voice.

She turns and grabs him by the collar and kisses him very suddenly, and his arms come up automatically to meet her. When she releases him, he has an endearingly mussed quality about him, and she wonders how long she could make that last. He looks surprised, and pleased. It's a good combination on him, and she'd make him wear it every day if she had the right to.

"Okay," she says, and returns to her task of chopping spring onions.

He glances sideways at her.

"How much time do we have?"

She glances at her cell phone.

"Not a ton. Nicole's coming over early with Owen to heat something up in the oven."

She moves off to the sink, when he suddenly catches her in his arms.

"Not what I meant, crackerjack," he says, and she vaguely registers that he's got two nicknames for teasing her now—*sweetheart* for filth, *crackerjack* for something sweeter. "How much time do we have, you and I?"

She stares back into his eyes and thinks she's so close to falling into them, she might have already done it.

"Enough," she says.

"I'm not so sure about that," Grant answers slowly, rubbing

his thumb on her forearm, and the doorbell chimes. He lets her go. "Saved by the bell."

Nicole and Owen bring baked brie and charcuterie and demands for wine.

Owen slaps Nicole's arm when he sees Grant gently brush back Helen's hair as she stoops to open the oven door.

"Nothing, nothing," he cackles, when she turns around quizzically.

Grant covers her pinkie on the counter with his own, and she looks up at him for just a second before they hear Owen fake a heart attack, put up a staying hand, and say as he walks away, "This is too much. I need to gather myself."

Grant laughs and drops a kiss to Helen's shoulder. Nicole lifts a brow.

"Well," she says. "Hot."

And she leaves too. Grant turns to Helen, and they both laugh.

"I think maybe people were invested," she murmurs.

"Fucking TV writers," Grant laughs. "They should know better."

Tom and Eve arrive with a chocolate lava cake and Saskia brings bruschetta. No one says anything when Grant touches the small of Helen's back, or when her fingers hold on to him until the last possible moment when he leaves her side to check the carrots.

When he returns, he rubs her shoulder and his hand travels up to brush the nape of her neck. Helen catches his hand automatically and brushes a kiss against it without thinking.

"Now, come *on*," Tom says plaintively. "Someone else has to have seen that!"

The room bursts into laughter, and Helen feels herself

laughing too as Grant loops his free arm around her and presses a kiss to the side of her head.

This is what it would feel like to love Grant Shepard, she thinks, and it aches.

AFTER DINNER, EVERYONE leaves one by one, staggered, cheeks flushed with conversation, until only Tom and Eve are left.

"He's going to gloat about this forever," Eve says, and laughs, as they head to the hall. "He's been telling me I don't know what a 'soft launch' is for weeks."

"Hey, you guys should come over for dinner," Tom says, sounding slightly sloshed. "And if you get married, I should officiate—"

"Okay, let's get you home, Tommy," Eve says, and pushes him out the door as she mouths an apology at them. Grant shuts the door with a click behind them.

Leaving them alone together. Again.

Helen looks up at him, grinning. "Did you have a happy birthday?"

He laughs, and he can feel her laughing too when he kisses her.

"Helen," he says softly, and he watches her expression go from hazy and dreamy to wary and alert.

"No," she says. "Let's not talk anymore."

"I have something to tell you." He nudges her gently with his nose.

"Unless it's about—something else, I don't want to hear it," she says, and walks away.

He exhales and follows her into the kitchen. She's cleaning up, putting dishes in the dishwasher, her hair in a messy, frustrated ponytail. He's so in love with her it hurts.

"We can't not talk about this forever," he says.

"Sure," she says, rinsing things. "We won't be talking in a few weeks, anyway, so we can absolutely not talk about this . . . forever."

"That's crap and you know it," he says, annoyed he sounds like a 1950s movie gangster. "March is right around the corner and neither of us is going to want to be done with each other in a few weeks."

"You don't know what could happen in a few weeks," she says.

"It was a slow fall but a pretty permanent crash, Helen," he says, and he can't help the acid note in his voice. "I'm in love with you."

"No, you're not," she says.

"Yes, I am," he says softly. "It's my birthday, and I say so."

Helen shakes her head and walks to the opposite corner, out of grasp.

"You just think you are," she says, studying her hands. "This isn't . . . you care about me, but . . . some fucked-up thing in our past is what's tying us together. We never would have started this otherwise, and you're confusing the two things—"

"That's not what this is," he says. "This is about who you are and who I am, right now, in the present. Why won't you let me just—"

She kisses him then, cutting him off from *love you*. It's a hungry, angry kiss, and he returns it.

"Fine, then," he says against her mouth, and he's suddenly cold despite the kitchen heat. "It's my birthday. Lie to me. Treat me like you love me back."

His kiss slows and she pulls away from him. She's staring up at him and there's something crashing in her chest at his expression.

"Grant," she says, and reaches out a hand to his face.

When she kisses him, it's slow and deliberate. It broods into something bruising and searching in seconds.

"Is it so hard to pretend you love me, Helen?" he asks softly, kissing a trail up to her forehead.

"This is very," she breathes, "melodramatic."

"We're artist types," he answers. "Humor me. I'll even take back what I said. I'm not in love with you at all, Helen. There, we're even. Now we can both just . . . act like it."

"Should I put on my best Katharine Hepburn?" she says, softly affecting a transatlantic accent.

"Yes, sweetheart," he murmurs, returning it in his best Jimmy Stewart.

Helen laughs softly. "You're so fucking corny," she says, and kisses him sweetly. "I love you."

SHE'S LYING, SHE'S pretending, this isn't real.

"You did that so well," Grant says, as some knife of a feeling twists in his chest.

Helen lets out a half-embarrassed laugh and ducks her head.

"I would have fallen in love with you sooner, if you'd let me," he says, and lifts her chin so he can watch her hear it. "You're so easy to love, Helen."

She kisses him then, and he thinks to himself *still counts still counts still counts* as he loves her back.

HELEN WAKES UP in the blue light of four a.m. and gets in her car. She pulls up a Spotify playlist—"driving away from the stupid damn love of my life"—and heads home.

HE SHOWS UP at her condo Sunday afternoon, looking tired and drawn.

"I'm sorry," he says first, and reaches out. She buries herself in his arms in a crushing hug, and he rubs a soothing hand down her back and up the nape of her neck. "Won't bring it up again, crackerjack. I know the rules, I promise."

"This is all I can give you," she whispers. "This is the best I can do."

"I'll take it, you know I'll take it," he says gruffly into her hair, thinking some senseless, endless stream of *want, need, give, take, please.*

He kisses her then, and she kisses him back.

Twenty-Six

The night before the first day of filming, Helen can't sleep.

"That's normal," Grant tells her sleepily, when she shows up on his porch at one a.m. "It's like Christmas, or the night before open-heart surgery."

He won't be on set in the morning; he'll be in the writers room still, as they finish breaking the last episode of the season. For the best, probably—ever since his birthday, it's felt like they're on borrowed time and she's trying to get used to the idea of not having him around always. It's almost March—and in a few weeks, he'll be done and ready to move on to a new show and *it'll be the most convenient time to let him go*. But she can already feel herself coming up with more excuses—why not wait until they're done with production in late April—even as she knows it'll only hurt more the longer they wait to break things off.

She starts crying when he hugs her and he laughs into her hair.

"You really hate being comforted that much, huh," he says, and she nods into his shoulder.

He kisses the side of her face first, then the salty tears off her cheeks, before he reaches her mouth. "Helen, I'm not trying to comfort you. I'm trying to seduce you."

She laughs and kisses him back, her arms twining behind his neck as he lifts and carries her into the bedroom. She has to be on set at seven a.m., and she lets him keep her up until almost three in the morning—laughing, gasping, touching.

When she slips out of bed at six a.m., he's still half sleeping, his hair tousled and a slight frown on his face from the early-morning light.

"You're always leaving me," he mumbles, and she walks off before the squeezing in her heart makes her do something foolish, like stay.

HELEN CALLS AS she drives home from set—it's just after six p.m. and they wrapped almost an hour early their first day.

"That's a good thing, right?" she says anxiously. "It means the director knows what she's doing? Or is it, I don't know, leaving things on the table . . ."

"It's a good thing," Grant says. "Production can be brutal if you're going a full twelve hours every day. Wrapping early on your first day sets a good tone."

She tells him about meeting the crew and how she thinks the first assistant director hates her but she has an ally in the director of photography, how the wardrobe team had questions for her that she was able to answer (*surprising!*), and how the cast looked so different in costume and full hair/makeup, she was thrown.

"It was like they stepped out of my brain and into reality—it was so weird in a good way. I felt like I was starstruck by my own characters."

Grant smiles at this and feels a strange sense of pride. A memory from high school randomly comes online—Helen, standing at the front of their AP English classroom, reading her essay to the class at the request of the teacher, as an example of good writing. He remembers no one paying much attention, himself included, and feeling a little bad about it. It had obviously meant a lot to her to be chosen.

He thinks people will pay attention this time, when the show comes out. It's a good one, and they've done a lot of work to keep what's special about her books in the series while letting it grow into its own thing. One of his favorite storylines isn't in the books at all, and Helen had surprisingly agreed it was one of her favorites too.

"Good first day, then?" he asks, when he opens the door and she's on the porch, still on the phone with him.

"Mm." She nods, and falls into his waiting arms. "Missed you, though."

He smiles into her hair and wonders how much longer they have.

HELEN HITS THE stop button on her phone alarm, telling her it's time to drive to LAX.

She's spent the last six hours obsessively cleaning her apartment, scrubbing the floors and checking through her closets and laundry, making sure they're free from any trace of *anything*. She doesn't think her mother will go through all her individual drawers looking for drugs under the vague pretense of missing a sweater like she did in high school, but Helen checks through them all herself just in case anyway (there's nothing, of course), just as she did then. Her mother had always seemed so certain Helen was hiding *something*, that sometimes Helen herself wasn't sure she wasn't.

"Next time you fly, there's an easier airport to pick you up from, in Burbank," she tells them as her parents load their suitcases (twenty years old and "They work just fine!" despite a broken wheel and stuck handle) into her car. "LAX is kind of chaotic."

"Next time, next time, what next time," Mom grumbles, looking out the window at construction signs and closed-off traffic lanes. "You are only in LA a short while."

Helen ignores the growing tension headache and drives them to a Radisson hotel nearby.

"A car will come and take you guys to set in the morning," she says. "There should be a drive-on pass for you at the gate, but you can call me if you have any problems."

"I don't know any of the words you are saying," Mom says. "My head hurts."

"Are you hungry?" Helen asks. "We can go get food."

"Yes, we should get food," Dad agrees. "Unless you already ate."

"I haven't eaten yet."

"You haven't eaten?" Mom's brows snap together. "It's almost eight p.m."

Helen wants to smash her own forehead into the steering wheel. "Let's get food," she says, and grips the wheel as she maneuvers them out of the hotel parking lot.

She takes them to In-N-Out and thinks about explaining the secret menu to them, but thinks better of it. When they sit down to share their meal, Mom unfolds herself happily, taking out napkins and packages of nuts she got on the plane from her purse.

"Thanks, Mom," Helen says wearily.

"So," Mom says, eating a plain french fry. "How are things?"

"They're good," Helen says automatically. "The first week of production went well. I was nervous at first, but everyone's doing a really good job and the showrunner's really happy."

"I don't understand why you don't run your own show," Dad says, biting into his burger.

"Because I've never done it before," Helen explains for the millionth time. "But Suraya's really great. It's like we're two brains in a pod."

It's a play on a familiar expression that's almost certainly gone over their heads. Helen often wonders how much of her relationship with her parents has been lost in translation and how different things would be if they'd never moved to this country. But then maybe she wouldn't have become a writer, or at least this kind of writer, telling these kinds of stories, with these specific people, at this specific time in her life, and she finds herself familiarly grateful that her parents made the decisions they made.

They go to her condo afterward ("just to have a look") and Helen feels a small surge of pride when Dad looks out the window and says, "You have a nice view."

Mom pats down each couch cushion to inspect its softness before she sits down, then bounces up and down slightly as if she's testing wares at a mattress store.

"The studio pays for all of this?"

"Yep," Helen says. "Until production's over."

"Very nice," Mom says approvingly. "This is very nice."

And it *is* nice, Helen thinks—letting her parents see her thrive on another coast.

See, she tries to silently communicate, *you don't have to worry about me. I'll survive.*

They stay for exactly one pot of tea, Dad quietly walking from room to room while Mom starts doing dishes even though Helen protests she has a dishwasher for that.

She had felt slightly itchy and nervous about having her parents in this space—imagining them moving within the scenes of her California life played slightly wrong in her brain, like a poorly done double exposure. But as she listens to Mom gossip idly about their old friends while toweling off plates and Dad flicks lights on and off in various rooms, she feels a sense of *home* wash over the condo, and finds she doesn't mind it as much as she thought she would.

She walks them down to the lobby to wait for their Uber, because Mom insists it's too late for Helen to drive them to the Radisson and back, and Helen's grateful because it *is* getting late.

She waits until their car is out of sight before she calls Grant.

"How'd it go?" he asks, his voice low in a way where she can tell he's lying in bed.

"Good," she says. "They came to the condo, like I said they would. They liked it. They came dangerously close to saying they were proud of me out loud."

Grant chuckles and she thinks, *I would keep this feeling, if I could.*

Twenty-Seven

Helen's parents *love* visiting the set.

A production assistant sets up chairs ("What, just for us?") at video village and Mike, the sound guy, gets them head-sets so they can hear the production audio. Suraya introduces them to the cast and crew as the parents of the brain that created the brainchild of this show. "So really, it's like they're the grandparents of our show."

Mom preens even as she protests the fuss and Dad spends most of his time wandering back and forth from catering to bring Helen snacks that she didn't ask for.

"You're a big deal here," Mom says when they get ushered to the front of the lunch line. "So much special treatment."

"They're all just trying to impress you," Helen mutters, a little embarrassed. "It's really the crew that's the big deal. I've never seen so many people work together so smoothly. It's kind of amazing."

She had found the concept of production and shooting to be intimidatingly foreign, a strange beast with strange terms she was still learning. And if working in a writers room with seven other writers was a strain on her introvert-leaning resources, surely a behemoth of a crew of hundreds of strangers with very specific jobs she couldn't even begin to fathom would be even worse?

Yet Helen has found set life to be unexpectedly appealing.

It works like a cross between an army regiment and a fine Swiss watch, each person reporting to someone else, each person doing a job that keeps the heart of production ticking. She finds it's easier to talk to people individually this way—chatting with Cherise, the second camera assistant, about the short film she's shooting over the weekend as she cleans lens filters, or having Jeff, the gaffer, show her photos of the elaborate lawn display he's putting together for St. Patrick's Day. She likes getting to know people as they do the jobs that they're so good at—she remembers something Suraya once said about comfort zones, and realizes that the set is a comfort zone for a lot of interesting, highly skilled artists and technicians, who fill the place with a thrilling buzz of activity between every *cut* and *action*.

She's enjoyed finding her own place on set. Suraya sits next to the pilot director, occasionally whispering something in her ear before the director nods and shoots off to pass along notes to the actors. Department heads come up with questions for upcoming episodes and Suraya leaves the big wardrobe and set design questions to Helen, while she deals with calls from the studio and network and postproduction.

"I told you we'd make a good team," Suraya says, and grins at Helen as they finish their dual creative sidebars at lunch.

Helen doesn't actually remember Suraya ever saying they'd make a good team, verbatim, but she's grateful nonetheless.

"She is a good boss," Dad says after Suraya leaves their lunch table to confer with the director and line producer about something they're shooting tomorrow. "She knows how to handle many things at once. You should learn from her."

"I am," Helen says.

Suraya dismisses Helen from set a few hours early ("Your parents are in town. You don't wanna bore them with four more hours of this—go treat them to dinner!") and Helen takes them to a trendy sushi spot in Studio City for dinner.

"What was your favorite part?" Helen asks as she pours them tea.

"Seeing your stories and words come to life," Mom says. "It was very wonderful and amazing."

"All those people, there to make *your* TV show," Dad says.

"It's not *my* TV show," Helen protests. "I have a shared 'created by' credit, but Suraya's the showrunner, and we have a whole team of writers, and—"

"Yes, but none of it would exist if you didn't write your books," Dad says. "We're very proud of you."

Helen thinks her heart might burst from the feeling of hearing him say it and excuses herself to the bathroom so they don't see her inexplicably start crying. She's quite sure she wouldn't know what to do if she ever saw her father cry. The least she can do is return the favor.

She washes her face in the bathroom, touches up her makeup, and smiles at her reflection tentatively. *It's been a good day, spending time with my parents, letting them into my life.* She spends so much of her time experiencing a low-grade resentment toward them, over a million little injustices from childhood that don't *really* matter anymore, she's forgotten this feeling—when she's happy, and they're happy, and they feel like what she thinks of when she thinks of a happy, loving family.

She returns to their table and Mom and Dad are fighting in low, hushed Cantonese.

"What's wrong?" she asks.

Dad shakes his head at Mom, Mom says something in Cantonese, and Helen is able to pick out the phrase "*Let me talk to her.*"

"What is it?" Helen repeats, a sense of foreboding growing in the pit of her stomach.

"Why," Mom says, her fingers white-knuckle gripping her own cell phone, "is there a writer with this . . . this name working for you?"

She turns the screen to Helen and it's a prep-schedule email from the production office, plainly listing "Episode 102, Day 1 of Prep: Director: Kasey Langford / Writer: Grant Shepard."

Helen stares blankly at the shape of Grant's name on the screen. *Why is his name on Mom's phone?*

"Your mom asked them to put us on the email list for everything," Dad says slowly. "She was so worried we wouldn't show up to the right place at the right time."

Helen blinks at Mom's cell phone.

Grant Shepard, it seems to repeat accusingly.

An old memory comes back online, of Mom sitting at the edge of Helen's bed: "Grant Shepard, that's the name of the boy who killed your sister. Do you know him?"

"I . . . it's not . . . it wasn't on purpose," Helen says finally.

"So it is *him*," Mom says, and it sounds like she's spitting out *him*.

"He's not . . ." Helen trails off, because she doesn't know what she can say to make this better. *He's not that bad. He's not that important to me. He's not going to be around much longer.*

"*Why?*" Mom hisses.

"I didn't know he was going to be on the show. Really, I didn't. I told you, I'm not the showrunner."

"*What other secrets are you keeping from us?*" Mom bursts out, sounding hysterical.

Dad reaches out to calm her and Helen feels the blood rush to her cheeks.

"I'm not . . ." Helen inhales and exhales. She doesn't want to lie to them. "I didn't want to keep this a secret. I just didn't know how to tell you."

"My own daughter," Mom says in disbelief. She stands.

"Mom."

"I will *not* eat here," Mom says, and after a quick, harsh word to Dad in Cantonese, she exits.

Helen looks back at her dad, who suddenly looks so much older and more tired than she remembers him.

"Dad," she says.

He puts up a staying hand.

"You should have told us," he says firmly. And stands, and leaves.

Helen blinks back tears and waits a few minutes, until she's certain her parents have left in an Uber. She pays for their meal to be boxed up and gets in her car and drives down the freeway until she's over the hill and in the familiar winding streets of Silver Lake.

She rings the doorbell and keeps ringing until the door swings open. Grant appears in sweats; he has headphones around his neck.

"Sorry, I was writing . . ." He trails off when he looks at her face. "Something's happened."

"My parents . . ." she says, and tries not to cry. He pulls her into a hug wordlessly and she feels suddenly like she's in a twilight zone, driving to the homecoming king's house to cry about her parents. *If my seventeen-year-old self could see me now*, she thinks humorlessly.

They separate, and she finds somehow they've crossed the threshold into his house. He shuts the door and she brushes the moisture from her face. She owes him a better explanation.

"They saw your name on an email."

"That's . . . unfortunate," Grant says, a muscle ticking in his jaw.

"They don't even know . . ." Helen trails off as she thinks about how her mother would react if she knew the full truth of the past several months. "And they just . . . it was exactly what I thought would happen, if they ever found out. It was *exactly* what I thought it would be."

Grant reaches her side again and strokes her back soothingly. "You didn't do anything wrong. You tried to get me to quit, remember?"

"I should have known how much this would hurt them," she says, shaking her head. "I shouldn't have . . ."

She looks over to him and finds he's watching her intently, a frown between his brows.

"How could I do this to them?" she asks, and she's not sure who she's asking.

"You didn't do anything to them," Grant answers, and she knows he doesn't understand. "They're your parents. They'll be mad for a while, and then they'll come around. It's not . . ."

He trails off, and she gives him a look. "Please don't say 'It's not that bad.'"

"I was going to say, it's not the end of the world," he says.

He CAN SEE she's turning over all this information in her head and it's driving her to an inevitable conclusion.

"Helen," he says, trying to pull her out of it. "I know you didn't want this to happen, but they were going to find out eventually. If not during production, then once the show aired. They were always going to find out."

Helen nods slowly and he wishes she would look at him.

"Maybe it's better this way," he says.

She looks up at him sharply then.

"We can't do this anymore," she says. "Obviously."

"Obviously," he repeats, stunned.

"It's bad enough you're working on the show; it's just pure dumb luck they haven't found out about . . . about us."

About us. What could anyone even know *about us*, Grant wonders, when he's not sure himself. It's been just over two months of having the confusing right to claim an *us* with Helen, and he feels like he's still untangling the knots in his brain from that first night they spent together in his childhood bedroom.

"I disagree," Grant says, then adds as an afterthought, "Obviously."

"We knew this couldn't go anywhere—we said that from the start," Helen says, standing, and he has the horrible feeling she's already made up her mind, maybe before she even walked through the door. "It's the only reason I agreed to it."

"Not the only reason," Grant says, and he can't keep the harshness out of his tone. "I remember some other reasons you found compelling enough."

"Why are you fighting me on this?" Helen says, and she seems so genuinely confused, it's a stab to the gut.

"Why the fuck do you think?" Grant answers, and walks to the kitchen for a glass of water.

"If this is about"—she waves a hand as she follows him into the kitchen—"about your birthday party . . ."

"When I said I was in love with you, yes," Grant mutters, and drinks his water.

"You knew," Helen starts, and there are tears of frustration in her eyes. He wants to kiss them away, which is stupid because she hates being comforted. "You *know* why it's impossible."

"You keep saying words like *impossible* but I think maybe you thought it was impossible to tell your parents I was working on the show until you had to do it," Grant says.

"Okay, but doesn't my parents' reaction to that prove my point exactly?" Helen says. "If I told them everything, it would be . . . it would be the end of their world."

What about mine? he thinks dramatically, but doesn't say it.

"I don't know what their reaction would be, if you told them everything," Grant says finally, trying to keep his tone measured. "They're your parents. If you think it'd be bad, you're probably right. But . . . we're grown adults, Helen. We don't need permission from anyone but each other."

"Right, because all the healthy relationships are the ones where they have no one but each other." Helen laughs, short.

"That's not what I'm saying."

"I never . . ." She looks away from him, as if she'll find the right words in his cabinets somehow. *Good luck*, he thinks, *those cabinets work for me.* "I never wanted this to be anything but temporary. It was fun, and convenient, and maybe the fact that it was a little taboo made it exciting—"

"Don't fucking do that," he says. "Don't cheapen this."

"The point is, I never saw a future here," she says. "I was upfront about that. If your feelings changed, that's . . . unfortunate, but there's nothing I can do about how I feel."

"Unfortunate," he mutters darkly. "That's me, Grant Shepard: Unfortunate."

"There's literally a million other people out there we could be happy with," Helen says softly.

He looks up at her sharply then. Helen feels the air leave the room.

"Do you want me to beg?" he asks. "I'll beg. Please, Helen."

Grant closes the distance between them in a few short strides and suddenly she's in his arms, and he's kissing her forehead, then her cheek, her neck, her shoulder. She can feel the shape of *please*, *please*, *please* forming against her skin with each kiss, and he's sinking onto his knees, kissing her hands, and her heart is breaking.

"You said once it'd be easier if we could say nothing's happened," he says softly. "We can still do that. We don't ever have to . . ."

Helen laughs humorlessly.

"*Something's* happened," she says. "This, this thing between us, it's the farthest thing from *nothing*."

A muscle ticks in Grant's jaw.

"I'm in love with you," he says.

Helen pulls her hands away from him. She sinks down to the floor and leans back against his cabinets, tired. "I wish you wouldn't say that. It makes things so much harder."

Grant laughs to himself. "Right."

He stares sullenly at her shoes and Helen wishes she could reach out and touch him.

"We said either of us could end this, at any time," she reminds him, instead. "It was supposed to be . . . painless."

"It doesn't feel painless," he says. "Does it?"

He looks up at her then and her breath catches in her throat. There's something piercingly vulnerable about his expression, and she can't bring herself to lie to him.

"No." She swallows. "It doesn't."

"I'm not crazy—you felt it too, right?" he asks. "This thing between us, it's different, it's . . . special. That sounds so fucking lame. It's not special, it's . . . it's a feeling, in my gut, like—like I've been waiting for this. For *you*."

Helen nods mutely. "I felt it too," she whispers finally.

"So what, we're supposed to just . . . give it up?" he asks, grimacing. He drinks his water and she wishes she'd asked for a glass too.

"I want to be happy. I want to be healthy," she says softly. "I can't do that with you. There's always going to be some part of me that wonders if the reason it's happening at all is because of some fucked-up thing in our past."

Grant shakes his head. "That's not the reason this is happening."

"Maybe if things had been different." She swallows. "Maybe if we'd met again later, or if we'd never known each other in the first place."

Grant laughs shortly. "I'm glad we're together now," he says. "I'm sorry it didn't happen sooner."

"I think you'll be glad we ended this in a few months," Helen says, and he's already shaking his head. "You'll meet someone who's fun and interesting and who can love you back without . . . without all this tortured drama."

"I like your tortured drama," he says plainly.

Helen isn't sure how much more of this she can take, but she also doesn't want to have this conversation with him ever again. So she stays. He looks at her, and all the warm, buried emotions she's glimpsed in his eyes before are there now, blazing quietly.

Grant tilts his head back against the wall. "Could you have loved me back, do you think? Or was it . . . always doomed?"

Helen swallows. *I do, I do, I do*, her heart seems to say with every beat.

"You know me," she says softly. "Always with the doom and gloom."

"I love you," he says again, staring at her. The corner of his mouth lifts. "It's kind of nice to say it out loud. Even under the circumstances."

Helen wipes moisture from her cheeks and realizes she's crying. In an instant, he's next to her, pulling her into his arms, stroking her hair, and whispering soothingly to her, "It's okay, you don't have to say it back, it's okay, I love you, I love you, I love you."

She kisses him to stop the words in his mouth, but she can still feel the shape of them against her lips as he kisses her back, in his hands coming up to cup her face. She can feel it radiating from the heat of his fingertips on her cheek, in the desperate sweep of his tongue, and the insistent tattooing rhythm in her chest echoing *I love you, I love you, I love you*, until she's no longer sure if it's coming from him or her.

Grant attempts to end the kiss first, slowly, coming back for a last kiss, then another, and another, until he's almost laughing against her mouth.

"Helen, we have to stop," he murmurs, and kisses her nose.

"This can't end on my nose," she answers, and he lets out a short "*ha*."

She holds him by the chin and presses a final (*really*) kiss against his mouth—it's short, firm, and unbearably *warm*—then she stands.

He looks up at her, and she looks down at him.

"You're leaving, then," he says.

She nods.

"Don't come back now, ya hear?" he says, in a terrible Jimmy Stewart drawl, humor in his eyes. The laughter dims, and he stares at her with a bleak expression of hopeless *wanting*. "I mean it."

She nods again and swallows, then leaves the kitchen.

He doesn't follow her, but he does stand and watch from the doorway of the kitchen as she gets her coat and bags. She looks back at him when she opens the door and he lifts two fingers in a half-hearted goodbye. She wishes instantly she hadn't looked back—the image of him is too easy to memorize, and she's already trying to forget the shape of him standing there and how easily she would fit into the crook of his neck.

"Bye," she mutters so quietly she's sure he can't even hear it, and walks out the door.

She doesn't listen to anything as she drives home and cries so much she briefly thinks it's raining from how blurry her vision gets at a stoplight on Sawtelle Boulevard. It's not, though, and she keeps her emotions in check long enough to get home in one piece.

Twenty-Eight

The biggest fucking joke of all is that they start prep on his episode the next morning, so Grant scrubs his face raw, puts on clothes and shoes and aftershave like it's a normal day, and goes into work.

He stops by the production office to introduce himself to the prepping director, who he knows a little because she worked on another show he did a few years ago.

"It's a great script," she says with that air of friendly distraction all episodic directors seem to carry, a million plates spinning in their minds. "It's gonna be a fun one."

"Yeah," he says, and laughs at himself. "It was a love letter. To the books."

She waits for him to say something else, anything else, and he realizes he's keeping her from her work. There are giant blueprints of all their standing sets on the walls behind her, and he's alarmed to find them starting to swim and blur in his field of vision. He rubs his eyes and clears his throat.

"There's, um, a thing at the top of the third act, that's setting up something later in the season, not sure if it's obvious, but I'm sure it'll come up at the tone meeting," he says, mostly for something to say.

"Great." She nods. "I'll keep an eye out for it, then."

"Great," he says stupidly, and walks away.

He spends the rest of the morning reading through incoming notes from Suraya about revisions on Owen's script that she doesn't have time to do, so could he please take care of them, and Saskia's new draft, and emails from his agent sending him books for his consideration to adapt, because apparently working on *The Ivy Papers* has proven he can work around intellectual property and that opens a whole new world of doors.

He doesn't go to set with the director for her initial walk-through of their soundstages, because he isn't sure if Helen's parents will still be there. Helen herself almost certainly will and he can't tell if that makes the decision harder or easier. He tries not to search for her every time he looks out his window at the studio lot below, and is irritated by the fact that he's a little devastated every time she's not there.

He's partially relieved when Suraya swings by his office at lunch to tell him she doesn't need him to cover his own episode on set, that she'd rather have him take charge of the closing weeks of the writers room.

"You got it, boss," he says, reminding himself who he works for.

He turns on the video feed to the soundstages at the end of the day, because they're still filming and some surviving idiotic thread of hope in him insists, because maybe, maybe she'll walk in front of the camera during a rolling reset and he'll get to see her.

She doesn't, of course, but he finds the familiar sound of production soothing anyway.

"You can forget about this, right?" a pouting, blond mean girl says to her mousier costar. She leans forward and grows hazy, then her face breaks into a nervous smile as she looks into camera. "Sorry. Totally blew past my mark."

The bell rings and the screen goes to black as the camera cuts, only to return again, the same setup, take two. The crew's moving fast now; everyone wants to go home.

"You can forget about this," the actress repeats. "Right?"

Grant has never liked this line. He thinks Suraya has a tendency to write the subtext of a scene into dialogue, a leftover habit from a decade of working on the most networky of network procedural dramas. She hits a note, then she hits it again, and then *one more time* for good measure, though he'll grant that sometimes it works for dramatic effect, in end-of-episode closing monologue montages paired with good needle drops.

"I'm sorry, is it my line? I thought she had more. . . ." The other actress glances over her shoulder at the camera and he knows Suraya's probably thinking about ways to rewrite the finale so they can murder her.

"No, I do, I was just taking a lil dramatic pause," the blond actress says with a self-deprecating eye roll. "We can take it back from the top."

"Whenever you're ready," a voice says from off camera, and he knows it's the director, but he still listens closer anyway, in case he can hear anyone else.

You can forget about this, right?

Helen's mother doesn't come to set on the second day, but her dad does.

He's quietly supportive and smiles and nods at the crew members who welcome him back for another round at the circus. He's on a first-name basis with their craft-services department and he brings Helen a cup of tea when they're going into hour thirteen of their longest shoot day yet.

"Thanks, Dad," she murmurs, and means it.

He nods and sits back down in a black folding chair, his knees cracking as he does.

They haven't spoken about dinner last night, but Dad tells her between setups for the last shot of the day that Mom will be there tomorrow.

"That's good," Helen says, and manages a smile.

There have been at least two more emails from production today that contain the name *Grant Shepard*—she knows he'll be at the table read tomorrow at lunch and in the tone meeting afterward, and she's dreading it almost as much as she's looking forward to it.

She thinks maybe she can bear it, if she can catch glimpses of him for now, before she has to give him up forever. They won't even be in the same room; production is shooting on location tomorrow so everyone will just be Zooming in from trailers and offices across town. She wonders if he'll be in his office or working from home. She wonders if he'll keep his camera on.

Part of her can't believe her life is this dramatic—more dramatic, it feels, than even the scenes of the soapy teen drama they're filming. Or maybe that's just how it feels *right now* and she'll be able to look back on this time with some kind of detached fondness someday. That even this keen sense of *missing him* will be something she grows to appreciate, because it throws every moment of this time in her life into sharper relief and maybe she'll even be grateful because it found its way into the art somehow.

It would be such a fucking waste if the art was bad too, after all this hurt and drama.

So she focuses on the work. She nudges Suraya when she thinks a phrase could be tweaked to help the actors, she sends references of random micro-influencers to the costume designer, she creates a whole Pinterest board for a single location that's being used only once for the production designer.

"Don't work too hard," Jeff, the gaffer, calls out to her after they wrap, and she knows now it's his daily send-off to everyone. "We need you here tomorrow."

"See you tomorrow," she says, and gives him a little salute as she packs up.

"Good day," Dad says as they walk out the giant barn doors of the soundstage. It's always jarring, leaving the fake afternoon light and walking into pitch darkness. "You got a lot done."

Helen laughs at the way he says it, as if she's the only one responsible for it.

"Yeah, well," she says. "I work with some great professionals."

"Everyone is working very hard," Dad agrees. "Your mom will be glad to hear about it."

Helen lets out a soft "*ha*" at that. She has no idea what kinds of private conversations Mom and Dad have within their marriage. She's never seen them kiss or flirt or drop so much as an *I love you*. She imagines they must hold some kind of love for each other she doesn't understand, for them to still be together after all this time and all this pain. But she doesn't want that kind of love for herself, and then she stops thinking about it because she can't bear to contemplate what kind of love she *would* want.

She drops Dad off with the sleek black shuttle to take him back to the hotel and he gives her a gruff, one-armed hug. It's probably the third hug he's ever given her in his life—she remembers one at her college graduation, and another awkwardly coached one by a photographer at one of her book events. They're just not the hugging type. But she smiles, pats him awkwardly back—anyone watching would think he was an old favorite professor of hers and maybe that describes her relationship with her father the best—and waves as he's driven off.

As she walks to her car, she briefly considers the dinner options waiting for her at home—she stupidly left all the takeaway sushi at Grant's house last night and she doesn't have the energy to cook something from scratch.

She isn't ready for it when she sees his familiar gray convertible in its designated parking spot across from hers—he's still *here*. She looks back toward the building containing the writers room and wonders what's keeping him here so late. A last-minute meeting with Suraya, maybe, or revisions ahead of the table read. She tries not to think of all the late nights they've spent here, flirting across a table, or playing a game where he tries to distract her as she works.

Some traitorous part of her tugs at her feet and she takes a half step toward the building.

But then the rest of her—*mind over matter*—wrestles back control of her disloyal limbs and she gets in her car and drives off the lot.

She has a long enough drive back to Santa Monica to talk herself into and out of various drive-through options, finally concluding that the leftover chicken salad in her fridge will have to do, and she probably has a protein shake in there somewhere too.

She's still vaguely entertaining a left turn into an upcoming McDonald's—*she would like fries with this sadness, please*—when there's a thundering *boom* that makes her think for a moment of a theme park roller coaster, a slow-motion surrealness as her surroundings seem to spin away from her, and then her world flips upside down once, twice, and then there's a horrible, metallic *screech*, before it all crashes into splintering black and crunching glass.

Twenty-Nine

She wakes up to the faint beep of a heart rate monitor and Suraya's frowning face.

"Good," she says. "You're awake."

Helen looks around and sees she's in a clean, if very pink, hospital room, and the dull ache in almost every bone in her body reminds her why. She's wearing a yellow patient gown, the air smells like lemon cleaning products, and she feels strangely color-coordinated to the room's pastels, as if she *belongs* here.

A doctor—a very pretty one, and Helen wonders vaguely if she's ever considered acting—comes in before she can muster a proper response to Suraya. The doctor briskly recites a catalogue of the ways Helen Zhang has been broken—broken arm, broken clavicle, and a fractured rib that narrowly missed becoming something more serious and potentially fatal.

"And whiplash," she adds. "That's pretty common. We put you on a lot of pain medication and sedation so you could sleep. Your parents are outside, asking to see you."

"No," Helen says, and realizes it's the first time she's spoken out loud in—however long she's been out. Her voice is croaky from lack of use. "Not—not yet."

The thought of her mother's white-lipped *concern* is more than she can bear right now and she doesn't feel even a little bad about preserving her peace a bit longer.

"Suit yourself," the doctor says, and leaves to see to some other injured, pastel patient in need of care.

Leaving her alone with Suraya.

"I'm sorry," Helen says automatically.

Suraya waves a hand. "What do you have to be sorry for? It's not your fault that truck blew a red light out of nowhere."

Helen suddenly wants to cry and she's not sure why. She smiles apologetically at Suraya instead. It hurts unexpectedly and she realizes there are bandaged cuts on her face. "You shouldn't have to be here right now. I know how busy you are."

"Well, the fact is I'm here now. Meetings get pushed all the time for less," she says. "But why am I your emergency contact?"

"Oh." Helen flushes with hot embarrassment.

Of course. Suraya didn't come just out of friendly concern; she came because someone looked up Helen's records and *called* her. The sting of humiliation at this hurts more than the rib fracture.

"I didn't really know anyone in LA, when I was filling out all those forms," she says. "I should have asked. I'm sorry."

"It's fine," Suraya says, with a glint of humor. "A little weird— I wouldn't recommend doing it on your next job—but then, I think you have more friends in this city now. Nicole and Saskia are out there. Saskia's been crying her eyes out, the poor girl."

"Oh," Helen says, and some warm feeling takes her by surprise. She has friends waiting for her.

"Grant's here too, obviously," Suraya says, and Helen tries to unpack every word of that brief sentence.

"Right," she says blankly.

Suraya gives her a half-hearted smile. "I like you, Helen, and you seem strong enough to take this, so if I could give you a little unsolicited advice?"

Helen nods.

"There's two things someone told me at the start of my

career. One—get your house in order." Suraya tilts her head. "You can't really prioritize the things you need to if you're wasting precious energy on your tortured personal life, as romantic as it may feel in the moment."

Helen coughs and feels another hot flash of embarrassment. *Is that how you see me?*

"The second thing, talk to a shrink about your mommy or daddy issues. Because the most important thing to remember about anyone you're working for is—I'm not your mommy and I'm not your daddy. I'm not still going to love you at the end of the day if you make that day miserable, because I already have my own kids for that."

Suraya's eyes flit to her phone and she adds, as an afterthought, "Not that my kids make me miserable. It's just . . . you're never really able to stop thinking and worrying about them, once you have them. All those awful clichés about your heart living outside your chest."

"Okay," Helen says softly. "I'll talk to my therapist about my mommy issues."

Suraya smiles. "I always thought mommy issues were more powerful than daddy issues," she says thoughtfully. "Certainly more motivating. But we can save that for a season two discussion. Who do you want me to send in first?"

Helen thinks, and chooses cowardice. "Nicole and Saskia, if you don't mind."

"I'll let them know." Suraya nods. "I'm heading to set. I think they're just getting the first scene off now. You can watch the production feed on your iPad if you want. Your mom brought it for you from home."

"Thanks," Helen says.

"Get better," Suraya orders with reassuring briskness, and leaves.

GRANT WATCHES NICOLE and Saskia head down the hallway and Suraya gives him a brief nod before she walks over to him.

"You're taking today off, then," she says matter-of-factly.

"Yeah," he says, and his voice comes out in a low rumble that sounds foreign to his own ears. "I, um—I sent in the revisions last night, and if you send me the studio notes after the table read, I can—"

"Grant," Suraya says, and tilts her head. She looks at him in a slightly pitying way that makes the lump in his throat hurt. "Don't worry about it. I can handle it."

"Thanks," he says. "Let me know if . . . if you need anything."

"I will," Suraya says, and reaches out to touch his arm in a way he assumes is meant to be comforting.

"How's she doing?" he asks, and realizes his mouth feels dry.

"She's awake," Suraya says. "Injured, and on a shitload of pain meds, but . . . it sounds like she'll be fine."

"Good," he says croakily. "That's good."

"It is," Suraya says. "How are you doing?"

Grant laughs but it comes out in a short, humorless gust of air.

"I'm fine," he says. "I didn't get hit by a truck last night."

Suraya's gaze sweeps over him.

"Maybe not, but you look fucking terrible," she says finally. "Take care of yourself. I need you whole tomorrow."

"Thanks," Grant says. "I'll try."

She nods, glances at Helen's parents (in the far corner of the room that Grant doesn't look at, because he isn't sure he can handle *this* being the second time they've ever met), then heads down the lobby for the elevator.

NICOLE AND SASKIA come bounding into the room with flowers (Saskia), dirty magazines (Nicole), and tears (Saskia again).

"Oh my god, you're such a drama queen," Nicole says, slinging an arm around the crying girl. "She's fine, look, she's fine."

Helen smiles and waves, then grimaces because that fucking *hurts*.

"I just thought, what if you died, and I never got to tell you I'm sorry for being such a bitch to you that last day in the writers room," Saskia wails.

Helen looks to Nicole in confusion. Nicole mouths "no idea" and rolls her eyes.

"Oh, don't worry about it," Helen says. "I . . . I haven't thought about it since. Honestly."

"You're so nice," Saskia says, and Helen would laugh if she couldn't feel the fracture in her ribs every time she tried.

"So Grant looks like shit," Nicole says, smoothly changing the topic. "In case you were wondering."

It's amazing how her stupid dumb heart still trills at the sound of his name. Like she's in high school, with a crush. The fact that everyone else can hear it too through the beeping heart rate monitor feels cruel and unusual. Nicole glances at the monitor, but wisely says nothing.

"I'm surprised he's still here," Helen mutters to her hands.

"Are we really?" Nicole makes a skeptical sound. "I told you he was in love with you."

Saskia giggles nervously. "He did seem very . . . distraught," she says. "When he called us."

"He called you?" Helen raises a brow.

"Yeah, he thought you might not want to see him," Nicole says. "Crazy, right?"

"Ha," Helen says weakly. A thought occurs to her then. "Has he been out there with my parents, this whole time?"

Nicole nods. "They aren't talking or anything, if that's what you're worried about. There's definitely a Sharks and Jets thing going on out there in the waiting room—no one's crossing to each other's sides."

"Oh." Helen nods. "That's good, probably."

"Though who knows what's happening now that we're not out there as buffers," Nicole says thoughtfully. She laughs at Helen's expression. "Don't worry! I'm pretty sure everyone's mostly worried about *you*."

"Right," Helen says weakly. "Me."

GRANT FROWNS AT the ground in front of him, willing it to stop swimming.

A cup appears instead and he looks up to see the older man he knows is Helen's father holding out a takeaway cup of tea.

"You should drink something," he says.

"Thanks," Grant answers thickly, and takes the tea. It's lemon ginger, and warms him from the inside. He glances over to the chairs where Helen's parents have been sitting and sees that her mother has disappeared—to the bathroom, probably.

"You've been here a long time," Helen's father says, his mouth a grim line.

"You've been here a long time too," Grant says.

"We're her parents," her dad says simply.

"Yeah." Grant nods, and looks back down at the floor.

There's an unspoken question between them—*We're her parents. Who are you to her?*—and Grant can't answer it, to Helen's father, to Helen, to himself. He doesn't *really* have a right to be anyone to her, but he also doesn't think he'd be useful to anyone else, anywhere else, right now. He wants to laugh at the way Suraya dismissed him summarily from reporting to work today and feels even more worthless.

Get it together, Shepard.

Grant tries to think of something, *anything*, he could say to Helen's father that would fix everything, and realizes *he doesn't even know this man's name*. Helen really never wanted them to meet. *Would it be better to respect her wishes or try something desperate?*

Helen's father casts an appraising look at Grant, sighs heavily, then returns to his chair across the room. Maybe he's thinking the same thing—*he should talk to Helen first.*

Grant tries for the hundredth time this hour to think of what he'll say to Helen when he sees her, if he sees her.

He's never really believed in writer's block—his dad had laughed at the idea once, saying something like, "Well, car mechanics don't get to have mechanic's block, do they?" And Grant had been determined to treat his job with the same un-romantic steely air.

The thing is, he's not so sure mechanics *don't* feel blocked sometimes. Grant has tried and failed to repair his own car enough times to respect the amount of creative thinking that goes into finding elegant solutions in the art of car maintenance.

But words have never failed him—at least not dialogue. Prose was trickier; he couldn't hold a thought long enough to expand it into a proper paragraph, let alone a novel. But dialogue he's always been able to hear as if the people he's writing are in the room with him.

He tries to imagine Helen's voice now but his brain stub-bornly continues to avoid all paths leading to hypotheticals.

Let's not experience this more than once, his psyche seems to suggest. *It's for your own good.*

NICOLE AND SASKIA stay long enough to annoy the nurses, and then they act as if they always planned to leave after Helen's hospital brunch of pudding and a fruit cup.

"Heal fast, babe," Nicole says, and kisses the top of Helen's head. "Who are we sending in next? The sad, hot man, or the sad, worried parents?"

"Your mom is really worried," Saskia says. "I mean, it's fine, just, you know, a lot of . . . 'My baby, they won't let me see her' kind of thing."

Helen huffs slightly. "Yeah, I'm sure."

Nicole leans against the doorway, jacket in hand. "I vote for the broody, hot one. You're already injured, you deserve a little fun."

"Fun," Helen repeats. "Right."

Nicole shrugs her shoulders and drops her voice. "Helen. Helen, I love you. Helen, hmmm . . ." She cracks a smile. "That was my Grant impression, in case you couldn't tell."

Helen laughs, genuinely, and winces.

"You've convinced me," she coughs, in a way that makes Nicole actually look worried for a second. "Send in the broody, hot one."

They slip out and she has the horrifying realization that she should have asked them to borrow a mirror first. She briefly tries to adjust her hair using her distorted reflection in the chrome railings of her hospital bed, then gives up just in time to hear familiar footsteps approach.

"Well," she breathes, and he's *here*. "You look terrible. What happened to you?"

Grant laughs then (she missed that sound, when's the last time she heard it?), leaning against the doorway. His T-shirt is a wrinkled mess and he looks like he hasn't slept in days, and she can see the crick in his neck from the way he unfolds himself strangely to drop into the chair nearest to the door, a long ways from her bed.

"You look worse," he says. "Like you got hit by a fucking truck."

"Ha," she says. "Funny."

"Hilarious," he agrees.

"Why did you come?" she asks.

"Isn't that obvious?" he says, and looks at her in that way he does.

"I don't have the energy to play this game right now," she says softly. "Would you come closer?"

He stands and reaches the chair closest to her in surprisingly few strides. She turns to look at him, close enough to touch now, though not quite yet touching. She reaches out lamely and he takes her left hand between both of his, then bows his head to kiss her thumb. It makes her heart ache painfully, but at least the heart rate monitor doesn't seem to pick up on it.

He kisses her wrist, then her palm, then each finger. She smiles slightly at that.

"Are you thinking of that time on my couch, with the yearbook?" he murmurs, as he presses a lingering kiss to the tip of her left pinkie.

"No," she says. "I was thinking I missed you."

He huffs softly.

"You gotta stop saying things like that out loud," he says gruffly. "It's fucking killing me."

She lifts her hand to press it against his scratchy cheek and he covers her hand with his own, pressing her closer.

"Grant," she starts, and he shakes his head.

"Maybe we shouldn't talk so much, crackerjack," he says softly. "Can I kiss you?"

She knows she shouldn't say yes, but she's on enough pain meds that she thinks maybe it's not such a terrible idea after all.

"You probably owe me one anyway," she mutters, and she can feel his laugh against her mouth. She lets out a shaky sigh as it evolves into a slow kiss—it feels like the first real breath she's taken since their last kiss. His lips linger—warm, sweet, *longing*—until it's over, and he's back in his chair, watching her.

Some searing pain in her chest tells her this is what it would feel like to be safe, and loved, and healing under the watchful gaze of Grant Shepard.

He chuckles.

"You're about to say something that's going to piss me off," he says.

He's so annoying.

"This doesn't change anything," Helen starts, and Grant holds out a hand, like *there it is*. "Take me seriously right now."

"As a heart attack," he says, his voice sounding raspier than she remembers it. "A cute, pastel one."

She ignores that.

"I'm glad you're here. I'd be lying if I said otherwise," she starts.

"Glad we're on the same page," he says coolly.

"I wish you wouldn't do that," she says.

"Tell the truth?"

"*Interrupt*," she says.

"Sorry, sweetheart," he murmurs, and she rolls her eyes.

"My parents are out there."

"Yes, they are," he says.

"My mom's probably having a minor meltdown at the hospital staff because I haven't let her in to see me."

"She's had a few," he acknowledges. "Very tiny, perfectly reasonable meltdowns, in my opinion. You can be frustratingly . . . opaque. When you want to be."

"Sorry," she says irritably.

"S'okay," he says quietly. "I'm used to it."

"How was it out there, with them?" she asks, pushing onward past the bruising pain. "Did you guys bond over my intake forms, are you besties now, did my mom invite you to Christmas dinner?"

Grant's jaw tenses. "No."

"Did Mom even acknowledge you?"

Grant lets out a short exhale. "No."

Helen sinks into her pillow sullenly. "Nothing's changed, Grant. I got in a car accident. People get into car accidents and break bones all the time. You know that."

"*You* don't, though," he says, his voice a dry rasp. "Do you know what it felt like, to get that call from Suraya last night? By the way, good job picking your boss as an emergency contact, that's not pathetic at all, Helen."

The quiet anger that's been simmering in him since their kiss ended is nearly at the surface now, she can tell. *Good.* She can deal with an angry Grant better than a sweet one.

"I didn't know anyone in LA," she says.

"You knew *me*," he hisses. "We filled that paperwork out week three, I remember, I was there. It was right before the camping trip."

"We weren't friends then," she answers.

"We aren't friends now!"

Helen exhales shortly. "You're being unreasonable. Who gives a shit when we filled out some stupid employment forms?"

"I don't know," Grant says, and pushes a hand into his hair in frustration. "I can't—I can't think straight when I'm around you."

"Maybe I *should* have put down someone else. Saskia or Nicole probably wouldn't have called you first."

Grant glares at her then. "Suraya called me because she knew I'd want to know. That's how she put it. I almost didn't pick up, because I hadn't slept in thirty-six fucking hours, because I kept replaying our last conversation trying to figure out if I could have said something, anything, that would have changed the outcome. Thank fuck I *did* pick up, Helen. Do you know what it would have done to me if you'd *died* and I'd been sleeping?"

Helen stares at him mutinously. "You shouldn't drive when you haven't slept for that long."

"I took a fucking Uber." He gives her a disgusted look, as if unable to bear the sight of her. "You know what I figured out on the ride over? All that talk about me being grateful in a few months, and finding someone else, and being happy and healthy, all of that—it's *bullshit*."

Her breath catches at the despairing look in his eyes. A memory suddenly comes online, of meeting eyes with him in that church at Michelle's funeral, all those years ago. It seems to reach across time and space, reminding her who they are and why they've been leaving each other for so long.

"You could keep me your dirty little secret, come to me tasting like other men, I'd still take you back every fucking time," he says, a muscle ticking violently in his jaw. "I'd rather have a *fraction* of you than all of someone else."

Helen swallows. "I don't want that for you. For either of us. It's not—it's not healthy."

"I don't *want* to be healthy," Grant says, and his chest is heaving as if he's just run a marathon. "I just want you."

She stares at him and knows if she told him she loved him back, there would never be any hope for either of them. They'd keep coming back here, over and over, holding on to less and less of each other each time, until they had nothing left but a lifetime of regret and resentment over old heartaches and missed chances.

"I'd like you to leave now," she says quietly.

"What's wrong, getting too honest?" Grant murmurs softly.

"Please," she says.

"You're a coward, Helen."

She's crying now, she realizes, and he sees it too. He doesn't move to comfort her (*she hates being comforted*), but he doesn't leave either. He stares at her, and folds his arms across his chest.

"Am I dismissed?" he asks bluntly.

"Yes," she says, and wipes her face. "You should go."

"Yeah, I'm going," Grant says, his voice low and dark. "Have a nice life, crackerjack."

"Grant," she says, and he stops in the doorway. He turns and watches her with shuttered eyes. She misses him so *fucking much* already. "I hope you're wrong. I hope you're able to . . . to get over this someday."

He stares at her for a long beat, and it feels like he's memorizing her.

"You can keep hoping for both of us. I won't be," he says grimly, finally, and leaves.

HELEN ASKS A nurse to take her to the bathroom and uses the time to clean herself up. She wipes the tears from her face and reminds herself she can cry more later, every night for the rest of her life, if she wants. She just has to keep it together long enough for her parents to see she's going to be okay—maybe a little scratched and banged up, but nothing time and bed rest won't fix. She has the terrible thought just then that Mom will probably insist on staying longer, maybe even move into her condo to take care of her until she deems Helen healed enough, and Helen tries wildly to think of the best arguments to deter her. *I have friends who'll come take care of me, the building's security keeps an eye on entries and exits and it's only my name on the sublease, if you move in, I'll jump out the window.*

She's only darkly amusing herself with the thought of saying that last one out loud. Maybe there are mothers out there who could hear that and laugh or at least tut dismissively and move on with the conversation. She knows her own mother would stare back at her, ashen-faced, and ask, *Why would you say such a terrible thing?*

Helen knows the hospital staff probably think she's a terrible person, that she doesn't care about her own parents, that they're treating an awful, unfeeling robot. As she looks down at her hands, which were shaking when she came into the bathroom yet seem oddly calm now, she wonders if she is.

She used to think it was her superpower, her ability to identify her upset emotions and set them carefully aside. *This anger isn't serving us right now; put it aside and deal with the facts. This sadness isn't helping; turn it off and look for solutions.* It made her effective, productive—powerful, even.

But she's found lately that she's much more emotionally fragile than she used to be. All it takes is a hug while she's trying to keep it together and the dam breaks, and the tears flow. No one's going to hug her now, though.

So she steels herself against the emotions that aren't helpful in this moment, practices the right kind of *it's okay, it looks worse than it is, I'm fine, really* smile in the mirror, and hits the bell for the nurse to help her back to her room. And finally she says, "I'm ready for my parents."

Her father enters wearing a grim expression, her mother a drawn, glassy-eyed one. She can tell Mom's been crying and she feels a stab of guilt. Mom holds out Helen's iPad and a bag of chips.

"They said you might be hungry," she says, and drops the bag on Helen's bed.

"Thanks," Helen says. She takes the chips but doesn't open them. She tries out the best *I'm fine* smile in her repertoire. "So obviously something happened. Ha. But I'm fine now.

Sorry I kept you waiting. I didn't realize so much time had passed."

"How are you feeling?" Mom asks, and a tiny line of worry appears between her brows.

"Good," Helen says. "I mean, not *great*, but pretty good, under the circumstances."

"The doctors said you have broken bones," Mom says, her eyes scanning Helen's limbs.

"Yeah, but I've broken bones before and gotten better. Remember that time I fell on my chin in fourth grade?"

Helen remembers it. She had been on the swings at Mom's friend's house and decided to try jumping off the swing like she saw the older kids doing. She'd fallen chin-first onto the ground, and she can still see the way Mom's eyes went comically aghast at the sight of all the blood gushing down her chin. She'd driven Helen to the ER, completely silent, radiating panic from the car to the parking lot to the waiting room. Helen remembers Mom asking questions in soft, broken English to the doctor until they found a nurse who spoke Mandarin and could explain Helen just needed a finger splint and fourteen stitches on her chin.

"You were younger then," Mom says.

"My point is, you were worried then too, and it was fine. I'm going to be fine."

"Fine, fine, all you ever are is *fine*," Mom says. "You don't tell us anything."

"I tell you things," Helen says, and can't keep a petulant tone out of her voice that makes her sound exactly seventeen years old.

"Listen to our daughter, listen to how she lies," Mom says, turning to Dad. "So easy for her."

"She needs to rest," Dad says.

"She says she's fine!" Mom snaps, then rounds on Helen. "I know what you've been doing with—with *that boy*."

She says *that boy* with disgust and Helen's brain wearily thinks, *I can't do this right now.* None of her surprise or shock synapses seem to be firing—all Helen can muster is *tired.*

"I saw your *text messages*," Mom says. "I had a lot of time to wait for you with your iPad."

Helen blinks furiously. She mentally runs through the entirety of her texts to Grant in milliseconds and tries to remember anything incriminating. The fact that she texts him at all is incriminating. But they didn't text *that* much—they spent most of their waking hours together.

"The way you talk to each other, *come over, I miss you, happy birthday*—"

"Oh my god, this is such an overreaction, Mom—"

"*I know what he is to you!*" Mom cries. "You let him in here before your *own mother.*"

Helen looks away then. She'd forgotten, somehow, that Mom would have seen that. The hospital's ability to wield a magical legal boundary between her and her parents' access to her must have driven her mad with power, or she'd never have forgotten something like that for even an instant. She remembers the last time she slipped up—in high school, when she'd come home one day in freshman year to find her diary open on the kitchen table and Mom waiting for her with an expression of betrayal. *How could you write these things about your own mother?*

"What would your sister say?"

Helen shakes her head silently and looks out the window.

Michelle would probably high-five her and say, *I never thought you had it in you.*

"You have no idea what he is to me," Helen says finally. "Anyway, it's over. He loved me, and it's over, and I really don't want to talk about it."

She's slightly horrified to find she's crying again and swipes furiously at the tears that refuse to stop silently rolling down her face.

"Helen. This is a *sickness*."

She's heard this one before, it's her mom's favorite phrase—when Helen would stay up past three a.m. reading by flashlight under the covers, when she found pages of Helen's diaries where she'd scrawled *four more years four more years four more years* in cursive script until she ran out of ink, as a way to calm the pounding in her head when her parents had done some now forgotten thing that probably had her best interests in mind but had felt wildly unjust at the time. *This is a sickness.* Yet Mom had balked when she'd first heard that Helen had started seeing a therapist regularly in her late twenties—"Why? What's so bad you need to see a therapist?"

Helen knows her parents have always done their best by her, that they just want an easier life for her. *They aren't that bad*, she reminds herself. *They let you become a writer, when everyone else's kids became doctors and pharmacists. They're supportive. They show up.* It's just that they don't have *context* for her and it makes her feel like they're talking in opposite directions in every conversation.

But I didn't choose this, she thinks. *You decided to move to another country and start a family. You should have known that not fully understanding your own kids would come with that territory.*

She loves her parents, she does, but it's a prickly, complicated love, and suddenly Helen is swept up in a hopeless feeling that maybe all she's capable of is prickly, complicated loving. Maybe even with Grant Shepard permanently, safely in the rearview mirror, she'll never be able to love simply and without disclaimers.

Helen feels a clawing sensation in her gut, a panicked kind of *trapped* feeling, and when she opens her mouth, the words come out in a choked gust—

"It's *suffocating*, being loved by you."

It sounds so awful and dramatic out loud, she almost can't believe she's said it. Helen lets out a shaky exhale. "You don't leave me an inch of space to breathe."

Mom stares at Helen, stunned. "I'm your *mother*," she says.

"I fucking know," Helen snaps.

She looks up, and she's never seen Mom look at her like this—like she wants to reach out and slap her. (Dad has retreated to the chair in the corner and is studiously watching the production feed on Helen's iPad.)

"You read my diary in high school, you read my texts now, you don't leave me *anything*," Helen says.

Mom stares back at her. "Because you give us *nothing*. What else am I supposed to do? How else will I know what's going on in your *life*?"

This would be the part of the episode, Helen thinks idly, where mother and daughter finally have a heart-to-heart. Walls come down, they finally, truly *see* each other, and all is resolved at last. It's the all-American fantasy she's been peddled by every episode of her favorite Emmy Award–winning, syndicated television dramas featuring tough-but-loving families.

But for some reason, she and Mom always seem to miss each other.

"We should let her rest," Dad says from the back of the room. "This conversation doesn't have to happen here."

Mom stares at Helen, her fingers balled in tight fists at her sides. Dad stands then, and returns Helen's iPad to her. He nudges Mom.

"Come on," he says.

Helen watches Mom's throat working, her eyes glassy with fresh tears.

I don't hate you, she wants to say. *I just hate the way you love me.*

But Mom wouldn't be able to hear that. Helen watches silently as her parents move toward the exit and knows this is the end of the scene, there's nothing else left to work out between them. *There's no point.* They're almost out the door when—

"Wait." Helen clears her throat, desperate to tell them *something.* "I'm not writing YA anymore."

Her parents stop, confused.

"What, you have a new book deal?" Dad asks.

"No," Helen says, her heart pounding. She isn't even sure she means any of the words she's saying and thinks suddenly maybe this is the thrill other teens experienced when they shouted "I hate you!" and slammed the doors to their childhood bedrooms. "I don't know what I'm going to do. I just know I don't wanna write about teenagers anymore."

Mom and Dad exchange a bewildered look.

"I don't care what you write about," Dad says slowly. "But maybe it is not so good to jump without knowing first where you will land."

"Michelle did," Helen says, hurling the words like knives across the room. "Maybe it'll work out better for me."

Dad grips the door handle as if he's been hit. Mom stares at her with an expression of horrified betrayal. *"How could you say such a terrible thing?"* she hisses.

Helen laughs and wipes at tears that are flowing inexplicably down her face.

"I don't know, Mom, I'm probably very broken inside. I wonder why."

Then Dad tugs at Mom's elbow, and her parents leave.

Finally.

Thirty

Grant has three weeks off between his last day covering *The Ivy Papers* and his next show, a high-budget Netflix reboot of one of his favorite hard-fantasy book series from childhood. He'd been genuinely excited when he first landed the job, and he remembers taking Helen on a trip to his favorite bookstore in Los Feliz to buy her a copy of the first book.

He'd spent the better part of their lunch afterward trying to explain the complex mythology of it. She'd asked follow-up questions and wrinkled her nose at a few outdated plot points *they would obviously fix in the adaptation*, and by the time they got to his car, he'd said, "You're not gonna read it at all, are you?"

She'd laughed, smiled up at him in that way that made him feel like he could do anything, and said, "I'll just read your version of it."

It's not going to be *his* version, though. He'll be the number two, but he's pretty sure if he does a good job on this one, he'll be able to leverage it into some kind of development *somewhere*.

"You're always creating so many extra steps for yourself," she'd said in passing. "Why don't you just tell your agent you want to take some time and develop something of your own?"

It had stopped him in his tracks, just for a beat. Of course Helen would think that—she always seemed so sure of her next steps. *Graduate high school. Major in creative writing. Write a novel. Sell it. Turn it into a bestselling series. Have writer's block?*

Turn the series into a TV show and negotiate a spot in the writers room. She always had a solution, and once she'd unlocked how to apply that skill in the writers room, she'd been pretty damn magnificent to watch work every day.

He had felt a bit like a fraud, standing next to Helen. He'd picked his college because California was as far away from New Jersey as he could imagine getting, and he signed up for a screenwriting course only because he'd had to fulfill an English elective requirement. LA was an industry town, so everyone had just assumed he was an aspiring screenwriter and he went along with it because it had seemed easier than coming up with a whole dream of his own. Eventually, it *did* become his dream, and he discovered the terrifying feeling of wanting something for himself and not being sure he would ever get it.

He's always been so sure his next job could be his last job that he's said yes to practically every meeting, every new show submission Fern has sent him. He thinks maybe he's spent more time on the craft of *getting* the job than on the craft of writing itself, and every time he hears himself pitched as *good in a room*, he feels the sting of what it implies.

Good in a room, but not a creative genius by any means.

Good in a room, if you need someone to fill an empty seat for a while.

Good in a room: he'll win you over and convince you just how much you need him, when really, he's the one who needs you.

He isn't even sure which of his own ideas he *would* want to develop into something real. He has old pilot samples that, combined with his list of credits on other people's's shows, have been good enough to get him meetings. He remembers being excited about those pilots once, years ago, when he wrote them. But when he scans them now, they feel like an outdated snapshot of his brain and he isn't sure he could re-create that version of himself if he tried.

He knows he has the kind of career now that if he showed his IMDb page to his twenty-two-year-old self, *that* Grant Shepard would think he could drop dead tomorrow and have achieved his life's ambitions.

But that was before *her*.

Before he'd had the maddening, exhilarating experience of loving someone who casually thought he could and *should* do better, that he hadn't reached the peaks of his potential yet.

"It's a curse," Helen had said to him once, when he had expressed admiration that she always seemed to create new goals for herself as soon as she achieved them. She'd smiled, a little wistfully. "I'll never truly be happy. I know as soon as I have the thing I want, there'll be something just . . . peeking into view over there, that I want just as desperately."

He thinks of their Forest Falls trip, back in early November, and how she'd called up to Suraya, "I hate hiking anyway."

Helen is a mountain climber if he's ever known one, and he thinks he would have been happy to climb mountains with her for the rest of their lives. He would have reminded her to stop sometimes, to look back on how far she'd come and take some time to enjoy it. And she'd have helped him to keep walking past the familiar peaks he'd already climbed and circled before, urging them both onward. *Come on, there's a better view just around the corner.*

He wonders if maybe he could do that for himself. If loving Helen—even if it was never really his right to love her in the first place—means he gets to carry some version of her with him forever. *She hopes he'll get over this.* He doesn't want to get over this, over *her*, at all. He wants to hold on to this hurt and wrap it in plastic and store it somewhere safe, because it's probably all he'll ever have left of her.

The last day his badge gives him access to the lot, Grant packs up his laptop and walks through the soundstages on his way to the parking lot. The main unit is filming on location somewhere else and the scent of sawdust is thick in the air, as the art director oversees the construction of a new set for the last six episodes of the season.

They're tearing down a coffee shop set they built weeks ago for his episode to make room for it, and his footsteps leave a trail in the sawdust as he walks through the space. On the other side of the now defunct coffee shop is a bedroom set for the main character of the series—it's Helen's favorite of their standing sets. He remembers her hitting him on the shoulder the first time the writers room did a walk-through of the soundstages and they reached the bedroom.

"It's *so good*," she kept saying. "It looks *exactly* like how I pictured it. They're so *good*."

And the art team *is* good. He's pretty sure they've won their fair share of Emmys in the last decade.

But he thinks it's also a credit to Helen, that when she pictures something—a bedroom, a goal, a *future*, she finds a way to turn it into a reality. He wishes she'd been able to picture a future with him in it. If she'd wanted it enough, he's certain, *somehow*, they would have found a way to make it work.

He sits down on the floor of the fake bedroom and listens as the walls of the coffee shop fall down on the other side, the buzzing chain saws filling the air with even more sawdust.

His phone rings then, and it's his mom.

"Grant, sweetie, you'll never believe what's happened."

He listens and reacts appropriately as she tells him that the sale on the house closed *very* suddenly over the weekend, and they have some contractors (*she Yelped them this time!*) coming to do some work, and so she has just three weeks until she's off to Ireland. The sheep farm isn't even *ready* for her, but it'll give her a chance to explore all the parts of the country that aren't close by.

"Now, I still have some boxes of your stuff, if you want them, or I can put them in storage, it's no problem. There's just some things that are too heavy to ship, you know? Like your night-stands and the couch in your bedroom, which I tried to donate but, honey, no one wants them."

He's about to tell her not to bother, to just toss it, when it suddenly occurs to him that he might never see his childhood home or have any reason to return to Dunollie, New Jersey, ever again after this.

"No," he finds himself saying. "I'll come pick them up. I'll drive."

The next day, he leases a fuel-efficient SUV he's been con-templating purchasing for a while and puts his convertible up for sale on a used-car group. He packs a week's worth of clothes and realizes Helen still has his favorite T-shirt. He decides she can keep that souvenir.

He opts for the faster, slightly less scenic route that takes him through the red rocks of Arizona and reminds him of Saturday-morning cartoons, watching the Road Runner *meep meep* through desert landscapes and roads that seem to stretch for infinity.

He sees the signs for the Grand Canyon and impulsively makes a detour, because he can't remember the last time he saw it with his own eyes. He buys a disposable camera at a gas sta-tion and has a mental image of himself asking random strangers to take his solo photo at the Grand Canyon, and them looking at him with pity. *They don't know I was homecoming king in '08*, he thinks, and laughs to himself.

He forgets the camera in his car when he gets there, but it doesn't matter, because he doesn't think photos would do the scene justice anyway. He sits on a craggy rock and stares out at the sweeping vista, full of burnt reds and blue-purples and the slightest hints of green peppering the carved valley below him.

He decides he'll either get over Helen by Chicago or buy a plane ticket and move to some remote island in Greece that's accessible only by boat and build cabinets for the rest of his life.

Neither of those things happens, of course.

He thinks about calling her when he takes a wrong turn in Oklahoma and ends up driving late into the night through the flat plains of Kansas. He doesn't, but the thought keeps him alert and awake enough to make it safely to his hotel in Wichita. *Thanks, crackerjack*, he thinks, and it barely even hurts that time.

He gets on the road early and, after ten hours of driving, reaches the apartment of Julie Swain, a college friend who moved to Chicago for the improv scene and offered up her couch when she saw him posting scenes from his cross-country trip on Instagram.

They run down the block to a convenience store so Julie can pick up some toilet paper—he thinks it's for him and insists on paying for it, but it turns out it's for her sketch comedy group that's meeting tomorrow. She buys a six-pack of beers and they put on a nature documentary in the background when they get back to her living room.

"So what's next for Grant Shepard?" she asks as he twists open a second bottle for each of them.

"Well, I was thinking about finishing this beer and then using some of that toilet paper I bought your sketch comedy troupe."

She laughs and shoves him on the shoulder. "You know that's not what I meant."

"I know, I'm such an avoidant bastard, aren't I?" Grant grins and sips from the glass bottle. "No, I have stuff lined up. This big Netflix thing I signed so many NDAs for I may have sold them my left nipple somewhere in the mix. And then after that, I don't know. Something'll come up."

"That's great," she says, and their shoulders touch lightly.

He thinks maybe there's a world where something could have happened between them once, back in college. But enough time has passed and they've settled into something easier and more comfortable—the companionship of old friends. He wonders if enough time will ever pass for him to have a conversation like this with Helen.

"What's up?" she asks, looking sideways at him. "You're, like, a million miles away."

"Nothing," he says, then thinks better of it. "Can I ask a weird favor?"

She nods, and maybe it's the beer, but he plows ahead: "Can I borrow your phone to make a call, and if they call you back tomorrow, just say it was a wrong number or try to sell them car insurance or something?"

Julie stares at him for a beat, and he detects a pitying note when she silently pulls out her phone and hands it to him.

He takes the stairs up to the roof to make the call, even though it's still cold enough in late March for there to be puddles of melting snow up there. He knows Helen doesn't answer unknown numbers, so he's surprised when he hears a laughing "Hello? Shhh—I'm on the phone! Hello?"

He swallows hard and listens to the sound of music—"*cooking with friends,*" *probably*—and her breathing in the background. He stands there for what feels like forever, stupidly grateful to hear her existing at the same time as him, before the phone clicks and she hangs up.

His call log tells him the call was four seconds long.

HELEN HANGS UP, and there's a funny feeling at the back of her neck when she sets her phone down.

"Must've been a wrong number," she tells Nicole.

Defying all expectations, her parents left LA the day after Helen got out of the hospital. She hasn't called them since, and they haven't called her. It's been almost five weeks. She isn't sure what to make of the silence and she gets an uncomfortable feeling of shame and guilt in her stomach when she thinks about it too much—like she did whenever she made a messy spill as a kid and tried to hide the results from her parents.

She hasn't heard from Grant either, not since the writers room officially ended and there was no reason to look forward to seeing his name in her inbox every day, even if it was just on a distro list for the daily prep schedule. She hasn't talked to him since that day in the pink hospital room and her heart still speeds up just thinking about it.

She knows he's on a cross-country trip and is somewhere in Chicago eating tacos with someone named "Julie" right now. It's embarrassing how much she knows. She's been watching his Instagram stories from the official *Ivy Papers* account and she thinks she'll probably always associate tapping to log into that shiny, pre-verified account with stalking Grant Shepard.

Nicole has all but moved into her condo to help her around as she heals. At this point, Helen can mostly get everything she needs for herself but Nicole insists on staying anyway.

"Your place is nicer than mine and I can't come over if you accidentally slip and die in the bathtub," she says, and Helen's honestly grateful for the company. She hasn't had a roommate in seven years and she's forgotten how nice it is to have someone to share chores and meals and thoughts with.

Nicole tells her about the new show she's writing on, some *godawful* mockumentary about suburban parents in a competitive e-sports league, but the people running the show are really great and her reps think it'll establish her more firmly in the comedy space, which she's been trying to break into since, *oh forever*.

"Not that I don't appreciate our dramarama time together." Nicole pats Helen's arm. "It brought me to this condo."

Helen laughs and wonders what she'll do next month, when production's over and she has to either find a place of her own in LA or move back to New York. Or move somewhere else? She isn't sure at all where she's going next and thinks randomly of Lisa Shepard and her Irish sheep farm plans.

"How do you feel, when you think about New York?" Nicole asks, when Helen mulls over her impending decisions out loud.

"Well, it's where I lived for so long. And it's a great city," Helen says. "There's always something happening, people living their lives out in the open right in front of you. It's kind of relentless but also kind of good, if you're a writer? And it's beautiful in the fall, and at Christmas. Walkable, which LA isn't."

"I didn't ask for facts. I asked for feelings," Nicole says. "Like how do you *feel*, in your body?"

This is the kind of LA hippie question Helen's New York friends probably would have laughed at, then written into a novel, alongside references to green juice and hiking. But Helen tilts her head and closes her eyes.

"I feel . . . even," she says. "Like something's tugging down a little, and up a little, and I'm right . . . here."

She touches her chest, opens her eyes, and feels slightly embarrassed. But Nicole nods, like this makes perfect sense.

"How do you feel when you think about staying in LA?"

Helen's breath gives an involuntary shudder and she closes her eyes tightly. She can feel the frown and tries to smooth it, but somehow that makes her think of *Grant*. She takes a heaving breath then, and swallows, and it feels like too much, like her chest is full and her head is too tight and she wants to gasp for air, and then she *does* and she's crying suddenly, out of nowhere, and her eyes aren't even shut anymore but she can't see anything, all she can see is the floral pattern on Nicole's navy pajama pants, and Nicole says, "*Oh, honey*," and strokes Helen's hair soothingly like an anxious pet in her lap.

"I loved him, I really did," she babbles stupidly into Nicole's pajama pants.

"I know," Nicole says softly.

"I loved him, and he loved me, and it's over now, and I'll never get it back," she cries.

"You don't know that," Nicole says.

"I do, though," Helen says. "He hates me now. And I hate me now. I'm such a stupid—dumb—crying *mess*."

"Yeah," Nicole says sympathetically. "I mean, I don't know. Maybe don't hate yourself."

"The worst part is I think he meant it," she says. "I think he *would* take me back if I asked, but eventually, he'd meet some cool LA director chick who really *gets* him and doesn't come with the—the *family* and the *history* that I do and he could be happy with her and he wouldn't really even consider it but *I* would know deep down I was keeping him from who he was really meant to be with, and, and . . ."

Helen takes a few deep, shuddering gasps.

"This is some wild fanfic you're spinning, babe," Nicole says, and rubs her back gently. "I can't wait to hear where it goes. And?"

"And it would kill me," she says. "Knowing I was standing between Grant and his happily ever after."

"Well, that's why you did what you did," Nicole says.

"I never told him I loved him back," Helen says.

"He knows, though."

"But I never *told* him, why couldn't I tell him?"

Helen knows she isn't making any sense and she cries for the loss of her good words and *him* and how *just out of reach* everything feels, and eventually she runs out of tears and Nicole brings her a mug of tea and says gently, "So it sounds like New York takes the lead."

DUNOLLIE, NEW JERSEY, in the spring is mostly muddy gray skies and fog, especially at the top of the mountain, but Grant finds he doesn't mind it so much.

"I was hoping you'd bring the California sunshine with you," his mom says as she kisses him on the cheek. He feels like he's been stooping lower for her kisses lately and the thought makes him sadder than anything about closing up their big old house for good.

The house is covered in cardboard boxes and awkward lengths of leftover Bubble Wrap, and he has no idea how Lisa Shepard intends to be out of here completely in two weeks. When he goes downstairs to check the basement, though, he's startled.

"Wow," he says involuntarily.

"I know," she says next to him, and they both stare at the empty space.

Grant used to be jealous of his friends with finished basements, where they could hang out and their feet would stay warm because they had carpeting and recessed lighting in the home theater section. His own basement was a cold, always slightly damp room, where everything his parents didn't want to find a home for ended up. His old bicycles, Dad's old receipts, Mom's boxes and boxes of family photos and the ghosts of Christmas party decorations past.

It looks like a blank space now, and maybe the next family to live here will add carpeting and heating and a home theater of their own. He frowns, and some homesick feeling pings in his chest.

"Who bought the house?" he asks, his voice coming out scratchy and unfamiliar.

"Oh, this *charming* couple," his mom says, and leads the way back upstairs. "Newlyweds, and so obviously in love. They met in college and broke up and got back together and it all sounds very tortured but they make it sound so *funny* now, I think their kids will be stand-up comics."

Grant nods and follows her up past the boxes to the second floor.

"I put all your boxes in your room." She waves a hand at the second door on the right. "I sold your bed, because I didn't think you'd be coming back. But there's the couch, and I still have your old sleeping bag somewhere."

"From when I was in seventh grade?" Grant lifts a brow.

"Point taken," Mom says.

Grant ends up driving to the local A&P to buy himself a blow-up mattress, figuring it'll be useful enough to take back with him. Mom sends him out with a list of short-term groceries—frozen pizzas, rotisserie chicken, that kind of thing. He remembers hanging out in the parking lot of this A&P with Lauren DiSantos his last summer in Dunollie before college, and he suddenly wants to get out of New Jersey as soon as possible.

"Excuse me, can you get that cake mix for me?"

Grant looks down and the sight splashes over him like a bucket of ice water. It's Helen's mother, and she looks equally surprised to see him, standing here in the lazy baking aisle of their local A&P. He remembers then that he's wearing a baseball cap and wonders vaguely if he should apologize for accidentally hoodwinking her.

He reaches up for an angel food cake mix on the top shelf. "This one?"

He looks back at Helen's mother, half expecting her to be gone. But she just nods mutely. He hands it to her, and she takes it. She doesn't look up at him, but stays rooted to the spot, staring at Betty Crocker's name. She opens her mouth and shuts it a few times, and he's not sure if she's gasping for air or trying to say something.

How is she, he wants to ask, but doesn't.

Helen's mother puts the box in her cart and turns around sharply, leaving him alone in the cake mix aisle.

He thinks maybe this is the first time he's heard her real voice.

HE BLOWS UP the mattress in his bedroom and stares at his couch for so long, he thinks he could summon the ghosts of his and Helen's past selves if he tried hard enough. He swallows when he thinks of that night—it's one he's revisited so many times in his memory, it's probably haunting him all the way back to LA.

The following Monday, he decides to take a train into the city, and his mom stares at him in surprise.

"But you hate the city," she says, and she's not wrong.

When he exits Penn Station, his feet start walking automatically up Seventh Avenue. He takes a right at Times Square, passing tourists and comedy show promoters and Broadway marquee signs, and keeps walking until he reaches the green picnic tables at Bryant Park.

"I used to write at the public library next to Bryant Park," Helen once said on a podcast, which he had listened to out loud to annoy her because he'd loved the embarrassed pink tinge on her cheeks. "Then I'd take lunch breaks in the park and watch old men play chess."

He buys a sandwich from a kiosk, even though it's only a quarter till eleven and barely any old men are playing chess. He wonders if there's any world where their paths could have crossed differently. He's been to the city half a dozen times in the last six years for work, usually against his will, hating it the whole time. He's even been to Bryant Park, sat at these very picnic tables. But would he have recognized her in the crowd? And if he had, would he have done anything about it? What if they hadn't known each other at all in high school, what then? Would some essential part of him still have recognized some essential part of her?

He spends the following hour in the library next door, wandering from floor to floor of the labyrinthine building, wondering which spots were Helen's favorites. He can see how their show was inspired by these Beaux Arts marble halls, the gilded ceilings, the church-like atmosphere that has everyone speaking in hushed tones as soon as they cross the front doors.

A librarian informs him there isn't a young adult section in this research library, so he buys a tote bag and a magnet from the gift shop downstairs and walks out the door to a depressingly modern lending library across the street. He looks for the Ivy Papers on the shelves. There's only two volumes from the four-book series available on the shelf, and the corner of his mouth lifts at this. She's in demand. He plucks the thicker of the two available options, the second book (her *least favorite*), and heads in search of an open chair.

He spends his afternoon reading Helen Zhang's writing. He thinks he can hear her voice sometimes in the best friend character, and her love interest. It feels like the most he's held of her in a long time and he savors the feeling, though it aches too.

The sun is low in the sky by the time he leaves the library, and he walks slowly back toward Penn Station.

He's about to drift off to sleep on the train, when he looks out the window and his heart stops.

Standing there on the platform, just disembarking from an opposite train—*surely it isn't*, except *yes, it is*—it's her.

Helen, in the flesh. She's wearing a familiar gray wool coat and a sling for her arm. Her hair is down and she looks annoyed and he knows in his gut *it's her*.

The train whistles and she looks up in his direction just then, as if she knows exactly where to find him. He registers the surprise on her face, the way her mouth drops a little, and her brow furrows.

He stands immediately and moves down the train compartment.

She walks toward the train too, and the motion is so smooth, he realizes the train is already leaving the station. He feels a certain panic rise, that he might never see her again, that she's not really even there and this is just an apparition of her he's conjured up from haunting her old haunts.

But she sees him too, and he knows it's real. He slams the window when he reaches the end of the train and watches as she reaches the end of the platform. She grows smaller and smaller, and he thinks he sees her pick up her phone, and he looks down to see his own has no signal. A voice on the intercom tells him "This is the 4:13 p.m. Raritan Valley Line, bound for Secaucus."

When they leave the tunnel and the electric-blue light of the sky filters into the train, he pulls out his phone and dumbly stares at it, waiting for bars of reception to appear. Nothing. As the train carries him farther and farther away, he becomes less and less sure he saw her at all. He doesn't have any missed calls or voicemails or texts appearing with his increasing signal. By the time he reaches Westfield and has three full bars of reception, though, he doesn't care anymore and—*fuck it*—calls her.

"Hello, this is Helen. Please leave your message after the tone."

He registers the fact that it rang twice before it went to voicemail and feels the brutal sting of rejection. He swallows.

Enough.

When he gets off the train at Dunollie, he deletes her number from his phone.

HELEN SHOOTS AN apologetic look to the librarian of the New York Public Library, then checks her phone. *Missed Call—Grant Shepard.*

She hasn't seen the shape of his name on her phone in so long, she almost has a heart attack. It *was* him, on that train on the too-hot platform with too many people and too many millimeters of glass for her to be sure she hadn't just seen a ghost. She shoves her notebook into her bag with a trembling hand and fumbles with her coat. She walks out of her favorite library in the world as fast as she possibly can, which, as it turns out, isn't very fast at all.

By the time she's finally on the ground floor, her breath is coming out in panicked spurts and when she gets outside to Fifth Avenue, people glance at her like maybe they need to call someone for her.

She pulls up her call log and her thumb hovers over his name.

He'd pick up, she's sure of it. She'd call, and he'd pick up, and she'd tell him she's moved back into her old apartment in New York that doesn't feel like home anymore, and she misses him so much her heart hurts all the time, and she loves him so much she sometimes can't fathom a world where she's ever truly happy again. He'd come back and she'd blow off her plans for a reconciliation dinner with her parents tomorrow, and she'd be able to *touch* him again, and—and—*and* . . .

. . . she would make it impossible for either of them to move on.

Let him go, she reminds herself sharply. *He deserves a happy, normal life with a happy, extraordinary someone.*

The kind of woman who deserves Grant would have found him on the right coast, the one he calls home, and he would have opened his arms and she would have fallen into them for the first time and known it was her favorite place in the world right away. She wouldn't have had to fight a terrible, confusing mixture of compulsions to flee and burrow at the same time, choosing ultimately to flee. The kind of woman who deserves Grant would have known what she had when she had it, and wouldn't have waited until weeks later to weep and wallow over the loss of him in a bathtub for so long, she now knows what her toes would look like if she drowned. *The kind of woman who deserves Grant would be capable of the kind of love that keeps little sisters alive.*

Grant Shepard deserves a Hollywood movie ending, with swelling music and sweeping camera movements and kissing in the rain. This movie would have an epilogue with warm lighting and dad jokes and family dinners in a summer garden over the end credits.

And Helen Zhang has never been built for that kind of uncomplicated happily ever after.

Thirty-One

Helen shows up to dinner at her parents' house with cupcakes from Magnolia Bakery, and she remembers trying to re-create the buttercream frosting in their kitchen with Michelle one Christmas morning, the air sweet with the scent of warm vanilla. Helen isn't staying here tonight, she's decided boldly to branch out into the world of Airbnbs in her old hometown.

The house she's picked isn't in a part of town she's overly familiar with and the fussy floral curtains and pink carpets remind her of Mrs. Stover, the fussy, floral geometry teacher from her sophomore year of high school. The owner is a Polish man in his late fifties whose kids are now off to college, and he brings Helen warm cookies when she checks in. He asks her what she does for a living and writes down the titles of her books so he can send them to his daughter at Columbia.

Mom opens the door when she rings and her eyes sweep from Helen's face to her toes.

"I already made a cake," she says, but takes the box of cup-cakes from Helen anyway.

"Nice to see you too, Mom," Helen says as she takes her shoes off.

She resists the urge to run upstairs to Michelle's old bed-room and instead follows Mom into the kitchen, where various pots and pans sizzle and steam deliciously with soy sauce and ginger and green onion. Dad's sitting on the couch, watching some bootlegged Chinese historical drama series on his iPad. He gives her a casual wave.

"How's work?" she asks him first.

Dad tells her it's not going very well at all. He thinks he's gone as high in the company as he can go because of his English, and he's getting too old to be as impressive as the kids coming straight out of college. He tells her he's been thinking of getting into the start-up business back in China, that there are more opportunities for someone like him, and his English language skills would be more appreciated back there.

"I think your English is great," Helen says, and means it. Dad grumbles, and asks how the show is going.

Helen tells him about postproduction and how the program she's using to sit in on the edit sessions remotely is glitchy and terrible and sometimes she isn't sure it's really worth her being there at all. She tells him about how occasionally, an edit session will go long and Suraya will leave the session to make dinner for her kids, and then Helen takes point, and those are her favorite sessions of all, when she and the lead editor unfold their bodies on opposite coasts and talk random shit about their lives while they wait for sequences to render for playback.

It's like therapy, in some ways—sitting on a couch and revisiting all the mistakes of production and highlighting the good parts and then cutting and trimming out the awkward pauses, then finding perfect takes blown by the most inane things like a fly landing in the actress's hair, and getting mad all over again at someone off camera dropping an apple box during the big climactic speech. Watching the editor reshape and polish a scene until it resembles the thing in her brain the closest, she feels like she experiences a million cycles of excitement (*the raw footage is so good!*), disappointment (*why did the director pick that take?*), frustration (*oh, that's why*), fuck-it-I-don't-care-anymore (*throw in the weird take with the fly, maybe no one will notice*), and pleasant surprise that no, actually, with a few creative strokes of the keyboard, it all worked out in the end.

"And your next book?"

Helen doesn't have an answer for that yet. Her agent did tell her she could probably staff as a screenwriter on someone else's show, if she wanted. "We'd have to bring on someone to represent you full-time in that area, if that's something you're interested in."

She flirted with the idea of really trying it out for a while, but the truth is, she has no idea what that would look like. She isn't sure she *could* casually float from show to show and let go of things because *it's not her baby* and *she's just here to do a job*. She thinks maybe she could learn something working under someone else, another Suraya maybe, but then she wonders—does she even want to learn whatever vague lesson that might be, or does she want to find a way to fix whatever's blocking her from doing her *real* job, that she loved so much once (*loves still*, her heart insists reflexively, and she thinks, *be quiet, we're not talking about him*), so she can deliver on the promise of the premise of herself as a novelist.

"I'm still trying to figure it out," she tells Dad, and Mom claps her hands in the other room to announce that dinner is ready.

She finds herself repeating most of the things she told Dad to Mom across the dinner table, and Mom nods and blinks rapidly and sometimes looks like she's thinking about a million other things while Helen's talking, but finally she says, "You will figure it out soon. You always do."

Helen's surprised by the warm gust of air that seems to blow into her chest from that and she says, genuinely, "Thanks, Mom."

Mom waves off the acknowledgment like it's a fly in the air, and Helen feels something familiar settling into place. *This is what reconciliation looks like, in our family.*

"I'm sorry," Helen says, suddenly gripped with a need to say it out loud. "For what I said in the hospital that day. I was angry and hurting, and I—I wish I'd handled it better, instead of trying to make you hurt like I did."

Dad gives Helen a short, embarrassed nod. Mom stands abruptly to clear their bowls.

"It's time for cake," she says briskly, without looking at Helen.

The cake is a Betty Crocker angel food cake and Helen remembers making this with her mom when she was little—so little, Michelle was too small to help. She had watched her mother crack the eggs and marveled at how magical they looked, their golden yolks trapped in a clear *aura*. She had learned that word from some animated movie and it radiated such a perfect elegance that she looked for excuses to use it everywhere for an entire year.

Mom had shown her how to use chopsticks to mix up the eggs and cake flour, introducing her to the concept of *bonding agents* and *chemistry*, and she had sat cross-legged in front of the oven as delicious, golden-brown, sweet smells filled the air. *This is what it feels like to be truly happy*, she remembers thinking, and Helen wonders if some part of her remembers this feeling every time she walks past the boxed cake mixes in the grocery store and doesn't buy them.

Something flickers in Mom's expression when Helen asks if she can bring some of the cake back to her Airbnb host, but Mom just sniffs and says, "Suit yourself."

She moves off to hand wash all the dishes and place them in the dishwasher for storage, and Helen sits with her cake and tea across from Dad as he frowns at things on his phone. After she finishes her tea, she goes to the kitchen and starts toweling off the cups that Mom is setting down.

"You don't have to do that," Mom says.

"When has that ever stopped you," Helen answers, and she thinks she almost catches a smile at the very corner of Mom's mouth.

They clean in silence and finally Mom gets out a stepstool. Helen tries to do it for her but Mom insists—"I know where everything is"—and pulls down their old Tupperware from the top cabinets.

"Why do you put stuff you need so high out of reach?" Helen marvels, and Mom lets out a soft "*ha*" to herself.

"We need a lot of things, and there isn't enough space for everything to be convenient," she says. "I get them when I need them."

Helen thinks sometimes Mom sounds like she's talking in metaphors, but the Tupperware is thoroughly rinsed and carefully dried with a paper towel before Mom cuts off a large chunk of the cake.

"For your Airbnb host," Mom says, her eyes blinking rapidly.

Helen feels like she wants to cry just then, thinking suddenly of all the fruit and cake and sugar they've exchanged over the years instead of *I'm sorry* and *I love you*, and she excuses herself to use the restroom before she gets on the road.

When she arrives back in her temporary bedroom, she puts on her favorite stolen T-shirt (she has a flannel button-up he left at her apartment too, but she didn't pack it) and brushes her teeth.

As she crawls into the creaky bed, she thinks about that old haunted hard drive and ugly last words she can't delete.

Sometimes I wish you weren't my sister.

If it were up to me, I wouldn't have one.

Helen thinks of what she'd say to Michelle if they could have one more conversation, now. They wouldn't linger on the past. She would tell her about Dad and how she's worried about him getting older. She'd tell her about Mom snubbing her cupcakes, and Michelle would say *that bitch* while rolling her eyes. Helen would admit she didn't go upstairs to pay her respects this trip, and examine the strangeness of wanting to apologize for that. She'd tell Michelle about Grant, and ask her sister if she thought she'd fucked up horribly where he was concerned, and Michelle would say, *yes, obviously, and I forgive you for fucking him so many times and falling in love with him.*

Maybe not that last part.

Helen opens Facebook on her phone and scrolls back through her old profile pictures, watching herself age in reverse until she lands on one of the earliest photos, from 2007. Her own too-thin eyebrows and aggressive side bangs greet her, and her head is tilted, pressed against her sister's. Michelle wears impressively applied winged eyeliner, considering it was an age before beauty tutorials and YouTube. Her hair is piled into a ponytail at the top of her head, and she still looks *so cool*. Helen wears a cardigan and pearls in the photo, and she vaguely recalls them snapping this before heading out the door to her National Honor Society induction ceremony.

That had been a promising day that had soured at dinner, she remembers, when Michelle had gotten into a fight with Mom and Dad because of something she said to their waitress. Helen had been pissed at her little sister for always finding a way to make things about *her*. But she'd still made the photo her profile picture, because she had liked the way her cheekbones looked.

I miss you, she thinks, and it doesn't feel as unbearable to admit anymore.

Helen takes a deep breath and does the only thing that seems to make sense now.

She opens the notes app on her phone and starts typing.

Dear Michelle,

She pauses and tries to think of how to continue.

How to address her dead little sister, after all this time.

Dear Michelle,

You dumbass idiot.

No. That's more likely how Michelle would respond. Helen laughs at her phone screen—it sounds strange in this cold, empty room, devoid of even the hope of old, familiar ghosts—and she starts over.

Dear Michelle,

It's been a minute . . .

Thirty-Two

Four Months Later

Helen flies into Bob Hope Airport in Burbank when she returns to LA in August for the press tour and premiere. It's a much smaller airport than she expects, possibly the smallest airport she's ever been to that still deserves the name. The walls have a sandy beige carpeting to them that looks like it's been there since the days of *Mad Men* and hasn't been cleaned since. There's exactly one kiosk with no good food options, and she thinks better of buying a five-dollar bottled water at the last second. But she gets from her gate to the baggage claim in under a minute and it's an easy shuttle ride to pick up her rental car from the structure up the street. She probably could have walked, honestly.

It's a good airport and she's glad she specifically requested it. She's in LA for just two weeks—the studio is covering her expenses and they've given her a packed ten-day itinerary of interviews, photo calls with the cast, breakfasts, lunches, dinners, and drinks with people (executives, publicists, actors). She barely has time to think about Grant Shepard at all, and when she does, her thoughts always seem to cluster around the *Ivy Papers* premiere night (*next Wednesday, August 24, seven p.m., the Hollywood Roosevelt hotel*) and whether or not he'll attend.

Helen tries to focus on things like what she's wearing (Nicole convinces her to work with a stylist), what she wants to say to the room at large (she writes a speech, a short one about *gratitude* and *dreams come true*), and what she'll do with her hair (*what would Grant like more?* she wonders, then ignores the thought, then decides to wear it down—no, up).

She wonders if he'll *bring someone* to the premiere, then viciously reminds herself *this is what you wanted for him*. She isn't foolish enough to think someone like Grant Shepard would stay on the market for long (*You're getting me for below market price, at great value,* he once told her). If this happens, she will *smile* and *nod* and *be friendly*.

Over the next week and a half, as she's driving to meetings and walking up to alfresco dining establishments, she has entire conversations in her head with Grant and his fictional date.

It's so great to meet you, she tells this faceless, effortlessly perfect creature. *Grant's so lucky to have you in his life.*

Yes, Grant and I knew each other in high school, she confirms to this woman who definitely exists. *No, we didn't talk much back then. We got to know each other a little better in the room, though. What a funny way to run into someone from your past.*

No, I'm not in love with your future husband, she tells this feminine paragon who has the face of Natalie Portman and the charitable nature of Mother Teresa. *If you invited me to your wedding, I would totally come.*

I'm so happy for you, she tells Grant in her head over and over and over. *Me? I'm doing really well, actually.*

She never gets the delivery quite right. Maybe she should try something else.

Me? I'm not sure I know how to feel things anymore.

Helen *is* doing well, though, if anyone asks anyone else. Her New York life has resumed as she once hoped. Going away to Hollywood and returning has made her something of a prodigal friend in her old author circles, and Helen has found it surprisingly easy to revert to an earlier draft of herself.

"We missed you!" Pallavi had exclaimed over their catch-up brunch, as if there had never been any strange distance between them at all. Maybe it had all been in her head.

"It's nice to have the old Helen back," Elyse said, when she came over for dinner. "Glad to see you didn't go all Hollywood on us."

Helen gazes out a window overlooking Hollywood Boulevard now, on the eighth floor of the historic (and supposedly haunted, her publicist noted conspiratorially) hotel where they're hosting the *Ivy Papers* press junket. She mentally maps the familiar streets she'd take to get to Grant's house from here. She'd drive down that long stretch of boulevard lined with palm trees and billboards, and in just fifteen short minutes, *she'd be there*.

But then the elevator *dings* its arrival, the doors open and she heads toward the press junket on the mezzanine floor instead.

Wednesday, August 24, 8:15 p.m.

IT'S THE NIGHT of the premiere and Grant is on his second—maybe third? fuck, who cares—glass of scotch. It's been four months since that day on the train, and he's spent every day since telling himself to *move the fuck on*, that Helen Zhang clearly wants nothing to do with him, that someday he'll probably see she's gotten married to some nice, *normal* guy her parents probably *love* and Grant will be happy she got what she wanted after all, because he's healed and moved on too. And every night before he drifts off to sleep, he resolves, *I'll try harder tomorrow.*

He thinks maybe he was holding out his last, barely there

thread of hope for this night. He's sitting in his home office, wearing a tailored suit he put on two hours ago with every intention of walking out the door in. He still might.

He had received the emailed invitation to the *Ivy Papers* premiere party weeks ago and given it a few moments' consideration before thinking *fuck it* and RSVP'ing for one. He had watched as that bulleted event on his calendar drew closer and closer—that looming green dot on his iCal was a better jolt of *wake up!* than caffeine. He watched Helen's Instagram stories like a shitty montage of self-inflicted misery, from her touchdown at Bob Hope Airport on Sunday to her whirlwind press tour reposts to vague snapshots of meetings and lunches at various Beverly Hills restaurants and rooftops, all *in the wrong goddamn direction*.

Grant reminds himself *this was part of the deal*, that they would cut off direct contact once everything ended. The days passed with nothing to contradict this in his inbox.

He couldn't sleep last night—he blamed it on a third act problem he was having in the new pilot he was breaking. He'd gone into his office, stared at the Scrivener document where he kept all his notes and outline drafts organized, and then suddenly remembered the only reason he even knew about Scrivener in the first place was because of a time he and Helen had been working at a coffee shop together. He'd been tabbing back and forth between an outline in Google Docs and his script in Final Draft and noticed she was using writing software he had never seen before.

"It's easier to track all the chapters when I'm drafting a novel," she'd said, and shown him the spine of a story in the left-hand panel. "I've been keeping a separate file for the show—I create a new 'chapter' for every day's notes." It had seemed like a genius way to organize his thoughts without cluttering up his hard drive, and Grant had downloaded it immediately.

He feels a weird itch to delete the program from his laptop now.

Grant loosens his tie and stares at his shoes across the room. *Get up and put them on*, he tries to mentally command himself.

Instead, his brain decides to play its new favorite game—*what scene comes next?*

Grant tries to redirect his thoughts, but the movie starts anyway—

```
INT. SOME FANCY FUCKING VENUE - NIGHT

Grant enters. He sees Helen right away. She
sees him too.

                    GRANT
          Helen. I know what you said in
          that hospital, and I know you
          ignored my call that day on
          the train, and I know I haven't
          heard a goddamn word from you
          since, but . . . I'd let you
          break my heart a thousand more
          times in exchange for just one
          more night.

Helen reaches out and places a hand on Grant's
heart. She smiles at him sadly. He covers her
hand with his.

A beat. She smiles, he frowns, and she pushes
her hand farther, farther, until there's a POP
and a CRUNCH and her hand is in his fucking
chest.

                    HELEN
          Does this hurt? Sorry.

Helen pulls out Grant's bleeding, still-beating
heart with a triumphant smile. She holds it
between them, then spikes it on the ground.
```

Grant snorts. He sips his scotch and mentally switches to the next film reel.

```
INT. / EXT. GRANT'S HOUSE - NIGHT

The doorbell rings. Grant opens the door. It's
Helen. They stare at each other. Words aren't
necessary.

They move toward each other at the same time—
lips meeting, hands searching, bodies crashing.
He pulls her into his house and out of her
clothes.

The rest of this movie goes full NC-17.
```

Grant glances at the door stupidly, hopefully. Nothing.

He glances at the clock. It's a quarter past nine p.m.

The screening's over. They're probably at the after-party by now.

His phone *dings* and his heart leaps and it's the old writers room group chat, resurrected by photos of Owen, shirtless, wearing sunglasses and a shit-eating grin. Happy premiere night from Bali xx, the text reads.

Grant thinks about chucking his phone off a cliff. But that would require getting up and walking out the door.

He tries one last scenario—

```
INT. GRANT'S OFFICE - NIGHT

Grant sits at his desk, replaying every memory
he's ever had of Helen, drinking away the taste
of her.

He texts the group chat—looks like a hell of a
party, sorry to miss it!!!
```

He looks up the hotel where they're hosting the
premiere. He sends her roses, without a note.

Grant pours himself another drink. He gets
mind-numbingly drunk alone. Tomorrow, he will
download Hinge and swipe until he fucking
feels something.

He decides to go with the last one, in the end.

Wednesday, August 24, 9:30 p.m.

> looks like a hell of a party, sorry to miss it!!!

HELEN STARES AT the text in the old group chat—the first contact
of any kind from Grant since that missed call in the New York
Public Library—and an awful, drowning sensation floods her
chest, overflowing from that one locked room of unwanted memories and useless emotions. She looks around at the loud, glamorous party that's celebrating the culmination of so many years of
hard work and *mind over matter* and *productive uses of personal pain*.

They're in a ballroom that's hosted nearly a century's worth
of glittering, glamorous parties, and the vintage dress she's
wearing is a constricting, beautiful thing made from layers of
cinched black tulle and tiny hand-sewn crystals. It felt perfect
when she put it on hours ago, and it feels utterly pointless now.

The room is decked in a fortune of florals and ice sculptures and
she has the strangest thought just then, that they're all dancing on
a sinking ship and she's the only one who knows. A waiter passes
by with a platter of oysters, and the disco ball above the dance
floor casts tiny, rippling reflections of the blue party lights. Helen
realizes with sudden dread, *maybe it's too late and we've already sunk.*

What else did you expect?

She searches for a way out of this mental spiral and discovers instead a small, secret compartment of hope she must have deliberately ignored these last four months—some tiny part of her that must have whispered this whole time, *maybe just seeing him again will fix everything.*

She hates herself for her own inconsistency. *Foolish, stupid Helen*, she admonishes herself. *Haven't you already filled your quota of pointless regret?*

Across the dance floor, the lead actors are having a dance-off with Suraya, Tom, and Nicole, while Eve and the rest of the cast hold up comically large scorecards from the sidelines. The blue-purple party lights cast an otherworldly glow on the bizarre scene, and Helen thinks she could probably go over there and smile and laugh and dance and ignore this numbing dead feeling growing inside her for another fifteen or twenty minutes.

But what if it's too late by then?

If she ignores her feelings for another moment, *she might never feel anything again.* Helen suspects she knows this because she's done it before, and the long stretch of time between Michelle's funeral and those first thudding starts of emotion with Grant were marked by a vast stretch of *nothing, nothing, nothing.*

So she slips off her designer heels and heads for the elevator, dodging overly familiar producers and curious strangers as she goes. The elevator doors open, then close, and she finds herself trapped in a mirrored box gasping back sudden tears as the floor jerks upward in that slow, creaking way old elevators have. The doors open again, and a wall of framed black-and-white photographs of the not-so-distant Hollywood past blurs as she rushes down the carpeted hallway to her room at the end of the floor.

There are roses and a bottle of champagne waiting outside her door, along with a note.

congratulations on a job well done!

With love from,
Suraya, Grant, Owen, Nicole, Saskia, Tom,
Eve, and the entire Ivy Papers family <3

Helen isn't sure why this note is instantly the bleakest thing she's ever read in her life, and she hastens to open the heavy mahogany door before anyone sees her ugly cry over *absolutely nothing*. She opens the champagne and drinks straight from the bottle. She takes the bouquet of roses, opens her window, and viciously deheads them one at a time—fluttering red bombs of petals onto the boulevard below. *He hates me, he hates me not.*

She opens her laptop and pulls up the document she's been working on for the last four months—the one she still hasn't told her agent about in case it all falls apart.

Letters You'll Never Read.scriv.

It's a working title, a placeholder for a pithier, more audience-tested title, if she ever reaches the finish line. *When* she reaches the finish line. Each chapter is a letter to Michelle, the completion of an old therapy prompt (*and what would you say to your sister, if you could talk to her now?*) that Helen resolutely rejected for the last fourteen years as she combed Michelle's hard drive looking for a suicide letter instead.

She's written of old gossip and future plans, catalogued childhood memories and collected lessons learned into a rambling one-way correspondence to be edited into something resembling a book later.

But she doesn't have an ending.

Helen opens her Scrivener file to the blank last chapter, labeled—*Here's Where I Leave You.* It's the one she's been putting off.

Why not now, why not here. Helen takes another swig of champagne.

Her cursor blinks back at her.

Then she starts typing.

Dear Michelle,

~~I've finally given up on hearing from you first.~~

Dear Michelle,

~~More than an afterlife, I hope someday I'll turn a corner~~
~~and there you'll be. I'll get everything right this time.~~

Dear Michelle,

*Before I say goodbye, I want you to know that I've been
doing just fine without you. I don't feel any guilt at all
because it wasn't my fault, and fuck you one more time by
the way, and I refuse to miss someone who didn't want to
be here in the first place.*

*I want you to know all of that, but I'm starting to suspect
it's my own bullshit that I have to get better at detecting.*

*I'm not fine. I haven't been for a while, and I blamed
you for so long because the last thing you ever did was
teach me how much loving can hurt.*

*I loved you and you left anyway. I tried not to dwell
on it, tried not to ask myself how I could have done
everything better, tried not to feel anything. And then two
months after you died, I went to college and I told a boy I
loved him, a week after we met. He was embarrassed, and*

I laughed out loud and told him I didn't mean it of course, it had just felt like too perfect a moment to pass up saying it out loud. I never had before, not even to you. I wasted my first I love you, and after that I didn't want to say it to anyone else, ever again.

Then I fell in love for the first time, for real.

It made me want to fix something I'd been pretending wasn't broken: my own barely beating heart.

The problem is, I don't know where to begin.

If I was writing one of those science-fiction novels Dad used to read to us, I'd start by inventing time travel and going back to our last fight in my bedroom. I'd come knock on your door and I'd tell you I'm sorry, and I love you.

And then I'd push that lever back even farther, and I'd find our grandparents and I'd teach them how to say those things to our parents first.

And then I'd come back to the present day to see what was different.

Maybe nothing.

Since this isn't a science-fiction story, I'll start here instead:

I'm sorry for all the ways I hurt you while you were living, and I wish you could be sorry for all the ways you've hurt me since you died. If I had a second chance, I would do so many things differently. But I couldn't get behind the steering wheel of your life that night and force you to stay, and I've been mad at you for so long without it changing a damn thing.

That's suited me fine up till now. You're the demon I don't want to exorcise. If I heal and move on, I'm worried I'll finally lose you for good. But I want to be healthy. And I want to be happy, though I've never trusted happiness.

To me, happiness is a fleeting, heartbeat-to-heartbeat experience that comes and goes and hopefully comes back. I worry happily-ever-afters don't exist for people like us.

So here's the ending I'll try to write instead:

The kind of ending where I don't have to leave you behind even as I move forward, because you're always a part of me—even if that part feels like a hole in my heart. (Loving can hurt, and I want to do it anyway.)

The kind of ending where someone else sees the best and worst of me and loves me back. We'd be happy together, we'd be sad together, we'd be everything together. And when it's all over and we've reached another ending, my ashes would be scattered over the tree that grows from his body because till death do us part wouldn't be enough, because I'd need more than one brief eternity with him.

I've always found endings harder than beginnings, goodbyes harder than hellos. When I was a kid, I had this idea—a hope, really—that life and death were two sides of the same door, and that when you died, there would be a long hallway in the afterlife where you would walk past the doors of all the lives you'd lived before. My theory was that in that hallway, you'd be able to remember every single life you'd ever lived, and if you concentrated all your effort on it, you could take a single intention or lesson with you, before opening the next door and starting your next life.

I don't know if we'll ever see each other again. I don't have much faith in heaven or an afterlife these days. But I've been wrong about many things in this life so maybe I'm wrong about that too. I don't think anyone living can know, and I'm not in a rush to find out.

Still—I hope this is the kind of story where there's an

epilogue. One day I'll turn the last page, and suddenly—there you'll be. And I'll walk up to another chance to get everything right, this time.

I'd start by telling you, "I love you."

I'll keep hoping for the both of us.

Helen

HELEN HITS EXPORT on the document and attaches it in an email to her agent before she can think better of it.

To: Chelsea Pierce
Subject: I've been writing

could be something, could be nothing. wanted to write it anyway.

Helen pauses, then clicks *forward email.*

To: Grant Shepard

I don't want to surprise you later, so I'm sending you the manuscript I'm working on now. The last chapter is relevant. If there's anything you'd like me to take out, I'm happy to have a conversation.

Will be in town through the rest of the week, if that's helpful to know.

Yours,
Helen

Thirty-Three

Grant stares at the text on his screen and wonders if this is some kind of fucked-up reading-comprehension quiz he's hallucinated into existence from sheer pent-up *yearning*.

Yours,
Helen.

Thirty-Four

It's one a.m., and the phone is ringing. Helen flicks on the light.

"Hi, Miss Zhang, this is the front desk—"

"It's one a.m.," she mumbles.

"Yes, there's a, um, *a very insistent gentleman* here to see you. I wanted to check—"

Helen sits up. "Who?"

THE ELEVATOR DOORS open on the eighth floor and Grant looks up, his heart pounding.

Room 805. It's down the longest hallway in the world, in a fancy historic Hollywood hotel that smells like *you can't afford this*. Every step he takes seems to be punctuated by the plush green carpet telling him to *give up, give up, give up*, and his heartbeat sounds like his own last frayed and battered thread of hope answering, *no, no, no*.

The door with the metal plaque *805* is in sight, *he hopes this isn't a mistake*, and suddenly it's in front of him, *now or never*, and he knocks.

SHE OPENS THE door, and *it's Grant*.

There's a feral glint in his eyes and he's wearing the disheveled remains of a sharp black suit, his tie lost to the ages. His jaw is clenched and his hands grip the door frame—he has the look of a looming, Byronic hero approaching the edge of a cliff he doesn't expect to return from.

"Helen," he says, in a low, predatory voice.

"Grant," she says, and swallows a lump in her throat. "I've missed you."

He nods shortly, and his eyes sweep over every detail of her—she's suddenly very aware of her messy, post-premiere hair and the gray waffle-knit hotel bathrobe she's wearing.

"I read your manuscript," he says. "From start to finish. All I want to know is what you meant by this."

Grant holds up his phone and it's her own email burning brightly back at her on the screen. Her eyes flicker over it, then fall in disappointment. *Oh. The legal disclaimer part.*

"I meant I wanted to send it to you early, in case—"

"No," he interrupts, and her hands itch with nervous wanting. It's been so long since she's been close enough to touch him. "Not that part. Lower. Read that back."

He taps the relevant part of the screen.

"Out loud, if you don't mind," Grant adds softly.

Helen's heart trips over two short words. She chances a look up at him then—his gaze is shuttered and she has the sudden, humiliating thought, *maybe he came for some kind of vengeful purpose, to give her a taste of her own medicine before telling her never to contact him again.*

"'Yours, Helen,'" she reads, finally.

"Are you?" His voice is hard and his words are cold. "Now or never, Helen."

Now or never. Helen contemplates a few eternities of *never*s she's already experienced. She never told her sister she loved her. She never told her parents unpalatable truths. She never felt as loved as she did the first time Grant Shepard held her in his arms.

Bring Grant Shepard back to the present tense, where he belongs.

"Yes," Helen says finally, and she sees a flash of heat behind his eyes. "If you still want me."

Grant doesn't move any closer—though his knuckles have turned white from gripping the door frame.

"That day in the hospital," he says slowly, carefully. "I think I lied to you. I told you—and I can't seem to stop replaying it in my mind, whenever I think about it—'I'd rather have a fraction of you than all of someone else.'"

Helen swallows a lump of regret. "I remember."

"The thing is . . . I had a fraction of you then, and it damn near killed me."

"Oh," she says, and nods in understanding. *He's saying it's too late.* "I'm sorry."

He takes a step forward and her world seems to tilt on its axis.

"I want all of it this time," Grant says, his voice harsh and impossibly close. "I want the nights and the days and the weekends and the holidays and I want you at my side and in my bed and in my life. I want to meet your parents and I want to take you to a sheep farm in fucking Ireland and my dad's place in Boston. I want to see what kind of person you are when you're eighty. I want to do this for real, and I want to call you *mine* so badly it's a fucking *joke*, but if you can't sign up for the whole show this time, then don't—"

She surges forward and kisses him then, and he tastes like whisky and surprise. His hands immediately pull her *closer*, *closer*, *closer*, his desperate heartbeat crashing against hers.

"I want all of that too," she murmurs, and he seems to take offense to her separating from him long enough to even say it out loud. He lets out a growling "*hmmph*" and chases her lips closer. "I'm still so afraid of messing things up. I don't think I've completely healed yet, and you deserve someone whole—"

"Helen," he exhales, his forehead against hers. "You don't have to be completely healed to be everything I want. To be *mine*. I love *every part of you*, you silly, *infuriating* woman. I love the parts of you I haven't even met yet."

"I love you too," she says, and her cold, broken heart suddenly seems to glow from the feeling of saying it out loud to someone else and meaning it *so damn much*. "I love you so much, it doesn't make sense to me in words."

"In that case," Grant says, and lowers his head to kiss her again, "let's talk less."

Thirty-Five

Around 6:25 a.m., a magnitude 6.8 earthquake hits fifty miles off the coast of Northern California. At 7000 Hollywood Boulevard, the tremors last for 39.73 seconds, and Helen wakes up to the feeling of Grant's arms wrapped firmly around her as the entire room rattles and jolts and she has the fleeting, half-dreamed thought that they're on a rickety roller coaster ride that's about to take off through the ceiling and also maybe *Grant never showed up at her hotel room* and it's all been some terrible, wonderful dream. *Don't wake up*, she commands herself.

"It's just an earthquake," Grant murmurs in her ear, and she discovers a new fear—he's here, and she's about to lose him again. There's an awful, clattering sound as the ground shakes the foundations of the building and everything inside of it, from wooden furniture and porcelain dishes to star-crossed lovers, newly reunited. "You're safe."

"I've never been in an earthquake before," she says, and suddenly it ends. She turns around to face him and she's relieved to find that Grant's still *here*, watching her with a sharp alertness. She reaches out and presses her palm to his cheek, and he waits patiently as she checks his solidness: *he's real*. "You've been through a lot, I bet."

Grant takes her hand and kisses her palm, then reaches out to trace her cheek, like he's checking that she's real enough to touch too.

"Sometimes there's aftershocks," he says finally, once he's satisfied. "If you're really staying here, we should probably go over earthquake safety at some point."

There's a hint of doubt behind these words, and her heart breaks for it.

"I'm really staying," she tells him.

"Good," Grant says simply, and his hand drifts down her neck, then travels a slow, warm path to her shoulder. She's naked beneath the sheet and he seems fascinated by his own hand disappearing beneath the sheet too.

"Grant," she exhales shakily, as his knuckles graze her ribs.

"Helen," he returns evenly, and his brown eyes stay locked on hers as his fingers explore hidden curves and valleys beneath white fabric.

"Should we"—she inhales sharply—"leave the building, or something?"

She glimpses a flash of humor in his eyes.

"No," he answers, and leans forward to kiss his way down her stomach. He takes her hands and places them on his head, and she tangles her fingers in his hair reflexively. "The first rule of earthquake safety is if you're in bed, you're supposed to stay there while it's shaking."

"Oh," she says. *Oh.*

"Then you're supposed to curl up and protect your head," he continues, from between her thighs.

"That's, um," she says, and loses her train of thought, as his tongue strokes just *there*. "*Ah.*"

"Drop down, cover your head, and hold on to something solid," Grant says, his low voice reverberating against the hot core of her.

"Grant," she pants needily. "Please."

He gives her what they both know she needs, and she bites

her lip as the mounting tension breaks and an orgasm sweeps over her.

Grant resurfaces above her then, and his arms are braced around her in a way that makes her feel *safe* and *loved*, even as she isn't sure if the tremors are coming from her body or the building.

"Think you'll be able to remember all of that?" he asks as he repositions himself at her entrance.

"Yes," she gasps as he pushes himself inside.

"Good," he says in a strained voice. She loves watching him like this, when he's wrapped in her heat and he's close enough for her to watch every expression flicker across his face. His eyes are laughing even as the muscles at his throat work rather spectacularly. "Practice saying that for me."

Helen squeezes him with her inner muscles, and his lips wordlessly form her name as he fills her to the hilt.

"You want me," he prompts, and her breath hitches as he withdraws from her.

"Yes," she answers, and he surges back in.

"Louder," he demands, and withdraws again. "You love me."

"Yes," she says, *louder*, and he rewards her.

"You'll stay with me, then?" he asks, burying his face in her neck.

"*Yes, yes, yes,*" she echoes, as he drives into her in a primal kind of rhythm, until her world splits apart and reassembles to the sound of his echoing climax.

Afterward, the air seems to be thrumming with something warm and familiar—a glowing, unspoken thing between them. *Want me, love me, have me, keep me,* her pulse races to communicate.

"We'll have to figure out what to do about your parents," he says then, and she laughs, out of breath.

"My parents are the last people I want to think about right now," she says, and covers her eyes. "We'll figure it out."

IT's A RAINY, early-September morning in Dunollie, New Jersey, when Helen announces Grant's reappearance to her parents over FaceTime two weeks later. She can see the sparse branches of the trees rattling outside the windows behind them, and she thinks, *the weather is so different here.*

"I, um, I started seeing someone, in LA. I'm moving to LA. It's serious. It's . . . it's him, it's Grant. I'd like you to meet him. He'd like to meet you, when we're getting my things in New York in a few weeks. But if you can't be nice to him, then we won't come."

Mom blinks and laughs and makes that low, clucking sound she sometimes makes of *scathing disapproval*, then stands from the couch abruptly and leaves.

"I thought you were done with that," Dad says. "Anyway, you don't even know what's going to happen. Who knows, in a year, maybe you will feel different. You shouldn't bring up these things until you are more sure."

"I am sure," Helen says.

"You are very young," Dad insists, and she thinks, *I'm 32.* "Don't make decisions so quick."

Grant squeezes her hand when she hangs up and looks over at him, an apologetic expression on her face.

"Let's go to the beach," he says, before Helen can apologize for family histories and complicated backstories that can't be rewritten. "The weather's perfect."

IT's SNOWING OUTSIDE the New York Public Library in January, and she's pretty sure he's going to propose. He knows she knows, she's certain, because he keeps glancing at her and shoving his hands in his coat pockets, only to produce his phone.

"You're so annoying," she mutters as they present their bags to security and Grant makes a show of hiding his bag from her.

"You love me," he answers, and whisks ahead of her to the reading room.

They sit beneath perfect blue skies painted on the gilded ceiling and pull out their laptops at a long wooden table in the back. Helen's working on revisions for her memoir—her book of essays sold to her YA publisher's sister imprint and has been newly retitled *Sending All My Love*. Grant has a pilot he's revising, a heady, straight-to-series sci-fi world of his own creation. His spec script sold in a heated auction and has been cited hopefully in the trades as proof of the lingering value of original ideas in a marketplace of perpetual adaptation.

The two of them have been talking about coming to work here together for months—a chance to rewrite over the memory of their last near miss. Helen loves the silence of this place, the church-like atmosphere among fellow bibliophiles typing away in quiet industry. After about ten minutes, she realizes Grant absolutely hates it.

"Hey," he whispers, and earns a few glares from the studious patrons around them. To be fair, it's his third time speaking in the last minute, and it's always been something mundane like "Can you move your chair?" or "Do you have the Wi-Fi password?" or, right now, "Can I borrow a pen?"

Helen hands him her best pen silently. He works out story beats in a black notebook, his laptop abandoned for a few moments before he starts tapping his foot with idle, pent-up energy. She covers his foot with hers, and he looks up.

"Sorry," he whispers against her ear, bumping her shoulder as he leans in to say it, and she shivers despite the heat.

He stops tapping his foot, but five minutes later, his left hand starts tapping restlessly against her planner. A librarian clears her throat in a pointed way, and Helen covers his hand with hers and gives him a quieting look. Grant rolls his eyes, then glances down at her hand.

He flips his captured hand up beneath hers, and suddenly she's the one who's caught.

He looks up at her, and her heart jams in her throat. He presses a *shushing* finger to his lips with his free hand, then reaches into his shirt pocket and produces a ring.

It's a simple round-cut diamond in a platinum, Edwardian-looking setting.

It's perfect.

He holds it out to her casually and lifts a silent shoulder. *What do you think?*

Like they're in silent study hall, and he's asking her to prom.

Helen blinks. Time seems to be moving differently.

This is how Grant Shepard proposes to you, she thinks, and can't quite believe it's really happening. *He's the homecoming king!!!* her seventeen-year-old self adds, unnecessarily, and she can feel the moment slipping away even as she wants to laugh at some future joke they'll tell their friends about *how many words does it take for a screenwriter to propose to an author?*

Then she looks up and sees some flicker of nerves in his eyes, despite his casual posture, and her heart seems ready to collapse with the weight of loving him.

Yes, she nods.

Grant lets out a short, relieved gust of air, laughs roughly, and slides the ring onto her finger. He raises her hand and kisses her knuckles, then leans forward, their knees touching as he presses a kiss to her flushed cheeks, her nose, and finally her waiting lips.

They're engaged.

It's SLEETING WHEN they meet Helen's parents a week later, at a dim sum restaurant off Route 22 that Helen remembers going to from ages eight through eighteen. On their way in, they pass a surly thirteen-year-old Chinese girl reading a thick novel while ignoring everyone else at her table, and Helen nudges Grant with some excitement.

"That one was me," she says.

Grant keeps his eyes on the table ahead, where Helen's parents are waiting for them. Her heart pinches at his grim expression.

"You're going to be fine." She squeezes his elbow. "A herd of wild horses couldn't keep me from marrying you."

The lunch goes as well as could be expected, which is to say, not great.

Mom refuses to place orders for the table, waving a hand toward Helen as if to say, *have it your way, order what you want, I see how it is.*

Dad tries to make conversation with Grant about his work, but mostly uses it as an opportunity to roast his entire filmography. "I saw that show you did, before Helen's show. None of my friends have heard of it."

When the check comes, Grant offers to pay, and Mom says stiffly, "Thank you, that's very kind."

Helen suppresses a despairing laugh—she remembers every world war her parents have started over their right to pay a dinner bill. They sit in silence waiting for the waitress to return for Grant's signature, and Helen wonders if it was a mistake, insisting he not ask her parents for permission before proposing. *Isn't my permission the only one you need?* Maybe she'd been wrong about that.

Her parents share a speaking look and Helen feels a foreboding twinge.

Mom sighs heavily, then says, "At least he's tall. My sister, her daughter Alice married so short."

She shakes her head and Grant looks to Helen like, *This was not in the flowchart of possible responses.*

Helen closes her eyes and mentally laughs until she cries.

"We're thinking a summer wedding," she says out loud.

Mom sniffs disdainfully, as if to say, *of course you are, who am I to stop you*.

"You will have to pay your respects to Michelle," she finally says, her gaze trained on Grant.

HELEN HANDS GRANT two sticks of lit incense, and they both stand in front of Michelle's smiling portrait on the bookshelf. She's still thrown by the sight of Grant standing in her childhood home. It seems so impossible an image, her brain keeps commanding her eyes to *check again*.

"I don't really know the proper way to do this," Helen says. "I just know what I do. I hold the incense, I face her, I say, *Hi, Michelle*, and, um, whatever else comes to mind. And I bow. That's kind of how it's always worked in our house."

Grant takes the incense from her and faces the portrait.

"Hi, Michelle," he says. "I'm sorry you're not here. I wish we all could have hung out together."

"That would have been so weird," Helen mutters beside him. "You know, usually we don't do this out loud."

"I don't mind if you hear what I have to say," Grant says quietly, and bows his head toward Michelle's portrait again. "I want you to know I'll take care of your sister. And thanks for having me here."

"Then you put the incense sticks in the pot next to the photo," Helen adds.

Grant follows her instructions. Helen smiles and shrugs.

"That's pretty much it," she says. "I'm never totally sure I'm doing it right."

"You do it fine," Mom says briskly, from the hallway. "It is not that complicated. Helen thinks too much. The important thing is we still have a connection to her. Chinese people care about this kind of thing, the living and the dead—we are all still connected, so we honor that connection."

THEY GET MARRIED outdoors in late August, on a sheep farm in Ireland. It's a smallish, intimate affair of just under sixty guests, mostly immediate friends and family. The weather is suspiciously perfect.

"I feel like I'm in a fucking Thomas Hardy novel," Nicole says as she sweeps up her bouquet and peeks out the window of the seventeenth-century croft house where they've been getting ready. "Lots of people and a couple sheep arriving out there."

"Haha," Helen says, and tries to ignore the churning sensations in her stomach. She's wearing a simply structured dress of ivory silk crepe, with a long row of silk buttons up the back that had taken the better part of an hour for Nicole to hook up with a hairpin (making jokes all the while on the odds of whether Grant would torture her with his patience or "really lean into a bodice-ripper vibe" at the end of the night).

"I think these could probably seduce a dashing farmhand

if the situation called for it," Nicole murmurs, adjusting her boobs in a gilt mirror by the entrance. "Right?"

"Your tits look great," Helen says. "I feel kind of like I might be dying."

Nicole blots her lipstick. "Say the word, I'll get the getaway car."

Helen shakes her head. "No, I think this is normal. Right?"

Nicole shrugs. "You tell me, babes. How's it feel, standing on the precipice of happily ever after?"

Helen lets out a strangled noise that sounds like a laugh, maybe.

She's terrified of it. She's terrified that she's incapable of wanting something and getting it, of real life obliterating perfect weather and happy endings if she goes on for an extra chapter, or even an extra sentence. *That just means you really want it*, she reminds herself, as her heart hammers in agreement.

So she nods and says, "I'm ready. Let's go."

ALL THINGS CONSIDERED, it's a pretty *normal* day.

The string quartet has some trouble finding a spot where both the guests and the bridal party can hear them, the florist forgets to add forget-me-nots to Helen's bouquet, and there are some pesky wrinkles that Nicole just can't steam out of the heirloom veil that's been in storage for the better part of a century.

Still, when Helen takes her father's arm and the sounds of Canon in D fill the air, she can't help but feel the thrill of something *a little extraordinary*. They're standing just out of view and Helen has to remind herself how to breathe, and they take a step forward.

"Slow down," Dad says as they approach the makeshift aisle

created by a profusion of chamomile flowers planted by Grant's mother months ago, in anticipation of this day. "You're walking too fast."

"I'm walking a normal pace," Helen says.

They're walking down the aisle now, and with every step, Helen can see familiar faces who have known her at various points in her life. She feels a strange kind of nostalgia–sensory overload, as every smiling face unlocks some memory from the past—*drinking champagne out of plastic cups, celebrating her first book deal at a hotel bar, laughing in a hospital over dirty magazines, crying in a bathroom over a bad book review, falling from the swings in a backyard, baking banana bread for the first time.*

She looks up then, and—it's *him.*

Grant Shepard. *Grant Fucking Shepard, good in a room, great in a bed, and the improbable love of my damn life.*

He grins, like he can read her mind. When she finally reaches him and he lifts the blusher of her veil, he whispers in her ear, "It's nice to see you."

She shivers a little and looks back at the crowd. She sees his mom first, her heart in her eyes, clasping the hand of the Irish sheep farmer she married six months ago. She sees her own parents, sitting in the front row, holding hands. Mom wears a brittle expression, and the corner of her mouth can't seem to decide if it wants to turn up or down. Dad looks like he might cry at any minute.

Helen looks to the other side of the aisle and sees Nicole eyeing Grant's father with blatant sexual interest. Nicole spots her and gives Helen a winking *nice.*

Grant squeezes her hand.

"Come hang out here with me," he says quietly, and she looks up into his laughing eyes. "I missed you all morning."

She smiles and feels a tug at the back of her dress.

"Shelley, no!" Grant's mom exclaims, as a rogue sheep wearing a flowery collar chews on the silk crepe of Helen's wedding dress.

Grant leans closer and her hand itches to reach out and touch his hair.

"The sheep's name is Michelle," he says. "If you can believe it."

"Hold for wardrobe," their officiant, an episodic director, quips.

They wait as Nicole wrestles Helen's train from the sheep and Helen looks up into Grant's eyes and thinks, *This is it*. She thinks wryly of how much easier things could have been for them in a different timeline, where they made a few different decisions, where *everyone* made some slightly different choices along the way. *It would have been an entirely different story*.

She thinks of the infinitely different love stories they could have lived instead—and she decides she'll write them all. She'll fracture this feeling into a million shards of glass reflecting back the same, unbelievable love story so she can capture it for the days when she needs to read it back to herself and to him—when they're sad, or tired, or annoyed, or hurting. *Or happy*, she reminds herself. Loving him is poetry, and she thinks she'll try her hand at that too.

"This is my favorite part of the day I married you," Helen says, smiling.

"So far," Grant agrees, and her heart—*that reliable organ*—beats loudly in agreement, in *want me, love me, have me, keep me*, in *happilyeverafter*.

Acknowledgments

This book was born in the dark and it took a lot of people and a lot of drafts to bring it into the light.

First: Zack Wallnau, my husband and creative soul mate, who I forced to read this book in front of me, every night before we went to sleep, as it was being drafted. Thank you for taking care of me and our cats while I was writing, and thank you to our cats, Canary and Eloise, for being the best lap companions.

Next: Ginger Jiang, my childhood bestie and the first person to read a complete draft. Thank you for telling me I had something worth reading. Thanks also for becoming a doctor and someone I can text for fictional medical inquiries.

My "first real draft" readers: Meghan Fitzmartin, Julie Ganis, Priyanka Mattoo, Whitney Milam, Anna O'Brian, Rosianna Halse Rojas, Rebecca Rosenberg, and Scott Rosenfeld. Your support and encouragement and gentle nudges for clarity helped me find the path to improvement. Shoutout also to Vicki Cheng and Heather Mason for moral support and answers about press tour logistics.

My "go long draft" readers: Alison Falzetta, Tim Hautekiet, and Stephanie Kim Johnson. You read the early extended-cut version of this book and told me what I could lose and what was worth keeping.

In a class of her own: Sarah MacLean. I forced this manuscript in front of your eyeballs via the Romancing the Vote auction and you went so above and beyond in your support and championing of this story and these characters, it makes me want to cry when I think about it too much. I've learned so much from reading your books and listening to your romance podcast (*Fated Mates*! Everyone who tells kissing stories should listen to this!) and I'm so glad a twist of fate (me, bidding frantically on a manuscript critique from you, for democracy and also my own selfish purposes) brought you into my life.

My agent, Taylor Haggerty. You represent a constellation of literary stars, and I continue to be beside myself that you chose to represent me. Thank you for giving me notes that whipped this manuscript into submission shape in ways I never could have done on my own, thank you for being my champion and fairy queen guide in the foreign land of publishing, thank you for knowing exactly how to sell this book.

My editor, Carrie Feron. When I was told you were leaving Avon once we finished this book together, I spent twenty-four hours crying my devastation about it and I don't think that was me being dramatic at all. You will always be the first editor I ever worked with in this business, and what a mark you've left on me as a writer! Thank you for wanting to bring this book into the world with me, and thank you for shaping me into the kind of author I didn't even know I could be.

The whole team at Avon: First, thank you for making the world a more romantic place through the books you publish. It's an honor to be published by you. Thanks especially to Asanté Simons, DJ DeSmyter, Jessica Lyons, Ellie Anderson, Alessandra Roche, May Chen, and Liate Stehlik for making me feel welcome and answering my many questions throughout this process. Thanks also to my proofreader, Katie Shepherd, for being patient with my creative commas, and copy editor Stephanie Evans for your keen eye and the truly humbling gift of getting to read my sex scenes described back to me in a style sheet.

Massive thanks to the wildly talented people who turned this docx file of a manuscript into a beautiful object on the shelf: illustrator Alan Dingman, art director Jeanne Lee Reina, interior designer Diahann Sturge, and managing editor Brittani DiMare. You have phenomenal taste in aesthetics and I am so grateful for your time, energy, and creativity. Thanks also to Henry Sene Yee, whose early sketches and hard work on this book gave me a crash course in the art of cover design and helped set us on the right path.

My sensitivity reader, Anna Akana. Thank you first for being a generous friend and kind soul who I'm so lucky to have in my life. Thank you also for reading this book in its thorny ugliness and guiding me to find a version that felt more emotionally honest and in line with the story you knew I was trying to tell. I am so very grateful.

Thank you to Kimberley Atkins, Lily Cooper, and Jo Dickinson at Hodder & Stoughton, Heather Baror-Shapiro at Baror International, Kristin Dwyer, Jessica Brock, and Molly Mitchell at LEO PR, Holly Root and Jasmine Brown at Root Literary, and Kassie King at The Novel Neighbor for steering me along my first publishing journey.

Thank you to my teams at UTA (Jenny Maryasis, Amanda Hymson, Greg Iserson, and Mary Pender) and Kaplan/Perrone (Alex Lerner and Ben Neumann) and my attorney, Phil Klein, for working tirelessly to turn me from a passionate creative artist type into an artist with a career. Your advice and steady guidance over the years is one of the greatest unfair advantages I have.

Thank you to all the smart women who've given me good

advice over the past decade, and all the smart women who gave them good advice first—this book wouldn't exist without you.

Thank you to anyone who ever read and reviewed my old fanfic and told me I should write a book someday. It took me a long time to get here, but I hope you find this.

Thank you to my parents, Ron Kuang and Sumei Ruan, who supported my dreams in ways big and small since I first announced at the dinner table that I wanted to be an author someday and wrote Lisa Frank fan fiction for a school assignment. I love you and am sorry for all the ways I've made your lives difficult over the years. If you have turned to the acknowledgments to make sure you're in them *before* reading the novel, I suggest you skip chapters 14, 15, 16, 17, 18, 20, 21, 24, and 35. And if you've read them, I don't ever want to know. <3

My sister, Olivia Kuang—fourteen years younger and so much cooler than I ever was at your age, at every age. I love getting to watch you grow up. Thanks for being cool about this plot when I called to tell you about it.

Finally, to the authors who first entrusted me with adapting their work for the big screen: Maurene Goo and Emily Henry. I will always be grateful to have found that shard of glass reflecting back a piece of me in your beautiful writing.